CHASING DEVILS

THE JACKSON CLAY & BEAR BEAUCHAMP SERIES
BOOK 3

B.C. LIENESCH

Copyright © 2023 by B.C. Lienesch & Liquid Mind Publishing, LLC. All rights reserved. No part of this publication may be copied, reproduced in any format, by any means, electronic or otherwise, without prior consent from the copyright owner and publisher of this book. This is a work of fiction. All characters, names, places and events are the product of the author's imagination or used fictitiously. For information contact:

www.liquidmindpublishing.com

For Dawn
Friend
Mentor
And now, Angel

THE JACKSON CLAY & BEAR BEAUCHAMP SERIES

The Woodsman

Country Roads

Chasing Devils

Happyland

Safe Harbor (Coming Soon)

ONE

NATHALIE GRACE MCKENNA lay in bed with her eyes closed until she heard the door to the condo shut. Her husband, Brad, left their palatial Georgetown abode just before five every morning like clockwork to swim laps at the Four Seasons Health Club. After that, he'd hold court at the Old Ebbitt Grill, or Hey Adams, or any other iconic downtown eatery, expensing meals to his company's account. If he knew Nathalie wasn't really asleep, he didn't let on.

It wasn't always like this. In fact, she used to sleep through the night. Easily, too. She'd wake up refreshed, enjoying a long morning usually all to herself before strolling into work sometime before noon. But that all changed the day she received the phone call. *That* phone call.

Rising cautiously, Nathalie peered out the bedroom door, ensuring the place was as asleep as she should be. Nothing stirred. She went to her wardrobe and slid on a pair of Lululemon running tights and a hoodie, then took their private elevator up to the rooftop running track.

As she opened the outer door, the wintry air squeezed her in a brisk embrace. Recoiling, she pulled the zipper up on her hoodie and slid a beanie on. Nathalie took the first lap slowly, almost at a leisurely pace, but increased her speed with each succeeding lap. A few laps in, she was running as fast as she could, her body pounding at the steel track with all the anxiety and anger and fear that had built up inside her the past couple weeks. She'd come up here countless times trying to exorcise the worst of those emotions, never once finding success. Now, it only made her run harder.

At every corner of the rooftop, the track—and her view—turned ninety degrees. First, there was the Kennedy Center and Watergate Hotel with the Washington Monument peeking out just over the top. To the north was Wisconsin Avenue, making its way up past Embassy Row and into the heart of Tenleytown. Turning again, she could see up the Potomac River carving an aquatic border between Virginia and Maryland. As she made the fourth turn, she followed the Potomac past Rosslyn, across the way.

Nathalie ran on until she lost count of the laps. Everything got lost in the monotony of repetition. This glorified hamster wheel crowning their multi-million-dollar condo. She ran until either the run or the thoughts—or both—proved too exhausting and she collapsed against the cold metal railing. Breathing hard, she looked out over the Potomac River, her warm breath forming small clouds every time she exhaled.

"Today," she told herself. "Today I tell him. This morning."

Nathalie knew such a conversation had to be done in person, especially after all these years. Taking the elevator back down inside, she grabbed a quick shower and changed into a pair of designer jeans and a sweater. She paused for a moment to look at herself in the bathroom mirror. Nathalie was model slim—her boss called her gaunt, but that was just her boss worrying—with auburn hair, fair skin, and icy blue eyes that looked even frostier contrasted with the dark circles around them. Contemplating throwing on some makeup to help the situation, she decided against it. To hell with it, she thought. He knows what I look like. For better or for worse. That had been a part of their vows in another life.

She put on her coat and went over to the desk to grab the Post-It note she couldn't forget. Slipping that and her car keys into her purse, she walked out the front door, taking their other private elevator down to the lobby. From there, she took the residential elevator down into the parking garage. Nathalie slid into her black Tesla Model S and drove it up to the street. Still before six, the sky had yet to lighten and S Street, pressed up against the Whitehurst Freeway, was little more than a dark corridor of faceless facades. She flicked on her headlights and turned onto the street, illuminating the dark.

As Nathalie headed for the freeway, she didn't notice the car that pulled out behind her and began to follow.

———

NATHALIE CROSSED the Key Bridge and took Interstate 66 into the heart of Northern Virginia. The highway was practically deserted, with only the occasional car whizzing past in the opposite direction, headed for the city. The slowly rising dawn painted a brilliant golden horizon in her rearview mirror, interrupted only by the headlights of the car behind her.

She looked down at her phone, double-checking the GPS app. The place she was headed, his home she supposed, could only be found by coordinates. That's how remote the area was.

Forty miles later, the congested sprawl of the DC suburbs gave way to rolling country. Both the clusters of buildings and the highway exits between them grew further apart. As the interstate took a lazy right turn around a large mountain, Nathalie's phone spoke up, informing her to take the next exit. She did as she was prompted.

The ramp dumped her onto a quaint two-lane road. She took it north, barely noticing the car behind her coming off the highway to make the same turn. The road climbed easily, winding its way up a hillside, and a thick forest of leafless trees ran its fingers across the rising sun, flickering the morning light as Nathalie drove on.

When the road straightened, her phone chimed once again, telling her to follow the road for another couple of miles. As Nathalie checked it and looked back up, she noticed the headlights in her rearview mirror. A large, dark car—maybe an SUV or truck—was gaining on her. She told herself it was probably a local, used to speeding down these back roads. But as the car caught up to her, it didn't pass. Instead, it edged closer to her rear fender.

Nathalie tried to make out the driver, but the person was an opaque blob. She tapped at her brakes, warning them to ease off. Instead, the pursuing car revved its engine and gunned into the back of Nathalie's luxury sedan. The collision forced a sharp cry out of her, and she switched her foot back over to the gas and sped up.

She tried desperately now to get away from the dark car, but it stayed with her. As the road began to bend and sway again, Nathalie didn't slow down. Her tires screamed, struggling to stay on the road. Her breathing became quick and shallow as panic took hold. The other car hit her rear fender again, and this time Nathalie nearly lost control.

Her Tesla fishtailed left, then right, sliding around a banking turn before straightening out just as the road did. Tears formed in the corner of her eyes and her hands trembled as they gripped the steering wheel.

Nathalie could see the straight stretch of road would be short-lived. She knew she had to slow down, but as she did, the other driver pulled out into the opposite lane and went faster. Finally, Nathalie thought, maybe they're passing and going away. She took her foot off the gas and allowed the car to overtake her.

Only, it didn't.

The menacing car veered left for a moment before swerving back right and smashing into the rear flank of Nathalie's car. She shrieked. Her car began to careen off the road, and she jerked the wheel left, fishtailing again. With her Tesla drifting right, the dark car gunned it forward one last time and slammed into her quarter panel.

The crash played out in slow motion for Nathalie. She felt the backside of her sedan swing around and whip across the road, tires wailing even louder as they slid sideways. She could see the other car pull up and begin to slow down.

Finally, a part of her thought, this was ending.

Nathalie looked to her right to see where her car was headed, but all she saw was the darkness of the woods bordering the road. In a horrific collision of metal and rubber and glass, the Tesla slammed side-first into a large hickory tree. Nathalie didn't lose consciousness, but the impact left her woozy and disoriented. She tried to piece together what had just happened, but the thoughts eluded her. She could hear dripping, a sputtering flow plinking against metal. Gasses hissed from the engine. She tried to look and—Oh god, she thought—she couldn't see. Something was in her eyes. She wiped at them, felt something warm and wet. Was it blood? She tried to wipe it away, but her vision didn't improve.

She was reaching for her seatbelt when she heard the dull thump of footsteps approaching.

Was it whoever had run her off the road? Or someone there to help? Either way, Nathalie's pleas were the same.

"Help me," she said softly, gazing blindly toward the sound.

She heard something that sounded like cloth moving. Nathalie reached out, but whoever was there brushed her arms away. She started to reach again when she felt a sharp pain in her stomach. She pawed at it, only to find herself grabbing at a hand. A fist. It pulled away and punched again. Another sharp pain, this time in her side. And then again, squarely in her chest.

With that blow, Nathalie felt herself begin to go weak. Something inside her told her the truth: She was being stabbed. Someone was killing her. This was the end.

Her mind drifted to the reason she was even out here. To the conversation she'd been putting off. The one about the phone call.

About her past. About *their* past. She wasn't going to make it there. To him. But he—he had to know. With the last bit of her strength, she reached into her purse and grabbed the Post-It note. Someone would find her body. That someone would have to tell him. They wouldn't know it all, but it'd be enough for him to find the rest. He'd done it for them once before. She knew he could do it again.

Nathalie Grace McKenna exhaled one last time. No subsequent breath came. Somewhere beneath the blood and matted hair, her pupils affixed and dilated and she was gone.

Amidst the carnage, a crimson red creek of blood streamed its way down her arm, drops dripping one by one off her thumb and onto the yellow Post-It note she held, underlining the name she'd hastily written over a set of GPS coordinates:

JACKSON

TWO

AMY CHO SAW the wreckage as her ambulance rounded the bend. The black sedan, or what was left of it, reminded her of those totaled cars her high school would put out as an ominous reminder of the dangers of drunk driving.

"Looks like a bad one," said Tommy, her fellow EMT.

"Yeah," Amy said.

She followed the fire engine ahead of them up to the accident. A woman stood between the mangled mass of metal and a separate car parked with its hazard lights on, her hand over her mouth in horror. Must be who called this in, Amy thought.

"I'll get the stretcher," Tommy said as he opened his door.

Amy nodded and climbed down from the ambulance as well. With a gear bag slung over her shoulder, she walked calmly but quickly over to the accident, her ponytail of black hair bobbing in unison with her steps.

The first few firefighters from the engine company had beat her over to the totaled Tesla and were beginning to examine its driver, but yielded to Amy as she approached. She dropped her gear bag and leaned into the car. The driver was a woman, somewhere in her forties, if Amy had to guess. She was covered in blood and bruises.

"Ma'am, I'm a paramedic," she said. "Can you hear me?"

The woman didn't move.

Amy pulled on a pair of latex gloves and placed two fingers under the woman's jaw. "No pulse."

She pulled her hand back and looked at the woman. A few more things would confirm it, but Amy could tell the woman was gone. As Tommy began rolling the stretcher over to her, she looked back and shook her head. Tommy sighed as the firefighter next to him relayed the news of the dead woman over his radio.

"Doesn't look like there's anyone else in there with her," said another firefighter.

Amy nodded, still focused on the woman. Her sweater had a clean cut across the chest, one that didn't fit with the chaos of a car wreck. Amy reached in and examined the cut in the sweater with a gloved finger. Beyond, she could feel a puncture wound in the woman's skin. She reached her other hand in and tore the sweater open more.

"Holy hell," said a firefighter, "is that a stab wound?"

"Looks like it."

Amy began looking the woman over more closely. A car door closed somewhere past her, and out of the corner of her eye, she saw the first sheriff's deputy had arrived. He was a large man, with a thick waist and marine-style buzz cut. He shifted something on his belt and began slowly walking toward the accident.

By then, Amy had discovered two more puncture wounds on the woman's body, one down low on the left side and another squarely in the stomach.

"Is she gone?" the deputy asked.

The firefighter next to Amy nodded solemnly.

Amy stepped back and snapped off her rubber gloves. "Yes, she's dead. But you're going to need to get someone out here—I don't think the crash alone killed her."

IN THE HOURS THAT FOLLOWED, authorities closed the road around the crashed Tesla as emergency vehicles clogged the thoroughfare. Starting with more police and first responders, the scene now included journalists and television trucks as word began to spread that the wife of one of the capital's premier real estate developers had died under suspicious circumstances.

Amidst the commotion, Special Agent Booker Moore maneuvered his state police Explorer through the pandemonium, parking as close to the taped-off crime scene as the traffic jam would allow.

Climbing out, he could hear a couple of field reporters behind him broadcasting to their cameras. The vans beside the reporters identified them as local DC network affiliates. Moore shook his head. Vultures, he thought.

Moore slipped into his state police windbreaker and walked over toward the crash itself. Two men nearby were looking down and punching furiously at their phones. One of them noticed Moore approach, nodded and smiled at him, and slid his phone into his pocket.

"How's it going?" the man asked.

"Alright," Moore said. "Which one of you is Detective Ransdell?"

"I am," the other man said. "Good to meet you."

Ransdell extended a hand. Moore reached out and shook it, his large, dark brown hand enveloping Ransdell's pinkish paw.

Moore took off his glasses, placed his hands on his hips, and surveyed the crash. Now in his 50s, he wasn't as slim as he used to be, and cheeseburgers hung onto his sides more than he cared for, but he wasn't the type to be self-conscious about it. He took the signs he was getting older as certificates of experience, from his bald head down to the orthotics he wore in his shoes.

"It didn't take you long to get out here," Ransdell said. "We only got word a half hour ago that State was taking over the case."

"Order came from the governor himself, apparently," Moore said.

"I guess that's what you get when someone with the right last name ends up dead."

Moore fetched a toothpick from the small cartridge in his pocket and slipped it between his lips. "Guess so. Why don't you walk me through what you've got here?"

"Sure thing." Ransdell pointed at the skid marks on the road. "Looks like the car lost control as it headed north. You obviously know we've ID'd the driver as Nathalie Grace McKenna of Washington, DC. Her vehicle came to a stop right where it is now, wrapped around that tree. She has injuries synonymous with a crash of that magnitude, but as they examined her, medics also found several puncture wounds across her torso. Stab wounds."

"Was she stabbed before or after the accident?"

"We can't say for certain. That's something the medical examiner will have to answer."

"Do we have a cause for the crash yet?"

"Crash Investigation is still en route, but there's debris all up and down the road for a mile or so. My guess is another vehicle struck hers and she lost control."

"A hit and run?"

"That's what I'm thinking. But I guess that's on you now to figure out."

Moore made a sucking sound between his teeth and nodded. He hadn't taken his eyes off the crash since Ransdell started talking. Specifically, he hadn't looked away from the body of Nathalie McKenna. She sat there, in the driver seat of her Tesla, slumped over. Her hair, matted with dried blood, obscured her face. He'd seen the woman's DMV photo on his phone on the drive over. She was younger than him. And pretty. Nothing like she looked now.

How did you end up here? He wondered.

"One other thing, kind of strange," Ransdell said. He grabbed an evidence baggy from the man next to him and held it out for Moore to see. Inside was what looked like a Post-It note smeared with blood. "The rescue squad found this in her hand. There's a series of

THREE

BY NOON, Moore was back at Division Two Headquarters in Culpeper, going over everything that had been collected at the scene of the crash. Most of the Bureau of Criminal Investigation staff were working on the case in some capacity, the governor having called the Division Two commander and making it clear the McKenna case was now their top priority. Moore even suspected "reinforcements" would arrive by the end of the day.

He was wrapping up a phone call, liaising with Metropolitan Police in DC, when a tall and scholarly-looking man with reddish-brown hair knocked on his open door. Moore waved the man in as he hung up the phone.

Special Agent David Cotton stepped in and shut the door behind him. "You're going to want to see this."

He tossed a thick folder onto Moore's desk. Moore promptly opened it.

"I was running down possible leads on who or what *Jackson* could be," Cotton continued. "Mrs. McKenna wasn't always Mrs. McKenna. At one point she was Mrs. Nathalie Clay."

numbers on it. Looks like they could be coordinates. And a name, or a place, I guess. *Jackson*."

Moore took the bag.

"When we contacted the husband, Brad, we asked him about it," Ransdell added. "Said she didn't have any friends or family named Jackson, first or last name. We're not sure who or what Jackson is supposed to be."

Someone does, though, Moore thought. And it was his job to find them.

"She was married once before," Moore clarified.

"That's right. She was married to one *Jackson* Clay."

The revelation caused Moore to look up briefly at Cotton before he remembered all this information was already sitting in front of him. With his glasses on the bridge of his nose, he looked back down and continued reading as Cotton spoke.

"Mr. Clay is an interesting person. Former Army Ranger that hasn't had any real gainful employment for almost a decade. He doesn't have much in the way of priors, but that doesn't mean he hasn't kept busy. Flip the page."

Moore did as Cotton suggested. The next page was a report from the Harrisonburg Police Department. A paper clipped to it was a print-off of a news article.

ATF, POLICE INVOLVED IN SHOOTOUT WITH LOCAL MILITIA

"Two years ago," Cotton went on, "our Jackson Clay was mixed up in that mess with the Kingdom of Solomon clan. His name was also flagged in reference to that Bobbie Casto case out of West Virginia last year. He was wanted for aiding and abetting in connection to it, though charges were eventually dropped."

"He has an awful lot of run-ins with the law for someone with few arrests," Moore said.

"He does. And here's the kicker: His last known address is a P.O. Box in The Plains."

"That's maybe three or four miles from the site of the crash. Do we have a physical address?"

"Possibly. No house number or anything, but he's listed as the owner of a deed of land. The lot is north of the crash site, also just a few miles away."

At that, Moore sprung out of his chair, closed the folder, and tucked it under his arm as he opened his office door, leaving Cotton in his wake.

"Where are you going?" Cotton asked.

"To brief the Captain. I want this guy in a room this afternoon."

"What about Mrs. McKenna's husband?"

Moore didn't look back as he answered. "I'll settle for the *ex*-husband living off the grid like the Unabomber for now."

FOUR

SPECIAL AGENT JEN BAILEY parked her car in her usual space in front of the Division Seven State Police Headquarters, hopped out, and walked briskly across the parking lot. She hated being late. She hated it as a quality in other people, so she especially loathed herself on the rare occasion she was guilty of the same infraction.

An hour spent trying to coax her indoor cat back inside had forced her to skip her usual pre-work trip to Compass Coffee for her daily caffeine fix. It had made up some of the lost time, but not all of it. That stupid fucking cat, she thought. The little shit could drop dead for all she cared.

Her mind was flipping between cats and coffee as she waltzed through security and pushed open the doors to the Bureau of Criminal Investigation with enough force that a number of fellow special agents turned to see what was happening. Bailey waved and quietly mouthed an apology to her colleagues as she turned and made for her desk.

She'd just gotten her computer turned on when she heard the distinct tap-tapping of men's Oxfords behind her.

"Rough night last night?" a voice asked.

Bailey rolled her eyes. Ben Reeves was another agent at the bureau's office in Fairfax. Reeves was just under six feet with chestnut brown hair, but that's where the similarities between him and Bailey ended. Bailey was slim and leggy while Reeves was pale and doughy. Bailey wasn't exactly tan, but she looked downright bronzed compared to Reeves' pallid complexion. He stared at her with his usual smarmy smile. It made Bailey nauseous. She had the distinct feeling Reeves badly wanted to sleep with her, but the same was probably true for every other woman in the department as well.

"Something like that," Bailey grumbled. "What's up, Reeves?"

Reeves planted his rump on the empty portion of Bailey's desk. Bailey hadn't invited him to do so, but that didn't seem to bother Reeves.

"Not much," Reeves said. "You see the big news this morning?"

"No, I haven't."

"10-70 over in Division Two. Homicide."

Bailey turned back to her computer and rolled her eyes again. "There's five hundred across the state every year. I don't know why you think another one is news."

"How many of those were some multimillionaire's wife?"

Bailey glanced back at Reeves. That bit had gotten her attention more than anything Reeves had said so far. "Who? Where?"

"Some real estate developer's wife. Apparently, he's a big shot in DC. She ended up in her crashed Tesla with a bunch of stab wounds a ways northwest of Haymarket."

"A stabbing?"

"Yep. Division Two is working it. Request came from the governor himself."

"Do you know who at Two caught it?"

"I imagine about half the office is on it. Booker Moore's name came up, though, when I was talking with Cap."

Bailey leaned back and frowned. "Book, huh?"

"Yeah. You know him?"

"I've worked with him before. He's a good one. I'll have to give him a call. Wish him luck."

Bailey reached for the phone on her desk and punched in a number. Reeves' eyes started to work their way down from Bailey's head.

"Anyways," he said, "you doing anyth—"

"I'm on the phone, Reeves." She shooed him away, and Reeves left reluctantly. Bailey took a deep breath in and sighed as the phone rang.

After the second ring, the sound of a noisy room came through the other end, followed by a familiar voice. "Moore, BCI."

"Book, it's Jen Bailey at Division Seven. How are you?"

"Busy, actually."

"Yeah, I heard you caught a big one. It's loud on your end, are you out at the scene?"

"No, I'm in a meeting. We're about to brief one of our tactical teams."

"Wow, that was fast. Must've been the husband then, if it was that easy."

"Nothing's done, just bringing a POI in for questioning. Not the husband. Ex-husband, actually. Listen, really, I do have to run."

"Yeah, yeah. Sure. No problem. Go get 'em. Be safe out there."

"Will do. Let's talk later."

"Uh-huh."

They hung up. Interesting, Bailey thought. Moore was good, but having a person of interest that quick was fast by anyone's standards. It piqued her curiosity.

She got on her computer and pulled up what information was already there. When she read the victim's name, she leaned back in her chair, thinking. The name Nathalie Grace sounded familiar. How did she know it?

When it hit her, the revelation came with a surge of panic. She brought up the information on her computer, looking for marital records. There were two entries. The first was for Bradley Trent McKenna. The second was for Jackson Clay.

"Oh, *fuck*."

She hopped out of her desk chair and left the office quicker than she had come in. In less than a minute, she was back across the parking lot and at her car. She got in, closed the door, started tapping at her phone furiously, and put it to her ear.

"Goddammit," she said as she listened to the line ring. "Pick the fuck up, Clay."

THE BELL WAS the first thing that alerted Jackson Clay someone was coming. An old school-style bell rigged to a perimeter alarm around his property—a nifty innovation a survivalist friend had shown him—clamored in the living area of his cabin, rattling the wood siding and shaking dust off the support beams that criss-crossed below the cathedral-style ceiling. Jackson had just gotten out of the shower and pulled on a pair of boxer briefs when he heard it ring through the door to his bedroom.

He opened the door, grabbed his M9 Beretta from his gun safe, and moved to the window, peering out to see if he could spot who or what had set off the alert. There was nothing. He reached over, flicked the bell's kill switch, and listened. Everything was quiet save for the continued ringing in his ear.

Jackson opened the front door and stepped onto the porch. The hot water came off his body as steam, condensing in the chilly air. Practically naked, his six-foot-three frame was a tapestry of scars, trophies earned through a life lived hard. From the old bullet wound above his knee to the two slash marks across his chest, they dotted his body practically all the way up to his jawline, where a graying brown beard and fawn complexion joined his wet, unkempt hair.

Again, Jackson listened. Somewhere in the distance, he could hear the rumbling of vehicles navigating the dirt road leading up to his house. Someone was coming. He was listening so intently he nearly jumped when his cell phone began ringing inside the cabin. He reached through the door, grabbed it off a side table, and put it to his ear as soon as he saw who was calling.

"Hello, Bailey," he said.

"Jesus Christ, Jackson, tell me you didn't do it." Bailey's voice was frantic.

Jackson had met Bailey not long after he began this, his new life. He'd found salvation in finding those who needed his help most or those who reminded him of what he'd lost: his son. Bailey was an ally with a badge, willing to get him the information he couldn't on his own.

"What are you talking about?" Jackson asked.

"Your ex-wife, Clay. Tell me you didn't do it."

"Bailey, I have no idea wha—"

His brain processed what Bailey had just said. His heart sank. "What happened to Nat?"

Bailey met his pause with one of her own before answering him. "You really don't know."

"Bailey, what's happened?"

"She's ... she's gone, Clay. She was found in her car this morning. The car was wrapped around a tree off a highway."

"Where?"

"I don't know exactly. Northern Virginia. Somewhere between Haymarket and The Plains."

"That's where I am."

"I know."

There was a sharpness to the way she said the last part. As if it were accusatory. Now the beginning of their conversation was starting to make sense to Jackson. He closed his eyes, his mind following everything she'd just said to the part she hadn't said yet.

"Tell me," he said.

"The crash wasn't all. It looks like she was stabbed. Repeatedly.

It's been handed over to the State Police out that way. BCI, Clay. They know about you."

Bailey continued to speak, but Jackson didn't hear any of it. Everything went quiet in his head as he watched the first State Police cruiser turn down the dirt drive in front of his cabin, followed by another, then an unmarked SUV and a large, armored vehicle.

"Did you hear me, Clay? They're coming for you."

"Apparently so."

He watched as uniformed troopers spread out across his yard nestled in the barren trees. Beyond them, men in olive green tactical gear pointed their automatic rifles at him as they moved up to support the troopers. Jackson spread his arms and hands away from his body, holding his cell phone and pistol out for everyone to see.

"State police!" someone shouted. "Drop the gun!"

Jackson slowly bent over to his left and placed his pistol on the porch. Behind the troopers, a man climbed out of the driver's seat of the SUV. He was black and older, though Jackson thought his bald head helped make him look young for his age. The man's khakis and windbreaker told him he was probably a special agent, most likely the one in charge.

"Jackson Clay," the man said through a megaphone, "we have a warrant to search the property."

"Can I put pants on first?" Jackson asked.

The man seemed to confer with someone in the car before speaking again. "We need to detain you for our safety."

"Then detain me."

"I need you to get down on your knees and drop the cell phone like you dropped the gun."

Jackson did as he was told.

"Stay there with your hands in plain view," the man said.

With that, a pair of troopers approached Jackson. *They think I murdered Nathalie*, he thought. If they really found her out this way, and she didn't have another reason to be out here, he couldn't really blame them. He'd pursued people off of less. Of course, he hadn't always been right, and neither were the police in this matter. He knew it, he just needed them to know it.

To his right, he could hear Bailey's garbled voice still saying something. Jackson realized he'd put the phone down but never ended the call.

"Bailey," he said without turning to the phone, "If you can hear me, I need you to do something."

He paused to see if Bailey stopped talking. She did. The two troopers were ascending the steps to his porch. Jackson looked at them as he talked to Bailey.

"Call Bear Beauchamp."

FIVE

JACKSON SAT ALONE in an interview room at the Division Two offices, waiting for someone—anyone—to talk to him. After the troopers had detained him and moved him away from his house, the man in the windbreaker—who had introduced himself as Special Agent Booker Moore—asked if Jackson would come willingly to answer a few questions. Jackson didn't object.

From that point on, the collective police force had said little more than a few words to him. Jackson wondered if they were anticipating he'd lawyer up right away, but Jackson had no such plans. He couldn't decide if that was smart or foolish, but he also didn't know any lawyers, which made the decision rather easy.

A knock on the door came and Special Agent Moore stepped in with a white Styrofoam cup.

"Here's some coffee," he said. "Do you take cream or sugar?"

"Neither, but I'll take a water if you've got it," Jackson said.

Moore stepped back out. A few minutes later he was back—this time without knocking—and brought another man with him. Moore placed a bottle of water on the table in front of Jackson, who promptly took it.

Moore motioned to the man beside him. "This here is Special Agent David Cotton. He'll be joining us if that's alright."

"The more the merrier," Jackson said.

Moore and Cotton sat in the metal chairs across the table from Jackson and opened up a pair of folders. Cotton pulled out a notepad and placed it beside them.

"We're still going over your place," Moore began, "but we should be done by dinnertime, and we'll give you a receipt for whatever we take."

"Take your time," Jackson said. "Whatever you're looking for, it isn't there."

Moore took off his glasses, put his elbows on the table, and folded his hands in front of him. "Mr. Clay, do you know what this is about?"

"I'm guessing it's not about that parking ticket I didn't pay."

Moore snorted, both amused and annoyed by Jackson's sarcasm. "You're single, aren't you, Mr. Clay?"

"I am."

"Ever been married?"

"Once. But you already knew that."

"Yes." Moore consulted the papers in front of him. "A ... Nathalie Clay."

"I believe she changed her name back to Grace after we divorced."

Moore smiled. Jackson could hear him breathing through his aquiline nose, and thought the man sounded like a bull. Jackson wondered if that made him the putz waving the red cape.

"Did you know she remarried?" Moore asked.

"Not specifically," Jackson answered.

"What do you mean by that?"

"We lost touch after we separated. So, no, I didn't know as a matter of fact, but it doesn't surprise me to learn she did."

"What makes you say that?"

"People remarry. People do lots of things, for that matter. So, are you going to cut to the chase and tell me why I'm here?"

Moore glanced at Cotton. He shrugged.

"Mr. Clay," Moore said slowly, "your ex-wife, Nathalie, was found dead this morning."

Jackson's face remained emotionless. "Someone did something to her."

"Why do you say that?"

"Because you're here asking the ex-husband questions. I'm not exactly next of kin. Two plus two equals four."

Moore nodded. "Unfortunately, you're not wrong. She was found in her car. It was wrecked off of Route 601."

"Near me."

"That's right."

"Do you think someone ran her off the road?"

Moore looked at Cotton again, who looked up from his notes. Jackson knew about the stabbing and they knew about the stabbing. It was only a question of who would put their cards on the table first.

"Yes, it appears she was involved in a hit and run," Moore said.

"But," Jackson said, pausing as if he was reading the man, "that's not all, is it?"

"No. It also appears she was stabbed. Several times, I'm sorry to say."

Moore waited for a reaction from Jackson, but nothing came. Cotton flipped over a printout and placed it in front of Jackson.

"The crash site," Moore continued, "was just a few miles from your house. And to the best of our knowledge, she didn't have another reason to be out there."

"You mean besides me."

"Yes, besides you."

"I already told you. I haven't had contact with her. I don't know why she was out there, but it wasn't to see me."

"Are you sure about that?" Moore pulled his hands in and

brought them close to his chest. "You seem to be a pretty smart guy. I'd even venture to say you know more than you're letting on. But the thing is, Mr. Clay, we know things, too. So why don't you just level with us? Why would your ex-wife come to see you?"

"I told you. She wouldn't."

Moore leaned back in his chair and sighed. Cotton fished out a plastic bag labeled *Evidence* and held it out for Jackson to see. It was the duo's "gotcha" moment.

"This was found in her hand, Mr. Clay," Cotton said. "She made it her last action on this earth to hold onto it."

Jackson looked at the bloody Post-It note in the bag. His name was scribbled down above a set of coordinates—a set of coordinates leading directly to his cabin.

"I honestly don't know why she would have this," Jackson said.

Moore sat up straight. For the first time since they'd met, Jackson looked visibly rattled. He'd been waiting for this and wouldn't miss his opportunity now. "I'll ask you again, Mr. Clay. When was the last time you spoke to your ex-wife?"

Jackson sat back, still looking at the note from afar. What is this about? he wondered. Had Nat really been looking for him?

He looked up at the two agents. They were waiting for an answer. Jackson thought for a moment, then leaned forward.

JACKSON WATCHED *as Nat signed her papers. The whole thing didn't make any sense to him. Years spent together, making memories—making a life—all dissolved with a few strokes of a pen. At least legally, anyways.*

"Excellent," the lawyer said as Nathalie finished. "And now, Mr. Clay?"

Jackson leaned forward and placed a thick yellow envelope on the table. "Already signed. You can make sure I did it right, though."

The lawyer gave him a professional smile and took the packet. Nat

27

looked at Jackson as if he'd committed some faux pas. Jackson shrugged. Had they agreed to do it together in the office? He couldn't remember.

The truth was the last two weeks had been a blur. Packing things and moving them into storage. Searching for a one-bedroom or studio apartment. Taking meetings with said lawyer. Ending a chapter of your life proved to be rather time-consuming.

Jackson and Nat had no interest in trying to best each other in a contentious divorce but had agreed to hire a lawyer to help them both navigate the process. As it turned out, ending something that all started with a couple "I do's" and a piece of paper was rather difficult, even in cases where the two sides weren't interested in fighting. For one, nothing could happen until the two were separated for some time. In Virginia, that was six months or a year if the two had a child between them. The six months were yet another devastating reminder of what they had already lost.

"Everything looks good," the lawyer said. "Let me take these to get everything finalized, and I'll have you on your way."

The lawyer stood and trotted out his office door, leaving Nat and Jackson alone. They both glanced around the office, trying not to acknowledge the awkwardness.

"Well, I guess that's that," Jackson said.

"I guess so," Nathalie agreed.

"Are you going to keep staying with your parents?"

"Until I find a place."

"Yeah."

"What about you?"

"I'm going to a motel tonight. I'm out of the house. Don't worry."

"That's not what I meant." Nat folded her arms and legs and sighed.

"Sorry."

Nat shook her head in reply.

"I just ... I guess I'm still trying to do right by you. Even though this is over. Maybe I owe you that much."

"I've told you a thousand times, Jackson, you don't owe me anything. I don't blame you for ... it."

The lawyer returned with the same zest he'd left with and plopped back into his chair. "Great, everything is good to go. Here are copies for each of you. I'll get this all filed and squared away. And ... I think that's it. We'll be in touch."

Nat and Jackson rose out of their chairs and thanked him. One after another, they somberly filed out of the office and shared an elevator down to the lobby in silence. As they got outside and the brisk fall air blew dancing leaves between them, Nat and Jackson stopped and faced each other one last time.

"So, I guess this is goodbye," Jackson said.

"Yeah," Nat said, unable to meet his eyes. "Um, goodbye."

Jackson offered a hug, and Nat took it. They embraced each other for a moment before Nat pushed herself gently away.

"Can I ask you a question?" Jackson asked.

"Sure.".

He looked out at the parking lot. A few miles beyond it, out of view, was their house, empty and ready for sale. At one point, it had been a home. A home they'd built together. Now, it was just a reminder of everything that had gone so horribly wrong.

"Do you think we would've made it? You know, if he hadn't ... if we hadn't lost him."

"We didn't lose him, Jackson. He—"

"You know what I mean."

Nathalie folded her arms and put a hand over her face. The question breached the levees, and she began to sob. "I'm sorry, I can't. I can't do this anymore. Not right now."

"Okay. I'm sorry."

"Listen, the realtor, um, she said she'd let us know when there was an offer and, um—"

"I'll take care of it."

"And she knows our situation so—"

"Nat, I said I'll take care of it."

Now Nat looked up at him. She nodded and mouthed what Jackson thought was "thank you" before placing a hand on his arm.

"Bye," she said.

"Bye."

Jackson stood there and watched Nat get into her car. She turned the ignition, pulled out of the parking lot, and took off down the road.

"I think so," Jackson whispered to himself. "I think we would've made it."

SIX

BY THE TIME the two special agents had finished up with Jackson, the sun was setting behind the large field in front of the Division Two offices. It had been a long, miserable day, but the knot in Jackson's chest undid itself a little when he saw a burly bearded man leaning against an old red Chevy Suburban in front of the building.

Bear Beauchamp and Jackson had met as Jackson searched for a missing girl a couple of years back. Bear followed that through to the end with him. Now, they were both friends and business partners, as they co-owned a hunting supply store in Martinsville. Bear—thick in every aspect of the word—came off his truck and slid one hand into his denim overalls as he scratched at his thick brown beard with the other.

"So, what's the verdict? Firin' squad?" Bear asked.

"No," Jackson said. "Not yet, anyway."

Jackson extended his hand. Bear took it and used it to pull the man in for one of his namesake hugs.

"Good to see ya, brother," Bear said.

"You, too."

"That cop lady ran me down. Special Agent Whatsherface. Told me a little about what's goin' on. She said if I couldn' find ya at your place you were probably here. I went in and asked, but the asshole in there told me to kick rocks. I told him I paid his salary, and I wasn' goin' nowhere."

Jackson snorted. "They asked if I'd come here for some questioning. I agreed."

"You got a ride home?"

Jackson shook his head.

"C'mon. I'll give ya a lift."

FOR THE FIRST twenty minutes or so, neither Jackson nor Bear spoke. Jackson sat in the passenger seat, watching the road ahead. Bear was willing to do the same for a while, but eventually the quiet got to him.

"So, this is about your ex-wife, right?"

"Yeah," Jackson said. "She was found dead this morning. In a wreck. Someone also stabbed her."

"And are we happy about this? Sad about this?"

Jackson looked at him as if he'd said something horrible.

"What, Jacky Boy?"

"She was killed, Bear. Stabbed to death. She didn't deserve that."

"My bad, my bad. All I'm sayin' is I know plenty of guys that'd be goin' out for drinks if they learned their ex was dead."

"It's not like that. She was a good, decent person. It just didn't work out between us. Too many bad memories after Evan."

"I got ya, brother. Like I said, my bad."

Bear got off the interstate and started up the winding roads that led to Jackson's cabin.

Jackson, realizing where they were, had a thought come to him. "I want to make a quick stop."

"Sure thing. Where to?"

"There's a left up ahead. Take it."

Bear did as he was asked. He continued for a couple of miles before Jackson asked him to slow down. Jackson leaned forward and studied the area as they drove through it.

"What are we lookin' for?" Bear asked.

"Where Nat crashed," Jackson said.

Bear cruised down the road slowly. Dusk had come, leaving the Suburban's headlights as the only real means to see anything. A half-mile down the road, a grouping of four black skid marks slashed across the road in a long, sweeping arc.

"Pull over," Jackson said.

Bear put the SUV on the grassy shoulder of the highway and the two of them hopped out. He reached into the cab of the truck, grabbed two flashlights from behind his seat, flicked them on, and came over to Jackson, who was following the skid marks in what little light the waning day had to offer.

"You think this is the spot?" Bear asked.

"The marks look pretty fresh," Jackson said.

He walked diagonally across the highway, following the four skids. They crossed over one another, indicating a car had spun. When he got to where they ended on the other side of the road, Jackson aimed his flashlight forward. In front of him was a large hickory tree. On one side, most of its bark had been stripped away. Jackson walked up to the tree and examined it more closely. Inside the scraped bark were little flecks of metal and paint. Black paint. The special agents had told Jackson Nat's car was a black Tesla.

"Looks like this is the spot," Jackson said.

"I'm sorry, brother," Bear said. "Looks like she spun out. Lost control."

"No. Someone forced her to lose control."

He began scanning the surrounding area with his flashlight. Bear wasn't sure what Jackson was going to find that the police hadn't, but he was happy to let Jackson do what he felt he needed.

"She was driving northbound."

"Okay. So, what does that tell us?"

"She was headed for my place."

Bear slipped his free hand into the pocket of his overalls and sighed. "That's possible. But you don' know that she was out here for ya. Din' ya say ya haven't talked to her in years?"

"Well over ten. But she was. She was looking for me."

"And how do ya know that?"

Jackson stopped scanning and now shined his flashlight down the road in the direction Nat had been heading. Bear stood behind him, both of them in the middle of the road, looking at the deserted two-lane highway.

"She had a piece of paper with her," Jackson said. "It had my name written on it, and the coordinates to my place."

"How would she even get that sort of thing?" Bear asked. "Was she the kind of person that would know stuff like that? Coordinates and whatnot?"

"Not really, no. In the time that I knew her, she was a paralegal. A bookworm. She'd take a cozy night in over camping in the woods any day."

Bear scratched at his beard. "So, you're supposin' someone gave her those coordinates to ya?"

Jackson nodded as he turned to Bear. "And I'm starting to think it got her killed."

SEVEN

AT A LITTLE PAST eight that evening, Moore was the only one still in BCI at Division Two in Culpeper. With everyone else gone, his desk lamp cast a low, ominous light over the rest of the open-concept workspace, like a match in a dark cavern.

He was reviewing files for the McKenna case when he heard one of the doors to the office swing open. Moore looked up to see Special Agent Jen Bailey walking toward him, armed with a warm smile and a bottle of brown liquor.

"Good evening, Book," she said.

"Jen Bailey," Moore said. "What are you doing here?"

"I come bearing gifts."

As she walked up to Moore's desk, she held the bottle out for him to examine.

"Booker's Bourbon," he read aloud.

"Yeah," Bailey said. "You've never had your namesake?"

"Can't say that I have."

"It's good bourbon. Made in Kentucky."

"Most of the good stuff is."

"You got a pair of glasses around here?"

"There's Styrofoam cups in the break room."

"That'll work."

Moore pointed over to a small enclave in the corner of the office. Bailey nodded and stepped away before coming back with two cups. She opened the bottle and filled each cup halfway, then slapped the corked top back into the bottle.

Bailey sat down and extended her cup toward Moore. "Cheers."

Moore echoed her and sipped from his cup. It tasted like gasoline to him, but he pretended to enjoy it for his company's sake.

"So, you pick that guy up?" Bailey asked.

It took Moore a moment to remember he'd briefly read her in on what was happening during their phone call that morning. "Oh. Yeah. Yeah, we talked to him."

"I'm guessing by the lack of activity around here it didn't pan out."

"There was nothing at his place tying him to the scene. We haven't cleared him yet, but we had nothing to hold him on, either."

Bailey nodded as she took a swig from her cup. "You check his phone records yet?"

"Not yet." Moore eyed Bailey quizzically. It was a rather specific question for small talk. "It's on my to-do list. He was talking to someone on the phone when we rolled up. Been meaning to see who."

With that, Moore started to shift the papers around in front of him, looking for Jackson Clay's phone records. Bailey watched him do this and wondered if she should let him find out for himself or tell him like she'd come here to do.

"I know whom he was talking to, Book," she said.

Moore stopped sifting through the papers. "What are you talking about?"

"Your guy, Jackson Clay. I know him. He's ... a contact of mine. Of sorts. I guess. It's hard to explain."

Moore tossed the few papers still in his hand aside and leaned back in his chair. The springs on it whined. "Well, you better start," he said, "because I've got a body in the medical examiner's office and just about everyone ranked higher than me looking for answers."

"C'mon, Moore. You're an old pro, same as me. You work people just like me. Sometimes they need something. Sometimes we need something. Everyone needs their back scratched now and again."

"But are you scratching the back of my killer?"

"Clay didn't do it."

"How do you know?"

"Because I know. I would bet … I'm almost certain he didn't do it."

"So first you know, and now you're 'almost certain'?"

Bailey shook her head and flashed the kind of smirk she gave when she grew frustrated. Moore waited for her to continue, but she didn't. Then, he started to put the other puzzle pieces together.

"It was you. You were on the phone with him this morning."

"I called him, yes."

"Good god, Bailey! You called him and what? Warned him we were coming?"

"Not specifically for that, no."

"Then what?"

"I don't know. To ask him if he did it. For fuck's sake, Moore, I found out in a matter of minutes you liked him for his ex's murder and that you were executing a warrant. I didn't exactly have time to weigh my options."

"That was stupid, Bailey. Damn stupid. What if he decided he didn't want to go? What if I had to spend this afternoon calling a spouse or spouses to tell them their loved one got shot and wasn't coming home?"

"He wouldn't do that. That's not him."

"Yeah, well you seem to be betting a lot of people's lives on what this guy is and isn't capable of. Including my vic."

Moore's raised tone hushed Bailey. The two of them sat for a moment, staring into their cups. Moore swirled his around, bucked his head back, and took the rest of his bourbon in a single shot.

"Be honest with me, Book," Bailey said. "You kicked him free. You could've held him at least overnight, you could have everyone here, at battle stations, burning the midnight oil on him, but you don't. Because despite whatever circumstantial evidence you have, your gut tells you he didn't do it."

Moore didn't look up from his empty cup. "Maybe."

"Maybe?" Bailey leaned forward and put an elbow on Moore's desk. "C'mon, Book. Level with me."

Again, Moore leaned back in his chair. He took a deep breath in and sighed, looking over everything on his desk before coming back to Bailey. "Do I like him less for it than when I picked him up? Sure. He was calm. Controlled. Barely showed any emotion. That doesn't sync up with how Nathalie McKenna died. But the fact of the matter is, of the leads I've got in front of me, he still looks the best for it. And I'm going to work it accordingly, no matter what you came here to tell me."

Bailey gave a terse smile and nodded. "Fair enough. Just keep it all in mind."

"I will. And for what it's worth, I appreciate you coming to tell me in person about the phone call."

Bailey nodded again and headed for the door. Moore stood and watched her as she headed out.

"Even if he didn't do it," he said, "your boy has a knack for being a pain in the ass."

"Yeah," Bailey said, pushing the door open, "he's good at that."

She turned the corner and disappeared down the dark hallways of the building. Moore eased back in his chair, alone again. He surveyed the chaos that was his desk. On the edge of it, the bottle of bourbon caught the light of his lamp and taunted him. With another sigh and a shake of his head, he grabbed the bottle and poured himself another cup.

EIGHT

THE NEXT MORNING, Bear woke up to find himself alone in Jackson's house. Getting up from the couch he'd crashed on, he peeked through his friend's open bedroom door to find the bed perfectly made and empty.

Left to his own devices, Bear found a warm pot of coffee in the kitchen. He rifled through the cabinets until he found a mug, and poured himself a cup. He wandered throughout the cabin for a moment before coming around to a front window. Jackson was jogging down the dirt drive that led up to the house.

Bear opened the door and freezing cold air rushed past him, an unwelcome house guest in the otherwise toasty cabin. He let the door shut behind him and stepped onto the deck. Jackson, dressed head to toe in sweats, thumped his way home in a hearty trot. When he got to his front stairs, he stopped and doubled over, catching his breath. Bursts of hot air plumed from him before wafting harmlessly away and joining the morning fog overhead.

"Mornin'," Bear greeted.

Jackson nodded in reply. He stood upright, placed his hands on his hips, and began to slowly circle the yard directly in front of the stairs.

"Couldn't sleep?" Bear asked.

Jackson shook his head, still trying to slow his heart rate down to its efficient resting rate of sixty beats per minute. Bear had heard Jackson tossing and turning the few times he'd gotten up to relieve himself in the night. He supposed now Jackson had eventually grown frustrated and opted to run off his stifled emotions.

"I was gonna whip up some breakfast, but you don' have much except beer and granola bars," Bear said.

"Don't sweat it," Jackson said.

Bear snorted at the irony of the statement. "I don' mind runnin' to the store to grab a few things. Maybe some other meals? More beer and bird food, if that's what ya want."

Jackson didn't laugh at Bear's attempt at humor. He shook his head, still pacing. "No need. Thanks, though."

Bear nodded and drank from his mug. He watched his friend continue to pace back and forth. The man looked like a cheetah at the zoo, pent up and anxious.

"You know, you could run all the way to her place in DC and back and not feel better."

Jackson scowled at Bear. "I'm not running from this."

"Never said you were. At least, not in the way ya mean."

The cheetah prowled, leering at its onlooker.

"What I mean is, you're not going to exercise what you're feeling out of your system. You've got to do what you do. What we do. Fix this thing."

"There's nothing to fix here. She's dead. Nat is dead. You can't fix that."

"Your head's still on the chopping block, brother. And even if it weren't, whoever killed Nat is still out there."

Jackson locked eyes with Bear and shook his head again.

"C'mon. Don' act like you haven't been thinkin' where to start since the cops kicked ya free."

Jackson stopped pacing, his walk slowing steadily until he stopped altogether, his breathing following suit.

He took one more deep breath in and sighed. "The husband."

"What?"

"The husband. Brad or something. She doesn't have any family left, and I don't know if she has friends or anything. He's the only point of contact for her I know."

"Then we go to the husband."

"The police will be all over him. Either working with him as the widower or watching him as the suspect."

Bear snorted again as he took another sip of coffee. "Fuck 'em. Let 'em watch what we do. When do we get to work?"

NINE

A QUICK GOOGLE search didn't turn up an exact address for Brad and Nathalie McKenna, but an online *Washingtonian* article mentioned their posh penthouse condo at the Omni Lofts & Residences. That was plenty for Jackson to work with. He hopped into Bear's Suburban and together the two of them headed for DC.

An hour later, Bear was leaning over the steering wheel as they circled an impressive brick-and-glass building tucked within the sloping hillsides of Georgetown. The narrow streets were lined with cars, giving Bear a sense of claustrophobia in his large SUV.

"I think this is the place," he said.

"Okay. I can hop out here. Just find a place to sit," Jackson said.

"Uh-uh. I ain't lettin' ya go in there alone."

Jackson looked at him, confused. "What do you mean?"

"You may be the cops' prime suspect, but I know who's on top of *your* shit list. That dude in there."

"I don't know who killed Nat."

"But I know who you want it to be. I'm not goin' to let one thing come to another and you take a swing at the guy. Or worse. C'mon, I'll find a spot and *we'll* go in. *Together.*"

Jackson sighed and sat back in the passenger seat. A few minutes later, Bear found a spot a block away, and the two doubled back on foot.

The lobby of the Omni Lofts & Residences was long but spacious, cutting the bottom floor of the building almost in half. Cream-colored marble or granite—Jackson honestly wasn't sure—made up the floors and most of the walls, as well as the large L-shaped desk where two clerks stood expectantly behind computers.

"In't this somethin'," Bear said.

Jackson motioned for Bear to follow. "Come on, over here."

He walked up to the nearest clerk, a tall bespectacled man with a long head and round chin.

The man gave Jackson an unctuous smile. "Hello, welcome to the Omni. Are we here for a resident?"

"Yes, actually," Jackson said. "I was hoping to speak with Mr. McKenna."

The clerk stared at Jackson blankly.

"Brad McKenna," Jackson clarified.

"Yes, I know who resides on our top floor. May I ask, what is your business with him?"

"It's a private matter."

The man exchanged a look with the other clerk and Bear started to get the feeling they were being quietly mocked by the lobby staff. He elbowed in next to Jackson and placed his beefy hands on the front desk.

"Listen, Jeeves," he said, "we're here to have a chat with the man. So are ya goin' to show us the way, or do we need to figure it out for ourselves?"

A security guard near the front door heard Bear's agitated voice and began to approach, but the clerk waved him off.

"Sir," he said to Bear with the same ingratiating grin, "Mr. McKenna isn't in. And even if he were, we don't simply allow ... *strangers* to approach our guests. Privacy is valued here."

43

"Uh-huh. And where, exactly, could we find Mr. McKenna now, then?"

"I'm afraid even if I knew, that wouldn't be information I'd be able to share with you."

Bear was about to escalate the situation even further when the spinning doors to the front came around and a small woman walked into the lobby. Drowning in a winter parka, she carefully brought a vase of flowers over to the front desk.

"Delivery for Mr. Brad McKenna," she said.

The tall clerk nodded, stepping away from Jackson and Bear to take the flowers. "Thank you."

He slid the vase across the desk before lifting it and carrying it into a back room. As it came past them, Jackson saw the tag with the order information:

Maria Wilkins, The Hallvard Project

When the clerk returned, Bear was ready to continue his crusade, but Jackson cut in. "Thanks, anyway."

The clerk said something in farewell as Jackson and Bear made for the door, but neither of them heard it. When they were through the swinging doors and out on the street, Bear hastened his gait to catch up to Jackson, who was already walking briskly toward the Suburban.

"We're givin' up that easily?" Bear asked.

"No," Jackson said. "I have another place we can ask around. Come on."

TEN

THE HALLVARD PROJECT was located on the top floor of an office building on K Street directly across from McPherson Square. Jackson Googled the organization as Bear drove across downtown to the address.

According to their website, The Hallvard Project was a non-profit organization providing underprivileged people with a legal defense against serious criminal charges. Maria Wilkins was listed on the website as the Executive Director.

Bear parked in the parking garage beneath the building and the two of them took the elevators up to The Hallvard Project offices. Beyond a pair of pristine glass doors, a young woman with fiery red hair sat behind a large oak desk. She smiled warmly as the two of them entered.

"Hello. How may I assist you?"

"Hi, my name is Jackson. I was hoping to speak to Ms. Wilkins."

"Mrs. Wilkins, yes. And what can I say this is regarding?"

"Nathalie McKenna."

"Oh, I'm so sorry. Did you know her?"

Jackson hadn't expected her to know what had happened or even who Nathalie was. Caught off guard, the most he could muster in reply was a solemn nod.

"We all just loved her here," the woman said. "Let me see if Mrs. Wilkins is available."

The woman swung to her side, picked up the phone on her desk, and pressed a button. She had a brief, quiet conversation Jackson could hear but couldn't make out, and then promptly hung up.

"She'd be happy to see you two now. Take that hallway there all the way down. The office is the last in the corner," the woman said.

Jackson nodded and thanked the woman.

The Hallvard Project offices were an unremarkable array of cubicles and conference rooms. Jackson assumed they could be mistaken for any one of a thousand offices around downtown DC.

As the two of them neared the corner office, a woman in a plum purple jacket and skirt stepped out and stood by the door. Jackson took her to be in her late forties or early fifties. Her salt-and-pepper hair was done up in a bun, tucked behind a set of reading glasses sitting atop her head.

"Hello, I'm Maria Wilkins. I don't believe we've met."

"I don't believe so. My name is Jackson Clay. This is Be—ah, Archibald Beauchamp."

Jackson felt Bear's nickname was perhaps too casual for this meeting. Bear, for his part, gave Jackson a subtle sneer.

"Clay," Maria repeated. Her eyes locked forward, and Jackson could tell her mind was making a series of mental calculations. "You're Nathalie's ex-husband. I had a feeling when I heard the name Jackson."

"Yes. I guess Nathalie must've mentioned me."

"She did, but it was the name Clay that put it together. That was Evan's last name, right?"

Hearing Evan's name out of a stranger's mouth hit Jackson like a body blow from a seasoned boxer. "So, she told you about Evan, too?"

"Yes, we talked a bit about each other's lives while she worked here. I considered Nathalie a friend. Why don't we come into my office here and have a seat?"

Maria motioned them in, and Jackson and Bear followed, sitting down in two chairs opposite her desk. Maria sat behind the desk in a computer chair and pulled herself forward.

"What did she tell you about Evan?" Jackson asked.

"At first, not much," Maria said. "She had a locket, and I once noticed the initials weren't hers or Brad's. When I asked her about it she told me she lost a son in a previous marriage. Then, of course, that phone call came and everything with that. She told me a bit more over these last couple weeks. About his disappearance and ultimately how you two separated. That sort of thing. I'm sorry, by the way, that happened to you two. It's unbelievably awful."

Jackson ignored the condolences he'd heard a hundred times. "What phone call?"

"Oh, I'm sorry. I thought she must've reached out to you and that's why you were here."

"Unfortunately, no. She was on her way to—no, we didn't speak before she died."

"Sorry to hear that. For what it's worth, she spoke well of you."

"Thank you. So, you mentioned a phone call?"

Maria didn't say anything at first. Her gaze shifted between Bear and Jackson as she tapped her fingers on her desk.

"Please," Jackson said. "What phone call?"

Maria sighed and leaned forward. "A couple weeks ago, we got a call from Keene Mountain State Prison in southwest Virginia. That in and of itself was fairly normal, given the work we do. However, an inmate asked for Nathalie. That *was* weird, since Nathalie did not handle any cases directly."

"Who called her?"

"Dale Jeffers."

A sharp pain formed in Jackson's chest. He felt his pulse quicken, his blood pressure rising.

Bear looked back and forth between Jackson and Maria. "Dale Jef—who ... who is that?"

"The man who took and killed Evan," Jackson said coldly.

"The man you—you were the one who found him, right? You found him with another boy?"

"A little boy named Oscar Quinones."

Maria sat back and recomposed herself. "Dale Jeffers is an inmate at Keene Mountain. And, yes. Though he was charged only with the abduction of Oscar Quinones, he is suspected of abducting—"

"And *killing*," Jackson said.

"—it's believed he's responsible for several children that were abducted and are now presumed dead."

"Like my son. What did Jeffers want?"

"Maybe that's a conversation for you to have with someone else. Later, when you've had time to process."

"I'm asking *you*. What did he want?"

Maria folded her arms across her chest. "He wanted ... to tell Nathalie he didn't kill Evan."

"So he wanted to lie to her."

"I don't know. I can only tell you what I know."

"Well, *I* know. He's lying."

"He called and said that he had started some program there at Keene Mountain. Therapy, basically, and part of it was to make amends for those that he had hurt. He also called the Quinones family and apparently apologized, admitting to what he did."

"But he bullshitted Nathalie."

"Like I said, Mr. Clay, I can only tell you what I know. I know Jeffers is not a good man. And he didn't want any sort of defense from us or this organization, not that we'd offer it. But he did seem, based on the phone call, genuinely concerned about letting Nathalie —and, I guess, you—live on with the belief that he killed Evan."

"Trying to clear a conscience he magically grew in prison."

"Maybe. And maybe it truly all is, like you said, bullshit. But I also can't think of a reason for him to come forward like this. He gains nothing from it."

Jackson was quiet. Inside, he was a fiery ball of anger growing larger by the second. He should've killed Dale Jeffers when he had the chance all those years ago. He couldn't bring himself to do it then, but if he'd only known the pain it'd save him now, maybe things would be different. If he had killed him, maybe Nat would still be alive.

"I imagine this is all a lot to take in," Maria said. "Sorry to be the one to tell you."

"I'm sorry, too." Jackson rose out of the chair and moved toward the office door.

Maria and Bear took that to mean their meeting had ended and followed suit. Jackson opened the door and started down the hall without saying goodbye, his mind cluttered with a thousand thoughts.

"Thank you for seeing us," Bear said to Maria.

But Jackson continued to walk. Halfway down the hall another thought ricocheted through his mind.

He turned back and called to Maria. "Her office—Nathalie's office. Can I see it?"

"Of course," Maria said. "Right this way."

Maria escorted Bear and Jackson through an array of cubicles until they arrived at one with a small pile of photos and flowers at its entryway. Most of the flowers were the same kind. Jackson recognized the large, curved petals, which gave the flower a concave shape like a satellite dish.

"Here," Maria said. "People around the office—mostly the women—wanted to make a memorial for Nathalie. Most of the flowers are—"

"Anemones," Jackson said. "Windflowers. They were her favorite."

"Yes, so I am told. Inside here, we've boxed up most of her things.

We weren't sure what to do with it all and Brad, her husband, hasn't returned any of our calls. You're welcome to look in and see."

Jackson nodded and smiled in thanks, but couldn't bring himself to look in the cubicle. He crouched down and admired the flowers. Where everything else in the office was colored in shades of beige and gray, the anemones were vibrant, a medley of scarlet and violet. They had a way of brightening up even the most morose settings—like a memorial to a beloved coworker. Nat had loved that about them, their ability to bring color to even the dreariest of times. She'd planted them all over their small front yard, and every once in a while, she'd collected a few for a vase in their front window. It'd been over a decade since Jackson could remember seeing windflowers like these.

JACKSON STOOD, *looking at the flowers in the window. They'd been there for a few days now and were starting to wilt. Even the most beautiful things died without proper care. Jackson couldn't help but see the parallels between them and his failed marriage.*

"The couch over there goes, too," *Nat told the two movers.*

The men in navy blue coveralls nodded and got on either side of the sofa before lifting it and carrying it out the door. All those years of happy marriage and it'd come to this, Jackson thought. The going-out-of-business sale on their lives.

"You can have the recliner, too, if you want," *Jackson said to Nat.*

"That's okay. You used it more. You take it."

Jackson and Nat had agreed to settle who-got-what themselves. Jackson thought it might make everything less painful, but if this was sparing him something, he couldn't imagine what.

Nat came up to his side, and the two looked out the front bay window of their home in Oregon Hill, Richmond, for the last time.

"So, what are you going to do?" *Nat asked.*

"Well, you said it'd be alright if I stayed here. At least until I found a place."

"No, I know. I meant about that other stuff."

There was an edge to the way she said 'stuff', cluing Jackson into what she meant. But Jackson would've known without the help. She was talking about him. Him and Dale Jeffers.

"I thought you didn't care," Jackson said.

"I care, Jackson. It's just ... ugh. I'm fucking exhausted, Jackson. I'm exhausted by all of this."

"I know. I'm sorry."

In the months since they had come to terms with the fact that their boy, Evan, wasn't coming home, the two of them had grieved in different ways. Jackson had taken to the pursuit of justice, determined to find who had done this to them. A fight with Nathalie outside the police station one evening had spurred the cause. Now, though, as he searched, Nathalie wanted nothing to do with it. When he'd brought her the name of the guy responsible for taking their son, she'd stormed out of their home. That had been the beginning of the end.

"What is it you'd like me to do, Nat?" Jackson asked.

"No, don't do that," Nat said.

"Do what?"

"Make this about me."

"I'm not."

"Jackson, don't you see? That's why you're doing this. Why you looked for that man. Why you needed to show me. You need someone to tell you it's okay to do what I know you want to do."

"So, tell me."

"No, I'm not going to do that. This is about you. You and this crusade you're on. If you've got to make it about this guy, that's about you, not me. I'm not going to be the reason you need. I'm not going to give you the permission you're looking for."

The movers had loaded the sofa in the back of the truck and now seemed to be avoiding coming back into the house. *They must hear our raised voices*, Jackson thought.

"It won't bring him back, you know," Nat said, her voice calmer. "Going after that guy."

"I know."

"Then why do it?"

Jackson thought for a moment. He'd wrestled with that very question the last few weeks. Who was he? Some wannabe vigilante? Or was he a father fulfilling his final duty? It's hard to know which side of the line you're on when you don't know where the line is.

"Because I have to," he said softly. "I can't move on until I do."

ELEVEN

JACKSON DIDN'T SAY a word the entire drive back to his cabin. Bear had made several efforts—giving his hot takes about the absurdity of city life—but they had all been in vain. Jackson just sat rigid in the passenger seat, staring straight ahead.

"Ya know, a cop's goin' to think I put a dummy in your seat to use these HOV lanes," Bear had said as they merged onto Interstate 66.

Jackson gave a small smile and nodded, acknowledging the humor.

When they pulled up to Jackson's cabin, Bear turned off the engine, but neither of them got out of the Suburban. For a moment, Bear joined Jackson in quietly staring out the windshield before turning to him.

"Penny for your thoughts?" Bear asked.

"What do you want to know?"

It was only mid-afternoon, but here in late winter, the sun was already low in the sky, trying hopelessly to stay afloat above the naked tree branches that stretched over the top of Jackson's home.

"What thoughts are pinballin' around in that head of yours? Shit, anythin'."

"Did I really get it wrong?"

"What do ya mean?"

"Dale Jeffers. And Evan. Did I really get it wrong?"

Bear swung his arm around the back of his seat, turning his body more toward Jackson. "I don' know, brother."

"Finding that kid, finding Jeffers, it fixed me. It got me right. And now, maybe it was all just ... wrong?"

"No. I don't know about your boy, but you saved the one ya did find. You put a shitbird away. One that deserved it. Plain and simple."

"One that maybe didn't kill Evan."

"He's a lowlife rotting in prison. Forget what that asshole said to Nathalie."

Jackson punched the dashboard. "I can't just forget it, dammit! Look at what it's done. Where we're at. Nat's dead, the police probably think I did it, and now the only thing that's kept me going since I lost my son, the only thing I have left to cling to, might be a goddamn lie. No, goddammit! I can't forget it!"

"Alright. Alright, brother."

Jackson slouched down in the passenger seat, placing his elbow up against the window and his head in his hand. "I don't know how we make this right."

"One step at a time. But whatever we do, we keep movin'."

Jackson nodded, and the two of them got out of the SUV.

The next couple of hours once again were quiet. Jackson changed back into sweats and left on another run, this time strapping a forty-pound rucksack to his back. Bear built a fire in the fireplace and polished off the last two beers in the house. After the sun set, Jackson grabbed another shower, and Bear drove into town to pick up dinner and a case of Miller High Life.

When he got back, he put out the spread of rotisserie chicken and microwavable sides from the supermarket and gave each of them a beer. The two men sat like that for nearly twenty minutes, content to eat silently in each other's company until Jackson finally spoke.

"I think I need to see him," he said.

"See who?" Bear asked.

"Him. Dale Jeffers."

"He's locked up."

"I know that."

Bear slurped on a chicken bone, pulling off what meat remained, and dropping it on his plate. "Are ya sure that's a good idea?"

"Like you said, keep moving. It's the only move I see."

Jackson gathered his empty bottle and plate and took them to the kitchen counter.

"Tomorrow," he said. "I'm going to Keen Mountain."

PART TWO
VILOMAH

"The truth does not change according to our ability to stomach it emotionally." — FLANNERY O'CONNOR

TWELVE

BAILEY'S PHONE buzzed on her nightstand, taunting her until she was somewhat conscious. Eyes still closed, she reached out, feeling everything from her clock to an empty rocks glass until she found the annoying little device. She rolled over, slid the green icon across the screen, and put the phone to her ear.

"Bailey," she mumbled.

"It's Jackson."

"Jackson. Wha—" Bailey looked over at her bedroom window. It was dark outside and the streetlight outside her house was still on, trying to creep through her curtains. "What time is it?"

"It's a quarter after six."

"On a Saturday. It's a quarter after six *on a Saturday*, Jackson. What's up?"

"I need a favor."

"I'm running low on those. The last one I did for you caught me up in a shitstorm."

"You mean warning me? I never asked you to do that."

"You're welcome, by the way. What's the favor?"

"I need you to get me in to see someone at Keen Mountain."

Bailey sat upright, pulling the comforter over her bare legs. The man next to her—the one Bailey had forgotten about until just now—grumbled something unintelligible before turning over and putting a pillow over his head.

"Keen Mountain is maximum security," Bailey said, rubbing her eyes. "It's not like getting you in at the local county jail."

"Can you get me in or not?" Jackson asked.

Bailey groaned. Jackson was being difficult, even by his standards. "I don't know, Jackson. Maybe. Probably. It's going to take pulling some strings."

"Start pulling them. I've got a six-hour drive ahead of me."

Bailey's hand moved from her eyes to her forehead and eventually down through her hair as she huffed, unamused. "Who are you trying to talk to, anyway?"

Jackson was quiet.

"Well?"

"Dale Jeffers."

"Dale Jeffers, as in the guy you helped put away?"

"That'd be the one."

"Why on earth are you trying to see him?"

"It's a long story."

"Well, I'm not calling anyone until I hear it."

The man next to Bailey poked his head up and grumbled something more. Bailey got out of bed and walked to the kitchen in nothing more than her underwear and a tank top.

"It's related to Nathalie," Jackson said.

"How so?"

"Jeffers called her. I think that's what started all this."

"Dale Jeffers called Nathalie? How did he even know where to find her? What did he say?"

"That he didn't kill Evan."

"Christ. You don't actually believe that crap, do you?"

"I don't want to, but I'm going to find out what it's all about. I need you to get me in there. Today."

"Alright, let me see what I can do."

The line went dead. The classic Jackson Clay goodbye.

Reaching into the fridge, she grabbed the carton of orange juice, and took a swig. Her head was pounding, partly from what Jackson had just told her, but mostly from the vodka sodas last night. It was too damn early for all of this. And on her day off, no less. But she knew Jackson Clay, knew how he operated. And she had a feeling that this—whatever all this was—was only just the beginning.

THIRTEEN

MOORE WAS at his desk the next morning when Cotton came knocking again. Like he did the day they caught the case, he held up a thick folder before plopping it down in front of Moore.

"Initial report from the crash investigation team," Cotton said.

Moore didn't look up from the papers he was looking over. "Give me the CliffsNotes version."

"Mrs. McKenna's Tesla had several scrapes of blue paint on it. They were able to pull some chips and get a match. The color is called Deep Impact Blue Metallic."

"Ironic, given the crash."

"Yeah, basically a dark blue. Anyway, it's offered on several different Ford models over several model years."

"So, it's a needle in a Deep Impact Blue haystack."

"Essentially. I guess it would've been too much to hope for something more exotic."

"Tire treads?"

"Only marks found belonged to McKenna's Tesla. Goodyear Eagle Touring tires. Clay doesn't happen to have a dark blue Ford registered to him, does he?"

Moore looked to his right and fished a paper out of a different stack. "Doesn't look like it. What about the husband, Brad McKenna?"

"The guy's a big shot developer, I don't think he slums it in a domestic grocery-getter like the rest of us."

"Well, confirm that."

"You got it. He's coming in today, right?"

"That's the plan. With his lawyer."

"That's ... interesting."

"Exercising your constitutional right doesn't make you guilty."

"Yeah. Still, though."

"Mmhmm."

Cotton stood in the doorway and watched Moore continue to skim over the papers in front of him.

Moore could feel his colleague's eyes on him and eventually looked up. "What else did the crash investigation get?"

"Uh, the multiple paint transfers indicate McKenna's Tesla was struck repeatedly. Both in the rear and the back left quarter panel. A hit to the quarter panel could explain ultimately how the Tesla lost control and crashed."

Moore leaned back, took his glasses off, and rubbed at his eyes. He'd been the last to leave the office the night before—shortly after Bailey's visit—and the first one in this morning. In between, he'd only gotten four hours or so of restless sleep.

Cotton noticed where Moore put his glasses down and saw Jackson Clay's DMV file in a folder open on the desk.

"You still like the ex for it?" he asked.

"I don't *like* anyone for it," Moore said. "That's the problem. But of the pieces that don't fit? Yeah, Clay doesn't fit the least."

Cotton nodded and folded his arms. "So, what do you want to do?"

"Keep on the car angle. Let's see if someone in Mrs. McKenna's life owns a vehicle that matches what we're looking for. Cross-reference friends, colleagues, the works."

"Got it. What about Clay?"

Moore shook his head. "I'll stay on Clay."

FOURTEEN

KEEN MOUNTAIN CORRECTIONAL CENTER was a maximum-security prison in southwestern Virginia, tucked away in the heart of the Appalachian Mountains. The complex, which was composed of three housing units and a long, rectangular administrative building, was watched over by four guard towers located at the corners of the prison's fenced perimeter. A main office was located just outside of the complex, on the other side of the security fences.

Jackson arrived just after noon, parked in the public lot, and walked into the main office. Shortly after explaining who he was, a corrections officer came and began escorting him through a series of hallways.

"You must be someone special for one of the assistant wardens to oversee you comin' like this," the officer said.

"Not really," Jackson said.

"More special than most, at least."

"Nope."

"Who are you here to see, anyway?"

"Dale Jeffers."

The officer shrugged as he continued walking. Keen Mountain's only well-known inmate was George Huguely, a University of Virginia student and lacrosse player who had beaten his girlfriend to death in 2010. Jackson doubted many had ever heard of scum like Dale Jeffers.

The officer led Jackson out a door on the side of the main office building and began walking toward the prison. As they walked, Jackson noticed a gun on the officer's hip. The bright yellow grip indicated it was a taser gun.

"I didn't realize you could carry weapons inside the prison," Jackson said.

"Can't." The officer looked at Jackson and rested his hand on the taser's grip. "Keen Mountain here's one of the few prisons that allow *nonlethal* weapons inside."

"Good to know, I guess."

"Why? You're not plannin' on startin' trouble, are ya?"

Jackson shook his head. He truly didn't, but no one here would know how much restraint that would take on his part.

They made their way through a pair of fences at the prison's perimeter, then on toward the administrative building. The walk was cold, with the wintry wind whipping its way down the plateau the prison sat on. Jackson tucked his hands into his coat. The officer, in short sleeves, seemed acclimated to the outdoor commute.

When they got inside, a thicker man, bald with a trimmed beard, was waiting for them. The officer stepped aside and Jackson held out his hand. The man didn't take it. Instead, he turned and began walking, motioning Jackson to follow him.

"Assistant Warden Jeffrey Jordan," the man said.

"Jackson Clay. Good to meet you."

"Wish I could say the same. We have over eight hundred inmates here, many of whom are so violent they are dumped off on us. Routine and procedure are how we keep safe and get my people home at the end of their shifts. I don't like people pulling favors and breaking procedure."

"Sorry if it ruffled some feathers."

The assistant warden didn't reply. Turning the corner, he approached a large steel door with a small window. With a loud buzz, the door clicked open.

"We'll set you up in our meeting room," the warden said. "We've cleared out visitation for this, so don't be surprised if you see some upset family members on the way out."

"That wasn't my intention."

"Never is with people coming down here and changing how we do things."

It didn't take a detective to figure out the man didn't like him, but Clay didn't much care. He needed to talk to Jeffers.

At the end of a long corridor, the warden led them into a large, open room. Stainless steel tables were laid out in a neat array, each with four round seats attached to them. Everything was bolted to the cement ground.

"Given the situation and Jeffers' history, I'm not going to let you be alone with him," the warden said. "That's *my* call. The guards will keep their distance, but they stay in the room with you."

"That's fine."

"Have a seat and wait here."

Jackson did as he was told, and the warden disappeared out a door on the far side of the room. Jackson closed his eyes and steeled himself for the encounter. He'd had enough reason to hate Dale Jeffers before, but now the sneaking suspicion he was the catalyst for Nat's death only compounded his vitriol. Jackson breathed in deeply and exhaled. He was here to find out what was going on, not for revenge, he told himself. There were too many people relying on him for this to go wrong. Special Agent Bailey. Bear. Nat. Even himself, though he cared very little about that at the moment.

A few minutes later, the same far door opened, and Dale Jeffers was escorted in by two corrections officers. Jackson expected the sight of him to reignite the rage he'd quelled within himself, but when he looked at Jeffers now all he felt was sadness. The man was older than he remembered—that much should've been obvious—

but it appeared he hadn't aged so much as he had *decayed*. He was emaciated—Jackson estimated he'd lost at least fifty or sixty pounds—with skin almost as gray as what little hair still grew around his head. His tongue lolled out of his mouth like he was panting, as he maneuvered his aluminum walker into the meeting room.

Jeffers shuffled his way over to the table and sat down. Breathing heavily, he braced himself by placing his hands in front of him. The metal shackles on his wrists clinked against the steel table.

"You're the last person I expected to see," Jeffers said, still trying to catch his breath.

"I never expected to visit you, either," Jackson said. "I promised myself I'd never see you again after that night."

Jeffers shook his head. "And yet, here we are."

Jackson watched as the man adjusted himself. His prison jumpsuit sat like a loose tarp on his bony frame. The white undershirt beneath his jumpsuit seemed to fit much better.

"I'd say you look well," Jackson said, "but that'd be a lie."

Jeffers huffed, amused. "Time and this place have not been my friends. When they found out what I was in here for … let's just say I haven't been the most popular person here."

"Even scumbags don't like child predators."

Jeffers raised his eyebrows and nodded as if Jackson had imparted a piece of truth he couldn't deny. "Well, luckily for them, the tumors on my liver will have me checking out soon."

Jackson nodded with a sneer on his face. "So that's what this is all supposed to be? Some sort of end-of-life mea culpa?"

Jeffers' shoulders sagged. A dejection came over the man—as if something he'd tried hadn't worked. "You know, I've had almost fifteen years in here and places like it. Fifteen years where you spend twenty hours a day in the same room. It gives you a lot of time to think. To think about the pain you've caused. Then, I get this." Jeffers grabbed at his torso, in the general vicinity of his liver. "I know now what it means to be perpetually in pain. I've thought about that, and the pain I've caused. And I realized I ought to end other people's hurt where I could."

"Wow. What a saint."

Jeffers looked down and shook his head again. "I realize nothing I'm going to say to you is going to win you over. But the least I can do is give you the truth. The truth that I kept from you."

"That you didn't take Evan."

"No. I never told Nathal—"

"Don't you dare say her name."

"I never told ... *her* ... that I didn't take Evan. I told her the truth. What had happened that night. And how, ultimately, I didn't do whatever it is she—and you—think I did."

"So, then tell me. What did you do?"

Jeffers took a deep breath in as he fiddled with the metal bracelets around his wrists, trying to find comfort. "You were right. I took your boy away from you. I saw you two that day at King's Dominion. The amusement park. You three, really. Your ... wife. She left to go on the Ferris wheel, leaving you with your boy. You were taking pictures when he got distracted. He stepped away from you and I saw my chance. When he was far enough on his own, I grabbed him."

Jackson's jaw was clenched, his face starting to turn red. "And you took him out of the park. A couple placed you with him outside the gates. They said a boy was struggling alongside a man matching your description."

"That's right. I took him out of the park and toward my car. It was crowded that day. I had parked far away and the lot was filled with people. The further we got from the park, the more Evan fought. Eventually, he started screaming. A man approached to ask what was going on. I let go of your son and went to the man to try to assure him everything was okay. But when I turned back, your boy was gone."

"What do you mean, gone?"

"He disappeared. I couldn't find him."

"Where did he go?"

"I don't know. I looked all over for him. In between parked cars, underneath them. You have to understand, I was terrified this boy was going to tell someone that I had just tried to take him. I got scared."

Under the table, Jackson's hands became fists. "What. Happened?"

"I told you, I don't know. That's the God's honest truth. I never saw him after that. The more I looked, the more I became paranoid someone had found him. After a while, I got in my car and left. I even stayed in a motel that night expecting the cops to show up at my house."

"Where did Evan go?"

"I'm telling you I have no idea. Hand to God."

"You're lying."

"I'm not. I'm trying to tell you the truth for once."

Jackson took a deep breath in and tried to push the tempting thought of placing his hands around Jeffers' neck out of his mind. Jeffers, for his part, stared directly into Jackson's eyes, almost begging Jackson to believe him.

"There's only one problem with this game you're playing," Jackson said.

"What do you mean?"

"You want me to believe you're telling the truth now? And the same for what you told the Quinones family. So you trot in here telling your cancer sob story like it's a dying man's last wish to get right with the world. But there's only one problem, Jeffers. What about the others?"

"What others?"

"Your other victims. I might have found you, and maybe the Quinones abduction is the only one they could pin on you, but there were others. The authorities liked you for at least a half-dozen other missing children when you went to trial. Where's the closure for them?"

"I didn't—"

"You're not trying to make amends—you're working a new angle. Same as always. I don't know what you're after. A commutation of your sentences, a pardon, a new trial? Whatever it is, spare me. Nat is dead now. Your lies are doing the only thing they ever have: taking lives."

Jackson stood. Two of the guards approached as if he might lunge at Jeffers, but instead, he backed up and began walking away.

"I'm ... I'm sorry," Jeffers said.

"No, you're not," Jackson said.

Jackson walked out of the meeting room without saying anything else. Two corrections officers came up and flanked him on either side. Together, the three walked out of the building, back through the prison's double fences, and on to the main office outside. There, the two officers stopped short, but Jackson kept on walking. Less than five minutes later he was back in his car and on the road, headed home.

IT WAS ALMOST eight that evening when Jackson got back. He opened the front door of his cabin and walked in to find Bear sitting in one of his recliners with a beer, watching television.

Bear scooted forward in the chair and turned to look at Jackson. "Welcome home, honey."

"Hey."

"I went out and picked up some fried chicken while you were gone. Left ya half the bucket. Well, almost half a bucket. There are some biscuits there, too. And beer in the fridge."

Jackson threw his keys down on the table and went to the fridge to grab a beer. He took the bottle over to the kitchen counter, placed the lip of the cap on the edge, and slammed his fist down, punching the beer open.

"So, how'd it go?" Bear asked.

"It didn't," Jackson said. "Complete waste of time. A day wasted."

"Oh, I don' know. I wouldn' say that."

Jackson looked up at him, confused. He came over and sat down on the sofa next to the recliner. "What do you mean?"

Bear nodded to the television, pointing with the remote in his hand. "Guess you haven't seen the news."

The news was playing footage of Jeffers, just as Jackson had seen him today, being marched out of what he recognized as the prison and into a waiting transport van. Below the video, the news chyron read:

CONVICTED CHILD PREDATOR CONFESSES TO SEVEN MURDERS

"You sure as shit did somethin'," Bear said.

FIFTEEN

JACKSON SPENT THE NEXT DAY, a Sunday, contemplating his next move. Though he and Bear never went out, Jackson had left on three different runs throughout the day. Bear awoke Monday, expecting to find Jackson out again on another run, so he was surprised when he sat up on the sofa to find Jackson at his dining room table with a forest's worth of papers in front of him. Slowly, Bear stretched and ambled over to Jackson, waking his limbs with each step he took. Jackson didn't pay him any mind.

"This all stuff you gathered about Nat?" Bear asked.

"No," Jackson said, "this is everything I had when I was looking for who took Evan."

It was only then Bear noticed the dusty banker's box with the words *Evan's Case Docs* hastily scribbled on it with black marker. "I'm guessin' this has to do with what happened yesterday?"

Jackson didn't respond. Bear rubbed at his eyes and made his way to the kitchen, reaching up and pawing around in a cupboard before coming down with a coffee mug. As he took the carafe from the coffeemaker and poured himself a cup, he turned back to Jackson.

"Need a refill?"

"No, thanks."

Bear shrugged, put the carafe back, then walked over and took a seat next to Jackson. Again, Jackson barely acknowledged him.

"So does this mean we believe that dirtbag now?" Bear asked.

After they'd watched the news last night, Jackson gave Bear a play-by-play of everything that had been said between him and Jeffers. When Bear asked why Jackson found Jeffers' story unbelievable, Jackson couldn't give him a good reason. Now, seeing all the files strewn about, Bear supposed Jackson was looking for one.

"I don't know," Jackson said, leaning back and looking at Bear. "I've been over this stuff for hours now. I want to find something that pokes holes in his story, but I can't."

"What, specifically, are ya lookin' at?"

"The stuff that led me to Jeffers. The stuff the police wouldn't move on."

Bear took a large slurp from his coffee mug and scooted his chair forward so he could better see everything on the table. "I guess we never really talked about it. How'd ya end up IDin' Jeffers?"

"The police questioned and checked everyone at the park. Evan wasn't seen leaving on any cameras, so the thinking was it was someone who knew alternate ways in and out. No one who worked at the park looked good for it. But I started to think about deliveries and delivery drivers. I figured out what distributors the park worked with and began calling them, pretending to clear an issue up with a delivery. That got me personnel that delivered to the park. When I started cross-referencing names with the Sex Offender Registry, Jeffers' name came up. I went back to the park and started asking around. Two guys who worked security told me they remembered seeing Jeffers, but not in his work clothes. That stuck out to them."

"Shit, that's good work. Did ya ever show that to the police?"

Jackson shook his head. "By then, it was weeks later. And any time I came to them, they looked at me like I was a grief-stricken father grasping at straws. I was, but that didn't make me wrong. I even tried to show Nat, and she didn't want to hear it, either."

"So ya handled it yourself. That's when you went after him."

"His current address was with his info in the offender registry. I decided I was going to see what he had to say about it."

"But instead, ya found him with that boy."

"And the rest is history."

Jackson leaned forward and thumbed at a photo of Evan. Evan was looking up, smiling at the camera in his tee ball uniform. His hat and mitt looked gargantuan on his little limbs.

"Suppose Jeffers is tellin' the truth," Bear said. "Where's that leave us?"

Jackson sighed. "I have no idea. All these years later? I'll probably never know what really happened."

"But there's got to be some sort of connection between the two."

"What do you mean?"

"I mean, play it out. Jeffers tells Nathalie he din' end up takin' Evan. At least, not farther than that parkin' lot. Nathalie decides to reach out to you and finds where you are, but someone kills her on her way out here. What's that tell ya? Someone din' want you knowin'. Or involved."

"That's a lot of assumptions, Bear."

"Is it any more than you askin' around about delivery drivers?"

"I guess not."

"I bet ya dollars to donuts she told her husband what she was plannin' on doin'."

"Maybe, but take it back a step further. Who do we know knew about the phone call?"

Bear thought for a moment. "Her boss at that place. That Wilkins lady."

"Yes, Maria Wilkins."

"I don' know, man. Ya really think she had somethin' to do with it?"

Jackson stood and pulled his phone from his pocket. "Probably not. But she'll know who else knew about the call."

SIXTEEN

MOORE WAS WRAPPING up a morning meeting with everyone working the McKenna case when he noticed Cotton at the back of the room, checking his phone. Cotton looked up at Moore, gestured with a finger that he'd be right back, and stepped out of the room.

Moore returned his attention to the rest of his team. "Alright, any questions?"

No one spoke or raised a hand.

"Great. You all have your assignments. Let's get to it."

The team of special agents and civilian personnel stood and gathered their things. Some began filing out of the conference room as others hung back, talking with one another. Moore organized his stack of files and stepped out to find Cotton. From the door, he scanned the office and found Cotton standing in the corner by his desk. The two of them locked eyes and Cotton nodded. Moore walked over.

"Alright, got it, thanks," Cotton said, ending his phone call.

"Who was that?" Moore asked.

"A new wrinkle."

Moore looked at him quizzically.

"You texted me yesterday after the Jeffers news to see if it had any tie-ins with the McKenna case..."

"Right. Jeffers was believed to have abducted Nathalie McKenna's late son."

"Exactly, so I called the prison. It turns out Jeffers had a visitor earlier in the day. The last-minute, favors-got-pulled-to-make-it-happen kind of visitor."

"Who?"

"Jackson Clay."

Moore's brow furrowed, and he shook his head. "Wait, Jackson Clay was at Keen Mountain? *Saturday*?"

"According to the name he gave and his ID."

"That's confirmed?"

Cotton shrugged. "The corrections officer verified the visitor's name was Jackson Clay. I doubt anyone would be stupid enough to use a fake ID at a prison, but I asked them to email me the video for us to confirm it was, in fact, Clay."

"Did you get the video yet?"

Cotton checked his phone. "Not yet. Oh, yep. Right here."

"Bring it up. Let me see."

Cotton loaded the video file attached to the email and angled his phone so Moore could see. Sure enough, there was Jackson Clay, sitting opposite an elderly-looking man in an oversized prison jumpsuit. The man's back was to the camera, but Moore had no reason to doubt it was Dale Jeffers. It certainly looked like the old man he'd seen on the news last night.

"And this was right before Jeffers just up and confessed to seven more abductions and murders out of the blue?" Moore asked.

"Timestamp puts it just a couple hours before."

"What on earth ..." Moore's voice trailed off. He stood there watching the video of the two men having a conversation. They went back and forth for a minute before Clay stood abruptly. The two guards in-frame reacted quickly and Moore thought for a moment something might happen, but Clay turned and walked away. As he did, Jeffers seemed to keep talking to him, even reaching out with his shackled arms.

"What the hell is this all about?" Cotton asked.

"I haven't the slightest clue," Moore said.

The video ended with Clay leaving the room. Jeffers collapsed back onto his seat, slouching as if he were slowly deflating. Moore felt like everyone else involved in this thing knew something he didn't, and he didn't like it.

He wanted answers—and he knew exactly who would have them.

SEVENTEEN

WHEN JACKSON and Bear arrived back at the offices of The Hallvard Group, Maria Wilkins was waiting for them. She nodded as they stepped through the double glass doors, and shook each of their hands before leading them back to a conference room. She took the seat at the head of the long, mahogany table and invited Jackson and Bear to take up the seats on her left side.

"Can I get you two anything?" she asked. "Coffee? Water?"

"I'd take a cup of joe," Bear said.

Maria smiled at him and motioned to someone outside the glass-enclosed meeting space. "So, what more can I do for you gentlemen?"

"First, I wanted to apologize for how I was last time," Jackson said. "That was a lot to process, and I could've handled it better."

"Please, it's no matter, Mr. Clay. I imagine this all is incredibly hard for you. I know it is for us."

"Yes, it's been tough. Still, that's no excuse."

"Again, no apology necessary. Let's get to what I can do for you now."

"Sure. I was wondering about the phone call Nat got from Dale Jeffers. How many other people knew about it?"

"Here? Probably just myself and a few others who worked directly with Nathalie. Why do you ask?"

"What about outside of work? Do you know who she would've told? Is that something she'd tell her husband?"

"I imagine she did. I'm sorry, I'm not sure what you're looking for here."

A young woman came in with a tray bearing a porcelain carafe, three coffee mugs on saucers, and cream and sugar. She placed it on the table.

Maria thanked the woman as both Jackson and Bear smiled and nodded. As the woman left, Bear reached for the coffee and began pouring himself a cup.

"Nathalie was killed near my home," Jackson said. "I think she was coming to see me."

"Oh, goodness," Maria said. "Do you think it had something to do with the phone call?"

"I don't know for certain but, yes, I do. I was hoping someone here might've known what she was thinking of doing with all that. Someone, obviously, who knew about the phone call."

"Well, I knew, and I had no idea she was planning to contact you. I could put together a list of people here who I think knew what had happened."

"That'd be great. What about outside of work? Any idea who she might have told?"

"I can't say for certain. Her husband, Brad, like you suggested, maybe. Oh, and her friend. Oh, what's his name? Adrien. Yes—Adrien Alva."

"Adrien Alva?"

"Yes, he's a friend of Nathalie. Or was, I guess. She met him at some sort of support group thing. From what I understand, they're pretty close."

"Do you know what he does? Like for a living?"

"I don't, sorry. Why?"

Jackson looked at Bear. Bear peered back at him from behind the mug. He put it down and shrugged his shoulders. Jackson turned back to Maria.

"Nathalie was found holding a note with my name and the coordinates to my property written down on it," he said. "The Nat I knew wasn't the type of person who'd work out those sorts of things. I'm thinking someone gave them to her. Someone with some considerable skills, since they were able to find me."

Maria winced and sighed. "Harry. Harry Spencer. He's a private investigator we use from time to time as we look into cases. Nathalie asked me for his contact info a week or so ago. I didn't think anything of it at the time. I thought it was related to work."

"Could I have Mr. Spencer's contact information?"

"I imagine it's out there for anyone but, sure, I can get it for you. He's a capable investigator. I imagine finding the coordinates to your property is something he would know how to do, but I don't know that he did that or anything else for Nathalie."

"Of course. Thank you. I think that's more than enough for now. Would it be alright if I contacted you again if I have more questions?"

"By all means."

At that, Jackson pushed away from the table and rose. Bear followed his lead. Maria also stood and extended her hand. Jackson took it and shook it.

"See Cindy, our receptionist, on the way out," Maria said. "She should have Spencer's contact info for you."

"Thank you," Jackson said. "I really appreciate it."

Jackson and Bear stepped out and walked themselves to the front of the offices. They stopped by the front desk, and Cindy printed off the information they were looking for. Jackson thanked her, then headed for the elevator.

"We goin' to talk to Spencer now?" Bear asked.

At the elevator, Jackson pressed a button with a large arrow pointing downward. "Now's as good a time as any. Seems like a solid lead."

"What about this Adrien guy?"

A bell chimed and the metal doors in front of Jackson and Bear opened.

"Adrien Alva, yeah," Jackson said. "Let's go see the PI first. Maybe he knows where to find Alva, anyway."

EIGHTEEN

HARRY SPENCER'S office was on the first floor of a red brick row house on Eighteenth Street, just a few blocks from the popular nightlife scene at the heart of the Adams Morgan neighborhood. As Jackson and Bear approached, they could see wrought iron bars covering the windows on the main floor, as well as the windows of the English basement below. Behind the bars on the front door, gold letters were etched into the window:

SPENCER INVESTIGATIONS, LLC

"Guess this must be the place," Bear said.

Jackson nodded and the two of them took the stairs up to the front door. Jackson knocked and looked up, noticing a camera above him. Bear looked up, too, and waved.

"Bear," Jackson admonished.

A moment later there was a loud buzz, and the door made a loud click. Jackson turned the handle and opened it. He stepped in to see a large man looking at the two of them.

"How's it going?" the man asked in a booming baritone voice.

Jackson thought the man had to be at least 6'6". He had slicked-back raven-black hair and stubble that said he hadn't shaved in a few days. He wore blue jeans and a buttoned-down workman's shirt—undone enough to flash some robust chest hair—that hung off his barreled torso. Jackson also noticed the man was wearing sandals in February.

"Harry Spencer," the man said, offering his hand.

Bear shook it. "Bear Beauchamp."

"And Jackson Clay," Jackson said. "But you already knew that, didn't you?"

Spencer nodded. "I guess we should talk."

He led them through what looked like a waiting area and a kitchen to an office in the back, each room messier than the last. In the office, a pair of barred windows overlooked a small yard overgrown with weeds and slabbed with broken concrete that stretched to the alley beyond. Spencer sat in an aging leather chair and propped his feet up on a precarious stack of binders and books piled atop his desk. Jackson and Bear sat in a pair of armchairs across from Spencer.

"I saw the news about Mrs. McKenna and where she was killed," he said. "I was wondering if it'd earn me a visit from you."

"Do you think I killed her?" Jackson asked.

"It never crossed my mind, to tell you the truth."

"Why's that?"

"Well, for one, she was looking for you. Generally, people don't willingly go looking for people that might kill them."

Bear chortled. Jackson shot him a look.

"So you gave her the coordinates to my place," he said to Spencer.

Spencer nodded. "I was hired to find you, and I'm good at my job—if you couldn't tell by all the lavish furnishings."

He gestured at his office and chuckled. The place was a graveyard of papers and filing cabinets and probably hadn't been cleaned this century. Frankly, the room looked like it belonged on an episode of *Hoarders*.

"Then I assume she told you what this was all about," Jackson said.

"She told me some," Spencer said. "That the man believed to have taken and killed her son—*your* son—called her out of the blue to say he hadn't. It made her very focused on finding you. 'Jackson found that man,' she would say. I told her I could look into the matter myself, but she was determined to get you involved. I guess you are, now."

"I guess so. Did she ever talk to you about Maria Wilkins or Adrien Alva?"

Spencer nodded as he rocked in his chair. "Maria and I go way back. I've been doing work for her for years. Obviously, she approves of it if she's referring other clients to me. And Mr. Alva came with Nathalie the first time we met. I gathered it was an emotional support sort of thing. I didn't see him again."

"What do you know about them?"

"Maria? Plenty. Alva? Very little. Maria's a strong woman. Has a family—they live in Chevy Chase, Maryland—with two kids and a dog. Built her organization up pretty much herself. She's a solid litigator, and she's passionate about her work. Can't say I don't relate."

"And Alva?"

"As I said, I just met him the one time. Seemed like a decent guy, if not a little awkward."

"Awkward? How so?"

"He was a bit antisocial. He was quiet, wouldn't make much eye contact. That sort of thing. But like I said, he seemed nice enough. Nathalie said they met at a support group for parents that had lost their children."

"Lost their children. You mean people whose children were abducted?"

"No. From what I understand, it's any kind of loss. Nathalie said there were all types there. People whose children overdosed, or died from cancer. Killed in traffic accidents. Pretty awful stuff."

"Do you know the name of the group?"

"It doesn't really have a name, apparently. Nathalie just called it *Vilomah*, or Support Group. Here, I'll write the information down for you."

Spencer grabbed an old piece of printer paper from his desk, tore it in half, scribbled on it with a pen, and handed it to Jackson. Jackson's brow furrowed.

"*Vilomah*," he said, reading from the paper.

"Yeah," Spencer said. "Apparently, it's quickly become the term for parents who've lost a child. Like widow or widower is the term for someone who lost their spouse."

"I guess that makes me one. A *vilomah*," Jackson said.

Spencer nodded solemnly, but didn't say anything. Neither did Bear. Jackson felt their collective eyes on him, and it made him uncomfortable.

"So who do you think did it?" he asked.

"Excuse me?"

"Nathalie. Who do you think killed her?"

Spencer shrugged. "I couldn't tell you. I haven't thought much on it, to tell you the truth."

"I don't believe that. She was your client. You gave her the information that sent her my way. You can't tell me you haven't thought about what happened."

"I have, but I'm not looking into it. That's what the police are for."

"Still, you have to have a theory. A hunch."

Spencer paused, thinking. "My hunch is ... the fact that there was something in all this worth killing for means it was much bigger than I ever knew."

"You knew it was about a dead kid taken from his parents, about the truth behind all of that. Maybe this is just some *vilomah* talking, but in my mind, there's nothing more worth killing for."

Bear looked at Jackson. There was a seriousness on Jackson's face he'd seldom seen before, and he'd seen him in all sorts of tense moments. It was a seriousness compounded by hurt and anger, by loss—and the loathing that came with it. At that moment, he realized this all had reopened his good friend's deepest wounds, and he was in a kind of pain Bear could never understand.

"Tell me about Nathalie's husband, Brad," Jackson said.

"I never met Mr. McKenna," Spencer said. "Nathalie seemed to imply he wasn't very much involved in all this. Like he wasn't to be kept in the loop if I found something."

"Why's that?"

"Because it's her thing? He doesn't care? He doesn't want her spending time on it? Who knows, maybe she was hiring me behind his back. Your guess is as good as mine."

"Seems like a pretty big thing to leave your spouse out of."

Spencer held his hands up. "What can I say? I'm an investigator, not a marriage counselor."

Jackson waited for more of an answer. When it didn't come, he stood up from the chair.

"Alright," he said. "I guess that's it, then."

Spencer got out of his chair and walked around his desk with an extended hand. "I hope I was some help. If you need anything else, feel free to reach out. I liked Nathalie. She seemed like a good person. If there's something I can do to help, I'd like to."

Jackson shook Spencer's hand. "I appreciate it. I'll let you know."

Bear led the way out. As they stepped out onto the street, Jackson pulled the lapels of his coat up against the blustery wind whipping down the corridor of close-knit buildings. The two of them walked briskly back to the Suburban, hopped in, and turned it on. Bear was about to put the old SUV in gear when he noticed Jackson sitting there with his eyes closed, taking a deep breath in before exhaling slowly.

"You good, bud?" Bear asked. "Ya want to call it a day and head home?"

"No," Jackson said. "I'm good." He pulled out his phone and began punching away with his thumbs. "Start driving. I'll look for an address for Alva."

NINETEEN

THE SLOG of the afternoon rush hour in the nation's capital added a good twenty minutes onto what should have otherwise been a fifteen-minute drive uptown. Adrien Alva's apartment was in Fort Totten, a neighborhood in Northwest DC named for the old Civil War fort built there. His building—a tan brick midcentury three-story complex—was situated directly across the street from the park that had taken the old fort's place.

As Jackson and Bear walked up to the building, an older woman wearing a thick parka and bandanna around her head was letting herself in. She held the door open for Jackson and Bear, mistaking them for residents.

The woman smiled. "It's nice to have young couples like yourselves around. The world's come a long way since I was your age. Terrific that you two feel comfortable being yourselves."

Jackson was about to politely correct the woman before Bear realized her assumptions had helped get them through the door.

"What can I say? I just love this guy," Bear said, throwing an arm around Jackson.

The woman grinned once more and tittered before turning and heading down to the lower floor of the building.

As soon as she was gone, Jackson shrugged Bear off. "Come on. We're not here to mess around."

Bear let out a hearty chortle. "She thinks we are, though."

Adrien's unit was on the second floor at the end of a long, drab corridor of browns and beiges that stopped being stylish years ago. Almost as soon as Jackson knocked, the door opened a crack. The man inside stared at Jackson for a moment and then smiled as if he recognized an old friend.

"Jackson Clay," he said. He opened the door completely. "This is a nice surprise."

"Thank you," Jackson said. "This is my friend, Bear."

"Bear?" Adrien asked.

Bear nodded. "Yessir. Good to meet ya."

"We were hoping to have a quick word with you," Jackson said.

"Uh, yes." Adrien stepped back and waved them into his apartment. "Of course. Please, come in. And make yourselves comfortable."

He motioned to a living area in the apartment before trotting into the kitchen. Jackson and Bear heard various cupboards opening and closing. Jackson thought the commotion sounded a tad frantic, but figured it was their unexpected company that had the man frazzled.

"Can I get you gents a drink?" he asked. "Some coffee or tea? Or water?"

Bear was about to speak up, but Jackson spoke first.

"No, thanks," he said. "We're okay."

Bear scooted back into the sofa he'd sat on and crossed his arms in protest. Adrien came out of the kitchen with a few bottles of water anyway. He was short, with an average physique. His square head was accentuated by his wide, flat lips. Thick-framed glasses didn't do his close-set eyes any favors, though they matched his short black hair almost perfectly.

"You recognized me almost immediately," Jackson said. "I suppose that comes from the time you'd spent with Nathalie."

"Yes, it does," Adrien said. "We talked about everything. I like to think we were very close. I'm sorry for your loss, by the way."

"Thank you. And I for your loss."

"Yes, of course. I'm going to miss her."

"How did you come to meet her?"

"At first we just went to the same support group together. But we got to know each other better, one on one. I think she really took a liking to me, you know? She even asked me to help her when she started looking into all this business with that awful man's phone call. I went with her to see a private eye, though I didn't think it was a good idea."

"Why not?"

Adrien shrugged. "She wanted him to find you, but she hadn't seen you in so long. People change, you know?"

"They never stop caring about the child they lost, though."

"Yes, that's true. But even so."

"And you met at this support group. For lost children?"

"Yes, I had been going there for almost a year when she started coming. I guess it was meant to be that our paths crossed."

"If you don't mind me asking, how did you lose your child?"

"I never lost a child of my own, actually. My sister Angela, and her daughter Laila, were killed when I was just a teenager."

"I'm sorry."

"Thank you. Yes, people think of the parents and grandparents of the lost in those times, but not about people like me, you know? There's not many places for grieving *uncles*. But I found a place for myself in that group. Fortunately, they were welcoming of me."

Adrien leaned forward and grabbed one of the bottles of water, opening it and taking a sip before sitting back. He may not have been classically handsome, but there was a smoothness about him. Jackson wondered what Spencer had seen to call Adrien antisocial.

"Were either of you two close with anyone else in the group?" Jackson asked.

"Not so much. Don't get me wrong, Nathalie got along with everyone, but she was quiet in a way. Like me, I guess. I think that's why she took a liking to me. Nathalie seemed … lonely. She had her husband, Brad, of course, but he wasn't often available. Emotionally or otherwise."

"What do you mean?"

"I mean, as I came to know Nathalie, it became clear Brad isn't—wasn't—really attuned to her needs. She still grieved the loss of Evan. She saw him in every boy that walked by. But it felt like, as far as Brad was concerned, their lives began when they met. He didn't want to deal with anything before him. Didn't even want to think about her being previously married. I think he's got a real jealous streak in him, if we're being honest. I met him only a couple of times, but he'd barely give me the time of day. I don't think that he liked that Nathalie and I spent time together."

"Sounds like he didn't like Nathalie focusing on the past. Could he be violent?"

"It's very possible, but I don't know."

"She never had unexplained bruises or injuries?"

"No, not that I saw."

Jackson felt that familiar anger begin to form in the pit of his stomach. Now he was starting to regret that he and Bear hadn't stuck it out more that morning and waited for Brad McKenna to show up. Bear took the lingering silence as an opportunity to say they had to get on the road. Jackson smiled and shook Adrien's hand when it was offered, but he didn't hear any of the pleasantries exchanged. His mind was focused on Brad McKenna.

They were just about out of the apartment when a thought occurred to Jackson. "One last thing, if you don't mind."

"Of course," Adrien said.

"The man that called Nat and said he didn't kill Evan. Dale Jeffers. Did she believe him?"

Adrien leaned against the door jamb and took a deep breath in, choosing his words carefully. "I don't know, to tell you the truth. I think a part of her couldn't face having to relive it all. She had started to accept what had happened. Any other story, true or not, would mean reliving Evan being taken. I don't think she wanted to face that."

Jackson nodded solemnly and turned to continue walking. Bear waved goodbye for the both of them. Neither of them said a word during the walk back to Bear's truck. Five minutes later, they were back on the highway and headed for Virginia.

"Ya want to grab dinner on the way home?" Bear asked.

"Sure, whatever you want," Jackson said. "I'm pretty beat, though. Mind if I grab some shut-eye until we're there?"

"By all means, brother."

Jackson pulled the hood of his jacket over his head and nestled himself into the corner where his seat met the car door, but he didn't close his eyes. Adrien's last words played on repeat like a broken record in his mind.

I don't think she wanted to face that.

He knew that side of Nat. Wanting nothing to do with Jackson's mad, personal quest to find whoever had taken Evan from them. Truthfully, his single-mindedness had precipitated the end of their marriage. He and Nat had broken in the same way when they lost Evan, but they required different things to heal. Jackson needed this: to know what had happened. To look the devil in the face and know he'd found him. Nathalie needed just the opposite.

Jackson looked out the window, watching office buildings and city streets roll by. In the distance, he could see the rotunda of the US Capitol building lit up against the darkness of the early night sky. As they came up on the Potomac River, he saw the Washington Marina and the top of the Thomas Jefferson Memorial.

This city, he thought. The loss of Evan had chased Nathalie away from everything they'd built for themselves in Richmond, and she'd ended up here. Now, she too was gone. Lost. To anyone else, those things were unconnected. A series of tragedies that had little to do with one another other than they'd hurt the same people. But Jackson saw the connections. Each moment was a domino, lined up in just such a way that it was guaranteed to knock the next one over. Evan's abduction had brought Jackson to this night, riding around this city, looking for now not one, but *two* killers.

And he'd been there the night the first domino began to fall.

———

THE KITCHEN WAS *silent save for the clock singing on the wall. It was a Disney cuckoo clock that had been given to him and Nat as a wedding gift. Nat had fallen in love with it when she saw it in an antique shop in Carytown. She had imagined it playing—singing "A Dream Is A Wish Your Heart Makes," from* Cinderella—*as iconic characters chased each other in a circle. Woody and Buzz, Pumbaa and Timon, Winnie the Pooh and Piglet. The idea is it would calm their little one. Now, it just taunted Jackson from across the room.*

Through the door, he could hear Nat on the phone with her mom, answering her questions.

"I don't know, Mom, for a while."

Jackson guessed her mom had probably asked her how long she'd be staying with them.

"He's going to stay here." Nat paused. "No, Mom. I told him to. It's fine. Not everything needs to be fought over."

Another pause. "I don't know. Maybe I'll look around DC. There's lots of law firms up there."

Now her mom was asking her about her plans.

"I can't stay here." Another pause. "Because I can't. I just ... can't."

At that, Jackson heard her begin to sob. There was a soft thud followed by the distinctive clink of their wood-and-glass coffee table. Jackson thought she must've slid down the side of the couch onto the floor. That was her go-to spot when she was upset.

"Everything here reminds me of him, Mom," she said between sobs.

"He's everywhere I look, except he's not. And it's killing me. It's fucking killing me."

Now it was Jackson who had to hold back tears. He knew what she was feeling all too well. It broke him all the same to go over the security footage he'd "borrowed" from the Kings Dominion offices, having to watch Evan be there and then suddenly not, over and over again.

"Okay. Okay, I'll talk to you tomorrow," Nat said. "I love you, bye."

Taking the phone call to be over, Jackson got up and pushed the door to the living room open slowly. Nat was, in fact, on the floor in front of their couch. Jackson sat precariously on the other side and together they stared forward at nothing until Jackson finally couldn't bear the silence any longer.

"So. DC, huh?"

Nat wiped at her face. "It was just an idea. Nothing I'm sure of." She chuckled in between sobs. "Like I'm sure of anything these days."

"What if we moved together? What if, I don't know. Maybe you're right. Maybe it's not us. Maybe it's just this place. All the memories. Maybe a fresh start would be good."

Nat shook her head. "It wouldn't work."

"Why not?"

"Because. It just wouldn't."

"Nat, there has to be a rea—"

"Because you, Jackson! It's you. As bad as all the memories are, they don't compare to you. I see him, Jackson. I see him every time I look at you. Those same eyes. Same nose. That laugh you two both have. Had. It kills me every time."

Jackson dropped his head into his hands. Her words were daggers stabbing him in his heart. He wasn't mad or sad or anything else. He felt nothing. It was a feeling he was having more and more often.

"And I hate myself," Nat continued. "I fucking hate myself that I feel that way. Believe me, I know how unfair that is to you. But just like I can't get my son back, I can't make us happy again. And it doesn't matter if it's here or DC or fucking Mars. Because as long as you're there, he's there. And I can't do that anymore. I'm sorry, but I can't."

Jackson's hands moved over the back of his head and slowly down to his knees. He nodded, staring at the floor. He rose, breathing in, holding back the tears welling up in his eyes. He rubbed at them and looked around, unsure.

"Okay, um, give me five minutes," he said. "I'll throw some things together and I'll let you have the space. Just let me know when you're done."

"Jackson, I didn't mean—"

"No, it's okay. I get it."

Jogging up the stairs to their bedroom, past all the framed memories on the wall, he threw a few clothes into a duffel bag. He grabbed his keys, phone, and wallet, and jogged back down. Nat was at the bottom, her arms wrapped around herself.

Jackson grabbed her with one arm and brought her in.

"I get it," he said again, softly.

He kissed her on the forehead, opened the front door, and left.

"Believe me," he said, trotting down the steps, "I get it."

TWENTY

IN THE TIME it took Bear to drive home by way of a pit stop at Sheetz for some subs, a storm system had formed over the Blue Ridge Mountains and was now peppering the area with icy sleet. As they pulled up to Jackson's cabin, the Suburban's headlights caught the little flecks of frozen water plinking off the roof and sides, dancing in the small yard nestled amongst the trees.

Jackson climbed out of the SUV and ambled his way up the front steps. Bear came around the front of the Suburban and trotted up behind him, using their dinner to shield himself from the sleet. Jackson fumbled with the keys in the shadow cast by his large friend.

"Ya want me to get it?" Bear asked.

"No, I'm good."

The key eventually turned, and the deadbolt clicked back, but just as Jackson started to step inside, a second pair of headlights flashed across the front of the cabin before settling on Jackson and Bear.

Jackson reached inside and grabbed the pistol he kept by the door. He couldn't make out the car, let alone who was driving it.

A shadowy figure got out of the driver's side door and

came around the front of the car, and Jackson tensed. When the car's headlights turned off, and the ambient light from Bear's SUV illuminated Special Agent Moore's face, he relaxed somewhat.

"Came with fewer guys this time," Jackson said. "But unless you've got another warrant, you're on private property."

Moore reached up and adjusted the toothpick sticking out of his mouth. "No, no warrant or backup this time. It's just me."

"Then, with all due respect, Special Agent, it's been a long day. What do you want?"

"I was hoping we could talk."

Jackson exchanged a look with Bear. "Like I said, I'm about all talked out tonight."

"You were up for a chat last time."

"Yeah, and you had about a dozen armed officers persuading me it was the prudent thing to do."

Moore grinned and stashed his hands in his coat pockets. "So how about you do it of your own volition this time?"

Jackson stared at the man but didn't say anything. Moore supposed he was deciding whether or not to go.

"Come on," Moore said, "It's freezing out here. You've got to know a place nearby that brews a decent pot of coffee. My treat."

Jackson looked at Bear again.

He shrugged. "Up to you, brother."

Jackson extended an open hand, and Bear gave him the keys to the Suburban.

"Do me a favor and throw my sub in the fridge," Jackson said. "I'll be back soon."

Navigating the icy front steps, he made his way over to Moore, pulling the hood of his coat over his head against the sleet. "Alright, follow me. And, yeah. You're paying."

DESPITE TAKING ALMOST HALF an hour in the wintry storm, Hart's Diner—located in a small town called The Plains—was one of the closest eateries to Jackson's cabin. One after the other, Jackson and Moore pulled into the empty parking lot and parked their respective cars in a pair of spaces directly in front of the diner.

"Looks closed," Moore said, climbing out of his SUV.

"Nah, Frankie's in there," Jackson said.

Jackson opened the door and found Frankie wiping down the eating counter.

He didn't bother looking up. "Sorry, we're closed."

"Hey, Frankie," Jackson said.

Frankie did a double take at the sound of a familiar voice and flashed his big, toothy smile when he saw Jackson.

"Hey, Jacks. I'm sorry, man, but the kitchen's already shut down."

"How about a couple cups of coffee?" Jackson asked.

Frankie eyed Moore suspiciously. His wariness grew more pronounced when he saw the badge and gun on Moore's belt.

"Yeah, I can probably do that." Frankie walked down the counter and made it a point to get close to Jackson. "You good, Jacks?"

"It's alright, Frankie. Just those coffees when you get a chance."

"Comin' right up."

Jackson almost religiously ate at the lunch counter whenever he visited Hart's Diner, but now he took a booth by a window overlooking the two cars in the parking lot. Moore followed his lead and took the bench seat opposite him.

"So, you wanted to talk. Talk," Jackson said.

"You boys got home late tonight," Moore said. "Out and about all day?"

"Something like that."

"Anywhere noteworthy?"

"Not really, no."

Moore grinned and took his glasses off. He fetched a handkerchief out of the breast pocket of his coat and began cleaning the lenses. "What about yesterday? You go anywhere noteworthy yesterday?"

Jackson realized Moore already knew about his visit to see Jeffers. "Just tended to some unfinished business."

Moore huffed. He finished cleaning the lenses and put the glasses back on. "And what kind of business did you have at Keen Mountain?"

Jackson stared at him. When Moore realized Jackson wasn't going to answer, he huffed again, but this time it was less amused and more annoyed.

"You're not stupid, Clay. You had to have known what I was getting at when I asked about yesterday. Why do I get the feeling you're playing games?"

"I don't know why you feel whatever it is you feel."

"Come on, Clay. Cut the shit."

His voice was sharp enough that Frankie looked back at them from across the diner. Moore looked over at him and raised a hand in apology before turning back to Jackson and leaning in.

"For the life of me, I can't figure you out," he said. "You say you know nothing about what's going on, and yet you end up everywhere you're not supposed to be. I can't figure out if you're so smart you're playing chess while we're all playing checkers, or if you only think you are."

Frankie brought over two mugs of coffee and set them down on the table between Moore and Jackson. Neither of them looked up at Frankie, their eyes locked on one another like two prize fighters.

"Everything okay here?" Frankie asked. "Do I need to call the Sheriff?"

"We're good," Jackson said. "Besides, we've got the police right here."

Moore grinned and took a sip of his coffee. Frankie walked away slowly, still watching them.

"Do you want me to level with you?" Jackson asked.

"I do," Moore said.

"Level with me first, then. Do you really think I killed my ex-wife?"

Moore took another sip of his coffee. "Honestly? I don't. Not for a lack of evidence, but you seem too ... controlled. You don't strike me as the type to run your ex off the road and stab her repeatedly, even if you wanted her dead. I'm guessing a bullet to the back of the head is more your style."

"Only if the person doesn't leave me a choice. So, why are you here with me and not looking elsewhere?"

"Because maybe you didn't kill her, but this involves you in some way. First the stuff with Special Agent Bailey, then your visit to Jeffers. And god knows what I just caught you and the big man rolling back from."

"Getting hoagies at Sheetz. Is that also suspicious?"

"Enough, okay? You've got cops watching your back, convicts confessing after talking to you, and an ex-wife you claim you haven't talked to in years who made it her last act on this earth to try to find you. Who are you, Jackson Clay? What makes you so damn special?"

"I'm no one."

Moore rolled his eyes and threw his hands up in frustration.

"No, really, I'm not. You think I want any of this? You think I want to deal with Nat's murder, or to go talk to the guy who may or may not have killed my kid? I'm handling this all the only way I know how. If that makes me special, I'd hate to see what normal is."

"What do you mean may or may not?"

"What?" He'd heard Moore perfectly well, but the question caught him off guard. He'd expected Moore to already know about the phone call between Jeffers and Nat. Moore asking him what he meant implied otherwise.

"You have reason to believe Dale Jeffers *didn't* kill your son?"

"I know he was never charged with it."

Moore leaned forward, his eyes narrowing as if he were trying to read Jackson's face. "Why were you really at Keen Mountain? No more bullshit. The truth, now."

"You haven't talked to people at Nat's work yet, have you?" Jackson said.

"I sent two agents there this afternoon, as a matter of fact. I've had to divide and conquer, what with people like you keeping my hands full."

"Then if they're any good at their job, they'll tell you Jeffers called Nat about two weeks ago. At her work."

Moore sat back. "What did he say?"

"He said he wanted to come clean. Said he hadn't killed her son—*my* son—Evan."

"So, you went to Keen Mountain to confront him about that?"

Jackson shrugged. "What would you do if it was your kid?"

"What did he say?"

Jackson told Moore about the whole exchange. The story Jeffers gave, Jackson doubting him, telling Jeffers if he was really interested in making amends, he would've confessed to all his crimes. Frankie came over and refilled their cups. He seemed startled by the subject of their conversation. Jackson realized when he saw Frankie's face, he'd never told him about Evan.

"Then Jeffers confessed later that day," Moore said.

Jackson nodded.

"So what do you make of that?"

"I think it doesn't really matter. He didn't kill Nat."

"Then the other confessions don't convince you. At least, not on their own."

"I don't trust anything that piece of shit says or does." Jackson looked out the window. He'd agreed to go with Moore because he wanted to ask the man something. Now was as good a time as any. "What about Nat's husband? Brad McKenna?"

"What about him?" Moore asked.

"You liked me for Nat's murder, some sort of domestic angle. Why not him?"

Moore put his mug down and shook his head. "I don't know what arrangement you have with Jen Bailey, but I'm not here to feed you information on our investigation. We're pursuing several leads."

Jackson shook his head at the cliché line. "I thought we were here to cut the bullshit."

"It's not bullshit. We *are* working a number of leads. But *we* are working them, not *you*. You hear me? Now, it's no skin off my back that you took a field trip down to Keen Mountain, but you need to lay off of this. I sympathize with what you're going through, I really do, but if you get in my way, I won't hesitate to book you on an obstruction charge."

Jackson slid out of the booth and stood to leave. "Well, it wouldn't be the first time you put me in cuffs in the past week."

"I hope you're hearing me, Jackson. I mean it," Moore said.

"Loud and clear. Thanks for the coffee."

He walked by Frankie, nodded goodbye, and headed out to Bear's Suburban. He'd heard what Moore had said, but he wasn't about to let that slow him down.

TWENTY-ONE

JACKSON AWOKE to the sound and smell of bacon sizzling in his kitchen. Bear must've started breakfast early, he thought. He rolled over and checked his watch. It was already after eight—grossly late by Jackson's standards. He sat up and swung his feet out of bed, stretching muscles that clearly resented his lifestyle.

From the kitchen, Bear heard Jackson stirring. He leaned toward the open doorway to Jackson's bedroom, cleared his throat, and said: "Mornin'! Breakfast is on."

Jackson nodded, pulling on a pair of sweatpants and a tank top. When he was dressed, he joined Bear in the kitchen. Bear had laid out a spread on the dining table rivaling that of a five-star bed-and-breakfast.

"Felt like we could have a big ol' breakfast," Bear said.

Jackson clapped Bear on the back and took a seat. Bear filled Jackson's mug with coffee, and sat opposite him at the table. He dove into the food as Jackson looked like he was unsure where to begin.

"So, who we seein' today?" Bear asked.

The two of them hadn't talked when Jackson got back from the meeting with Moore. Jackson had grabbed his dinner from the fridge and ate standing quietly at the kitchen counter while Bear had been fast asleep in one of the recliners, growling like his namesake.

"I want to find Brad McKenna," Jackson said, poking at eggs with his fork.

"Somethin' the cop say steer ya that way?"

"It's more what he didn't say."

"And what did he *not* say?"

"A lot."

Bear snorted and shook his head. "Well, the front lobby at his place wasn't much help last time."

"No. We're going to have to find a workaround."

"Like what?"

Jackson shrugged. "Don't know. Something. But it's got to be today."

Bear nodded as he chewed a mouthful of bacon. It was the closest Jackson and him had come to talking about it. At first, he wondered if Jackson didn't know, then he realized he had to and must just be avoiding the subject, so Bear had gone along with it. But now he couldn't help but take the opening Jackson had given him.

"Her funeral is tomorrow, right?" Bear asked. "Nathalie's?"

Jackson nodded as he chewed his eggs.

"We could just wait 'til then, I reckon. We know he'd be there, then."

"He'll be surrounded by mourners and well-wishers. I want him alone."

"There's gonna be a lot of eyes on him this week. On both of ya, for that matter."

"What are you getting at?"

"I'm just sayin' let's not do somethin' stupid here. Gettin' arrested for real this time isn't gonna help anybody."

Jackson looked up and met Bear's eyes for a moment before focusing back on his breakfast. "Deal. Nothing stupid. But we've got to talk to him."

Bear didn't say anything more. Jackson finished up the last

couple pieces of bacon on his plate before tilting the dish and scraping together the last bits of breakfast into one forkful. If nothing else, their conversation had reinvigorated his appetite.

Jackson swallowed the last bit of food, washed it down with a gulp of orange juice, and marched his dirty plates over to the kitchen sink with purpose. After a quick rinse, Jackson put the dishes into the dishwasher and came back to Bear.

"Grab a shower if you need to," he said, patting his friend on his back. "We leave in twenty."

Jackson went into his bedroom and closed the door behind him.

Nothin' stupid, Bear thought. Sure.

TWENTY-TWO

IT BEING the day before Nat's funeral, Jackson figured there was a better chance Brad McKenna would be at his condo this time. Bear drove them back to McKenna's building, and the two of them entered the lobby, steeling himself for another bout with the front lobby staff.

As Jackson approached the front desk, he heard the *whoosh* of the revolving door behind him, and a staff member said, "Welcome back, Mr. McKenna."

Jackson turned and came face to face with Brad McKenna for the first time. He was larger than Jackson expected, tall and broad-shouldered, with a jawline chiseled from stone, and silver hair cleanly tapered at the edge of his cleanshaven face. McKenna stared back at Jackson with eyes so darkly brown they almost looked black.

"Brad McKenna," Jackson said. "My name is Jackson Clay."

The other desk clerk looked up, saw the interaction unfolding, and trotted over.

"Sir, this is highly inappropriate," the clerk said, putting his hands up in front of Jackson. "You need to make a—"

"It's alright," McKenna said, waving the clerk away. "It's fine. Clay, you said? What can I do for you, Mr. Clay?"

The clerk stepped away from Jackson, nodding to McKenna in acknowledgment.

Jackson ran his hands over his coat, sorting himself out, before looking back at McKenna. "I was hoping we could go somewhere to talk. Privately."

"Sure, Mr. Clay," McKenna said. "What would you like to talk about?"

"Nathalie."

McKenna nodded solemnly and slid his hands into his pockets. "Well, I appreciate you coming to offer your condolences. Perhaps the funeral tomorrow is a more appropriate time for this."

"I was hoping we could talk now. Before the funeral."

"I'm sorry, I don't think I caught how you knew Nathalie."

"I'm her ex-husband."

A deafening quiet came over the lobby. A couple of people pulled out phones, anticipating an imminent altercation.

Instead, McKenna smiled warmly and extended his hand. "Well, I'm sorry it took this for us to finally meet. Why don't we talk upstairs?"

"I think that would be a good idea," Jackson said.

McKenna led the three of them to an elevator separate from the others. At first, he seemed confused by Bear following along, but Jackson's face told him that Bear was welcome to join them.

The elevator took the trio directly up to the penthouse floor. It opened onto a small hallway leading to a pair of large, beveled glass French doors. McKenna punched a number into a keyless entry pad and the doors clicked open.

Jackson and Bear stepped into a room that could only be described as opulent. White and gray marble made up the floor and ran up the walls before intersecting with a gilded ceiling. Grand square columns supported an open floor plan featuring an array of large windows overlooking the Whitehurst Freeway and the Potomac River.

"Nice digs," Bear said.

McKenna nodded. "Thank you. I like to think I've done alright for myself."

He placed his wool overcoat on a brass coat rack and reached out, offering to take Jackson and Bear's jackets as well. Both men declined.

"So," McKenna said. "You're the ex."

"I am," Jackson said.

"I've heard a bit about you."

"That's funny, that's not what I've been told."

"And who have you heard that from?"

"Adrien Alva, among others."

McKenna snorted and shook his head. He walked into his kitchen and fixed himself a glass of bourbon. Bear looked at his watch and noted it was still well before noon.

"I'm afraid Adrien and I haven't always seen eye to eye," McKenna said. "I could see how he might not be the most complimentary of me."

"Then you two didn't get along, I take it," Jackson said.

"Adrien is an odd fellow. From what I gathered from Nathalie, he didn't have many other friends. You can't blame a husband for being wary about another man spending as much time with his wife as Adrien did."

"Do you have reason to believe he had a thing for Nathalie?"

McKenna took a sip of bourbon. "Nothing specific. I guess it was just a feeling he gave me."

"Wasn't he friends with Nathalie before you two met?"

"Yes. What is your point?"

"Well if he wanted to be romantically involved with her, he would've had his chance. Before you."

"You're assuming Nathalie liked him like that."

"You're assuming she didn't."

Bear tensed. Jackson was clearly trying to push McKenna's buttons.

McKenna stared at Jackson for a moment, then flashed him a grin. "I see your point, Mr. Clay, but I don't think Adrien was her type."

"What makes you think that?"

"Well, for one, she married me. Adrien and I are obviously very different people. To suppose I was her type would mean Adrien probably was not."

Jackson returned the grin, but his was forced. He couldn't deny Brad McKenna had a charm about him. It'd probably served him well, especially with the ladies, though Jackson suspected McKenna's biggest fan was himself.

"Do you think Adrien would ever hurt Nathalie?" Jackson asked.

"I wouldn't imagine so," McKenna said. "If I had any suspicions, of course, I'd bring them to the authorities."

"Have you spoken with the police yet?"

"Not yet, no. Unfortunately, planning a fitting farewell for your wife proves to be rather time-consuming. That, coupled with my normal business obligations, has kept me busy."

"Some people might say a widowed husband avoiding the police has something to hide," Jackson said, segueing into the question he'd wanted to ask all along. "Do you?"

McKenna put his glass down and looked over at Jackson. "Excuse me?"

"Do you have something to hide from the police?"

McKenna shook his head in disbelief. "I'm sorry, you come into my home, where I invited you in, and you insinuate *I* had something to do with my wife's death?"

"I'm not insinuating anything. I'm simply asking. Since, apparently, the police haven't gotten the opportunity yet."

McKenna leered at Jackson, the grin on his face deteriorating into something less warm. A scowl, almost. Jackson returned his gaze, emotionless.

"Mr. Clay, I like to think I'm a gracious person," McKenna said, "but I'm afraid you've worn out your welcome."

"You didn't answer my question."

"I think that'll be all for today, My. Clay," McKenna said. He turned and began pouring himself a second drink. "Have a good day."

Jackson didn't move.

When McKenna realized the man wasn't leaving, he turned back around, his drink full. "Or do I need to get security involved?"

"Nah, that won't be necessary," Bear said as he grabbed Jackson's arm and began ushering him toward the door. "We were just leavin'. Thank you for your time."

Jackson reluctantly let Bear escort him out of McKenna's condo. The two of them called for the elevator, and they were back outside The Omni Residences & Lofts in a matter of minutes.

"Well, I don't think we'll get a Christmas card from him," Bear said.

"He never answered my question," Jackson said.

"You really think he had somethin' to do with Nat's death?"

"That's what we're going to find out."

"And how are we goin' to do that?"

"I'm going to have a look around that place. Without McKenna around."

"You're talking about breaking in?"

"We know when he'll be gone. Tomorrow, during the funeral."

So much for nothin' stupid, Bear thought.

They got into the Suburban. Bear fired up the engine but didn't pull out of the parking spot. Instead, he turned and looked at Jackson.

"I thought you would want to go to Nathalie's funeral," Bear said. "To hell with Brad McKenna or whoever else, if we're not invited."

Jackson looked out his window, wiping at his nose. Bear wasn't sure if it was the cold or emotions getting to his friend.

"I'll pay my respects when I find out who did this to her," Jackson said quietly. "I owe her that much." He wiped at his nose again. "Besides, I've buried enough loved ones to last a lifetime."

SAINT BENEDICT CATHOLIC CHURCH *was a massive red brick house of God that rose upwards toward the heavens from its foundation on Sheppard Street in Richmond's Fan District. Jackson sat alone on one of the back pews, tucked up against one of the massive columns that supported the vaulted ceiling above. Several rows ahead, an altar sat in an alcove carved out from the front of the chapel. In front of it was an all-too-small casket.*

Slowly, people began to file in, occasionally looking over at the grief-stricken father, but Jackson's gaze was affixed to the tiny casket. No one should ever have to build such a thing, he thought. He couldn't decide if the fact that it sat empty made things slightly better, or unbelievably worse.

But it all had come to this. The police had informed Jackson and Nat that they had exhausted their search and rescue resources, and any investigation moving forward would be treated as a recovery operation.

They would have to say goodbye without someone to say goodbye to.

Truthfully, Jackson wasn't much of a religious person. Neither was Nat. If they'd had it their way, they would've held a quiet memorial for Evan at their house, or perhaps even at Hollywood Cemetery, where Evan —or at least the memory of him—would eventually be laid to rest. This service, on the other hand, with all the rites and rituals that came with the Catholic diocese, was Nat's parents' idea. Jackson hadn't had the energy to fight them on it.

He continued sitting there, alone, when Nat saw him. She excused herself from a group, offering her their condolences, and bent over the pew in front of Jackson.

"We have spots reserved up front," she said.

"Are you sure you still want to be seen together?" he asked.

Nat sighed in frustration. Yesterday had been the day. The day they'd both known was coming for months, but had ignored. The day one of them spoke up. They'd both felt it, but someone had to say it. So Nat had, and she'd finally told Jackson she wanted to end things.

"Please, Jackson," she said. "Let's not do this here."

"I'm not doing anything," Jackson said. "I'm really asking."

"Yes. Of course I still want to be seen with you. No matter what is going on with us, you are the father of my child."

"I was."

Nat took a deep breath. She looked over at the people filing into the church. Many of them were looking their way, sensing their unpleasant conversation. Nat smiled at them before leaning in closer to Jackson.

"Look," she said, "Please don't—let's just get through this. Through today, okay?"

Jackson nodded solemnly, but he wasn't looking at her, he was still looking at Evan's casket. Nathalie followed his gaze and turned. She stepped out of the pew in front of Jackson and slid into the one he was sitting on. Two grieving parents looking on at a shrine to their lost son.

"I imagined a thousand things for him," Nat said, "but never this."

"No one would ever imagine this for their child," Jackson said.

Nat nodded in agreement. More people filed in. Less of them were noticing Nat and Jackson now that they'd lowered their voices.

"Do you ever think about it?" she asked. "How you'd want to be, I don't know, celebrated?"

"Only time I've thought about it was overseas. And even then, I just figured the Army would take care of it."

"I don't know what I'd want."

"I guess it won't be up to me to figure out. Not anymore."

"Jackson—"

"What?"

Nat sighed again. "Nothing."

Jackson shook his head sternly.

"Anyway, it's probably best," he said. "I could never imagine that. Laying you to rest."

"Why's that?"

Jackson didn't say anything.

Nat looked at him and could tell he was struggling with something. "Go on. Say whatever it is. Please."

"Losing Evan has been unbearable," *Jackson said. His shoulders slumped, and he leaned forward.*

Nat thought he might keel over and moved to catch him. Jackson rested in her embrace. It was the closest thing to a hug or kiss they'd shared in weeks.

A single tear formed in the corner of Jackson's eye before he quickly wiped it away.

"Married or not," *he said,* "I don't know what I'd do if I lost you, too."

TWENTY-THREE

BEAR SPENT the majority of the drive back trying to convince Jackson that breaking into McKenna's condo was a bad idea, but Jackson didn't want to hear it. When they got back to Jackson's place and Jackson immediately began to sketch out what he had in mind, Bear knew his lobbying had been in vain. For better or worse, this was happening.

Now, nearing dinnertime, Jackson and Bear stood over a couple of crudely drawn diagrams on the table, studying them with beers in their hand.

"Run it by me again," Bear said.

"This large bay door on the street gives access to the residents' parking," Jackson explained. "That's what some of those elevators in the lobby go down to."

"Okay, but there must be some sorta code or somethin' to get in."

"From what I saw, it looks like you swipe a key fob or card."

"A fob or card we don' have."

"Yes, but there's no security. They rely solely on this setup being the gatekeeper. There's a blind spot on the street here. Someone—*I*

—could wait here for a resident to leave the parking area and bring up the gate. Then I could slip in before it closes."

"And what if there's security inside?"

"There won't be. But even if there is, once inside, I'm a resident, just like anyone else. Then, from the lobby, I can take the elevator directly up to McKenna's penthouse. I watched him key in the code on the elevator and the keypad on his front door. I saw both codes."

"What if there's another code for the elevator from the garage to the lobby?"

"Then I loiter around until a resident comes and catch a ride up with them."

"And what if the front desk or a doorman spots ya in the lobby?"

"That's where you come in. You'll go back in, demanding to see Brad as I ride up. Their attention will be on you, not me."

Bear shook his head. "I don' know, Jacky boy. Seems risky."

"I don't think so. But it doesn't matter. It has to be done. Nat's whole life is in there. We need to have a look."

"What about her stuff at the office? It could have clues or whatever, too. And there we don' even have to break in. It sounded like that Wilkins lady would help us out."

Now Jackson shook his head. "The penthouse is a better bet. We have a definite time tomorrow when we know the place will be empty. If we waste it going back to Nat's work, we don't know when we'll get another shot."

Bear scratched at his beard, thinking. It was hard to know whether everything going on was affecting Jackson's judgment, or not. They'd been in more serious situations than this one, though, and Jackson hadn't steered them wrong. Bear trusted Jackson with his life. If he said this was the play, this was the play.

"Alright," Bear said with a sigh, "you're the boss."

Jackson nodded.

"Come on, we need to pick up a few things," he said. "We've got a big day tomorrow."

PART THREE
SKELETONS

"The past is never where you think you left it." — KATHERINE ANNE PORTER

TWENTY-FOUR

THE NEXT MORNING, Jackson and Bear were in position just after sunrise. The long shadows of the buildings overhead still covered the narrow street, but the sky above was cloudless and a bright glacier blue. Jackson had cornered himself in the blind spot by the gate to the resident's parking lot, and Bear was in his Suburban just down the block. They would communicate by phone, each of them outfitted with a wireless earbud. Jackson didn't know how far inside his cell reception would carry, but it didn't matter. Once he was in, Bear knew what he was supposed to do.

Just after eight, a black Escalade pulled up to the front doors of The Omni Residences & Lofts. Minutes later, Brad McKenna stepped out of the building and got into the back of the car as the driver opened the door for him.

Bear's voice crackled over Jackson's earbud: "Our boy just got into an SUV dressed for a funeral."

"Got it," Jackson said. "Next car to leave, I'm going in. Get ready to move."

The black Escalade left. As it turned and headed for M Street, Jackson heard the whine and rumble of the gate coming to life.

Slowly, it lifted as a silver BMW exited the lot and eased its way onto the street.

"It's open," Jackson said. "I'm going in. Start heading in."

Inside, the parking garage was well-lit with harsh fluorescent lights. Jackson didn't know if there were any security cameras, so he kept low to the walls, crouching and sliding his way past cars he'd never be able to afford.

The elevator was in a glass-enclosed entryway on the adjacent corner of the garage. Jackson passed a few more cars and made it to the glass windows. He peeked inside, making sure it was clear. Then, with the bill of his ballcap pulled low to conceal his face, Jackson stepped out and pretended to be any other resident heading inside.

To help him sell the idea, Jackson and Bear had run out to a nearby mall the night before and gotten a pair of designer jeans, boots, and a puffer coat that cost more than Jackson's first car. He felt he looked ridiculous, but the young lady behind the counter had assured him it was a nice look.

Now, Jackson wore the outfit as he snapped on a pair of nitrile gloves and took the elevator up to the lobby. As it turned out, there had not been a code for this first elevator, though he did notice his phone had now dropped the call with Bear. When he stepped slowly out into view of the front desk, he looked over and saw Bear having an animated conversation with both clerks. Their voices weren't raised, and it wasn't the kind of fracas Jackson knew Bear could cause when he wanted to, but the man definitely had the attention of everyone nearby.

Jackson moved to the private elevator for the penthouse. When it opened, he stepped in, punched in the code, and hit the button for the top floor. On the penthouse level, Jackson stepped out and moved to the large double doors. He entered the code he'd memorized, and the door unlocked with a metallic click. It was almost too easy.

Once inside, Jackson closed the door behind him and looked

around. The sun was just peeking out behind the skyline of Arlington, Virginia across the river, and it filled the condo with warm light.

Jackson began methodically making his way through the McKenna abode. From the living area to the kitchen, then down the hall to the office and library, and two bedrooms in back. The office had two computers in it, but a quick look over everything told him both belonged to Brad. It made him wonder if Nat had had a workspace of her own.

He stepped back out into the hallway and went over the condo once more, searching for a place that would be recognizably Nathalie's. Stepping past a gigantic master bathroom, he noticed a second door he'd passed over. Jackson tried the knob, and the door opened easily. Inside was a second living area; a den, of sorts. Immediately, it was clear this was where Nat had spent most of her time: Instead of large pieces of art, or photos of Brad posing with Washington's elite, the room had photos Jackson knew belonged to her. Photos of her and her friends in college; her and her mom; their family dog, Ozzie.

On a sofa, tucked partially under a blanket, Jackson spotted a MacBook. He opened it up and the laptop came to life. A photo of Evan smiling greeted him, grabbing at his heart and squeezing it. The computer prompted Jackson for a password.

He tried several iterations of Evan's name—and Brad's—to no avail. He looked around the room, searching for inspiration. Nothing came to him. Then, as he looked down at the end table, he noticed a Post-It notepad with something scribbled on the top note. The paper was the same highlighter yellow as the one the police had found Nat clutching when she'd died.

He reached over, grabbed the pad, and glanced at what was written on the top note.

BW
KING'S QUARTERS

Jackson wanted to tear the note off and take it with him, but he couldn't be certain Brad or anyone else wouldn't notice it missing. Instead, he snapped a photo of it with his phone and put it back where he found it. He half-tucked the laptop back under the blanket, then left the den and closed the door behind him.

He went through every room a second time. The bathroom and guest bedroom didn't offer anything interesting. At the very end of the hall, through a sliding barn door, was that cavernous master bedroom. The bed, immaculately made, lay centered at the head of the room. The pink eyeglasses case on the nightstand situated to the left of the bed told him that was probably Nat's side. He got down on one knee—opting not to disturb the bed or mattress—and began to slide the nightstand drawer open when his phone buzzed in his pocket.

Jackson pulled the phone out and checked it. Bear had texted him:

GET OUT!

Jackson jumped to his feet and ran. In a matter of seconds, he was down the hall, back to the main living area. He went to the front door and opened it. On the other side of the hallway, he could hear the elevator whirring. He hadn't called for it, which meant someone was taking it up. Frantically, Jackson looked around, but there was nowhere to hide. There had to be another way in or out. As he moved back into the condo's kitchen, he noticed a second elevator near the corner.

It'd have to do. Jackson pressed the button, and the doors opened immediately. Inside, the only button that wasn't an alarm or the emergency phone read ROOFTOP. Jackson punched it, and the doors slid closed just as he heard two uniformed police officers enter the condo.

The elevator took Jackson upwards and opened on a small access area with a door. The door opened to a flat roof lined with what looked like a metal catwalk tracing the perimeter. Jackson jogged down it, looking for another way off the roof. With his earbud in,

Jackson tapped it and commanded his phone to call Bear. Bear answered immediately.

"Jacky boy," he said, "where are ya?"

"The roof," Jackson said. "Police were entering the condo."

"Yeah, I guess ya din' spot the camera in the entryway off the elevator. I was at the front desk when Brad called, chewin' them out about someone breakin' into his place. They called the cops, so I bounced."

"Okay, I'm looking for another way down."

"I'm back at the truck. So far, only two patrol cars with a few cops are there. They all went into the lobby. As long as you avoid that, ya might be okay."

Jackson had followed three-quarters of the catwalk around the building when he found a ladder at the far corner of the roof. He looked over the side. The ladder led down to a lower roof hugging the level he was on. He took it down and started jogging around the lower roof looking for his next move. On the opposite side of the building, there was a door, but it was locked, so Jackson doubled back to the side of the building with the ladder.

"I'm on a lower roof now," he said, "but I think I'm about out of options. There's only one door, and it's locked."

"Lower roof?" Bear asked. "Well, what's below *that* roof?"

Jackson peered over the side. The Omni Residence & Lofts practically rubbed shoulders with the next building over, separated only by a narrow alleyway, but it was too far to jump. He'd just about given up when he noticed a fire escape at the far end. It had a small outcropping for each floor, connected by several staircases. Jackson couldn't see all the way down, but he was out of time and options.

"I think I found a way," Jackson said.

He placed himself underneath the fire escape. The first outcropping was several feet down. He had no choice: he had to jump and hope the landing would hold. Jackson shimmied over the side, lowered himself as far as he could with his arms, and then let go.

With a loud clunk, the fire escape caught him. Jackson shot down one flight of stairs after another, descending the building's side. It took him all the way down to what he guessed was the third floor before he found one last ladder. It had to be lowered. Jackson maneuvered it into position, but halfway down the sliding mechanism jammed. He raised the ladder and lowered it again, trying to release the blockage. It didn't work. The ladder, as is, would get him about fifteen feet off the ground.

Good enough, Jackson thought.

"Bear, there's a small alley on the east side of the building, between it and the tan building next door. Do you see it?"

"Sure do."

"I'm on an escape ladder in the alley. The Suburban should fit, get over here."

He started to descend the final ladder when Bear's red Suburban bounced on its loose suspension into the alleyway and pulled up underneath him. Jackson dropped down onto the roof of the Suburban, then rolled off and climbed into the passenger seat.

"You're buffing any scratches out," Bear said.

"Just drive."

Bear fired the large SUV down the small alleyway and flew out onto K Street, directly underneath the Whitehurst Freeway. They followed it up to M Street before looping around and taking the Key Bridge back into Virginia.

"I don' know if I have to tell ya this," Bear said, "but that was damn stupid."

Jackson let out a deep breath. "I know."

"Was it at least worth somethin'?"

Jackson pulled out his phone and looked at the photo he took. The bright yellow Post-It notepad stared back at him. "I don't know yet."

TWENTY-FIVE

OAK HILL CEMETERY WAS A 19TH-CENTURY, twenty-two-acre churchyard on the north side of Georgetown that started at R Street and made its way down to the banks of Rock Creek, just on the other side of Embassy Row. Moore watched from his unmarked SUV as the funeral procession made its way along the tiny avenues weaving their way amongst rows of tombstones. A large Cadillac hearse, escorted by a Metro DC Police car, led the convoy of black limousines and SUVs through a brick and iron main gate, their wheels nearly touching the hallowed grounds on either side of the pavement. The sight stirred up some deep-seated claustrophobia in Moore and he shifted in his seat, uneasy.

"Do you know how much it costs to get a six-foot hole here?" Cotton asked from the passenger seat.

"More than we'll make in this lifetime," Moore said. "Or the next."

Moore and Cotton had observed funerals for cases before, but this one was different. Not only was it not in Virginia, but for his part, Moore could not recall being present for one so cold. Even in their police-issued Explorer with the heat blasting, just the sight of naked trees looming over old headstones frosted with windswept snow made him shiver.

The procession followed the road as close to Nathalie McKenna's grave as it could get, then stopped for people to file out of their respective rides. A cluttered mass of mourners dressed in black followed a pastor and eight men carrying Nathalie's casket. At the head of the followers was Brad McKenna.

"Is that the husband?" Cotton asked.

"Yup." Moore shifted the toothpick in his mouth.

"You think the ex will show?"

Moore made an indiscernible grunt that Cotton took to mean his partner wasn't sure. Now, Cotton also shifted uneasily in his seat.

A black canopy tent was situated on a flat spot on the hillside, just ahead of a large, rectangular hole in the earth. The first few people—likely family and close friends—filed in under the tent and huddled together, seated in rows of folding chairs.

Cotton and Moore scanned the surrounding hillside for onlookers, a force of habit in their line of work. Aside from a pair of groundskeepers, the rest of the churchyard was deserted.

"Not much out of the ordinary," Cotton said.

Moore huffed, amused. "Nothing about this case is ordinary."

"Still, I don't see any unwelcome guests. I suppose Clay could be down there with the group."

Moore was about to convey his doubts on the matter when his phone buzzed in his pocket. He pulled it out and answered it. "This is Special Agent Moore."

Someone spoke on the other end of the line, and Moore sighed. Cotton wasn't sure if it was out of frustration or disappointment.

"When was this?" Moore asked. After listening a moment, he said, "Alright, thanks. Tell Metro PD we'll meet them there."

He ended the call and shook his head.

"What's up?" Cotton asked.

Moore turned on the car. "Someone just broke into Brad McKenna's place."

TWENTY-SIX

AS THE ELEVATOR doors opened on the penthouse level of the Omni Lofts & Residences, Moore and Cotton could already hear Brad McKenna shouting at people. The man must've left his wife's funeral awfully quick to beat them here, Moore thought. The French doors to his condo were open, and a couple of uniformed Metro PD officers stood with McKenna in the kitchen as he berated another man in a gray suit with a badge clipped to his belt.

"What are you asking me for?" McKenna shouted at the man. "I've explained to you a dozen times—*I wasn't here!*"

When Moore and Cotton stepped through the entryway, McKenna threw his hands up in exasperation.

"Oh, good," he said, "*now* the calvary comes. Please tell me you're someone more in charge."

"I'm Special Agent Booker Moore, Virginia State Police," Moore said. "This is Special Agent David Cotton. We have yet to meet, Mr. McKenna, but not for a lack of trying on our part."

"I just had to leave my wife's *funeral* to come and deal with someone *breaking into* my condo! What is it with this goddamn city? Someone broke into my place, and these guys let the guy get away!"

"I understand you're upset, Mr. McKenna, but—"

"You're goddamn right I'm upset! I'm supposed to be at the reception following my wife's funeral. Instead, I'm here dealing with this crap!"

Moore raised his hands defensively. "We know someone broke in, Mr. McKenna. That's why we're here."

"You think this has something to do with Nathalie's death?"

"We're not ruling anything out."

McKenna slammed his hands on his kitchen counter and looked down, shaking his head. The five police officers looked at one another, wondering if the man had finally calmed down.

"*Clay!*" McKenna spat, hammering the counter with a fist, eyes flicking angrily back to Moore. "He was here yesterday. He accosted me, accused me of having something to do with my wife's death! I bet this was him."

"Jackson Clay?" Moore asked.

"Yes, Jackson Clay. The gall of that man. Can you imagine? Accusing *me*? The *day before* my wife's funeral!"

"We'll make a note of that. Do you have the video camera footage from the front door?"

"Yes, I already gave it to these officers here, who *still* have not done anything with it!"

Moore raised his hands again. "Alright, Mr. McKenna, alright. Why don't I take a moment and talk with these men here, and we can figure this all out."

"I'm telling you, it was Clay. Jackson. Clay. He had to have been the one that did this."

"Okay, Mr. McKenna. Just give us a moment."

Moore motioned for the Metro DC police officers to follow him over into the living area, but Cotton peeled away from Moore and approached McKenna.

"Mr. McKenna," Cotton said, "would it be okay if I looked around the place?"

McKenna gestured Cotton was welcome to do whatever he

CHASING DEVILS

wanted. Cotton nodded at the two uniformed Metro officers and they followed him as he headed deeper into the condo. The man in the suit accompanied Moore over to the large windows overlooking the Potomac River.

"That guy's less than happy," he said. "I'm Detective Tim Plumlee, by the way."

"S.A. Booker Moore. My partner is S.A. David Cotton."

"I heard. You two are working the wife's murder. So you're looking at this as a part of it?"

"Can't say for certain until we know what we've got here."

"Pretty straightforward. An intruder came up the penthouse elevator and came in through the front doors about a quarter after eight this morning."

"How'd he get in? And how was he able to use the elevator to get up here?"

"Whomever it was had the code for both."

"How does one go about getting that?"

"Haven't figured that out yet. I was trying to ask McKenna when he started throwing his tantrum."

"Do you have the video?"

"Yeah, right here." Plumlee pulled out his phone, opened an email attachment, and held it out for Moore to see. "The building in general doesn't have a lot of cameras. I guess it's a privacy thing with the residents. But McKenna had one of those Ring cameras installed in the entryway, just over the elevator door."

Moore watched the video as a man, slightly taller than average, stepped off the elevator and approached the French doors. The camera, positioned over the man's right shoulder, just barely caught the intruder punching at the keypad before turning the handle and opening the door.

"Open sesame," Plumlee said.

"His back is to the camera," Moore said. "Do we ever get a better look?"

"Unfortunately, no. The Ring camera sent an alert to McKenna, who called the front desk here. They called us. Uniformed officers responded and took the elevator up. They think they scared the intruder up to the roof. After clearing here, they swept the roof and found no one. We're guessing the man found his way down somehow."

Cotton poked his head in from the hallway, looking suspiciously at McKenna before turning to Moore and gesturing him over. Moore excused himself from Plumlee and met Cotton just inside the hallway. There, Cotton handed him a folder of marketing material for McKenna's real estate company.

"Take a look at this," Cotton said.

A logo for McKenna Development, Inc. stretched across the top of the folder, just above a perfectly photographed office building bearing the same logo near the roof. Out in front of it, smiling people stood in business attire, with a fleet of company cars on either side of them.

"Notice the vehicles?" Cotton asked.

"They're dark blue," Moore said.

"Dark blue *Fords*. How much are you willing to bet they're Deep Impact Blue?"

Moore rolled the toothpick around in his mouth with his tongue. He looked over at Brad McKenna, leaning against his kitchen counter, staring back at them warily. "Did we ever find out where Mr. McKenna was the morning his wife was killed?"

"His lawyer told us he left for the gym before Nathalie was awake. His usual routine for a weekday. We haven't independently corroborated that, though."

McKenna turned and began fixing himself a drink.

"Let's do that," Moore said. "And get the info on those company vehicles, too."

TWENTY-SEVEN

BEAR HAD STARTED to head back into Virginia when Jackson told him he wanted to see Adrien again.

"Are ya sure that's the best idea?" Bear asked. "Ya just broke into Brad McKenna's place. Maybe we oughta lay low for a bit."

"Laying low isn't an option right now," Jackson said. "Come on, let's talk to Adrien."

Bear acquiesced, and fifteen minutes later they were back in Fort Totten. As the duo pulled up to the apartment building, they spotted Adrien stepping out the front door. Jackson got out before Bear had managed to park and jogged across the lawn, ignoring the signs asking people to keep off the grass. Adrien had started to turn and walk the other way when he spotted Jackson out of the corner of his eye.

Doing a double-take, he smiled warmly and waved. "Jackson. What brings you by again?"

"I have a couple more questions, if that's okay," Jackson said.

"You know, I'd love to help, but I'm actually running late at the moment. I'm headed for the metro."

"Well, can we walk and talk?"

"Sure, I guess."

Jackson looked back at Bear and motioned that he and Adrien were going to walk. Bear nodded and climbed back into his Suburban.

"I'm surprised you're not at Nathalie's memorial service," Jackson said.

"And I could say the same about you," Adrien countered.

"I spoke to Brad McKenna yesterday. It could've gone better. I don't think I would've been welcome today."

"I assumed the same for myself."

"Yeah, I understand now what you meant about Brad not being exactly fond of you. Even seemed to think you had the hots for Nathalie."

Adrien chuckled and shook his head. "I imagine Brad McKenna is a smart guy, but he couldn't be more off."

Jackson followed Adrien as he turned off the sidewalk and onto a paved path leading away from the street. The walkway bisected the woods to their right and a small community garden to their left, though in late February it was little more than dirt plots and frozen weeds.

"Listen, does BW or King's Quarters mean anything to you?" Jackson asked.

Adrien thought for a moment, then shook his head. "No, I can't think of anything. Why?"

"It's just something that came up, possibly related to Nathalie. I just wondered if you knew what it was."

"I can't say that I do, sorry."

"No problem. It may be nothing, anyway."

"I see."

"When we were at your place, you said you weren't sure if Nat's husband could be violent."

"I honestly don't know one way or the other. But, no, I didn't see anything that made me wonder."

"No bruises or marks or anything?"

"No, nothing like that."

"So, then, if you don't mind me asking, what makes you unsure?"

Adrien shrugged. "I don't know. You just don't know people sometimes. What skeletons they've got hiding in their closets."

Their walk had taken them past the community gardens, and they were now coming up on the street on the other side. Beyond that was the metro station.

"I'm sorry, but I really do have to catch the metro," Adrien said.

"Sure, no problem."

"It was good to see you again. Take care, Jackson."

Jackson stopped and waved as Adrien continued on. Adrien waved back before turning for the metro station. Jackson was watching him walk off when he heard a familiar rumble come down the street.

Bear pulled up curbside and rolled down the passenger window. "I drove around the block. Figured I'd save ya the walk back."

Jackson opened up the passenger door and climbed in. "Thanks."

"Can we get out of DC now? Before one or both of us is arrested?"

"Sure, Bear. Let's go."

TWENTY-EIGHT

BACK AT THE CABIN, Jackson spent most of the afternoon either on his computer or on his phone, making calls. Bear, for his part, was just happy they were home in time to catch the Baywatch marathon on TV. He was posted up in one of Jackson's recliners—the one quickly becoming *his* recliner—with his third Miller High Life.

"Okay. Thank you, again," Jackson said, ending a phone call. He dropped his cell phone on the dining room table and sighed in frustration. Bear didn't look away from the TV as he engaged the man.

"No luck?" Bear asked. He didn't take his eyes off Pamela Anderson jogging down the beach.

"No. Nothing about the Post-It note sounded familiar to Maria Wilkins."

"Did ya try that private eye guy?"

"Before Wilkins, yes. He didn't know anything about it, either. This is ridiculous—someone has to know."

"I suppose we could ask the husband, but I guess we kind of burned that bridge already."

Jackson glowered at Bear. Bear kept his eyes on the TV—he knew he'd made his point. Jackson walked into the kitchen, grabbed a bottle of water, and took a heavy swig from it.

"Have ya tried just Googlin' it?" Bear asked.

"It's two letters and a phrase. It could mean anything."

"Just sayin'. Ya said someone oughta know. Maybe the Internet does."

Jackson gave him another look, but went over and opened up his laptop, nevertheless. He typed *BW* into the search bar and hit enter. The first results that came up were for Baldwin Wallace University. Jackson shook his head, entered *King's Quarters*, and searched again. The top results were for an apartment complex in Missouri, and a hotel in South Carolina.

"Nothing," Jackson said. "*BW* returns info on some college in Ohio, and *King's Quarters* comes back with Midwest apartments and a hotel down south."

Bear took another hearty sip from his beer. "Did you try the two together?"

"What together?"

"*BW* and *King's Quarters*."

Jackson entered *BW King's Quarter* and hit enter. The search result sent a chill through him.

"Son of a bitch," he said under his breath.

He began clicking around. Bear chortled from the recliner, knowing he'd been proven right. He switched the recliner upright and scooted forward in his seat to look over at Jackson.

"What is it?" he asked.

"Best Western King's Quarter. It's the hotel right next to Kings Dominion."

"The theme park Evan was taken from?"

"Exactly."

"I'll be damned."

Jackson nodded. He couldn't find anything to say. Why hadn't he thought of that? As soon as the search showed him, he remembered the hotel. An afternoon asking people what the Post-It note meant, and he'd known all along. He just hadn't put it together.

He met Bear's eyes. "Do you think ...?"

"Do I think, what?" Bear asked.

"Was she looking into Evan's disappearance herself? Did she wonder if Dale Jeffers was telling the truth?"

"I don' know, brother."

"Yeah, I don't know, either."

Now it was Bear who got up and went to the fridge, though instead of getting a water he grabbed his fourth beer of the afternoon. He twisted the cap off in his meaty paw and took the first sip.

"Guess we're goin' to Kings Dominion tomorrow."

"Absolutely," Jackson said.

TWENTY-NINE

JUST AFTER SUNRISE the next morning, a week to the day Nathalie McKenna had been killed, a small convoy of police vehicles —with Special Agents Moore and Cotton at the front in their unmarked Ford Explorer—pulled up in front of a large, red brick warehouse-style building on New York Avenue in Northeast DC. A sign reading *McKenna Development, Inc.* hung over the front doors.

Moore and Cotton had learned overnight that the building photographed in the marketing material they'd found at McKenna's penthouse was the company's headquarters on Capitol Hill, but the work vehicles were kept here, at the company's auxiliary office. Now the two of them, escorted by Metro DC Police, had a search warrant for the property. Officers and agents filed out of the various vehicles and swarmed the building's entrance.

Cotton handed the warrant to the first office manager who tried to rebuff them, a stocky woman in a cream blouse and maroon skirt. After skimming it and giving it back to Cotton, she begrudgingly led the men to the garage.

Moore ordered a group of DC police officers and Virginia State

Police special agents to search the vehicles, then turned back to the office manager. "Where are the keys to the vehicles kept?"

"In that office over there," the woman said, pointing to an array of windows that looked into the garage. "They're kept in a lock box. People with access can open it with a PIN."

"Each person with access has their own identifiable code?"

"That's usually how PINs work, yes."

"Check the attitude. We're going to need to see records of who's accessed the box, going back the last two weeks."

The manager rolled her eyes and left to get the requested information. Moore stood back and took in the garage. It was a cavernous car park with ceilings stretching twenty feet overhead. The parked vehicles, all the same shade of Deep Impact Blue with the McKenna Development logo painted on the front doors, were arranged back to front in neat rows and took up most of the floor space. The rest was littered with automotive and maintenance equipment.

"Agent Moore, over here."

Moore turned toward the voice and noticed a fellow special agent across the garage, waving him over. He joined the man in front of a Ford Edge partially covered with a canvas car cover.

"This one was covered up," the agent said. "Check it out."

The agent and Moore each shined a flashlight on the exposed part of the car. It had clearly been in some sort of collision, with its grill and front bumper heavily damaged. Moore knelt and examined the scrape marks on the bumper.

"Black paint scrapings," he said.

He stood and looked around the garage for Cotton. His partner was at the front of the garage with the office manager, examining something. Moore walked over to him.

Cotton saw Moore approaching and waved a stack of papers at him. "Look at this. Based on the PIN code entered, Brad McKenna accessed the lock box with the keys just before five thirty in the morning last Thursday, when his wife was killed."

Moore's brow furrowed as he looked over the data log. He took the toothpick out of his mouth and twiddled it between the fingers of his free hand. "It's hard to be here when he's supposed to be at the gym."

"Downright impossible if you ask me," Cotton said.

"There's a work vehicle over there with front-end damage and black paint scraped across its fender."

"How much you want to bet it matches the black paint from Nathalie McKenna's Tesla?"

Moore turned back toward the special agent near the damaged Ford. "Get a sample of that black paint rushed over to our lab. I want it processed as fast as possible."

The agent nodded.

Moore turned back to Cotton. He sucked his teeth before putting the toothpick back in his mouth.

"We better go see about that alibi," he said.

THIRTY

BEST WESTERN KING'S Quarters was a two-story brown brick motel sitting cattycorner from Kings Dominion's massive parking lot. It'd seen a lot of business during the park's busy season. Now, though, as Bear and Jackson pulled up to it on a frosty Thursday morning, the motel seemed deserted.

Bear leaned over the steering wheel, taking in the place. "Looks closed, brother."

"Shit," Jackson said. "Yeah."

"I guess there's only one question: is it closed for the season or closed for good?"

Jackson shook his head before opening his door. "Doesn't much matter for us."

He and Bear climbed out of the SUV and the two began to wander around the empty parking lot.

"Why was this place important to her if it was closed?" Jackson asked.

"Don' know," Bear said. "Maybe there's more to it than that."

Jackson turned and looked across the way, at Kings Dominion. It was eerie out of season. Large, steel thrill rides lay dormant as they formed their own skyline. The park was the size of a small town. Here, in late February, it was a ghost town.

"The offices of the park and stuff are right there." Jackson pointed at a couple of buildings situated in a small sliver of the parking lot closest to them. "The motel here would be the closest thing not a part of the park."

"And?"

"What if Jeffers didn't leave the park through the front? He was used to making deliveries here. He might've used something like the employees' entrance. If he told Nat the same story about him letting Evan go in the parking lot, maybe Nat thought the motel was the most likely place for Evan to run to."

"That's great and all, but it's still closed. Ya sure it was open back then?"

"Pretty sure. Besides, look at it. That building hasn't been abandoned for fifteen years."

Jackson walked toward Kings Dominion, crossing the drive leading to the park's parking lot, and looked around again.

"Where else would he have gone?" Bear shouted to him.

"I don't know. The interstate is right there, so probably not west. We never found anyone else who saw him at the park to the south."

"And the motel is here, north of ya. So what's that leave?"

Jackson looked east. "More parking lot."

"Or what's farther north? Beyond the motel here?"

"That's a good question. Let's find out."

Bear locked up the Suburban, and the two of them began walking. On the far side of the hotel was a small lawn and a line of trees that must've marked the end of the property. Jackson and Bear crossed through the trees to a small field on the other side. They traversed the field and came to a service road that ran parallel to a six-lane road.

"I don' think he would've made it across this road without someone noticin'," Bear said.

"Me neither," Jackson agreed. "He was barely taller than this highway divider here. I doubt he could've even gotten over it."

He sighed and looked back at the motel. Another dead end. They'd already wasted nearly half a day. Jackson was starting to get frustrated.

"This is a waste," he grumbled.

Jackson started walking away, but instead of heading back toward the motel, he turned at an angle in the direction of the King Dominion parking lot. At the line of trees, he jumped a white wooden fence and headed toward the center of it. The area was a barren landscape. Nothing but asphalt and concrete for almost as far as the eye could see. Jackson walked on, a winter wind whipping at his face and piercing the thin layers he had on. He kept walking until he reached the grassy median that cut the front portion of the parking lot in half. Two lanes on either side of it ran headlong toward the front of the park.

He came to the end of the median and looked around, situated in the geographic center of the massive lot. The area was like another planet. Devoid of any life. Like Mars, but black and gray instead of red. A tarmac tundra, as bleak as it looked.

Questions pinballed and ricocheted around Jackson's mind. Why had Nat noted this place? Was Jeffers telling the truth? And if he was, where did Evan really go?

JACKSON STOOD *at the edge of the median, scanning the packed parking lot. His son had been missing for fifty-one minutes. Jackson was keeping precise time. He'd looked at his watch moments after Evan had first disappeared. Something told him time would be important.*

Nearing the hour mark, there was still no sign of his son. Park security had fanned out in the area locally where Evan first went missing. When that wasn't fruitful, the local police were called. Now, a larger search operation was going on around the park and its surrounding areas.

Behind Jackson, red and blue lights strobed from the police cars that dotted the entrance to Kings Dominion. Visitors pooled together, looking on, aware something was wrong. Jackson felt like all their eyes were on him.

"Where did you go, Ev?" he asked himself.

He stepped off the median and walked deeper into the parking lot. The sun was starting to set, but the humid Virginia air had yet to relinquish its hold on the summer heat. Jackson's shirt, damp with sweat, clung to his torso, sticky and uncomfortable.

A car honked and Jackson jumped aside, nearly getting hit. He turned to see Nat running over to him.

"What are you doing?" she asked frantically. "You're going to get yourself killed."

"I—I don't where he is, Nat," Jackson said. "I don't know where he went."

"Getting yourself hit by a car isn't going to do us any good. Let's go back to the park. He wouldn't have walked away this far."

It's not him walking off I'm worried about, Jackson thought.

He followed Nat back to the entrance. There, a small cluster of Kings Dominion Park Police had rendezvoused with Hanover County Sheriff's deputies and Ashland Police officers, preparing for a wider sweep of the area. One of the men—the chevrons on his sleeve told Jackson he was someone in charge—walked over to Jackson and Nat.

"We're waiting on one more team member, then we'll do a wider sweep of the area," he said. "Do you have a photo of the boy?"

"Not on me, no," Nat said.

She looked at Jackson, who pulled out his wallet and removed a small photo.

"It's about six months old," Jackson said. "He's grown a lot since."

"It will have to do for now," the officer said, turning to one of his peers. "Run over to the park offices and get copies of this photo made to pass around."

The officer turned back and continued to talk to Jackson and Nat. Jackson replayed the last hour in his mind in reverse, like a movie being rewound. He went back from being a distraught parent to having Evan safely by his side. He and Evan and Nathalie were happy, and all was right with the world. He wondered if he'd ever feel that way again.

"Jackson!" Nat snapped, bringing him back to the present. "Where are you? I need you with us. With me, here."

"Okay, I'm sorry," Jackson said.

At that, tears formed in the corner of his eyes. Nat was taken aback, but Jackson was even more shocked than her. He could count on one hand the number of times he'd cried. He'd had friends killed in front of him without shedding so much as a tear. He'd lost family members without ever needing a tissue. Now, he was on the verge of losing it. Grief was a wicked thing. And nothing compared to the thought of losing a child.

"I—I lost him, Nat," he said, the first tear streaking down the side of his face. "Not you, me. You left him with me, and I lost him."

Jackson dropped his head. Nat cupped it with both of her hands, lifting it back up.

"Listen to me," she said. "No one is lost. Evan is just ... missing. We're going to figure this out. You and I. Together, Jackson."

Jackson nodded. He looked up and his eyes met hers.

"Together," she repeated.

"Together," he said.

THIRTY-ONE

AS COTTON and Moore entered the Four Seasons Health Club, a posh fitness center just off Wisconsin Avenue, they were immediately greeted by an immaculately groomed gentleman, tall and tan, with long blonde hair tied back into a bun.

"Good afternoon," the man said with a big smile. "Welcome to the Four Seasons. How may I help you?"

Cotton and Moore flashed their credentials.

"Special Agent Moore, Virginia State Police," Moore said. "This is Special Agent Cotton. We wanted to inquire about one of your guests."

"Well, I must say our guests value their privacy here ..."

"That's okay, we're not looking for anything too ... *private*. In any event, we can come back with a warrant for your files if need be."

The man thought for a moment, no doubt calculating possible ramifications, then waved his hand dismissively. "That's alright. I'm Carson. Let's see if I can't help you out."

"Appreciate it, Carson," Moore said. "We're looking for some information on a Brad McKenna."

"Oh, yes. Mr. McKenna is here almost every weekday. A wonderful guest. We're lucky to have him."

"We're looking for someone to verify he was here last Thursday, a week ago today."

"Sure—I can verify that. Mr. McKenna was here every day last week."

"And what time roughly was he here last Thursday? Do you recall?"

"He usually comes in around half past five in the morning, maybe a little after. Works out for about an hour. He's usually out by seven. Last Thursday wasn't any different."

Moore looked up at the security camera over Carson's left shoulder. He turned and spotted another one just inside the front doors. "Do those cameras have video going back a week?"

"Yes—I mean, um, no. No, they don't, unfortunately," Carson said, tripping over his words.

Moore tilted his head forward and looked at the young man over his glasses, his eyes asking Carson if he was sure that was the answer he wanted to go with. "You know, we're serious about that warrant. We can go get it. For your files and your camera feed."

"Are you familiar with the term 'Obstruction of Justice', Carson?" Cotton asked. "You can do jail time for it."

Carson's shoulders drooped. He looked around before leaning over the desk toward Cotton and Moore. "Maybe we can talk somewhere ... *other* than here?"

Moore nodded. Carson disappeared behind a door momentarily, fetching someone else to man the front desk. When he came back, he had a coat with him.

"I'm going to run for a coffee real quick," Carson said to the other gym employee. "I'll be right back."

He put on his coat and motioned with his head for Moore and Cotton to follow. The three men stepped outside into the cold. Wisconsin Avenue was bustling with noisy traffic, making it impossible for the trio to have a truly quiet conversation.

"Mr. McKenna isn't always here in the morning," Carson said. "He wants people to think he is, though."

"Why's that?" Moore asked.

"I'm not entirely sure."

"Then how do you know he wants people to think he is here?"

"Because he asked me to tell people he was."

"He asked you?"

Carson's feet danced uncomfortably. "He sort of ... paid me."

"Paid you? For what?"

"To say he's here every morning, even when he isn't. He gave me $10,000. *Cash*. Said he wanted to help me with my student loans. Georgetown is expensive. All he asked is that I say he was at the gym during his normal hours. Even when he wasn't."

"And last Thursday he didn't come in?"

"No."

"At all?"

Carson shook his head. Cotton and Moore looked at each other.

"Alright, thank you, Carson," Moore said.

"I can still keep the money, right?" Carson glanced expectantly at Moore and Cotton. "The truth is, I kind of need it."

Moore shrugged. "I don't know what money you're talking about, son."

Carson looked at him, confused for a minute, then understood and nodded with a thankful smile. Moore nodded back. Carson thanked the two men before hustling down the block to a nearby Panera.

Cotton's phone buzzed in his pocket and he pulled it out. "Just got a message—that Ford back at the McKenna Development garage was completely wiped down. No fingerprints or anything. Like it'd been cleaned. The manager confirmed that is something they don't typically do with the vehicles."

"Get in contact with Metro PD, and see if we know where Brad McKenna is," Moore said.

"You want to get things going on an arrest warrant?"

Moore began dialing a number on his own phone. "I want Brad McKenna in custody by tonight."

THIRTY-TWO

THE QUESTION HUNG in Jackson's mind: Where had Evan gone? Standing at the top of the median with Bear now by his side, he looked around once more. If Evan went back to Kings Dominion, someone would've likely seen him. Same for the motel. The idea of him crossing the main road to the north unnoticed was equally implausible. Jackson looked to his right where the parking lot ended at a tree line.

"Do you know what's over that way?" Jackson asked.

"Beats me," Bear said.

Jackson started walking that way. Bear followed.

It was a couple hundred yards to the trees. When Jackson and Bear got there, they opted to climb the small hill nearby rather than try to traverse the thick underbrush. The other side of the hill—a mound, really—descended onto a small road littered with cracks and potholes. Beyond it, a field and more trees, with a cluster of large power lines running overhead.

"There's damn near nothin' over here," Bear said.

"Wouldn't be a lot of eyes this way. And with the sun going down? It'd be easy to miss a little boy."

"Ya think this is where he went?"

Jackson shook his head. "I don't know. Even if he did, how would we know? It's been almost fifteen years, and he could've gone anywhere from here."

"Well, what's around here?"

Jackson shrugged. Bear pulled out his phone and punched at it with his thumbs for a minute before looking up at the field across the road.

"Looks like there's a campground over that way," he said.

"How far?"

"Less than we've already walked from the parkin' lot."

Jackson started walking in the direction Bear pointed, but Bear begged him to double back and let them drive over.

"My dogs are barkin'," he said.

Jackson agreed, and the two of them returned to Bear's Suburban back at the shuttered motel, then drove down the road to the campground. The first thing they came upon was a small camp store and office. The few parking spots in front of the store/office were empty save for a pickup truck that had seen better days. Based on the logo on its door, it was a work truck for the property.

As Bear and Jackson parked and climbed out, a gray-haired older woman in a denim jacket and work pants came around the truck.

"Afternoon. You boys lookin' for a place to stay?" The woman's Southern drawl was thick, and her voice rasped and crackled like she'd been smoking since she'd been born.

"No, not us," Jackson said. "We're looking around the area and wondering maybe if someone here might be able to help us out."

"Help you out with what?"

"Well, let me ask: How long have you worked here?"

"Shoot, over thirty years, hon. Started in the summer of '91, the year the park put in the Anaconda coaster."

"Then maybe you can help us. Do you happen to remember a child that went missing from the park in 2007? It made a pretty big stir."

The woman nodded as she lifted what seemed like a heavy cardboard box into the back of the truck. "Sure. You're talkin' 'bout the night two of 'em went missin', right?"

Jackson exchanged a look with Bear. "You said *two* went missing?"

"Yep. Believe it was Labor Day weekend," the woman said. "Don't recall 'nother time that sort of thing happened."

Jackson's mind whirled. His skin went clammy, felt too tight on his bones. He'd worked with the park and local authorities for months, and searched for Evan for years after. This was the first time in all that time he'd heard about a second child gone missing that weekend.

"You're saying two separate kids were reported missing in '07?" he asked. "And on the same day—that Labor Day weekend?"

The woman nodded. "Sure am. I assume they were two separate incidents, anyway."

"What makes you say that?"

The woman stopped what she was doing and leaned against the pickup truck. She pulled a pack of Camels from her pocket, grabbed one, and lit it between her lips. "The park police officer that came over this way and got the one kid."

Jackson's heart thumped hard in his chest. The woman blew smoke out in front of her, where it intermingled with her warm breath in the frigid air.

"You're saying you had one of the missing children *here*?" Jackson asked.

"Why do you keep askin' what I'm sayin'?" the woman said. "Yes. Eugene, a guy who worked here with me, walked up on a Kings Dominion officer with the boy. We'd heard one'd gone missin' from the park. Eugene asked if that was the boy everyone was lookin' for and if he should call the Sheriff. The officer said it was a different boy, said he'd take him back to the park."

"This Eugene guy physically saw the boy? Did you see him?"

"No, Eugene told me 'bout it after. I was stuck here at the office all day."

"Where did Eugene see the boy?"

The woman pointed over her shoulder toward the park. "Back thataway. By the tent sites."

Jackson felt as if his knees were about to give out on him. "And you reported all this to the police?"

"Why would I? Didn't seem like there was anythin' to report. A kid went missin', but the park police found him."

Jackson took out his wallet and fished a small photo from it. "Do you remember what the boy looked like?"

"No. Like I said, I never saw him. Eugene did. He just told me 'bout it after."

"Does Eugene still work here? Can we talk to him?"

The woman shook her head as she took another drag from her cigarette. "There's no talkin' to ole Eugene, I'm afraid. He caught the big C a while back. Colon cancer. Passed away, oh, goin' on 'bout ten years ago, now."

Jackson rubbed his head. A flurry of emotions welled up inside of him. Mostly, he was angry at himself. He'd searched forever for Evan and had never discovered all this back when it happened. When it mattered. Would it have made a difference if he had? Pondering that question made him nauseous.

"The other boy," Jackson said, a thought coming to him. "His photo must've made the rounds. Did Eugene ever see it?"

The woman thought to herself. "I'm not sure. I imagine he would've. Like you said, it was a big deal at the time."

"Did Eugene ever say whether *that* boy was the boy he saw or another one?"

"Not that I remember. But if he recognized the missin' boy as the one he saw, he would've said something."

Jackson's heart sank. The woman was right. Could there really have been a second boy missing that day? He'd never heard about it. Jackson tried to think, but his head hurt. He was tired. Physically, mentally, and emotionally. It had been a long day in more ways than one.

"I'm sorry I can't help ya'll more," the woman said. "If y'all really want a place, I can give you a good deal. Make it up to ya'll. Bosses ain't goin' to tear into me too much for givin' a discount in the slow season."

Jackson was about to kindly turn the woman down when Bear stepped in close to him.

"It ain't a half bad idea, brother," Bear said. "C'mon. You're beat, I'm beat. Let's grab some brewskis from that truck stop back down the road and crash here tonight. My treat. We'll get you back home in the mornin'."

Jackson wanted to object, but fatigue was getting the best of him. The truth was, *not* having a ninety-minute car ride home sounded really good.

"Alright," he said. "Thanks."

Bear grinned and slapped Jackson on the shoulder before turning to the woman, prepared to haggle with her. Seeing Bear—a foot taller and considerably heavier than the old woman—hammer out the details for their stay made Jackson smile. Bear was a good friend. He knew he was lucky to have him.

He couldn't imagine facing all of this alone.

THIRTY-THREE

OFF THE RECORD was a bar in the basement of the historic Hay Adams Hotel. Plush velvet armchairs and benches filled the upscale watering hole, and colonial red walls with varnished wood trim held caricature portraits of DC's elite. A cocktail ran almost twenty dollars, and the steak frites could cost double that. It was everything people who loved being Washingtonians wanted it to be, and Brad McKenna was no different.

He routinely had drinks there after hours, almost always before running to a dinner reservation somewhere else across town. This Thursday night, despite Nathalie's funeral just the day prior, was no different. He laughed graciously as his company—one of the heirs to a famous chain of hotels and resorts—shared an anecdote about his trip to St. Kitts. Truthfully, Brad didn't care, but schmoozing is how wheels were greased in the nation's capital.

McKenna downed his third old fashioned, asked for the check, paid it, and stood to leave with his guest. The two of them pulled on their overcoats and made their way out the doors and up the stairs, back to city level.

As they stepped out onto the H Street sidewalk, the sun was low, hovering just above the trees of Lafayette Square. McKenna put a hand in front of his eyes to shield them, looking for his driver and the black Escalade that'd brought him here. Instead, all he saw were several black SUVs and sedans bookended by two Metropolitan Police squad cars.

"What's all this?" McKenna's acquaintance asked.

Before McKenna could answer, the doors of all the cars opened, and out stepped a small army of police officers. Some wore uniforms, while others wore Kevlar vests and windbreakers over their shirts and ties. Two men McKenna recognized exited the SUV directly in front of him. One, black, and the other, white, they both wore badges around their necks and vests emblazoned with the words *Virginia State Police*. The black man, bald with glasses, led the charge.

Unsure of what was happening, McKenna started to step back and raise a hand in objection. A uniformed police officer grabbed his wrist and twisted it behind him. McKenna was too confused to resist.

"Mr. McKenna, good evening," said the black state police officer. "Do you remember me?"

"You were at my place after the break-in," McKenna said. "Moreland-something."

"Moore, actually. Special Agent Booker Moore."

A second uniformed officer came up and grabbed McKenna's other wrist, holding it back while the first officer handcuffed McKenna.

"What the hell is this? You can't seriously think I broke into my own place," McKenna said.

Moore smiled, shifting the toothpick in his mouth. "This is not about your break-in. Mr. McKenna, you are under arrest for suspicion of murder in the death of Nathalie McKenna."

McKenna was incredulous. "*Murder?! Nathalie?!* You've got to be fucking kidding me!"

"I'm afraid not."

Moore nodded to one of the uniformed officers who began to

read McKenna his Miranda rights. A small crowd was gathering, and onlookers quickly pulled out their phones, trying desperately to video record their own piece of the action. McKenna's suit and coat screamed money, and everyone loved to see a rich man fall from grace. The two uniformed officers began to usher McKenna toward one of their squad cars and now McKenna, keenly aware of what was happening, began to resist. He tried desperately to turn back and look at Moore as he was led away.

"You're making a big fucking mistake," he shouted. "You hear me? A *big* fucking mistake!"

Moore ignored the man. He'd heard the same thing or some iteration of it a thousand times. Brad McKenna was no different.

Cotton came around to Moore and offered a congratulatory hand. Moore took it and shook.

"Good work," Cotton said.

"Not done yet," Moore said. "Let's get him booked and extradited to Virginia."

THIRTY-FOUR

SOME ONE HUNDRED twenty miles away, Jackson and Bear sat in a pair of Adirondack chairs in front of a fire pit outside of the small cabin they'd rented for the evening. Bear had run out and grabbed some hot dogs and a case of Miller High Life—the dinner of champions—at a grocery store in nearby Ashland. Now, they looked on, beers in hand, as the flames from the fire licked the early nighttime sky.

"Do ya think Evan was really here?" Bear asked.

"I don't know," Jackson said. "We may never know. Too much time has gone by. People who were there aren't here anymore."

Jackson looked past the fire at the area around them. Trees surrounded the campsite, but the tops of the Kings Dominion roller coasters craned overhead. Without cars or screaming riders whizzing by, they looked incomplete, like skeletal structures for something more, or the desiccated remains of a bygone era. For Jackson, who hadn't come close to this area in over a decade, that's exactly what they were. Skeletons of the past.

"I never thought I'd come back here, to all this," Jackson said. "Not after I'd moved on."

Bear nodded and finished off his beer. Rocking himself out of the chair, he rose gingerly, and plodded over to the gas grill that sat underneath the grape arbor in front of their cabin. He opened the lid, and the sound of sizzling processed meat filled their little camp area.

"What about Nat?" Bear asked. "Ya think she came down here? Lookin' for answers?"

"I have no idea. Fifteen years ago, I'd say no way. But now?" Jackson shrugged. "People change."

Bear nodded again as he poked at the hot dogs, rolling them over on the grill. "I'm sorry I never got to meet her. She sounds like she was a great woman."

"She was."

"I bet she'd get a kick out of me."

Jackson grinned and snorted. Bear let out his signature chortle. Closing the lid of the grill, he tossed his empty beer can into the receptacle next to him.

"I'm going to grab another, you need one?" Bear asked.

"No, I'm good. Thank you."

Bear ducked into the cabin.

Nat meeting Bear. That'd be a sight, Jackson thought. It had never crossed his mind. Thinking of Nat seeing any of his life now felt surreal. Not just because she was gone—that much was obvious—but everything was so different now. *He* was different now. The last she'd seen him, he was a wreck. He suspected she was, too, but she did a better job of hiding it, the things that troubled her. She always had. Slowly, though, he'd picked up the pieces and built something of a new life for himself. He hoped Nat had, as well. Truthfully, a part of looking into her death was him making sure that she had. Because no matter what, Nat, like Evan, wasn't coming back. It meant something to Jackson if he could know she'd found happiness in the end.

Bear leaned his head out the open door of the cabin.

"Jacky boy, you're goin' to want to see this, brother."

Jackson turned to look at him. There was a seriousness in his tone and on his face that alarmed Jackson. He got up and followed Bear into the cabin. They stepped into the small living space and Bear gestured to the television.

News footage of Brad McKenna being led into a DC police precinct played on the screen. Officers did their best to hold a swarming crowd at bay. Flashes from cameras gave the scene a chaotic strobe effect. Below it all, a breaking news chyron scrolled across the screen:

DC REAL ESTATE MOGUL ARRESTED ON SUSPICION OF WIFE'S MURDER

"Ain't that somethin'," Bear said.

The most Jackson could muster was a small nod in agreement.

"Guess that's one mystery down."

Jackson turned the other way and looked out the cabin's front window. In the last of the day's twilight, he could still see the haunting silhouette of the roller coaster tracks on the horizon.

"One to go," he said.

Bear nodded and slapped him on the back. Jackson smiled, but it was forced. In that moment, a sadness washed over him he couldn't shake.

"You know what? This has been a hell of a day," Jackson said. "I think I'm going to hit the sack."

"Oh, okay. Yeah, man. No problem. Have a good night."

Jackson forced out another smile before moving into his bedroom and shutting the door. He sat down on the bed and retrieved the photo of Evan from his wallet. Behind it was the first photo Jackson had ever taken of his son, then just a few hours old and swaddled in a light blue blanket.

THE DIGITAL CAMERA *flashed in little Evan's eyes and immediately he began to cry. Everyone in the room chuckled, including Jackson. Nat's mother, Janet, reached in and took her camera back.*

"I'm not the best at working these things," Jackson admitted.

"Heck, I'm not either," boasted Nat's dad, Tim.

Again, the group laughed. Evan continued to cry in Nathalie's arms. She bounced softly up and down, trying to calm his newborn son.

The five of them were in the Mother-Infant Unit at VCU Medical Center, on the edge of downtown Richmond. Jackson came around to Nat's bed and watched her calm their son. In less than a minute, Evan stopped crying and fell back asleep.

Calming a baby. Another thing Nat did better than Jackson.

A nurse came in with a fresh pitcher of water. "Okay, everyone, it's time for mommy and baby to rest for the evening. You guys can come back tomorrow during visiting hours."

Tom and Janet grabbed their jackets and then took turns kissing Nat and Evan goodbye. Jackson also stood, at which point the nurse looked at him, confused.

"Mr. Clay, you can stay, of course," she said.

"No, I know," Jackson said. "I'm just going to walk them to the elevator." He turned to Nat. "I'll be right back."

Nat smiled and nodded.

Jackson followed Janet and Tim out the door and down the hall to the elevators. There, Tim pressed the button to call the elevator up just as Janet put a hand to her cheek.

"Oh, goodness," she said. "I forgot the camera."

"Hon, we're coming back tomorrow," Tim said.

"No, no. I'll run back real quick and get it."

Turning back she did something between a jog and a fast walk back down the hallway. Her gait was awkward, and she waddled back and forth.

"That woman runs like a duck," Tim quipped. "So does Nat, though I'd never have the heart to tell her. I hope to God she doesn't pass that gene on to Evan."

Jackson and Tim chuckled.

"Hopefully he gets his physical acumen from you, Ranger," Tim added. "Or I guess I should say Dad, now, huh?"

Jackson grinned. "I guess so."

"It's a great thing, becoming a dad."

"Well, hopefully, I live up to you."

"Oh, you will. I don't doubt it."

"I don't know. Nat is ... amazing. I've told you that before. That came from somewhere."

"Her mother, mostly, probably. She raised that girl right. I was just there to steer the two of them out of trouble."

"I'll try my best to do the same for Nat and Evan."

"That's the thing, you know. When you have a wife and kid, they become your everything. The little things that used to rile you up, they don't matter anymore. Just your child and your wife. You feel like you could move the heavens if it only meant making sure they were safe."

"Yeah, I think I know what you mean."

Janet hurried back around the corner, camera in hand, and held it up to show her success. "Got it!"

"Oh, good," Tim said sarcastically. "We were on pins and needles over here."

Janet slapped his arm, and the two laughed. Tim called for the elevator again, and it came immediately. They filed in and turned back, facing Jackson.

"See you tomorrow, hon," Janet said.

"Have a goodnight, son," Tim added. "Dad."

Jackson grinned again and held up a hand in farewell before the elevator door closed. He walked over to the empty waiting area and plopped down into a chair. He closed his eyes, taking a deep breath in, then out. What a day it had been. A fantastic day. Up to and including that last conversation with Tim, his father-in-law. He thought again about what the man said.

They become your everything.

He'd told Tim he knew what the man meant, and he did. Nat, and *now Evan, were his whole world. It came naturally, with him not having much of anything else to leave behind. All that mattered were them.*

You feel like you could move the heavens if it only meant making sure they were safe.

Again, Jackson knew exactly Tim meant. Love wasn't a strong enough word for how he felt about Nat and Evan.

His life was theirs now.

PART FOUR
THE OTHER SIDE

"What gets us into trouble is not what we don't know. It's what we know for sure that just ain't so." — MARK TWAIN

THIRTY-FIVE

THE NEXT MORNING, Moore allowed himself to be ten minutes late for work, hitting snooze on his alarm once, and stopping at Einstein Bros. for a bagel sandwich and coffee. A small reward to himself for clearing the McKenna case faster than he had expected. However, his celebration and jovial mood were short-lived. Sitting down at his desk in the Division Two BCI offices in Culpeper, he was immediately confronted by his Captain, Raymond House.

"McKenna's lawyer called this morning," he said. "Gave me a mouthful."

Moore shrugged. "His client is about to be charged with murder. I imagine it's not a pleasant thing."

"He says we were overzealous in arresting McKenna."

"He can say whatever he wants. We have McKenna's PIN accessing the lock box to the garage shortly before his wife's murder. We have the car used in the murder *in* that garage, wiped down, with damage and paint scrapings that tie it to Nathalie McKenna's collision. *And*, not for nothing, we have an employee at McKenna's gym admitting Brad McKenna paid him to lie and give him an alibi for the time of the murder."

"But you never actually *questioned* McKenna."

"Because he kept dodging our attempts for an interview. If it weren't for the B & E at his condo, we probably would have never talked to him at all."

Captain House's brow furrowed and he shifted his belt. "Well, his arraignment is this morning. I got an earful about how bail wasn't set last night. The lawyer thinks it was done on purpose by us, that we should've contacted him and set up a time for McKenna's surrender, if not question him."

Moore turned his palms outward in frustration. "I've been trying to get McKenna in a room from day one. Tell his lawyer McKenna only has himself to blame. As for arresting him last night, it was as fast as we could move. Last I checked, we weren't in the business of doing murderers any favors."

"Still, we've arranged a sit down this morning before court. He was moved to the Adult Detention Center in Manassas overnight. You and Cotton will meet McKenna and his lawyer there."

"Fine with me. I've been wanting to talk to the guy for almost a week now, anyway."

"Just get it done. You and Cotton should probably get on the road."

With that, House turned and left. Cotton watched from across the room, waiting for the Captain to step back into his office before he approached Moore. Moore, seeing Cotton walk over, stood up and grabbed his suit coat off the back of his desk chair.

"In case you didn't hear that," Moore said, "we apparently have a date with Brad McKenna and his lawyer, and we're running late."

"Yeah, I know, Cap told me when I got in," Cotton said. "What do you think this is all about? His lawyer apparently raised a real stink."

"Beats the hell out of me."

THIRTY-SIX

JACKSON AND BEAR left the campground before sunup to beat the morning commuters on Interstate 95. They were back at Jackson's cabin by midmorning and, from there, Jackson hopped in his Dodge D100 and headed into DC, leaving Bear at the cabin to pack up his stuff.

Jackson called ahead and arranged to meet Maria Wilkins at The Hallvard Group offices to pick up Nat's personal belongings. With Brad arrested and no other family in the area, Jackson took it upon himself to settle what he could of Nat's estate.

Maria met Jackson at the building's loading dock with Nat's things boxed up on a push cart.

"Thanks again for doing this," Maria said. "We'd been waiting for Brad to claim her stuff, but he never came or sent anyone. Now, I guess he is ... otherwise engaged."

"You could say that," Jackson said as he began loading boxes into the bed of his truck.

"I still can't believe he did that—hurt her, I mean."

"He killed her."

"Yes. That's what I mean. It's ... unthinkable."

"It often is for people who aren't murderers."

Maria stepped off the loading dock and started to reach for a box, trying to help Jackson, but Jackson stepped in.

"That's okay, I've got it," he said.

"What are you going to do with it all?"

"I don't know yet. Hang onto it for the time being."

"Well, like I said, I appreciate it. Her parents aren't alive anymore, is that right?"

"No, they passed not long after we separated. One shortly after the other."

"And she was an only child?"

"Yeah." Jackson grunted as he lifted another box onto his truck.

"Well, I guess it's best you have it all, then. From the little we spoke about it, I gathered she still cared deeply for you."

"And I for her."

Maria folded her arms and looked down at the ground. She kicked at an old cigarette butt with one of her designer high heels. Jackson finished loading the boxes and closed the tailgate on his truck before patting the dust off his shirt and coming around to shake Maria's hand.

"Thank you again," he said.

"Happy to do it. Oh, before you go, Adrien Alva called this morning. I guess he's looking to get in contact with you and wondered if we had your information. I told him I could probably pull it from our call histories in the office, but I didn't want to pass anything along without your permission. He left his number and asked if I heard from you, that you give him a call."

Maria pulled a slip of paper out of her coat and gave it to Jackson.

Jackson took it and nodded. "Thanks, I'll do that."

"Great. Well, I guess that's it. Take care. And please, if you need anything more, don't hesitate to reach out. We loved Nathalie and would be more than happy to do anything we can for her."

"Sure."

The two waved goodbye. Maria corralled the pushcart and

steered it back toward a freight elevator. Jackson climbed into his truck and dialed the phone number on the slip of paper.

"Hello?" Adrien answered.

"Adrien," Jackson said, "it's Jackson Clay. Maria Wilkins said you wanted to get in touch with me."

"I did, yes. I'm sure you've seen the news about Brad."

"I have."

"Awful. Just awful. I wanted to know how you were doing."

"Nat's killer is getting his. I'm good."

"Yes. Well, that's good. Listen, if you're ever in DC again—"

"I'm here now, as a matter of fact. I came by Nat's work to pick up her stuff."

"Oh. Well, could you possibly meet me for a coffee or something?"

"I was just about to head out, actually."

"Ah. Next time then."

"I don't know if I'll be back, honestly. Not much reason to, now."

"I see. Then, before you go, would you please meet me? Let me send you off, for Nathalie's sake."

Jackson paused for a moment and thought. It had been an exhausting couple of days, and he was tired. But Adrien, apparently, was the closest thing to a friend Nat had here.

"Can you meet now?" Jackson asked.

"Uh, sure, yes," Adrien said.

"Great. Pick the place. I'll meet you there."

JACKSON MET Adrien at a sandwich and coffee shop just south of Washington Circle, a stone's throw from the Foggy Bottom metro station. He miraculously found parking on the street just out front and beat Adrien there. While he waited, Jackson got himself a hot black coffee and took a seat in one of the metal garden chairs next to a small café table outside on the sidewalk.

Several minutes later, Adrien walked up from the metro station, waving as he approached.

"Thanks for meeting me," he said. "I see you already got yourself squared away. Let me grab something real quick."

"By all means," Jackson said.

Adrien ducked into the small eatery. Jackson sat back and watched people and cars pass by. Commuters on their way to work. A small group of tourists looked on helplessly as they tried to navigate the maze of downtown streets. Ambulances rolled in and out of George Washington University Hospital, across the way. It was a mild enough day that everybody wasn't hurrying to beat the cold.

A few minutes later, Adrien came back out with a coffee of his own and sat in the seat opposite Jackson. "They have good coffee here."

"Yeah, it's good."

Adrien took a sip of his coffee and nodded in pleasure. "So, you packed up Nathalie's things from work."

"I did."

"What did she have in there? Anything important?"

"I haven't looked at it much, to tell you the truth."

"Ah, I see. Then you'll be on your way back home, I suppose."

"The city's not really my place. I was only here to find out what happened to Nat. But that's over, now."

"Yes. It's just terrible what Brad did. To think someone who loved her could do such a thing."

"He never loved her. You don't do that to someone you truly love. Maybe *for*, but definitely not *to*."

"You say that like you know from experience."

Jackson took a sip of his coffee. "I know how I felt about Nat. And I would never hurt her like he did."

Adrien shook his head. "I can't believe that man had the gall to stand there, accepting everyone's well-wishes as she was lowered into the ground."

"No one's wishing him well anymore. He'll get his."

"Still, it must bother you. We're probably the only two people left on this earth that truly cared for her. And neither of us was there to say goodbye."

Jackson didn't say anything. He'd been so focused on finding out what had happened to Nat that the thought hadn't crossed his mind. Now, a wave of guilt came over him.

"Are you going to go by and say goodbye on your way out of town?" Adrien asked.

"I think I might, actually."

"Good, good. In any event, I just wanted to see you one last time, make sure there's nothing else you needed now that this is all over."

"No, I think I'm good. Thanks."

"Well, it was nice getting to meet you. Probably the only good thing that came out of this horrible mess."

"Yeah. It was nice to meet you, too."

At that, the two stood up. Jackson walked his coffee over to a trash can near the front doors of the eatery and threw it away.

"Perhaps we can stay in touch," Adrien said. "You have my number now."

"Yeah. I'll call if there's anything else."

Adrien flashed a big smile, his lips curling. "And who knows? Maybe I'll come out and visit you on ol' Bull Run Mountain sometime."

Jackson returned his smile, but he was struck by Adrien's specificity.

"Take care, Jackson." Adrien extended a hand.

Jackson shook it. "You, too, Adrien."

The two waved goodbye and turned to walk their opposite ways. As Jackson climbed into his truck, the fact Adrien knew where he lived poked at him. Maybe he'd learned it from Nat or the private investigator, Harry Spencer. Spencer had run Jackson's location down for Nat, after all.

Still, it nagged at Jackson. He decided to call Spencer, but it went straight to voicemail. Jackson left a message asking Spencer to call him back and hung up.

It was strange, but there were a handful of simple explanations. He shook the worry from his mind. In any event, he appreciated Adrien's suggestion. He did, indeed, want to say one last goodbye to Nathalie.

Jackson pulled out of the parking spot and headed for the cemetery in Georgetown.

THIRTY-SEVEN

BY THE TIME Cotton and Moore got to the Prince William County Adult Detention Center, McKenna was already waiting in a private interview room with his lawyer. As the two special agents stepped in, McKenna's lawyer stood but didn't offer his hand. McKenna, clad in a hunter-green jumpsuit and handcuffed to a bar on the table, simply snarled at the two men from his seat.

"Well, you guys have really done it this time," the lawyer said. "Arresting a grieving husband as integral to the community as Mr. McKenna. We'll be filing suit not long after we move to dismiss. Unless you're here to talk about release and offer one hell of an apology."

Moore grinned and snickered at the arrogance of McKenna's lawyer. Adjusting the toothpick in his mouth, he slid into a seat opposite McKenna. Cotton followed suit.

"Why don't we start with some introductions," Moore said. "I'm Special Agent Booker Moore, this is S.A. David Cot—"

"Yeah, yeah. Brad McKenna, Richard Bremner." The lawyer gestured toward McKenna, then himself. "Are you releasing my client or not?"

Bremner remained standing, fists on the table. He was older—Moore guessed probably in his sixties—with slicked-back white hair and a jowly face.

"Please, sit down," Moore said. "And, no, we have no intention of releasing Mr. McKenna."

"Brad McKenna did not kill his wife."

"That's what you say. The evidence says otherwise. We have his personal code accessing the lock box for the keys to the vehicle used, we have the vehicle *forensically* tied to the crime scene, and we have witness testimony that Mr. McKenna paid an employee at the gym he goes to in an attempt to fabricate an alibi."

"That may be, but Mr. McKenna didn't kill his wife."

"The vehicle used, his PIN, and his fabricated alibi have *nothing* to do with his wife's murder? I'm dying to hear this explanation."

Bremner turned and looked at McKenna, implying it was his turn to speak up.

McKenna leaned forward, placing his elbows on the table. "I did access the lockbox, and I did take a vehicle from the garage—but it had nothing to do with Nathalie. I ... was ... *am*, I guess, seeing someone."

"And?" Moore asked.

"I leave my car at that office and take one of our fleet vehicles to see her. I assume Carson gave me up and told you I paid him. It wasn't for some alibi. Well, actually it was. Just not for Nathalie's murder. But to cover where I really was."

Moore shook his head. "When asked over the phone, your lawyer, Bremner, here, specifically said you were at the gym. You're saying that was a lie? Directly obstructing the investigation?"

Bremner held up his hands. "That is what he told me at the time. There was no deceit on my part."

"Yeah, well, *at the time*, I wasn't under arrest and facing murder charges," McKenna chided. "I thought I could keep my ... *affair* under wraps."

Cotton and Moore exchanged a look.

"And we're supposed to believe this new alibi?" Moore asked. "After you've already lied and paid someone to cover for you?"

"It's the truth," McKenna said.

"That's a long way to go to cover up a fling with another woman," Cotton said.

"Yeah, well, in a moment of stupidity, I married Nathalie without a prenup. Do you know how much I'm worth? How many assets I have to my name? If she found out and left me, she could rake me over the coals."

"I'm inspired by the romanticism," Moore said dryly.

"You want me to admit I'm an asshole? Fine, I'm an asshole. But being an asshole isn't a crime. And I certainly didn't kill anyone."

Moore sucked on his teeth as he stared at McKenna, trying to read him. His gut told him the man was finally telling the truth—and he hated what that meant for the investigation.

"Even if we wanted to believe you," he said, "what proof do you have? Because right now, you're still a suspect who can't vouch for his whereabouts."

"Call her," McKenna said. "Mandy. Mandy Bryant. She'll tell you."

"Just like Carson tried to tell us?" Moore asked. He shook his head. "You're going to have to do better than that."

McKenna tried to throw his hands up in frustration, but the shackles on his wrists kept him in place. He looked down at the floor.

McKenna's gaze settled back on Moore. "My phone. We ... *I* videotaped us. Her. When we were ... together."

"Jesus," Cotton muttered.

"We'll take that as permission to search your phone," Moore said. "We'll need any password or PIN information to unlock it."

Moore and Cotton rose quickly and turned for the door in unison.

"What does this mean for my client?" Bremner asked.

"Oh, he's not going anywhere. Don't worry, we'll be in touch," Moore said.

Bremner began to object, but Moore and Cotton left the interview room. As they stepped out into the hall, Vanessa Fernandes—the Commonwealth's Attorney for Prince William County—marched toward them. Her clacking heels upbraided Moore and Cotton with each step, a scowl darkening her face. Moore had worked with her before, and he and Cotton were aware she'd been watching their meeting with McKenna and Bremner via closed-circuit television.

"Is it true?" she asked.

"Is what true?" Moore said.

"His story. With the woman."

"No way of knowing. We just heard about it, same as you."

"Jesus Christ, guys. We're going to look like incompetent clowns if we arrest this guy only to turn around and release him."

"Vanessa, it was a good arrest. The evidence fit. It still does. You'd tell us to go pick him up if we showed you what we had, and you know it."

Fernandes put a hand to her forehead and sighed. "It doesn't change the optics here if it's true."

Moore shrugged. "Let's not get ahead of ourselves. We'll get into his phone and run down this Mandy girl. With a little luck, we'll know where we stand by the end of the day."

"I'm supposed to be in court with him in less than an hour. What am I supposed to do in the meantime?"

"That's up to you. But every minute we stand here is a minute we're not working."

Fernandes crossed her arms and studied Moore and Cotton before stepping aside. "Keep me up to speed."

Moore grunted in acknowledgment. He continued down the hallway with Cotton, working their way back through the detention center and out the front doors.

"Do you think he's telling the truth?" Cotton asked.

"Hell, I don't know," Moore said.

"What does your gut tell you?"

"That our case is one big turd, and it just met the fan."

THIRTY-EIGHT

JACKSON PARKED on the street outside Oak Hill Cemetery, then walked through the main gate. The burial ground sloped down into the trees lining Rock Creek, and Jackson followed a paved path as it switched back and forth through an array of headstones.

The path brought him to a large stone obelisk next to a red-brick mausoleum. Beyond, through the naked branches of the trees, he could see the rooftops of the neighborhood across the way. At the base of the obelisk was carved the name *McKenna*. Jackson knew it was legally Nat's name, but the sight still bothered him. A lasting reminder of the relationship that ultimately killed her.

Her name, *Nathalie*, had been etched in smaller letters below *McKenna*, and beneath that, *Loving Wife* was bookended by a pair of outlines of what Jackson thought might be doves. Snow had melted and refrozen in the crevices, obscuring the writing. Jackson squatted, wiping it away. He ran his fingers over the first three letters of her name.

Nat.

In all their years together, that was the only name he'd ever called her. Nat hated it, thinking it sounded like *gnat*, but Jackson loved it. Nat was the love of his life. He'd never known the name carved in stone before him now, this *Nathalie McKenna*.

Jackson stood and looked around, unsure of what to do. He'd never been mistaken for the most talkative individual, and talking to inanimate objects seemed particularly foolish to him. Still, there was no other way to talk to Nat. Not anymore.

He stared at the ground, trying to conjure something to say. Fragments of sentences popped around in his mind like kernels of popcorn would in that retro popcorn machine they'd gotten as a wedding gift. Pieces of things he'd imagined telling her if he ever saw her again. And the revelation that day would never come left him feeling numb.

"I'm sorry," he finally said.

Jackson shook his head, almost surprised by his own words. Still, he felt them. And meant them. He was sorry for a million things. Sorry he hadn't been strong enough to save their marriage in the wake of losing Evan. Sorry he hadn't made the effort to stay in her life after they separated. Sorry that Dale Jeffers called her and reopened those old wounds. Sorry that Brad McKenna, a man she must've loved, betrayed her—and killed her. More than anything, though, he was sorry he hadn't been able to save her.

He stood for a moment, waiting to see if he could bring himself to say anything else. Nothing came. The popcorn kernels were gone now, and the two words he had spoken hung over him like a black cloud in the otherwise unblemished sky.

Jackson placed a hand on the obelisk and closed his eyes.

"Goodbye," he said, lingering for a moment before turning to leave.

Jackson walked slowly through the cemetery, back up the hillside, and then down the brick sidewalk back to his truck.

He drove his way through the streets of Georgetown and eventually out to Virginia. The interstate was a parking lot, so Jackson opted to cut through the heart of Arlington, a trendy DC suburb. As he came to a red light, he looked across the street.

The intersection at Washington Boulevard cut the block at a sharp angle, and O'Sullivan's Irish Pub filled the corner. A tan and green building with red trim, patrons had ventured into the outdoor seating on this unseasonably warm day. Jackson smiled sadly. It would be March soon, and St. Patrick's Day not long after that. It had always struck him as a bit of a silly holiday. One day a year when everyone pretended to be Irish as an excuse to drink their livers into early cirrhosis. Except for the one time, way back when, in 2004, it had been one of the happiest days of his life.

JACKSON WATCHED *as Joe shimmied haphazardly through the crowded bar, holding all four of their drinks in his two hands. Mulligan's Sports Grille was a bar in Richmond's Fan District. While it didn't claim any particular Irish heritage like some watering holes, it had the vibe of a place that felt appropriate for St. Patrick's Day.*

Jackson and Nat were there with their neighbors, Joe and Sam Macy. The four of them weren't much for the bar scene, but the March holiday had felt like a good excuse to get out of their respective houses. Now, Joe came to their table with four beers dyed Kelly green, and as he approached, he tripped, nearly spilling everything.

"Easy, you klutz," Sam said. "It took you forever to get these. We don't need you taking another fifteen minutes getting replacements."

"I got them here, didn't I?" Joe said.

Jackson and Nat looked on, chuckling.

Joe raised one of the beers in a toast. "Here's to the land of Shamrock, so green. Here's to each lad and—"

"Joe!" *Sam tugged on his arm.* "You are half Honduran and half Italian. Neither of which is Irish."

"Oh, we're all Irish today, baby!"

Sam rolled her eyes as Joe downed half his beer in two gulps. He was a couple of shots of Jameson ahead of the group, and it showed. Sam finally managed to corral her husband, bringing him down and planting him in his seat. She tried to keep her voice down as she chastised him, but Jackson and Nat could hear.

Jackson put an arm around Nat, laughing as he looked on. Joe and Sam made a good couple.

"Okay, okay," Joe said. "Here, everyone take a beer. One for Jackson, and two for the ladies."

Jackson and Sam each grabbed a pint glass of leaf-colored lager, but Nat shyly pushed hers away. Joe, Jackson, and Sam looked at her, confused.

"It's alright," she said. "I'm just going to get a water from the bar."

"Nat, it's St. Patrick's Day," Joe said. "C'mon, have a drink. Live a little. We're doing Irish car bombs after this."

"Like hell we are," Sam countered.

Nat smiled politely but didn't take her beer. Joe downed the rest of his. When he looked back at her, he seemed miffed that she hadn't joined in.

"Jesus, Nat," he said. "What, are you pregnant?"

Sam slapped his chest with the back of her hand. Jackson and Joe laughed at the seemingly silly idea, but when Jackson turned back to Nat, he noticed she was simply holding the same polite smile.

"Nat?" Jackson asked.

Nat looked at Joe and Sam before coming back to Jackson. Her smile shifted into more of a bashful one, and she nervously brushed her amber hair behind her ear.

"I was waiting for the right time to tell you," she admitted.

"Oh my god! My boy's going to be a dad!" Joe shouted.

Sam slapped him again and the two fell into one of their playful arguments, but Jackson didn't pay it any attention. He locked eyes with his wife, his love.

"Really?" he asked, a smile growing on his face.

A single tear streamed down Nat's cheek as she lifted her arms and fell into him. Jackson caught her and embraced her.

"You hear that?" Joe called out to no one in particular. "Jackson here's a father-to-be. Drinks all around! On me!"

"I swear to god, I will divorce you," Sam said.

The two were laughing, but Jackson didn't see them. Or anyone else, for that matter. Just Nat. He felt hands pat and slap him on the back, people nearby wishing their congratulations, but they were a world away. Jackson leaned forward, touching his forehead to Nat's. The two of them closed their eyes and felt one another. In a crowded bar full of strangers and friends, everyone faded into the background. There was only them.

Jackson felt a warmth well up inside him. A kind of happiness he'd only experienced a few times in his life. Meeting and falling in love with Nat was one of them. Now, this was another. Nothing could make him happy as Nat could, and he knew the same would be true of their child.

There was only them. And nothing else mattered.

THIRTY-NINE

MANDY BRYANT LIVED on the sixth floor of a modern apartment complex on Massachusetts Avenue between Logan Circle and Downtown. Tan with blue trim, it stuck out from the other much older buildings around it.

Moore and Cotton took the elevator up to Bryant's floor and walked down the hall to her door. When they knocked, a young woman opened the door just enough to peer out at them over the chain latch lock. Based on the DMV photo of Mandy both Moore and Cotton had seen, it was safe to assume the woman behind the door was the very person they were looking for.

"Ms. Bryant?" Moore asked, flashing his badge. "I'm Special Agent Moore, this is Special Agent Cotton. We're with the Virginia State police."

"This is DC," the woman said.

"Yes, ma'am," Cotton said. "We're just here to ask a few questions. Are you Mandy Bryant?"

"What's this about?" the woman asked.

"A homicide that took place last week," Moore said. "We're looking for Mandy Bryant. We just have a few questions."

The woman sighed. She shut the door, unlatched the chain, and opened the door back up wider. "Yes, I'm Mandy. But I don't know about any murder or anything like that."

"May we come in, ma'am? We'll be quick, I promise," Cotton said.

Mandy's eyes darted between the two of them. She was tall, leggy, and slim, with honey-colored hair. Stepping back and away, she waved them inside. Moore nodded as he walked past her.

"This is quite a place, Ms. Bryant," he said, looking around. "What do you do for work, if I may ask?"

"I work at Ladylove."

"Ladylove? I'm sorry, I'm not familiar."

"It's a womenswear store in Georgetown. We sell lingerie, loungewear, that sort of thing."

"So, Victoria's Secret, basically."

"We're much more exclusive than that."

Moore grinned as he slipped a toothpick between his teeth. "And you're what there? A manager or something?"

"I work the floor."

Moore nodded as he walked around the apartment. "This is quite the place for a retail salesperson. Rent must be, what? Over two grand, for sure."

"I do fine for myself." Mandy folded her arms. "You said this was about a murder? No one was hurt at my work."

"That's correct. We're looking into a homicide that took place in Virginia, not Georgetown. Can you tell me where you were last Thursday morning? Say, between five and seven?"

"I was here, sleeping."

"Quick recollection of something that happened over a week ago. Are you sure?"

"I work Thursdays, and we don't open until eleven. My alarm would be set for eight. So, yes, I would've been here, asleep."

Moore continued to nod along as he walked around. When he

circled back to Mandy, who was leaning against what looked to be a dining table, he gestured at a chair. "May I?"

Mandy nodded. Moore pulled the chair out and took a seat.

"Ms. Bryant, do you know a Brad McKenna?"

"I've heard the name," Mandy said, "but I don't know him personally, no."

"Well, Mr. McKenna says otherwise. According to him, you two are seeing each other."

Mandy's eyes once again flicked back and forth between the two men. "Brad said that?"

"Well, he said he was having an affair with you," Cotton said, standing a few steps away from her and Moore. "But I think Special Agent Moore was trying to put it more delicately."

Mandy's shoulders slumped. Pulling out the chair across from Moore, she slumped into it. "We met when he came into the store once. I knew he was married. Knew it was wrong, but I also knew who he was. I liked that he was paying attention to me."

Moore pulled out his notepad and pen from his jacket and leaned forward. "Seeing a married man isn't a crime, Mandy. We're not here to jam you up. We're just trying to understand everything, how the puzzle pieces go together."

"Okay. Yes, I know Brad. I'm sorry I lied. We've been seeing each other, like you said. Mostly him coming here. I mean, he paid for this place."

"He got you this apartment?" Cotton asked.

"Yes. I was renting a bedroom in Petworth when he met me. After seeing me a few times, he said it was too risky for him to keep coming up there, so he moved me in here. I think it's officially paid for by his company or something. They built this place a couple years ago. I guess it's easier for him to explain why he's coming by one of his own buildings."

"And how long have you two been seeing each other?" Moore asked.

"I don't know," Mandy said. "Several months? I moved in here last August."

"So, circling back, last Thursday. You were here?"

"Yes. And he was, too. He came by early in the morning. That was his usual time on weekdays to see me. Early in the morning."

"You're saying Brad McKenna was here, in this apartment, last Thursday? What time?"

"I don't know, I guess he woke me up a bit before six? Stayed a couple hours. By eight, he was off to work."

Moore nodded along, jotting down notes, then looked up at Cotton. Cotton nodded and pulled out his phone.

"Ms. Bryant, we have a video that was given to us by Mr. McKenna," he said. "It's a little uncomfortable, but we need you to verify it's you in the video. It's very important to our investigation."

"Video?" Mandy glanced at Moore, then back to Cotton. "I—I don't understand ..."

Cotton opened the video file on his phone and played it, setting his phone on the table for Mandy to see. A naked man who was clearly Brad McKenna was laying on his back in a bed. A woman with Mandy's hair and physique was on top of him, straddling him.

"Oh my god," Mandy said. "That fucking asshole."

She tugged at her sweatshirt as if trying to cover herself up.

"Are you saying that's you in the video?" Moore asked.

Mandy couldn't look him or Cotton in the eye. "Yes ... that's me. I'm sorry."

"There's nothing to be sorry about," Cotton said, stopping the video and replacing the phone in his pocket.

"I'm sorry we had to show you that," Moore said, "but I hope you understand it was important."

"No, I'm glad you showed me. I didn't know about it," Mandy said.

Moore gave her a sympathetic half-smile and nod before standing up. "Thank you again for taking the time to talk to us. I'm

185

going to give you my card. If there's anything else you can think of that we should know, please don't hesitate to call."

Mandy took the card from Moore but didn't say anything.

"We'll see ourselves out," Moore added. "Thank you again."

Moore and Cotton left the way they came and took the elevator back down to the apartment building's lobby. When they got outside, Moore called Fernandes.

"What've you got?" she asked.

"Mandy Bryant corroborated McKenna's story," Moore said. "She says he came here, to her apartment, sometime just before six last Thursday morning and stayed until about eight."

"Did she verify that was her in the video?"

"Yes. She said it was her."

"The techs looked into McKenna's phone. The timestamp on the video adds up with the timeline Mandy gave you."

Moore didn't say anything.

"I'm assuming you understand what that means," Fernandes said. "McKenna was in DC when his wife was killed. He's not your guy."

"Respectfully, I think you mean *our* guy."

"I meant what I said. We're releasing McKenna."

Fernandes ended the call. Moore slid the phone back into his pocket, shook his head and sighed.

"What's up?" Cotton asked.

"They're going to kick McKenna free," Moore said.

Cotton nodded in disappointment. Moore placed his hands on his hips and looked down at the sidewalk. He kicked at a piece of broken concrete.

"Back to work?" Cotton asked.

Moore snorted. He shook his head again and moved toward their Explorer.

"Yep," he said. "Back to work."

FORTY

WHEN JACKSON ARRIVED BACK at his cabin, he expected to find Bear's bags all packed up on the porch, if not gone with him and his SUV altogether. Instead, he found his friend sitting on the stairs leading up to his front door with a beer in his hand. As Jackson climbed out of his pickup, Bear nodded at him.

"How'd it all go?" he asked.

"Pretty good," Jackson said. "Got Nat's stuff packed up. That Adrien guy got in contact with me, asked to grab a coffee."

"Did ya?"

"I did. And I stopped by Nat's grave, paid my respects."

"That musta been hard."

Jackson shrugged. Bear took another draw from his beer. Jackson got the sense there was something his friend wasn't telling him.

"So, you decide to hang around a few more days?" he asked.

Bear looked up at him. There was a funny look in his eyes, one Jackson hadn't seen before. A mixture of pain and regret and uneasiness. "Ya haven't had the news on, have ya?"

"No. Why? What's up?"

Bear pulled his phone out of his pocket, tapped the screen a few times, and showed it to Jackson. It was a news article.

AUTHORITIES DROP CHARGES IN MCKENNA MURDER,
DC REAL ESTATE TYCOON RELEASED

Jackson took the phone from Bear and scrolled the article for some sort of explanation, answers to the flurry of questions growing in his mind. There wasn't much. A look of consternation formed on his face as fiery anger began to well up inside him. His hands clenched the phone tightly as his mind spiraled. Bear reached for the phone and Jackson's hands, bringing his friend back to where he stood.

"We're gonna figure this out," Bear said.

Jackson let go of the phone and turned back for his pickup. Bear stumbled to his feet and tried to catch him.

"Hold on now, brother. There's gotta be a reason. We have to figure out the right way to deal with this."

"What right way? We tried this their way. Now we're doing it my way."

"Jackson, wait—"

Bear tried to intercept Jackson, but the man was too fast. Jackson had the engine on and the truck in gear before Bear could get to his door. The pickup tore backward down the drive before jerking left and turning around. Bear ran for his Suburban and hopped in to follow.

The two raced down the winding road leading away from Jackson's cabin. Jackson took the turns at speed, the tires on his truck screeching as they struggled to keep a grip on the road. Bear managed to stay on Jackson's back bumper. His mind scrambled for a peaceful way to stop his friend.

As they came to a T intersection, Jackson slowed to make the turn. Bear knew Jackson would be turning left, and he pulled out wide. As Jackson began turning, Bear flew past, then slammed on his brakes. The Suburban skidded to a stop, blocking the intersecting road, forcing Jackson to swerve to avoid T-boning Bear.

Jackson jumped out of his truck and stormed toward the Suburban. Bear came around the hood, his hands up. He honestly didn't know if Jackson was about to hit him.

"What the hell are you doing?" Jackson shouted.

"Stoppin' ya from doin' somethin' stupid."

"He *killed* her, Bear! He fucking killed her! And they're letting him go!"

"Okay, Jacks, okay. Just breathe, brother."

"No, fuck that! They had their bite at the apple! It's my turn now!"

Bear grabbed Jackson by the lapels of his coat and pinned him against the front of his pickup. "I know! I know. It hurts! You're hurtin' and there's not a damn thing I can do about it, brother. And it fuckin' kills me. But hell will freeze over before I let you do somethin' you can't undo. Somethin' I know you'll regret later."

Jackson looked at his friend, stunned. He couldn't recall another time Bear put his hands on him like that. Now, Bear looked into his eyes, desperate to get through to him.

"You want to do this, for Nat and Evan," Bear said, his voice calmer. "I get that. But ya go down there now, after McKenna, and all you're doin' is gettin' yourself locked up. Or worse. And you can't do nothin' for Nat or Evan if you're behind bars or dead."

Bear let go of Jackson but stepped toward the open door of his pickup, anticipating he might still have to stop his friend again. But Jackson just stood there, his gaze shifting between Bear and the darkening road beyond their two cars, weighing his choices.

"Okay," Jackson said finally. "Okay."

"Let's go home, and let's take a breather," Bear said.

Jackson nodded. Bear put a hand on his shoulder.

"We're goin' to figure this out," he promised. "You and I. Together."

FORTY-ONE

NEITHER JACKSON nor Bear slept most of the night. Bear, at least, pretended to be asleep while he kept tabs on Jackson, who paced restlessly throughout the cabin. When dawn came, he changed into some sweats and told Bear he was going for a run. Bear watched from a window to make sure he didn't head for his pickup. It wouldn't have mattered anyway: Bear had made it a point to block the dirt drive with his Suburban, just in case.

Now Bear sat in the recliner he'd adopted, watching SportsCenter, pretending he wasn't worried about his friend. He heard Jackson trot up the front stairs and walk across the porch. The front door opened, and Jackson came inside, accompanied by a whoosh of chilly morning air, before shutting the door behind him. Temperatures had plummeted overnight and Northern Virginia was out of its flirt with an early spring.

Panting, Jackson grabbed a bottle of water from the kitchen and chugged half of it in a matter of seconds. Stopping for air, he wiped his mouth with his forearm, and leaned against the kitchen island, staring at the floor.

"Good run?" Bear asked from across the room.

Jackson nodded. "I'm going to grab a shower."

He walked into his room but didn't shut the door. Bear heard Jackson start the water in his bathroom, then return to his dresser for clothes.

"You sure you don't want to check the window in here before I get in?" Jackson asked. "I might jump out it and make a break for it."

Bear snorted, shaking his head from the recliner. His friend was going to be okay. Ten minutes later, Jackson came out of his bedroom, dressed, and sat on the sofa next to Bear's recliner. He was still catching his breath from everything.

"I want to go talk to Special Agent Moore," Jackson said. "Be there this morning, before he gets in."

Bear looked over at him, worried.

"I'm good, I promise," Jackson said. "Obviously they had a reason to kick McKenna free and I want to know what that reason is."

"The story just broke last night. I'm sure we'll find out soon enough."

Jackson shook his head. "No more sitting around, watching the news. I want to hear it from the source."

"What makes ya think he'll tell us?"

"If McKenna isn't their guy, I've still got to be on the short list of suspects. Moore won't turn down an opportunity to get me talking."

"Well then, are ya sure it's a good idea to be talkin'? Without a lawyer?"

"I didn't actually kill her, remember?"

"Hate for ya to be sayin' that same thing, doin' twenty-five to life."

Jackson reached over and grabbed his boots, pulling them on. "I know what I'm doing. Trust me on this one."

Bear shook his head. "Famous last words of a thousand rednecks."

"Don't you mean *rural lifestyle enthusiasts?*"

Bear smiled and shook his head again.

"Anyway," Jackson said, "I'm no redneck."

"Brother, I hate to tell ya. But you're living off the grid in the mountains, wanted by the law, tryin' to take justice into your own hands. You're more of a *rural lifestyle enthusiast* than you know."

"Then let's get going before the banjo music starts."

Bear chuckled. Yeah, he thought, his friend was going to be okay.

FORTY-TWO

AN EARLY MORNING argument with his wife about having to work a second straight weekend already had Moore in a bad mood—and things didn't improve when he got to the Division Two headquarters. Spotting the red Suburban in the parking lot as he arrived, he knew immediately he had visitors. He'd wondered if McKenna's release would earn him another visit from Jackson Clay and his galoot of a friend. It appeared he had his answer.

Cotton intercepted Moore almost as soon as he walked through the double doors to the BCI offices. "You're never going to guess who showed up this morning."

"Jackson Clay," Moore said.

"Yeah, and his big buddy. Wait, how'd you know?"

Moore shook his head and walked past him. "Elementary, my dear Watson."

Cotton turned and followed him. "They were here pretty much before everyone this morning. They tried loitering by your desk, so I put them in a conference room."

"I appreciate it."

Moore walked over to his desk, dropped his bag, and draped his suit coat over the back of his chair. He could feel Cotton behind him, lingering. Moore closed his eyes, took a deep breath in, and turned to his colleague.

"Alright. Let's see what they want."

They crossed the office to an array of doors and floor-to-ceiling glass windows that lined the interior wall. In the first conference room, Jackson and Bear were sitting at the end of a long oak table.

Cotton opened the door and held it for Moore, who walked in first and took a seat across from Jackson. Cotton followed him in, letting the door close behind him, and leaned against one of the interior windows.

"Mr. Clay," Moore said. "To what do I owe the honor?"

"You're kicking McKenna free," Jackson answered.

Moore grinned. Reaching into the breast pocket of his shirt, pulled out a small cartridge, and fetched a toothpick to put in his mouth. "Actually, it was the Commonwealth's Attorney that failed to bring charges."

"Cute. What made you release him?"

"I can't comment on an ongoing investigation."

"By the looks of it, not much is going on anymore."

"The investigation into the death of Nathalie McKenna, your ex, is still very much ongoing."

"But clearly McKenna isn't a suspect anymore. So, level with me. Tell me why."

Moore shook his head. "That's not the way it works, Clay."

"Is that because I'm still a suspect?"

Moore didn't answer. He looked on at Jackson, rolling the toothpick in his mouth with his tongue. Jackson could tell the man was getting annoyed.

"Say, I gotta hit the head," Bear said. "You guys got a john around here?"

Cotton looked at Moore, who looked at Bear. Bear looked back and forth at both of them.

"Out the door, to the right," Moore said. "Special Agent Cotton can show you."

"I don' need a bathroom buddy," Bear said. "Just point me in the right direction."

Cotton opened the conference room door, leaned out, and pointed across the office. Bear nodded and headed in that direction.

"You didn't answer my question," Jackson said. "Am I still a suspect?"

"We are pursuing several leads," Moore said.

"Do you remember back at the diner, when you asked me to quit playing games? It's my turn. Cut the crap, Moore."

"I don't know if you've checked your chest recently, but there's no badge there, Clay. I owe you zero explanations."

"And I could've lawyered up instead of talking to you."

Moore leaned back in his chair and sighed. He and Jackson stared at each other. Jackson's eyes told Moore he wasn't going to concede on this.

Bear re-entered the conference room and joined Cotton in observing Moore and Jackson's standoff.

"Can we have the room for a minute, gentlemen?" Moore asked without shifting his gaze.

"Book," Cotton said, "are you—"

"Please. Thank you."

Cotton and Bear backed out of the room and shut the door behind them. Cotton tried observing through one of the floor-to-ceiling glass panes, but Bear stepped in front of him and started to give the man his unrequested thoughts on the upcoming NASCAR season.

Alone in the conference room with Jackson, Moore sighed heavily. "I don't have to do a damn thing for you, Clay. If I give you this, I want you off my back."

"Depends on what 'this' is," Jackson said.

"Fine. Brad McKenna has an alibi. A *hard* alibi."

"Bull."

"He does. Backed with a timestamped video. It's airtight, Clay."

"You booked him and everything, though. So what changed?"

"Him. His story. He wasn't as forthcoming before. But, facing murder charges, he played ball."

"Or just gave you a new story you haven't poked holes in yet."

"Clay, I'm telling you. It's solid. You think I like egg on my face? I wish it wasn't true. But it is."

Jackson shifted uncomfortably in his seat. "What's the alibi?"

"Not going to give you that. I've given you enough to explain why things are the way they are now."

"You're obviously off McKenna. Give me what you've got, let me worry about it."

"I said that's not going to happen."

Jackson tapped his fingers anxiously on the table. Moore stared him down. Now it was him with the eyes that said he wasn't going to acquiesce. Jackson stood up abruptly from the table.

"Fine," he said. "If that's it, then we'll be going."

Jackson walked the length of the conference table to the door and let himself out. He walked past Bear and Cotton without stopping and continued toward the double doors leading out of the BCI offices. Bear trotted after Jackson, leaving Cotton in mid-sentence.

Moore came out of the conference room and rejoined Cotton, watching Bear and Jackson leave.

"Clay, I mean it." Moore said loudly after them. "I want you to lay off now. I won't hesitate to put you in cuffs again. You and your friend both."

Bear turned back to Moore as he opened the door out of the office for Jackson. "Don' threaten us with a good time."

Moore shook his head, and the two were gone.

Outside, Jackson and Bear walked quickly toward the Suburban.

"What did Moore say to you?" Bear asked.

"McKenna has an alibi," Jackson said. "He wouldn't go into details."

"I wonder if it has to do with this."

Bear opened his phone and showed a picture to Jackson. It was an overhead view of a file on a desk. Jackson recognized the desk as the kind back in the offices they'd just left. The file looked to be a printout from the DMV, complete with a name, address, and headshot of a pretty, young woman.

"I snapped this off of Moore's desk when they thought I was takin' a leak," Bear said. "Her name's Mandy Bryant."

"Let's go see if Mandy is the reason McKenna is walking free," Jackson said.

FORTY-THREE

AN HOUR after Jackson and Bear left, the BCI offices at Division Two in Culpeper were full and bustling. Moore had requisitioned the same conference room he and Jackson had used and laid out pertinent case information on a large whiteboard. He and Cotton were effectively starting back at square one.

"Okay, Brad McKenna has a solid alibi, fine," Moore said to Cotton. "What *doesn't* that change in terms of what we know?"

"We've still got the car," Cotton said. "The Ford Edge with front-end damage at the McKenna field office on New York Avenue. Paint scrapings positively tie it to the collision with Nathalie McKenna's Tesla and, thus, her murder."

"We're positive there was no other traffic accident involving her Tesla and the Edge at another time?"

"Seems highly unlikely."

"Well, double-check. We've already been burned once on this case. I'm not interested in making a habit of it."

Cotton pulled out his phone. Moore stood staring at a photo of the damaged Ford Edge on the whiteboard. A thought struck him.

"The prints," he said.

"What was that?" Cotton asked.

"The prints. The Edge at the McKenna office was wiped clean. That seems a bit over the top for covering up an affair."

"It does. So, what are you thinking?"

"Hold on." Moore's gaze shifted to another photo of the garage at the McKenna office. It was from a wider angle, showing the whole fleet of vehicles parked there. "Brad McKenna admitted he used a company vehicle to go see Mandy Bryant. But we never confirmed he used *that* vehicle. The one tied to the collision."

"Do you think McKenna will tell us? He hasn't exactly been forthcoming. Hell, we had to arrest him just to get him to talk to us."

"Maybe we don't need him. We only worked over the one car. Let's get a team down there to go over *all* the cars."

"If McKenna's prints are all over a different vehicle, he was probably driving that one, and not the one in the collision."

"Exactly."

"But that would mean someone else accessed a vehicle in there. We have the records of who accessed the lock box to the keys. Only Brad McKenna's PIN was used."

"Maybe someone accessed it earlier and simply pocketed the keys. Or someone accessed the lockbox using McKenna's PIN."

"Like who?"

Moore turned and opened a cream-colored file folder on the conference table. He flipped through the papers until he found what he was looking for and slid a photo across the table for Cotton to look at. It was a still from the Ring camera outside Brad McKenna's penthouse condo, showing the back of the man who'd broken in while McKenna was at his wife's funeral.

"Perhaps someone who seems to already have McKenna's passcodes," Moore said.

Cotton nodded and headed for the conference room door. "I'll get a team down to that garage."

"Let's make this happen quick."

FORTY-FOUR

JACKSON COULDN'T FIND an address for Mandy Bryant as Bear drove toward DC, but he did find her Instagram account. On it, he noticed almost half the pictures were geotagged with the same place: a store called Ladylove, in Georgetown. Based on her profile picture, most of the photos didn't have Mandy herself in them, but in the few that did, Jackson noticed she was wearing professional-looking blazers or blouses. Work attire. He googled the address for Ladylove and plugged it into his Maps app.

The storefront looked like a townhouse nestled on a busy commercial part of Wisconsin Avenue, wedged between an eatery with a similar façade, and a bank. Its brick exterior had been painted white with black trim, and in its only window stood a partial manikin modeling a set of lacy underwear.

Inside, Bear and Jackson were greeted with warm, floral-smelling air and soft acoustic guitar music. A woman—not Mandy Bryant—approached them from behind the open desk that served as the store's counter and housed a single register.

"Good morning," she said in an Eastern European accent. "Can I help you gentlemen find something today? Perhaps for one of your missuses?"

"You got anythin' in my size?" Bear asked.

Jackson stepped in front of his friend. "Actually, we're looking for someone. Mandy Bryant."

"Mm, I see," the woman said. Her lips pushed upwards into a bit of a scowl and she now stared at Jackson and Bear for a moment as if judging them, disappointed they were not rewarding her effort with an easy sale. Turning, she shouted into the depths of the narrow store. "Mahn-dee, you have...guests."

The woman returned to her post behind the register as Mandy Bryant came around the corner. Tall and pretty, Jackson couldn't help but notice her hair was almost the same shade as Nathalie's. She was pencil-thin but wore the black skirt and cream-colored sweater she had on well. When the other woman pointed Mandy toward Jackson and Bear, she looked at them with confusion.

"I'm sorry," she said, "do we know each other?"

"No, I don't think so," Jackson said. "My name is Jackson Clay. I was wondering if we could talk for a moment."

Mandy looked back at the other woman, who was watching them scornfully. She turned back to Jackson. "Um, what's this about?"

"Brad McKenna."

Mandy immediately looked back again at her coworker. When the woman seemed uninterested, Mandy motioned for Jackson to follow her deeper into the store.

"I'll give you two some room." Bear said, peeling away from them.

Mandy led Jackson to a back area where a couple of dividers and drapes made up some changing rooms. Mandy stopped next to a rack of swimwear Jackson thought could not possibly be practical for swimming.

"Are you with the police?" Mandy asked. "The ones that came to my place yesterday?"

"No, I'm not a police officer," Jackson said.

"Then who are you?"

"My name is Jackson Clay. I used to be married to Nathalie, Brad McKenna's wife, who was recently killed."

Mandy looked down with a sorrowful expression, her voice sounding riddled with guilt. "So, you came to find me. The other woman." She brushed a tear from the corner of her eye. "I'm sorry. It's just been ... a lot."

"I understand, but the police released Brad McKenna yesterday. I need to know why. My understanding is it might have something to do with you.."

Mandy sighed. "I guess you could say that. At least, that's how I took it."

"What do you mean?"

"They asked me specifically about mine and Brad's whereabouts last Thursday morning. Then just a few hours later, it came out the charges were dropped against him."

Bear, making his way through the store, walked by a particularly bosomy manikin modeling a fancy bra. "My god, look at the honkers on that thing..."

Mandy and Jackson glanced over at him before looking back at each other.

"Was Brad with you last Thursday?" Jackson asked.

"Yes," Mandy said.

"What time?"

"From about six in the morning to just after eight."

"And that was it? They didn't ask for any proof or if anyone could corroborate that?"

Mandy looked down at the floor and folded her arms. She peered back to make sure her coworker wasn't listening. "Brad apparently made a video. Of us. They showed it to me, and, um, asked me to verify it was me."

"A video?"

"Yes, of us. You know, *together*."

"Oh. I see."

"Yeah. Anyways, that seemed to be good enough for them. Like I said, a few hours later I saw on the news he was released. Nothing like stepping out on your wife to prove you didn't kill her, I guess."

"That's tough, yeah. I'm sorry. But you must've known he was married. He didn't exactly live a private life."

Mandy nodded. "I did. Not at first, I swear. But I learned not long after we started seeing each other. Not from him, though. He never said anything about her. Never said anything, and I never brought it up. I guess we pretended she didn't exist."

Jackson wasn't sure what to say, so he didn't say anything.

Bear rifled through a rack of babydolls, flipping over a price tag on one. "Good lord," he said. "Where the hell is the rest of it?"

Jackson contemplated asking Bear to step outside until he was done, but his phone buzzed in his pocket with an incoming call. He was about to check it when Mandy spoke again.

"I saw her, though," she said. "Once."

"What do you mean?" Jackson asked.

Mandy patted down the front of her outfit as if she were suddenly uncomfortable in it. "After I knew he was married, curiosity got the better of me one day. I wanted to know who she was. Maybe if she seemed awful ... I don't know. I guess I was looking for a reason to justify Brad and I's relationship. So, I watched her."

"Watched her where?"

"I Googled her and saw she worked at this law office downtown. I waited around five in the evening for her to leave one day. She came out and met a friend outside. A guy."

"How did you know they were friends?"

"I meant they didn't seem like something more. I wanted them to be, I guess to tell myself it was okay what I was doing. But they were friends. He wasn't her type. At least, not if Brad is her type."

"What type was he?"

"I don't know, dorky-looking? Short and boxy and had these geeky glasses. He looked cross-eyed, sort of."

Jackson thought Mandy was describing Adrien Alva almost perfectly. And it made sense that Nathalie might meet him after work, seeing how close they apparently were.

"Anyways," Mandy continued, "they went to this little café, so I followed them. It sounds creepy now, but I even got a table next to them."

"I see."

"Look, I don't know, alright? I guess I wanted to see how the other side lived. What it was like to *actually* be Mrs. McKenna. Not just Mandy."

"And what was it like?"

"Strange. They didn't really talk about Brad much at all. Some other big thing. I gathered something had happened at her work. She was debating whether to go see someone about it."

"What do you mean?"

"I'm not entirely sure, I just heard bits and pieces across the way. I guess she had learned some troubling news and was deciding whether or not to tell someone else about it."

An uneasy feeling shot through Jackson's chest as he felt goosebumps form on his arms. "When did you say this was?"

"A week or two ago."

"As in the week before last? The week before she was killed?"

"I guess. I didn't have anything to do with her murder, if that's what you're—"

"No, not at all. But this man, did you catch his name?"

"Not that I remember, no."

"Describe him again. You said he was short? Wore geeky glasses?"

"Yeah. He had short black hair, balding. He wasn't big but wasn't like super skinny, either."

Jackson tried to remember if he had a photo of Adrien he could show her. He couldn't recall one. "And you're certain you heard them talking about whether or not to go see someone?"

"Pretty certain, yeah."

"Did they say who?"

"No, just someone in Virginia, I think. Sounded like they lived in the middle of nowhere. They were talking about GPS coordinates and stuff."

"They said 'GPS coordinates'?"

"Yeah. I thought that was weird."

Jackson couldn't form words. His senses numbed. The in-store music and Bear's commentary dulled and became muted. Nathalie had talked to someone who sounded a lot like Adrien almost certainly about where Jackson lived.

"Yeah, weird," Jackson finally managed to say. "Well, thank you for talking to me."

Mandy told him he was welcome, but Jackson didn't hear it. He was deep in his mind. He turned and left the store, paying little mind to Bear or the other salesperson. Bear, seeing him leave, followed him out.

Out on the sidewalk, Jackson just stood in place, thinking. Bear grasped Jackson's shoulder and brought him back to the present.

"What's up, brother?" he asked.

"Mandy. The girl in there," Jackson said, gesturing to the store. "She followed Nat one day. Nat and another guy talked about going to meet someone using GPS coordinates. She described Adrien almost to a tee."

Bear's brow furrowed. "That's weird. Din' that private eye guy say Adrien went only the first time to his office?"

"That's what I thought, too."

"Well, I guess she coulda told him about the GPS stuff after meetin' with the guy."

"Maybe, but there's something weird about all this."

"What are you thinkin'?"

Jackson didn't have an exact answer to that question. Remembering the phone call he missed, he pulled his phone out. Harry Spencer had called him. He pressed the button to call him back.

"Spencer Investigations."

"Spencer, it's Jackson Clay returning your call."

"Oh. Well, Mr. Clay. I was calling to return *yours* from yesterday. I'm sorry I didn't get back to you. Pretty busy here. What can I do for you?"

"I was trying to remember something. Did you say Adrien Alva only came with Nathalie to your office once? The first time?"

"That's correct, yes."

"Do you know why that was?"

"As I told you when we met, I gathered he was there for emotional support or something. But he also sounded like he didn't entirely approve of the idea, either. Nathalie made it clear to me she was prepared to go it alone."

"Do you know if she talked to him about getting my info after you passed it along to her?"

"I don't, no. But as I said, I got the idea she was going solo to find you."

"Okay. Alright, thanks."

"Let me know if I can help with anything else."

Jackson ended the call and slid his phone back into his pocket.

"What's up?" Bear asked.

"Spencer can't recall Nat telling Adrien about finding me, either," Jackson said.

Bear shook his head. "So, what do ya want to do? Are we still lookin' at McKenna, or diggin' into Adrien?"

Jackson looked across the street, then back over the top of the Ladylove storefront. To the south was the heart of Georgetown. To the north was the rest of DC: Adams Morgan, Columbia Heights, and beyond that, Fort Totten and Adrien Alva.

"I don't know," Jackson said.

FORTY-FIVE

LATE IN THE WORKDAY, Moore found himself still stuck at the office trying to delegate matters to colleagues. He knew it was the fastest way to get everything done, but he was restless. He wanted to be out in the field, hunting leads.

Cotton came by and knocked on his open office door before stepping in. "Techs ran over all the fleet vehicles at the McKenna offices. Your hunch was right: Brad McKenna's prints were all over the driver space of a different vehicle."

"Not the one we linked to Nathalie McKenna's collision," Moore said.

"Exactly. So, we questioned that manager again, specifically about the vehicle with front-end damage. She said she'd noticed it covered up when she got into the office that day, but didn't think anything of it at the time. She said no one used it or uncovered it while she was there."

"And we're sure the access log to the lock box shows only Brad McKenna's PIN was used."

"Yeah, though we did a deeper dive on that. The logged data shows the lock box being accessed twice between five and six that morning. Once at 5:19 and again at 5:26. Both times it was McKenna's PIN code."

"So, McKenna could've used his code, gotten keys to the car he took, and then someone else could've used his code a second time and taken the keys to our damaged Ford, using it to run Nathalie McKenna off the road."

"That's exactly what I was thinking."

"Still, it's a hell of a coincidence that they used Brad McKenna's PIN shortly after he did. At a time when, apparently, no one knew he was there."

"You think maybe McKenna had help? Hired someone to kill his wife and showed them where to get a clean vehicle?"

"Possibly, but he'd have to know that'd come back on him."

"Or, what if someone knew about McKenna's secret morning visits and was trying to use it against him? Implicate him in his own wife's murder."

"That's what I'm thinking. And something's been nagging at me. Where are those stills I showed you? The one with the B & E suspect at McKenna's condo?"

Cotton held up a finger and stepped out. He returned a moment later holding an 8x10 photo. It was a grainy image of the man breaking into the McKenna condo. He gave it to Moore.

Moore glanced at the picture, then held it back up to Cotton. "Tell me that doesn't look like Jackson Clay."

"I don't know," Cotton said. "Tall, fit, Caucasian. He fits the general type, but the guy's back is to the camera. It could be him, but it could also be someone else."

"But let's say for a moment it is Clay—he clearly has the codes somehow to get up to the penthouse. It's not much of a reach from there to think he's got McKenna's PIN to the lockbox at work, too."

"Maybe, but how do you prove it?"

"We work the theory. We already know Clay isn't happy McKenna was released. Maybe it's because he was counting on

Nathalie's murder being pinned on the guy. Now he's got to adjust. So we watch Clay and see what he does."

"The guy lives in the boonies, is ex-army, and at least *a little* paranoid. He'll spot surveillance a mile away."

Moore sat back in his chair and thought about it for a moment. He looked at the whiteboard he'd dragged out of the conference room and moved over to his desk. He'd used magnets to pin up a map of the DC metropolitan area, including Northern Virginia. Both Jackson Clay's property and the location of Nathalie McKenna's murder were marked on it. An idea came to him.

"Maybe," he said, popping out of his chair, grabbing a marker, and going around his desk to the map, "but what if we get clever about it? He'll either be driving his vehicle or his friends' vehicle. That red Suburban. Both are uncommon and easy to ID. If he's going to do anything, he'll go into D.C., almost certainly using I-66." Moore traced the length of the interstate highway with his finger as Cotton followed along. "The latest he'd get on 66 is here, at Haymarket. Let's talk to patrol division, see if we can't place a trooper just east of there on the interstate."

"If Jackson or his friend drive by, they'll just think it's a trooper running radar," Cotton said.

"Exactly. The trooper makes either Clay's black D100 or Beauchamp's red Suburban and alerts surveillance. Then we pick it up from there."

Cotton grinned. "I like it."

"Me too," Moore said. "Call Patrol Division. Let's get it set up."

FORTY-SIX

JACKSON SPENT most of the drive back to his cabin deciding what he was going to do next: keep looking into McKenna or shift his focus to Adrien. His gut still told him there was something wrong about McKenna, but he couldn't think of a benign reason why Adrien would lie about knowing where he lived.

As they pulled into the dirt drive, small pellets of sleet began to plink off the Suburban's windshield. The storm that had clouded the skies overhead was now opening up.

"We better get Nat's stuff out the back of your truck and inside before it all gets ruined," Bear said.

Jackson nodded, and the two climbed out of the Suburban and began grabbing boxes from the bed of Jackson's pickup.

"Careful, don't slip on the stairs," Jackson cautioned.

"What, are ya worried I'm goin' to sue?" Bear asked. "Here, you stand on the porch. I'll run boxes over to you."

Jackson did as Bear suggested. One by one, Bear carried box after box over to Jackson at a pace somewhere between a walk and a trot. Within a few minutes, Bear had the last box and was closing the back of the truck. He hurried over to Jackson, and the two of them slid it onto the porch. Finished, they hopped up the stairs, Jackson slumping into one of his deck chairs.

"Just let me take a beer break and we'll get them inside," Bear said.

"You don't have a beer."

"That's a problem, ain't it?"

Bear stared at his friend until Jackson realized what he was getting at. Jackson grinned, shook his head, and stood up.

"High Life?" Jackson asked.

"Is there any other right answer?"

Jackson laughed and ducked inside. When he came back out, he twisted the tops off of two beers and handed one to Bear.

"Thank ya," Bear said.

"No problem."

Bear cocked his head back and let the malty beverage pour down his gullet. Jackson took a much more moderate sip of his as he rifled through the things in the box directly at his feet. It was mostly office supplies and photos. Jackson recognized some of the faces, but most were strangers. People Nat had met in her new life, after him.

He shifted a couple picture frames over to reveal a small wooden box underneath, then pulled it out and opened it. Jackson's heart sunk into his stomach. Inside was a necklace: a cluster of round, marquis, and pear-shaped crystals arranged in an arc on a rose-gold chain. Jackson placed his beer on the porch beside his chair and picked up the necklace.

"Whoa, that's some necklace," Bear said. "You think McKenna gave it to her?"

"No," Jackson said. "I did. On our wedding day."

He ran his thumb over the crystals, feeling the sharpness of their shine. He spread his other fingers out and let the rose gold chain fall through them. He knew it was the perfect necklace for her the second he saw it in that small jewelry boutique in Richmond's Carytown. The rose gold complimented Nat's auburn hair perfectly.

Bear caught the sadness in his friend's eyes. "It's beautiful, brother," he said quietly. "She clearly loved it."

Jackson nodded. But inside, he was begging his mind to shift to something else. Anything else. Anything had to be less painful than *this*. He forced himself to focus once more on Brad McKenna and Adrien Alva. They didn't have the time or resources to look at both at the same time.

A thought occurred to him , and he pulled out his phone, punched in a number.

"Jackson," Special Agent Bailey answered on the other end of the line. "You doing alright? I saw the news about McKenna."

"Yeah, we'll see about him."

Bailey paused. That wasn't what she was expecting to hear from Jackson. "Book's a good investigator, Clay. If he let Brad McKenna walk, he had good reason."

"Everyone's wrong sometimes, but that's not why I'm calling. I wonder if you could do me a favor. I know it's the weekend."

"What's up?"

"Adrien Alva. He is—*was*—a friend of Nat. I need as much as you can find on him. He lives in an apartment in Fort Totten in DC."

"I'm guessing you're not going to tell me what this is all about."

"Nat, Bailey. This is all about Nat."

"Fine, I'll kick the tires on the guy."

Jackson hung up. He looked down at his hands. Phone in one hand, Nat's necklace in the other.

"We movin' onto Adrien?" Bear asked.

"Bailey is," Jackson said. "We stick on McKenna."

Bear nodded before polishing off the rest of his beer. He slammed the empty bottle down on the armrest of his chair in victory and propelled himself out of it. "I'll start gettin' these boxes inside."

"Thanks."

He continued to play with the necklace in his hand. The crystal glinted off of the light over his front door.

JACKSON HELD *Nat's hand just outside the pristinely white tent. They watched as, two by two, some of their closest friends danced into their wedding reception ahead of them. Jackson felt the ring on Nat's finger, the one he'd placed there just a half hour or so ago.*

Nat briefly let go of Jackson's hand and wiped hers on his pants.

"Your hand is so sweaty," she said with a chuckle.

"My bad," Jackson said.

June was always warm in Richmond, but their wedding day ended up being the hottest day of the year so far. With temperatures and humidity both in the nineties, Jackson felt himself sweating through his rented tuxedo as he walked down the row of white folding chairs laid out on the lawn. It didn't matter. Nothing was going to dampen the joy of the day.

He and Nat married on a sloping lawn in historic Maymont Park, a hundred-acre Victorian estate that was built for a Richmond philanthropist and deeded to the city after his wife's death. Now, Jackson and Nat were there, waiting to be welcomed into their reception.

When it was their turn, two attendants held the doors to the tent shut. Jackson looked at Nat. She was gorgeous in her flowing white dress. The crystals around her neck caught the sun overhead and shined like stars.

"Ready?" Jackson asked.

"Ready," Nat said, beaming.

A moment later, the DJ announced: "And now! For the first time anywhere, please welcome Mr. and Mrs. Jackson Clay!"

The attendants opened the doors. Inside, all fifty of Nat and Jackson's guests were standing and applauding. Jackson and Nat walked in, waving to everyone. An old Army buddy stepped forward from the crowd and slapped Jackson on the shoulder. Jackson turned back and pointed at his friend, laughing and shaking his head.

"Now, if you'd make room on the dance floor, please," the DJ continued, "Nathalie and Jackson will share their first dance as husband and wife."

The crowd parted and Jackson led Nat to the dance floor. He slipped his arms around the small of her back, and she reached up and put her arms around his neck. Behind them, John Michael Montgomery began crooning from the speakers. Together, Jackson and Nat swayed slowly to the rhythm of the guitar.

"Well, we did it," Nat said quietly to him.

"We sure did."

Jackson brought her in and held her even closer as Montgomery's baritone voice and Kentucky drawl filled the reception tent. As they turned, Jackson felt the toe of his right foot catch one of Nat's heels.

"Sorry," he said.

Nat laughed. "It's okay. It's what I signed up for, right? To have and to hold you, for better or for worse."

"For richer or poorer."

"In sickness and in health."

"To love and to cherish."

"'Til death do us part."

Jackson shook his head. "I don't know about that last part."

Nat arched her neck back and looked at Jackson quizzically. "Oh?"

"Oh. I'm yours forever, Nat. Death isn't going to stop that."

She looked deep into his eyes and smiled. "I love you, Jackson Clay."

"I love you, too."

Jackson looked up at the room, at everyone there to celebrate them. To celebrate their love. Some people found the idea silly. He didn't. For as much as he loved Nat, he knew that sort of thing was worth celebrating. Now, he took in everything around them. The world centered on them, if only for this moment.

"Whether you're gone, or I'm gone, or we're both gone," Jackson said, "that won't matter. I'm yours."

"No matter what?" Nat asked.

He looked back down at her, meeting her eyes. "No matter what."

PART FIVE
THE HORNET'S NEST

"There aren't demons flying around with horns, people are demons."
— CHUCK SCHULDINER

FORTY-SEVEN

OVERNIGHT, the weather had warmed just enough to turn the pelting sleet into a dreary, cold rain. At the Division Seven offices in Fairfax, Virginia, Bailey trotted across the parking lot, seeking cover and cursing the colorless weather. She didn't have any open cases at the moment, so the only reason she was coming into work on a Sunday was to run Adrien Alva for Jackson. Stepping into the lobby, she pulled her hood back and shook off the rain like a Labrador. A trooper walking by gave her the stinkeye, and she held up a hand in apology.

Bailey expected to find the place virtually deserted as she walked through the double doors leading to the BCI offices, but a good number of people were there, working. She scanned the room and noticed one of the adjacent conference rooms was full. Reeves, standing outside the conference room, was watching through the glass door when he turned and noticed Bailey. Bailey turned away to roll her eyes as Reeves walked over to her.

"You look like crap," Reeves said. "Someone burn the midnight oil with a handsome gentleman last night?"

"A lady doesn't kiss and tell," Bailey said. "Where's Cap?"

Reeves pointed across the offices to where he'd just walked from. "First conference room."

Bailey looked over. Inside the crowded conference room were her captain, two other Special Agents from their office, and Booker Moore and David Cotton. The room had enough papers, equipment, and whiteboards in it to tell Bailey they were neck-deep in something.

"What are Book and Cotton doing here from Division Two?" she asked.

"Cap said they'd be working out of here for the next day or so. They have some surveillance set up or something on I-66. I guess we're a convenient base of operations."

Bailey nodded, but she had an uneasy feeling. There would only be a handful of reasons they'd want to watch the interstate—and she knew one of them. Bailey grabbed a handful of papers off her desk to look busy and walked over to the conference room.

She knocked twice on the door before letting herself in. Everyone in the room turned and looked up at her. As soon as Moore realized it was Bailey, he cautiously closed the laptop in front of him. Bailey took notice of that.

"Hey, Cap," she said. "Weather's nasty out there today."

"Bailey, what are you doing here?" Captain Trask said.

Bailey ignored the question as she turned and waved at the table. "Morning, guys. Good to see you, Book. This the McKenna case, still?"

Captain Trask stepped in between Bailey and the rest of the agents. "Moore and Cotton will be working out of here for the next few days. If they need you, they'll let you know."

Bailey didn't like being brushed off so casually, but she forced herself to smile and nod anyway. "No problem. Good luck, guys."

The four men around the table returned to their work. As Bailey turned to leave, she glanced down at the papers directly in front of Cotton. On top was a vehicle registration for a black 1979 Dodge D100. She read the name below the vehicle information:

CLAY, JACKSON

The hairs on the back of Bailey's neck stood up, but she pretended not to notice. Instead, she coolly walked back to her desk and slid into her computer chair. There, she pulled out her phone and tried to call Jackson. The call went straight to voicemail.

"Fuck."

She bet almost anything Jackson Clay didn't kill his ex-wife. Helping Clay also helped Book and Cotton—the faster they were off of Clay, the better for everyone. But what could she do?

Jackson had asked her to see what she could find on Adrien Alva. She had no idea why but had to assume it was related to Nathalie's murder. If that would help Jackson, and in turn help Moore and Cotton, then that's what she'd do.

Bailey booted up her computer and got to work.

FORTY-EIGHT

JACKSON AND BEAR headed out just after nine the next morning. Driving down the lonely county highway, the wipers on Bear's Suburban whined each time they struggled to push water off the windshield.

"Hate this fuckin' rain," Bear grumbled.

"Well, it's only supposed to get worse throughout the day," Jackson said.

Bear shook his head.

Within twenty minutes they'd made it to the tiny village of The Plains, passing Frankie's Diner, and just a couple minutes later were approaching the junction of Interstate 66. Jackson groaned as he looked ahead: The eastbound lanes were a parking lot. Cars and trucks were jammed together, bumper to bumper. A couple of drivers were even out of their cars, braving the weather in an attempt to see what was causing the stoppage.

"Shit, must be an accident," Bear said.

Jackson pulled out his phone, opened up his traffic app, and checked it. "Yeah, about a mile east. Must be a bad one if it's this backed up."

"That's alright. Hold on."

Bear jerked the wheel, and the Suburban made a sharp U-turn in the middle of the road, cutting off a hatchback coming the other way. Bear doubled back to The Plains, then took a small county highway east.

"We can pick up 66 in Haymarket, after the accident," he said.

Jackson nodded, but kept his eyes on the road. Bear was suddenly in a hurry, racing some anonymous rival—the traffic on the interstate, Jackson supposed—and took the winding turns of the two-lane thoroughfare without slowing down. Jackson felt his phone buzz in his pocket, but opted not to answer it for fear he was about to meet his maker.

The highway dipped underneath the clogged interstate before coming around parallel to it on the other side. Jackson looked over and saw the accident come into view. A large semi had jackknifed across 66, pinning a small Kia underneath its trailer. Traffic was haphazardly getting by in a single-file line on the right shoulder.

"Nasty accident," Bear said.

"Yeah, let's not end up like them."

Bear ignored Jackson's critique of his driving. A few minutes later the road dumped them back into civilization and the small town of Haymarket. Bear flew by a gas station and hopped over to the on-ramp for I-66. The wreck had done wonders for freeing up everything beyond it.

As he pressed down on the pedal, Bear chuckled, clearly amused with himself. The eight cylinders under the hood opened up and roared to life. "We'll be in DC in no time."

"Careful—watch the cop," Jackson said.

He nodded over at a State Police cruiser parked perpendicularly on the median between the two sides of the interstate.

"I see him," Bear said, waving at the patrol car as they drove past.

Jackson leaned over and watched the road behind them in the side view mirror. Just as the cruiser came into view, he saw it pull out into traffic and begin following them.

"You weren't speeding, were you?" Jackson asked.

"No way. Barely had the chance to."

Jackson looked in the side view mirror again. He'd driven Virginia's interstates thousands of times in his life; it was rare a State Trooper left where they were posted up without pulling someone over or speeding off to a call. Still, this one seemed to hang back, driving casually down the highway with them. Something was strange about it all. He kept an eye on the cruiser as they drove on.

MOORE CHECKED HIS WATCH; it was a quarter to ten. He extended his arms up in the air and stretched. They'd been at the Division Seven BCI offices for almost three hours now with no action. To him, this all felt like fishing, and Moore hated fishing.

Cotton came around the conference table with his laptop and took the seat next to Moore. He positioned his laptop so Moore could see the screen.

"Check this out," Cotton said. "I've been looking for video on the outside of the McKenna garage on New York Avenue."

"We checked," Moore said, shaking his head. "They didn't have any cameras facing the street. No one around them did, either."

"Right, but I got to thinking about what's changed. We know now Brad McKenna went from the garage to Mandy Bryant's apartment. So, I started hunting down places with cameras in that direction. This is video from an Exxon station about a quarter mile west of the garage. It's pointed south at a couple of the pumps, but the westbound traffic on New York Avenue is in frame. Look."

Cotton pressed play. Beyond a portly Hispanic man filling his Camry, cars moved left to right on the dimly-lit New York Avenue in the pre-dawn hours.

Fifteen seconds in, Cotton paused the video and pointed. "There."

Frozen on the screen was a dark blue Ford Edge with the McKenna logo on it.

"Okay, that's great," Moore said. "You verified McKenna's alibi. But how does that help us?"

"The timestamp on the video is 5:39 a.m. Now, I'm going to skip forward four minutes. Watch."

Cotton cued the video forward and pressed play again. The footage, as Moore expected, was just like what he'd seen. The man gassing up was now a young Black woman, but cars continued to cruise down New York Avenue. And then Moore saw it. Cotton paused the clip. Moore felt his mouth droop open.

"*Another* blue Ford Edge with the McKenna logo," Cotton said. "*Also* headed west on New York."

"One of those is McKenna. The other is our killer."

"Exactly. And it gets better. The techs looked at the video and were able to get the plates off of both vehicles. We know which car is which. And get this: the first vehicle, the one that passes by at 5:39 is the same one that had Brad McKenna's prints all over the driver's side. The second one that goes by at 5:43 is the one we found under the tarp with the paint scrapings from Nathalie McKenna's Tesla."

Moore looked closely at the paused video. "There's no way to see the drivers, though. It's dark and the angle's all wrong."

"Yes, but this fits your theory. Brad McKenna accesses the lockbox in the garage, takes one car, and goes to see Mandy Bryant. Someone else follows right behind him, uses his code, and takes a second vehicle out, also heading west."

"Toward Georgetown."

"And further out, the spot where Nathalie McKenna is killed."

"And just beyond that is Jackson Clay's cabin."

Moore stood up, reinvigorated by the lead. He gave Cotton a friendly slap on the shoulder as he stepped around him and made his way to the conference room door, coffee mug in hand. "That's good stuff. Let's stay on it. I'm going to get a refill."

He stepped out, went over to the small kitchenette, and poured himself another cup. Moore would bet a good chunk of his pension that Jackson Clay broke into Brad McKenna's penthouse using McKenna's code. Now, if only he could prove Clay also used McKenna's PIN at the garage with the company vehicles.

Moore was reaching for the sugar when Cotton burst out of the conference room and jogged toward him. He had both of their jackets in his hands.

"State trooper just spotted an older model Suburban heading east on 66. Fire truck red. Two white, male occupants. The trooper is tailing them."

Moore left his coffee at the kitchenette and headed for the double doors out of the BCI offices. "Let's roll."

JACKSON CONTINUED to keep a watchful eye on the police cruiser behind them. Through open roads and what little congested traffic they encountered, the car kept its distance. He was about to say something to Bear when, as they passed the exit for the Fairfax County Parkway, the trooper slowed and pulled onto another paved strip across the highway median. Jackson leaned back, starting to think he'd been paranoid when he noticed two unmarked cars come up the on-ramp from the parkway at the same time and merge onto the interstate behind them.

The cars were black and dark blue—Jackson thought one was probably a Ford Explorer and the other a Ford Taurus—but their small silver dog-dish-style hubcaps gave them away as police vehicles. The Explorer slipped in two cars behind Bear's Suburban while the Taurus hung back further.

Bear noticed Jackson studying his side-view mirror, his brow furrowed. "What's up, brother?"

"I think we might have a tail."

Bear looked up into his rearview mirror. "I don' know. That trooper is gone."

"Yeah, but as soon as he stopped, two more got on the highway. One is a couple cars back. Black SUV. And there's a dark blue sedan behind it."

Bear checked his rearview again. "Ya sure?"

Jackson looked back over his shoulder and noticed a helicopter was flying low, also following the highway. "I don't know, yet. Keep driving."

COTTON AND MOORE caught the Fairfax County Parkway just past the Division Seven offices. Less than a minute later, they were merging onto the interstate. Behind them, in an unmarked patrol car, was another trooper. The plan was to keep a revolving tail on the red Suburban to avoid detection.

Cotton looked up at the Virginia State Police helicopter overhead, a Eurocopter EC45 sent from Chesterfield, and radioed it. "Five-oh-five, Forty-twenty-two. Do you have a visual on the vehicle?"

"Copy, forty-twenty-two," the helicopter radioed back. "Red Chevy Suburban, traveling eastbound in the number one lane. They're about a quarter mile ahead of you."

"I see them," Moore said, both hands gripping the wheel. "Tell Lewis to hang back."

Cotton radioed Trooper Lewis in the patrol car behind them. "Five-twenty-three, forty-twenty-two. We're up first. Target vehicle is in the number one lane a quarter mile ahead of us. Hang back and we'll have you rotate in."

"Forty-twenty-two, five-twenty-three. Copy all," Trooper Lewis responded.

Moore shot past a slow-driving Subaru and eased into the left lane two cars behind Jackson and Bear in the red Suburban. They were close enough that he could see the silhouettes of their heads through their rear windshield.

"You think they're going after McKenna again?" Cotton asked.

"Wherever they're headed, we'll be watching," Moore said.

JACKSON AND BEAR weaved in and out of increasingly heavy traffic on the interstate as they approached the nation's capital. When they passed through the city of Falls Church, Jackson watched the Ford Explorer disappear from his view in the mirror. Moments later, the Taurus came up and filed in a few cars behind them. As they drove on through Ballston and Arlington, the Taurus allowed traffic to overtake it and the Explorer came back to take its place. All the while, the helicopter stayed in view, hovering off to their right.

"It's a revolving tail," Jackson said. "A black Explorer and a dark blue Taurus. Every time one backs off, the other comes up."

"Who do ya think it is?" Bear asked.

"State police would be my guess. Moore."

Bear shook his head, annoyed. "What do ya want to do?"

"Stay on 66, don't take the Key Bridge into Georgetown."

Bear did as he was told. The interstate snaked southeast through Arlington before crossing the Potomac River into D.C. The Taurus and the helicopter left them, but the Explorer stayed in view, following them across the bridge.

As they entered the nation's capital, the highway split four ways, like a fork that had met the business end of a firecracker.

"Take the exit for Rock Creek Park, and then K Street," Jackson said. "Circle back to Georgetown."

Bear nodded, and he crisscrossed lanes, making one merge after another. The Explorer stayed with them. On K Street, they turned back west where the Whitehurst Freeway ran overhead. Jackson looked up and down the street, formulating a plan in his head. To his left, he saw Washington Harbour, a trendy shopping district on the banks of the Potomac. Lots of foot traffic. An idea came to Jackson.

"Turn in there," he said, "where it says Washington Harbour. By those taxis and Ubers."

Bear turned. The Explorer followed. Jackson looked for their next move. A small Prius backed out in front of them so quickly Bear had to hit his brakes hard to avoid smashing into the side of it.

"Sonofabitch!" he growled. "What kind of yuppie asshat—"

"No, good. Good. Pull in. Take that parking spot."

Bear pulled the large SUV into the cramped space. The Explorer moved into the traffic circle in front of the shopping plaza where it could see them.

Bear glanced at Jackson. "Now what?"

Jackson opened his door and hopped out. "You stay here with the truck."

"What are you goin' to do?"

"Go for a little walk."

Bear sighed, letting his hands drop from the steering wheel and onto his belly, but Jackson was already gone. The crowd at Washington Harbour was a mosaic of deployed umbrellas in the rain. Jackson filed in amongst them and walked down the main open-air corridor that bisected the shopping center. At a wishing fountain, he stopped, pretending to tie his shoe, and looked back at the Explorer. Special Agent Cotton climbed out of the passenger seat and wandered into the fray, scanning the crowd. Jackson shook his head. He knew it would be them.

As Cotton unwittingly walked toward him, Jackson glanced around. A corridor to his left went underneath the buildings and out the other side. He had another idea. When Cotton looked the other way, Jackson ducked down the shadowy corridor and disappeared.

Coming out the other side, he looked back. Cotton hadn't followed. Jackson jogged around the corner of the building and came back to the small parking lot where Bear was parked. In between was the traffic circle, and the Explorer facing away from him. He slowed to a walk, blending in among the other people moving around him, and slowly made his way to the Explorer.

MOORE AND COTTON took turns with Trooper Lewis, slingshotting forward and falling back as they followed the Suburban toward DC. Jackson and Bear didn't make it easy, constantly shooting the gaps between vehicles, bobbing their way through the ever-increasing volume of commuters. At least the rainy weather wasn't so bad that the helicopter couldn't maintain a visual on the situation, Moore mused.

"There goes the exit for 29," Cotton said in the passenger seat. "Wouldn't that be the way to Brad McKenna's condo?"

"The fastest way, anyway," Moore said.

As the interstate turned south, zigzagging its way through Arlington, the helicopter radioed in: "Forty-twenty-two, five-oh-five. We're approaching restricted airspace for Reagan National. We're going to need to break off here."

"Copy that, five-oh-five. Thanks for the assistance," Cotton said. He put the radio down and looked at Moore. "There goes our eye in the sky."

"We knew it was probably going to happen," Moore said. "It changes nothing."

Two minutes later, the interstate cut east again, heading across the Potomac and into the capital. The tops of the Jefferson Memorial and Washington Monument peeked their heads over naked trees, forming the iconic D.C. skyline.

"Forty-twenty-two, five-twenty-three. They're headed out of Virginia," Trooper Lewis said over the radio. "What do you want to do?"

"Tell him we'll take it from here," Moore said to Cotton.

Cotton picked up the radio again. "Five-twenty-three, you can break off, too. We'll maintain surveillance. Thank you."

Moore got into the center lane and gunned it forward as Trooper Lewis' patrol car slowed and took the next exit off the highway. Moore got clear of everyone else and eased in behind a pair of work vans following Jackson and Bear's Suburban.

Street after street, turn after turn, Moore and Cotton stayed on them. Eventually, the red Suburban took a quick left and pulled into the parking area for Washington Harbour. Moore knew following them in was a risk, but he also knew he and Cotton didn't have any more backup at the moment. By the time they drove past and doubled back, they could lose their visual on Jackson and Bear altogether.

Moore followed them in.

Stopping in the traffic circle out in front of the Harbour, they watched the Suburban deftly maneuver into a tiny parking spot. A moment later, Jackson Clay exited the vehicle and headed into the shopping complex.

"Hell of a time to go shopping," Cotton said. "Maybe he's meeting someone at one of the restaurants. Or that Starbucks there."

Moore looked at Cotton. "Only one way to find out."

Cotton stared back at him until Moore's insinuation clicked. He grabbed his radio from the center console and opened his door. "I'll be on the radio."

Moore watched Cotton get out of their car and slowly approach the crowd out front, looking around. Jackson had walked headlong into the thicket of rain-drenched shoppers and disappeared from Moore's view. He hoped Cotton hadn't been too slow.

Staying in his driver seat, his gaze shifted from the herd of shoppers to the red Suburban in the parking lot. Larger and older than every other car in the small lot, the SUV stuck out. This was now a town of beamers and Cadillacs, not a bygone era of Americana.

The tailpipe of the Suburban rattled, spewing out noxious exhaust. Bear hadn't left to join Jackson.

"What are you two up to?" Moore asked himself.

The back door of his car suddenly opened behind him. Moore

instinctively reached for the pistol on his belt and turned to see Jackson Clay jump in and shut the door.

"Jesus, Clay," Moore said. "I almost shot you. What the hell are you doing?"

"You seem so intent on putting me in the back of a police car, I thought I'd save you the trouble."

Moore shook his head and groaned. "So this all is a game to you? You have us running around, following you, just so you can pull some stunt?"

"You made the decision to follow me. I just dealt with it. I agree with you, this all is a waste of time."

"What are we doing here, Clay?"

"You tell me. I already told you I had nothing to do with Nat's murder. Every minute you spend on me is time wasted."

"Do you know how many killers have told me they didn't do it?"

"You swept my place and found nothing. Whatever evidence you had that led you to Brad McKenna in the first place obviously also excluded me. What reason have I given you to stay on me?"

"Gee, I don't know. You want to talk about the break-in at McKenna's penthouse?"

Jackson gave Moore a cold look but didn't say anything. He looked out the back window of the car.

"You're going to tell me that wasn't you?" Moore asked.

"If you think you can prove it, then arrest me."

Moore shook his head again. The two of them saw Cotton reappear. A head taller than everyone else around him, he was still looking around for Jackson.

"I'm telling you, straight up," Jackson said. "I didn't kill my ex-wife. You can waste your time while I do your job for you, but if I'm dealing with you, I can't be out there doing that. So stop jamming me up."

"That road goes both ways, Clay. I already warned you once, but I'll tell you again: stop interfering with our investigation. Don't think I won't slap you with an obstruction charge."

Jackson opened the back door of the car and stepped out. "I guess it'd be the first real arrest you've made this week."

"Asshole," Moore growled under his breath.

Cotton came through the crowd and trotted back to Moore in their SUV. He opened the passenger door and climbed in. "I lost him."

Moore sighed as he put the SUV in gear. "It's fine," he said. "We're wasting our time, anyways."

FORTY-NINE

WITH THEIR TRIP TO check out Brad McKenna again busted by Moore's surveillance, Jackson decided it was best to head back and rethink their next move. He got back into the Suburban with Bear, and they crossed back into Virginia. But in Arlington, with Bear's stomach grumbling loud enough to hear over the radio, the two stopped at a '50s-style diner for breakfast. Jackson was nursing a coffee when the waitress came around with two entrées, both for Bear.

"One Country Scrambler and one Lumberjack Breakfast with eggs over hard," she said, dropping off the food.

Bear grabbed an entrée with each hand and positioned them in front of himself. He looked up at the waitress and flashed a boyish smile. "Thank ya, ma'am."

The waitress looked unamused. "Mhmm. Don't see many folks ordering eggs over hard."

"Yeah, well, I like mine good 'n' dead."

The waitress gave him a crude look before walking off. Bear was about to dig into his double breakfast when he looked over at Jackson, staring out the diner window.

"Ya sure ya don' want anythin'?" Bear asked.

Jackson shook his head. His bout with Moore had left him hungry for very little, much less a greasy-spoon breakfast. He was content to work on his coffee and think. There was no guarantee Moore was going to let up, and having to shake a tail anytime they did anything would eventually become impossible. He needed to find a way to convince Moore they were truly on the same side. Perhaps Bailey could help with that.

The phone buzzed on the table. It was Bailey, as if conjured by the very thought of her name.

Jackson picked up the phone and answered. "I was just about to call you."

"I guess I beat you to it," Bailey said. "Listen, I started looking into that name you gave me."

"Yeah, Adrien Alva."

"Well, I've checked both the National Crime Information Center database as well as the DC DMV, and I didn't find any Adrien Alva."

"That doesn't make any sense. I've been in his apartment, in DC. Wait ... You know what, once after we spoke, he headed for the metro—he might not have a car."

"But he'd still need an ID to do pretty much anything. You know that. I even ran the name through the Virginia and Maryland DMVs for good measure. All common spellings. The only hit I got was an Adrian Alva—with an *a*, not an *e*—in Williamsburg."

"Do you have a photo?"

"Yeah, hold on, I'll send it to you."

A moment later, Jackson's phone pinged with an incoming text from Bailey. He tapped the message and opened it. It was a photo of a young Latin man with a full head of black hair.

Jackson put the phone back to his ear. "That's not him. This doesn't make sense."

And then it hit him. He said it under his breath as Bailey said it over the phone:

"Adrien Alva doesn't exist."

FIFTY

BEAR NEARLY CHOKED on his mouthful of bacon as Jackson muttered the words. He put a fist to his chest, trying to ease his breakfast down before coughing. "What did ya just say?"

Jackson held up a finger. "Okay, Bailey," he said into the phone, "can you do me one more favor?"

"Shoot," Bailey said.

"I'll text you the address of Alva's apartment building with the unit we visited. Can you do a little digging, see if maybe a landlord knows Alva's real name or something?"

"Sure. I have a friend in Metro PD who owes me a favor. I'll have him ask around."

"Make it quick if you can, please."

Jackson ended the call. Bear was looking at him, waiting to be debriefed.

"Adrien Alva doesn't exist," Jackson said. "At least not on paper."

"No shit?" Bear asked, wiping his mouth.

"There's only one Adrien Alva in DC, Maryland, and Virginia—a guy in Williamsburg. Bailey sent me the ID photo: it's not our Alva. Plus, he spells his name differently."

"Son of a bitch. Maybe it's a nickname? Or alias?"

Jackson shook his head. "Bailey's not new to this. She'd check for known aliases."

The two of them fell quiet. Their waitress came by with a coffeepot and asked if Jackson wanted a refill, but he shook his head. He looked out the diner window again, thinking.

"So, what do ya want to do?" Bear asked.

Jackson's sights had been set on Brad McKenna for so long that he hadn't really considered anyone else. But Adrien Alva had lied about knowing where Jackson lived and was apparently lying about who he was. Whomever the man that befriended Nat was, he had a secret. And Jackson wanted to know what it was. But they were late to the game and needed to catch up fast.

"Spencer," Jackson finally said. "We're going back to Harry Spencer."

Bear looked at him, confused.

"Come on, for real," Jackson said, sliding out of the diner booth. "Finish your food or get it to go. I'll call Spencer, tell him we're coming."

"Why are we goin' back to Spencer? To ask him more questions?"

"No. To hire him."

IT TOOK twenty minutes to get back across the Potomac and up to Spencer's office in Adams Morgan. As Jackson trotted up the concrete steps to Spencer's front door with Bear trudging along behind, he heard a loud buzz and the front door clicked open. Spencer must've been watching for their arrival on the camera overhead.

Jackson and Bear shook the rain off their coats in the entryway.

"Back here!" Spencer's echoed from somewhere deeper in the building.

Jackson and Bear maneuvered their way through the two front rooms and into the office in the back. Spencer stood up from behind his desk and offered his hand. Jackson shook it before sitting down in one of the seats facing the desk.

"So," Spencer said as he returned to his seat, "what brings you by?"

"Adrien Alva," Jackson said.

Spencer exchanged glances with Jackson and Bear, who'd taken the seat beside Jackson's. "Right. Well, as I told you before, I hardly met the guy. Just the one time."

"As it turns out, whoever came here was not Adrien Alva."

Spencer looked on, confused.

"There is no Adrien Alva in the metropolitan area," Jackson explained. "Whomever you met—whomever I met, for that matter—was someone else."

"Well, that is interesting. But, again, I met him just the one time. Obviously, he could've given me any name, and I'd have no reason not to believe him."

"It's more than giving you a name, though. Nat told her peers at work about Adrien. She *called him* Adrien Alva. So, he was going by Adrien Alva to everyone, including Nat, who was supposedly a very good friend. He's hiding something. I want to know what."

"I don't blame you. But I've told you everything I know."

"Everything you know *so far*. I want to hire you to look into him."

Spencer rubbed the stubble on his chin and grinned, but Jackson didn't smile back. He was all business.

"I assume you need a retainer to start," Jackson said. "How much?"

Spencer shook his head, still grinning. He scooted forward in his rusting computer chair and put his elbows on his desk. "When Nathalie hired me, she anticipated needing my services for more than just you. In fact, she paid a pretty hefty retainer—one she had not completely burned through when she was, well, killed."

"How much are we talking about?"

"Ten grand."

Bear's jaw slacked open, and an audible moan came out of his mouth. Spencer looked at him and chuckled.

"She gave you ten thousand dollars up front?" Jackson asked. "That's a lot of money to move. You said she was keeping her husband, Brad, out of all this. Did she tell you how she managed to move that much money without him noticing?"

"It wasn't his. I had the same concerns myself. The last thing I need is a real estate mogul breathing down my neck, but she said he didn't even know about the money. Said it was hers in a private account. She called it her 'rainy-day fund.'"

Those last three words pierced Jackson and sent a chill coursing through his body. He already knew what Spencer was talking about.

When Jackson didn't say anything, Spencer took it as his cue to continue. "I kept waiting for a next of kin to come and ask for the balance of her account from me, but no one came. I thought about reaching out to Brad, then thought better of it. She obviously had a reason to keep him out of the loop, and it wasn't my place to break that trust."

"You're saying you'd take what she has left as payment for us?"

"I don't know how deep you're thinking, but certainly to get started. She obviously wanted to contact you about all this, anyway. I'm thinking she'd want you to have it, especially if it meant finishing what she started."

Jackson's mind churned, processing everything. He rose and got up out of the chair. "Get started on Alva. I'll be in touch."

Spencer rose, too, and nodded. He began to climb his way out from behind his desk but Jackson didn't wait. By the time Spencer had freed himself, Jackson was opening the front door and leaving, Bear following behind. They trotted back down the front steps and walked briskly back to the Suburban. Bear had to break into a jog just to keep up.

"'Rainy-day fund,'" he said. "Do ya know what he's talkin' about?"

Jackson didn't answer.

"Okay. Well, where are we headed?"

"To get eyes on Alva," Jackson said. "Or whatever his name is."

FIFTY-ONE

BEAR PULLED up to the front of the apartment complex where they'd met the man they knew as Adrien Alva and slowed. Jackson eyed it briefly but motioned for Bear to keep going. Bear hesitated, confused.

"Keep driving," Jackson said.

"I thought we were gettin' eyes on the place," Bear said.

"We are, but not like this. Keep going."

Bear cruised down the street. A block later, they came to the entrance of Fort Totten Park.

"Pull over," Jackson said.

Bear pulled over. Jackson slipped on his ballcap before turning and rummaging around in the backseat of the SUV.

"Do you have a rain parka or something?"

"All the way in the back," Bear said. "If we're goin' back on foot, maybe I should park for real."

"I am. You're not."

Bear stared at Jackson, waiting for an explanation. Jackson didn't immediately offer one, but when he felt Bear's eyes on him, he stopped and came back to the front seat.

"We're not going anywhere until Alva or whoever the hell he is moves, or Spencer or Bailey gives us something to work with. We're setting up for the long haul. I want you to go back to my place, switch vehicles and get my pickup. Alva hasn't seen it, so he can't make us in it. Get everything we need to be here for a bit. Food, a change of clothes, the works. Get us some comms, too, in case we need to split up."

"Okay. Ya want me to get us some firepower as well?"

"No. Neither of us has stuff registered in DC. If we get jammed up by a patrol officer or something, we'll be screwed. We'll have to go without."

"Okay. Wait, what about you? Where are you goin' to be durin' all this?"

"Watching the building." Jackson nodded toward the park before moving to the SUV's tailgate. The park's woods extended back down the road across the street from the apartment buildings. He found the poncho and put it on.

"I'll be back as fast as I can," Bear said. "Play nice until then."

Jackson shut the tailgate door and jogged across the street. He took the paved pathway up a grassy knoll and walked deeper into the park. Behind him, he heard Bear's Suburban take off for Jackson's cabin.

In the drab downpour, the park was deserted. The only thing Jackson heard was the rain plopping against the nylon of the poncho he'd borrowed from Bear. The thing was three sizes too big for him, but he didn't mind. Disguising his figure would come in handy.

He walked to the back of the park, hidden from the street. He checked that no one was around one last time and slipped into the woods. The naked branches overhead darkened the area but also blocked some of the rain. He hiked his way through mud and dead leaves, eventually making his way back, parallel to the street.

A quarter of a mile later, he was there. Stepping up to the edge of the woods, Jackson dropped to his belly and tucked himself behind the trunk of a large maple tree. For the first time since the morning the state police came to search his property, he felt in control. He was in his element. The woods, the mud, the rain. It wasn't the city. It was familiar.

Jackson looked out across the street at Adrien Alva's apartment building, pinpointing which unit and corresponding windows were his. A light was on, but the shades were drawn.

A shadow moved across the curtains.

Adrien Alva might not be real, but *someone* was up there. Alva was a ruse. A lie. Sooner or later, the real man, and the truth, would have to reveal themselves. And Jackson would be waiting.

For a moment, he closed his eyes and just listened. Rain pitter-pattered all around him, and Bear's voice played in his mind.

"'Rainy-day fund.' Do ya know what he's talkin' about?"

Jackson hadn't answered Bear, but he knew. He'd been there the night she—*they*—received it as a gift. Even then, it had been earmarked for a rainy day. It was only fitting that it came into play now, during this deluge.

He opened his eyes back up and watched. And waited.

NAT LAUGHED SO *hard Jackson thought she was going to spit out her mouthful of mulled wine. She'd heard the punchline of her dad's go-to joke —the one with two cows talking in a field—a hundred times, but it was late. She was tired and tipsy and the corny quip got the best of her.*

"Easy there, Nat," *Jackson said.* "You're going to soak the sofa!"

Now, Nat's parents were laughing at Nat and not at the joke.

"I'm going to soak my pants if I laugh any harder," *Nat said.*

Everyone laughed harder. Nat's dad, Tim, wiped tears from his eyes. It was a week before Christmas. String lights lit up the plastic four-foot tree in the corner of the living room, and the decorations Nat had picked up from Five Below made the rest of the place feel homey and festive. Frank Sinatra's voice surrounded them with his rendition of "It Came Upon the Midnight Clear."

Jackson took another sip of his own mulled wine and let it linger in his mouth. The laughter died down, and a lull fell over the foursome's conversation.

Feeling the silence, Nat's mom, Janet, made a point to check her watch. "Well, it's getting late, Tim. Perhaps we should go. We've tortured the lovebirds enough."

"Oh, I suppose you're right," Tim said.

"It was great having you guys," Jackson said. "Thank you for coming over for dinner."

Tim scooted forward in the recliner he was sitting in and pulled an envelope out from the breast pocket of his blazer. "Well, really quick, we wanted to give you guys this."

"What is it?" Nat asked.

"Go on," Tim said, handing her the envelope. "Open it."

Nat grinned the way she did when she was surprised and began opening it.

"We haven't seen you all since Nat here said yes to you, Jackson," Tim explained. "This is just a little something from us to wish you well. Consider it a joint Christmas and engagement gift."

Jackson watched as Nathalie pulled a card out of the envelope and her eyes widened.

"Oh my god, dad," she said. "This is ... this is too much."

"Nothing is too much for my little girl," Tim said, beaming. "And don't even try to give it back. I won't have any of it. This is for you two. And your new life together."

Nat passed the card to Jackson. Inside the card, in Janet's handwriting, was a message:

Congratulations on your engagement! We love you two!
Love,
Tim and Janet

Below that, a cashier's check for ten thousand dollars was paperclipped to the card.

"Nat is right, you guys," Jackson said. "This is way too much."

"Oh, hush, dear. Think nothing of it," Janet countered. "We want you two to have it."

Jackson handed the card and check back to Nat, who placed it on the coffee table in front of her.

"You guys, it's so much," she said. "Where did you even get that much?"

"I sold the Spitfire," Tim said, his smile getting even bigger.

"Stop it! You did not!"

"I did! And I was happy to. We were going to give it to you guys, but I know you're not much into cars. We figured you'd all appreciate the cash more. Plus, this way I had a little something left over to get your mom and me a new washer and dryer."

"Dad, you loved that car. Really, it's ..."

Tim gave Nat a look that told her it wasn't up for discussion. Another quiet came over the room and now Jackson was the one who felt obligated to break it.

"Well, seriously, guys, we can't thank you enough," he said. "And we're treating you to dinner sometime next week. That's for sure."

"Jackson, you make everyone some of that mean coffee you brew Christmas morning, and we'll be square," Tim said, standing up.

Jackson laughed. He and Nat walked her parents to the door. The four exchanged goodbyes, Nat and Jackson thanking her parents again, and Tim and Janet walked out to their car. Jackson shut the door and turned to Nat, who was already back on the sofa, looking at the check. Jackson came over and sat next to her.

"That was really something of them," he said.

"Yeah," Nat agreed. "I guess we can use it to pay for the wedding?"

"I don't know. Maybe we hold on to it. Save it, you know?"

"Save it? For what? We already have our house."

"Maybe we get a bigger one. Or start a college fund. For when we have a little Nat running around here."

"Or a little Jackson. Jackson Junior."

Jackson shook his head and crinkled his nose. "No way, I wouldn't want a Junior."

"You wouldn't want a little boy?"

"No, a son would be wonderful. Just not a Junior. We'd name him something else."

Nat leaned over and tucked herself under Jackson's arm. Together, the two of them laid back and sunk into the plush cushions of their sofa. Frank Sinatra was now on to "Silent Night."

"Evan," Nat said after a while. "Like your father."

Jackson thought about it, and a soft smile stretched across his face. "I like it."

"Me, too."

"But we save this. Like for a college fund for him—or her. Or just save it in general. Squirrel it away."

Nat slipped the check from the card and held it out in front of them. "For a rainy day."

"Yes. Our own little rainy-day fund. I'll go to the bank tomorrow and put it in a savings account. To help us when we need it."

Nat put the check back down on the table before folding her arms into her body.

She closed her eyes. "Deal."

Jackson held Nat like that, under his arm, until they both drifted off to sleep.

FIFTY-TWO

LATE IN THE AFTERNOON, Moore and Cotton returned to their office. Not the conference room where they had set up camp at Division Seven in Fairfax, but their actual office at Division Two in Culpepper. There, Captain House was waiting for them.

"I heard the surveillance was a bust," he said, annoyed.

"It was," Moore said, shrugging. "Worth a shot."

House raised an eyebrow skeptically. "Was it?"

"What does that mean?"

"I mean it looks like you were grasping at straws. Looking at a guy you'd already moved on from."

"McKenna's alibi put us back at square one. You know that."

"That doesn't mean you waste time looking where you already looked."

"Cap, it was a solid lead. To be honest, Jackson Clay still can't be cleared."

House stepped toward the two men, getting so close Moore could smell the pastrami sandwich his boss routinely had for lunch on the man's breath.

"We're a week into this thing with little to nothing to go on."

House brushed back his suit coat and put his hands on his hips. "I got a call from the Governor's office while you were out, asking where we're at."

"What did you say?" Moore asked.

"I said we're close to making an arrest. A *real* arrest. One that'll stick this time. And I'm not going to be made a liar. So whatever overtime or resources you need, it's all approved. But close this thing. This week."

Moore and Cotton nodded.

House took one more look at each of them, then marched back to his office and grabbed his overcoat. "Now, it's Sunday night and my family expects me home for dinner. I want to hear we've made some real progress when I get in tomorrow morning."

Again, Moore and Cotton nodded. House stepped past them and walked out of the office. When he was gone, Cotton's shoulders relaxed, and he loosened his tie.

"Well, that was fun," he said.

"Cap's just under a lot of stress," Moore said. "We all are."

"So, what do you want to do? Go back to Division Seven?"

Moore walked over to his desk and took a seat, loosening his own tie. "No. No more surveillance on Clay. Just get someone to pick up our stuff over there tomorrow morning."

Cotton nodded. He was looking intently at something on his phone. Moore tilted his chair back and watched his colleague, waiting for him to share what was so interesting.

"I think we may have something here," Cotton said.

"What is it?"

"Remember that video I showed you? Of the two McKenna vehicles from the gas station? You said to keep at it, see if we could find somewhere along the route with the driver's faces."

"Yeah. We get something?"

"I had a couple of the guys keep at it while we were out. Check this out." Cotton came around next to Moore and shared his phone with him. "This is from a traffic cam on the Ninth Street bridge, over top of the rail yards. Watch this."

Cotton played the video. Thirty seconds in, a dark blue Ford Edge came up over the crest of the bridge. The camera was across the bridge but pointed directly at the SUV. As it got closer, Cotton paused the video and used his fingers to zoom in on the driver.

"That's not Brad McKenna," he said.

"It doesn't look like it. But the image is so pixelated."

"It's not clear enough for a positive ID, but that definitely isn't McKenna. I'd bet you anything that's our killer."

Moore nodded, studying the image. Cotton was right. It was hard to tell what exactly the driver looked like, but it certainly didn't look like Brad McKenna. The person in the image looked to be wearing glasses, plus their build was stockier, with a larger forehead. And they were bald, or at the very least bald-*ing*. They definitely did not have Brad McKenna's full head of hair.

"That's definitely something," Moore said. "Let's keep at it. If we found this, maybe we can find a better image. I'll order a pie for delivery. It's going to be a long night."

Cotton turned and looked at Moore with a smile. "Hey, Book."

Moore was punching in the number on his desk phone for the local Pizza Hut, but stopped and looked at Cotton.

"This is our guy," Cotton said.

FIFTY-THREE

BAILEY WAS JUST ABOUT to head home for the evening when her phone buzzed in her pocket. Pulling it out, she checked the caller ID—a DC number—and answered it.

"Special Agent Bailey," she said in her official-sounding voice.

"Jen, hey," said a man on the other end. "It's Tim Funkhouser over at Metro."

Detective Funkhouser was with the Metropolitan Police Department in DC; Bailey had called in a favor and asked him to look into whoever was claiming to be Adrien Alva.

"Funk," Bailey said, "hey, how's it going?"

"You know, another day, another dollar. Anyway, I ran down that guy for you."

"Great. What have you got?"

"I don't know if Adrien Alva is an alias, per se. This guy might just be going by his middle name. I talked with his renter—the full name on the rental agreement is George Adrien Alvanitakis. He's a licensed driver here in the district. Same name and address with the DC DMV. I don't know about the last name part. Maybe he shortened it because it's easier? You know, anglicized it, or whatever."

"Yeah, or whatever. Did you run him?"

"I did. He's got a handful of charges on his juvey record. Animal cruelty. Destruction of property. One serious one: Assault with a deadly weapon."

Bailey grabbed a scrap piece of paper off her desk and quickly jotted the information down. "That assault? You get anything more on it?"

"No. All the charges are out of Bath County out there in Virginia. I guess that's where he grew up. I don't know."

"That's alright. I'll get into it. Thanks."

"No problem, let me know if you need anything else."

"Will do. Thanks, Funk."

Bailey hung up and looked at her notes. The assault was sort of interesting, but less so without any context. Some people have rough teenage years—it wasn't necessarily something to hold against a person. Lord knows she certainly wasn't a saint growing up. But it also wasn't nothing. She wanted to know more.

Logging back into her computer, she started a deep dive into George Adrien Alvanitakis. Forty-seven years old, born at Bath Community Hospital in Hot Springs, Virginia, in 1975. He was 5'6" and 160 pounds, with dark, thinning hair and a round face. Bailey saw the charges Funkhouser mentioned, but there wasn't much else. She frowned.

Bath County would be policed by the County's Sheriff, but it was a quarter to seven in the evening, and any small county sheriff would be home and two beers in by now, especially on a weekend. Still, it was worth a shot. She found the number and called.

A squeaky male voice answered: "Bath County Sheriff."

"Hi, this is Special Agent Jen Bailey with the state police. Is the Sheriff available to talk?"

"No, ma'am," the man said. "He hasn't been in today. If this is an emergency, I can notify him."

Bailey bit her lip. She knew she'd personally hate it if someone bothered her off the clock for nothing, and she wasn't sure if this stuff with Alvanitakis amounted to anything. "No, no emergency. I'm looking for more information on some old cases from '89 to '92."

"Well, that's before my day. Sheriff Pickett might know, though. He's been a deputy here since the early '80s. I could leave him a message to call you when he gets in tomorrow if you'd like."

"That'd be great. Thanks."

Bailey left the man her information and hung up. It was, in fact, late. If the sheriff had to wait until morning, she could, as well. She got up and began packing up her things. As she went to shut down her computer, Alvanitakis' DMV photo was there, staring at her. She looked over at the conference room where Book had been running his surveillance operation. It had been hours now, and he'd never returned. Although he hadn't said it, she knew they were watching Jackson Clay.

She knew in her gut Clay did not kill Nathalie McKenna. Bailey didn't know if this Alvanitakis had anything to do with the murder, but she told herself giving Book and his team any reason not to waste more time on Clay would be helpful. Before she logged off, she printed off Alvanitakis' DMV and criminal records and slipped them into a manila folder, then stepped into the conference room and placed the folder with the rest of Book's things.

As she headed out of the office, she called Jackson.

FIFTY-FOUR

JACKSON SAT in the passenger seat of his pickup, finishing off his fries from Ben's Chili Bowl. Bear had returned with supplies and dinner courtesy of the DC eatery. Now, the two of them picked up what Jackson had done most of the afternoon: watching Adrien Alva's apartment.

The sun had set, and with it, the temperature had nosedived. The cold rain saturating the area all day had turned back into an icy mixture of sleet and freezing rain. Bear and Jackson had even seen a couple of trucks go by treating the road with brine.

To save gas and avoid detection, they were staking out the apartment with the engine off. Jackson, wrapped in a coat and hoodie, could see his breath in the cabin of the truck every time he exhaled.

"He's probably in for the night," Bear said. "Why don' ya get some shut-eye? We can take shifts watchin'."

"I'm good for now," Jackson said. "Plus, he didn't come out during the day. Maybe he does whatever he does at night."

The two looked on at the apartment in silence until Jackson's phone buzzed inside his coat pocket. He glanced at it, saw it was Bailey, and answered it.

"Hey, you find anything out?" Jackson asked.

"Yeah, hi, I did, actually," Bailey said. "The guy's full name is George Adrien Alvanitakis. He's forty-seven, from Bath County, Virginia. It's on the rental agreement for the unit you visited him in, and he's got a DC driver's license with the same name. I'm sending you everything I got in an email. You can see his DMV photo to confirm it's him."

"I'm sure it is. Did you run him?"

"Yeah. He's got a handful of charges from when he was a minor. Mostly boys-will-be-boys stuff, but there is one assault with a deadly weapon charge. I put in a call to the sheriff down there, to see if anyone can give me some more information on that, but they're home for the night. When they call me, I'll call you."

"I appreciate that. Anything else?"

"Not right now. But like I said, I'll let you know."

"Okay. Thanks."

Bailey hung up. Jackson's phone pinged with Bailey's incoming email. He scrolled through it while briefing Bear on what Bailey had just told him.

"His name is George. George Adrien Alvanitakis. He's from rural Virginia. Not much of a record except for when he was a minor. One was assault with a deadly weapon."

"It don' scream bad guy," Bear said. "But the dude's not a boy scout, neither."

"And it doesn't change that he's been lying to us."

Jackson finished scrolling through the email and came to Alvanitakis' photo at the bottom. Adrien Alva and George Adrien Alvanitakis were one and the same.

"So, how do ya want to play it?" Bear asked.

Jackson didn't answer him. Bear looked on as Jackson opened the call log on his phone and scrolled down to a number. He selected it and called it back.

"What are you doing now?" Bear asked.

The call was ringing in Jackson's ear.

"How do you get hornets out of their nest?" Jackson asked.

"I don' know. Kick the nest?"

Jackson nodded. "You kick the hornet's nest."

Alvanitakis picked up. "Hello?"

Jackson didn't say anything.

"Hello? Jackson?"

"Hello, George," Jackson said coldly.

Now it was Alvanitakis who went quiet.

"George Adrien Alvanitakis," Jackson said. "That is your real name, isn't it?"

Alvanitakis didn't answer, but Jackson could hear him breathing on the other end of the line.

"I don't know why you've been lying to everyone, or what game you're playing, George. But I promise you, I'm going to find out. For Nat."

Silence.

"Have a good night, George."

Jackson ended the call.

FIFTY-FIVE

JACKSON WATCHED the main door to the apartment complex. Six minutes after he called, the door opened and George Alvanitakis stepped out. Jackson put a wireless earbud in his ear and opened his passenger door.

"There he is," he said. "I'm going on foot. Stay with the truck. I'll let you know when to move."

"Remember," Bear said, "nothing stupid."

Alvanitakis crossed the courtyard to the sidewalk and began walking away from Jackson and Bear's position. Jackson, fifty feet back, followed at a casual pace with the lapels of his coat pulled up, and the bill of his ballcap pulled low.

Sleet pelted them as they walked, whipped around by a piercingly cold wind. Overhead, the sky was an eerie mauve, clouded and saturated with the light from the city below. Alvanitakis walked past his apartment complex and headed into the darkness beyond. Jackson couldn't see it, but he had a feeling he knew where the man was going.

"Heading east along the street," Jackson said to Bear over his earpiece. "I think he's going for the walkway to the metro station."

"Ya want me to move?" Bear asked.

"No, not yet."

Jackson allowed Alvanitakis to gain distance on him as they headed away from any lights. Pretty soon, the man was invisible, but Jackson knew the same was true for himself. And unlike Alvanitakis, he had something to help him see in the dark.

He pulled his FLIR monocle out from his coat and aimed it forward. The pocket-sized thermal scope highlighted Alvanitakis' warm frame in a fiery orange hue. Jackson watched him through the monocle as he diverged from the sidewalk and turned onto the walkway along the community garden.

"He just took the cut-through to the metro station," Jackson said. "Work your way around like you did the other day. I'll keep you posted."

"Gotcha. Movin'."

Jackson saw Bear's headlights shine on the barren garden in his periphery, but he paid little attention to it. He followed Alvanitakis down the path, checking every few moments with his monocle that the man was still headed for the metro.

On the other side, the Fort Totten Station was awash in light, a flame in the night as its tracks crossed over Galloway Street. Alvanitakis headed for the station, and Jackson followed.

"He's taking the metro," Jackson said.

"How do ya want to play it, brother?"

"We don't have a choice. I'm following him. Pull a map of the metro up. I'll let you know which way we go. You work your way to us."

"I think ya need a metro card or somethin' to get on."

"Well, then I guess I'm buying a metro card, aren't I?"

Alvanitakis entered the station. He swiped his card at the fare gates and took the escalator up to the platform running over the street. As Alvanitakis peered back over his shoulder, Jackson stopped at a fare card machine.

"He's going up to the red line," Jackson said. "Either toward Glenmont or Shady Grove."

"Looks like it runs like a *U*, runnin' out to Maryland each way. Should I head for Maryland?"

"No, he could be connecting somewhere. Start toward the closest highway."

With a *ca-chunk*, the machine dispensed Jackson a fare card. He took it, swiped it at the gates, and jogged up the ascending escalator, then slowed to an inconspicuous pace as he got to the top. He looked around slowly, spotting Alvanitakis standing at the far end of the platform.

"He's facing toward the Shady Grove track. Don't do anything yet, he could still switch."

"Roger that."

Jackson leaned against a large concrete pillar and studied Alvanitakis. He was standing just at the edge of the curved canopy overhead, watching the storm ahead of him. As a train approached, he stepped toward the tracks.

The train whirred into the station, lights at the edge of the platform signaling its arrival. It was nearly empty. When the doors opened, no one got off, and Alvanitakis immediately jumped in.

Jackson jogged up the platform after him. "We're getting on. Toward Shady Grove. Start moving."

"On it. It'll take ya deeper into the city before kickin' out to Maryland."

The train cars chimed, and a computer-woman's voice said, "Doors closing."

Jackson ran to the car before the one Alvanitakis was on and jumped in. The doors closed and the train slowly left the station. The inside of the train cars were lit, and Jackson could see Alvanitakis sitting by himself one car over. Jackson found a seat with Alvanitakis in view and sat down.

The train rolled on, floating just above the city it served. Together, Jackson and Alvanitakis rode in and out of metro stations without either of them moving. First Brookland and Catholic University, then Rhode Island Avenue and NoMa. Jackson relayed their status to Bear at every station.

After NoMa, the track dipped below the city and came to its first underground stop at Union Station, the rail epicenter of the district.

"We're underground, can you still hear me?" Jackson asked.

"Loud and clear, bud."

"We're at Union Station, staying on the train."

The doors closed, and the train slid headlong into a narrow tunnel. It rocked and rolled on the tracks, like an airplane hitting light turbulence. Lights along the tunnel blurred by.

Three stops later, they pulled into Metro Center. As the train slowed to a stop, Jackson saw Alvanitakis get up, brace himself with the overhead handholds, and move to the door of the train car. Jackson stayed seated.

"Hold up. He got up. We might be getting off. Metro Center."

When the doors opened, Alvanitakis walked out. Jackson got up quickly and left his own train car. As he got out, Alvanitakis walked down the platform toward him. Jackson quickly turned his back and looked down at his phone until Alvanitakis passed by without incident.

"We're out at Metro Station," Jackson said when Alvanitakis was out of earshot.

He stepped behind a large pillar displaying the next stops on each line and peered around it. Jackson thought Alvanitakis was headed toward the exit, but the man turned sharply around a banister and stepped onto the escalators headed down.

When he was gone, Jackson ran to the escalators. He looked up at the signage. "We're not leaving—he's headed to another train. The platform for the Blue, Orange, and Silver Lines."

"All three run west to east. From Virginia, through D.C., into Maryland. Which way is he headin'?"

Alvanitakis stood uncommitted in the middle of the platform. Jackson pulled up the Metro Map on his phone and studied it.

"If he were headed east, he would've caught the Yellow or Green Line back last station," Jackson said. "He's headed west."

"Unless he's circlin' around, checkin' for a tail."

The thought hadn't crossed Jackson's mind—he was sure he'd been so careful. At Bear's warning, he took a seat on a bench with his back to Alvanitakis. A moment later, a train arrived, headed eastbound. Jackson peeked over his shoulder. Alvanitakis didn't move.

In fact, he didn't move as a handful of trains went by each way. Jackson started to wonder if he'd been made and Alvanitakis was messing with him, but when a westbound Orange Line train came into the station, Alvanitakis stepped toward it.

"It looks like he's getting on the Orange Line. West."

The train doors opened and sure enough, Alvanitakis got on. Like before, Jackson made his way to the next car over and boarded.

"He's headed into Virginia."

"There's still a handful of stops in DC," Bear said.

Jackson knew Bear was right, but his gut told him Alvanitakis was headed across the Potomac. "It'll be Virginia. Get over there."

Just like on the Red Line, metro stations came and went without Alvanitakis moving. Jackson was seated across from a large map of the Metro system and followed their progress, all the while keeping an eye on Alvanitakis.

They pulled into the Foggy Bottom Station, and Jackson suddenly realized this was probably the exact same route Alvanitakis had taken when he'd met Jackson at the eatery in DC. This time, though, Alvanitakis didn't get off. Jackson looked again at the map.

"Leaving Foggy Bottom. Last stop in DC," Jackson said.

"Huh. You were right," Bear said. "He's headin' into Virginia. I'm on Constitution, headin' for I-66."

"Haul ass."

Alvanitakis and Jackson took the train through the next several stops. After Ballston, the tracks rose and climbed back to ground level, squarely between the divided lanes of the interstate.

"We're back above ground," Jackson said. "Next stop is East Falls Church."

"Roger that. I'm just a few miles back."

The train pulled into the station, and Alvanitakis got up. Jackson got up, too, and stepped toward his own set of doors.

"We're getting off at East Falls Church. There's no connection here. This is where he's getting out. Get here."

"I'm comin', I'm comin'."

Alvanitakis got off the train. Jackson stepped off the train, too, but hung back a bit to allow a reasonable distance to grow between them. They took the escalators down to the main level and exited the station through the fare gates. The station entrance opened onto a busy suburban street with the metro tracks and the interstate crossing overhead. Alvanitakis looked each way up and down the street before turning down the sidewalk.

Jackson pulled out his phone and opened up his Maps app to get his bearings. "He's headed down the street on foot. South on Sycamore."

"I'm two exits away."

Alvanitakis took the sidewalk past a fleet of waiting taxis, away from the metro station, and into a quaint suburb in Falls Church. Jackson kept his distance but never lost sight of him. Together, they walked through the night, Jackson following Alvanitakis, Alvanitakis following whatever he'd set his mind on.

They passed a large soccer field down a steep hill to their right. At the next intersection, Alvanitakis turned into a neighborhood. Jackson checked his phone.

"He made a right on Sixteenth. It's a residential area. Wherever he's headed, I think he's close. I need you."

"I'm minutes away."

When Jackson got to the street Alvanitakis had turned down, he stopped and watched. Alvanitakis disappeared and reappeared as he moved in and out of the glow of street lights.

Jackson pulled out his FLIR monocle. Alvanitakis walked almost a quarter mile before turning up a driveway to one of the houses. And then he was gone.

Jackson broke out in a flat sprint to get to where Alvanitakis had disappeared. "He went up a driveway. I'll get you a house number. Hold on."

In less than a minute, Jackson had made up the ground. A large hydrangea bush bordered the driveway Alvanitakis had gone up. Jackson crouched down behind the bush and peered out at the driveway. The house—a modest Craftsman with a newer addition—had a detached garage in the backyard. Jackson saw Alvanitakis now as he worked at opening a door on the side of the garage. He looked over at the main house.

"He's trying to get into a garage in a backyard. Twenty-six sixty-four Columbia."

"Two minutes. Give me two minutes."

But it wouldn't be enough. Behind Jackson, a door opened across the street and a middle-aged woman in sweats stepped out. She saw Jackson crouching behind the bush.

"Hey!" she shouted. "What are you doing? I'm calling the police!"

Alvanitakis turned to look at the woman. He saw Jackson's head poking out. At that, he turned and ran deeper into the yard.

"Shit!" Jackson said. "He's running, he's running!"

"I'm almost there, brother," Bear growled through the earpiece.

Jackson raced down the driveway after Alvanitakis. An elderly woman stepped out from the main house, but Jackson flew past her. Alvanitakis got to the end of the yard and climbed a fence at the back of it. Jackson got to it and, in one swift motion, jumped over.

"I'm turnin' onto the street now," Bear said.

Beyond the fence was a wooded community trail. Alvanitakis turned to his right and ran down the dirt pathway. Jackson, following, looked ahead and recognized the soccer field from the street.

"He's coming back your way, Bear," Jackson said. "Toward a soccer field."

"Roger. I see it."

BEAR SPOTTED the soccer field down a street to his right just as Jackson told him. He jerked the wheel and slammed on the brakes. The tail of the pickup whipped three-quarters of the way around and nearly missed the turn. Regaining control, he punched it forward.

The street dead-ended at a small parking lot for a dog park. Both the field and the parking lot were deserted at this late hour. So too was the dog park, for that matter. Bear stopped the truck in the middle of the lot and got out. He started trotting for the soccer field, expecting to see Jackson or Alvanitakis any moment. But when he got to the edge of the field without seeing either one of them, he did a quick three-sixty.

"I'm at the field," he said. "I don' see you guys."

"I lost him," Jackson said over his earpiece. "He was headed toward the field."

Bear stepped a little further into the open field, looking toward where the two of them should've been coming from. "I've got nothin', brother."

As the words left Bear's mouth, a shadow appeared at the opposite end of the field. It stopped and doubled over, looking as though it were catching its breath.

"Is that you over there?" Bear asked. "At the other end?"

"Yeah," Jackson said in between pants. "I see you."

"Hold on, I'm comin' to you."

He had just started to move toward Jackson when he heard a branch snap behind him. Bear started to turn, but it was too late. Alvanitakis stepped out from the dark and plunged a knife into Bear's side.

"Bear!" Jackson screamed.

Bear grimaced as a searing pain roiled through him like a tsunami wave. When it faded, so did his strength. He was confused, almost unaware that he had just been stabbed. He could see Jackson running toward him, but didn't fully understand why.

"Give Nathalie and Evan my best," Alvanitakis hissed in Bear's ear.

There was another sharp pain and Bear felt the knife come out of his body. Alvanitakis let go of him and Bear collapsed to the ground. Looking up at the night sky above, he heard footsteps running away and the faint sound of Jackson shouting. Coming for him. He told himself to wait, to hold out for Jackson, but now fatigue washed over him.

"I need an ambulance to the soccer field south of East Falls Church Metro," he heard Jackson say, certainly to a 911 operator. "My friend has been stabbed."

Good, Bear thought. Help was coming. Jackson was coming. He'd be here in just a few seconds.

But Bear closed his eyes and drifted off.

FIFTY-SIX

BEAR GROGGILY OPENED his eyes to the blinding white of harsh fluorescent lights. He had to squint to see anything. When he tried to block the light, he found his motion limited by the IV protruding from the top of his left hand.

Slowly, he became more aware of his surroundings. Machines beeped behind him; people talked somewhere in the distance; an announcement came through the speakers in the ceiling of his room. Bear tried to call out, but he couldn't—a large tube ran from a machine beside his bed into his mouth and down his throat. He tried to remove it with his other hand, but someone gently grabbed his hand and pinned it down.

"Don't grab at anything," Jackson said, reaching over from a chair at Bear's bedside. "You're okay."

Bear blinked a few times. Slowly, he glanced around the room, then came back to Jackson. He made a slight swirling motion around the room with the hand that didn't have the IV.

"Where are you?" Jackson asked, trying to interpret.

Bear nodded.

"The hospital. Virginia Hospital Center, in Arlington."

Bear pointed at the tube running into his mouth.

"They took you into surgery soon after you got here. They had to put you on a ventilator. To be safe."

Bear made a jerking motion with his hand.

"When will it come out? I don't know. I can ask someone."

Bear pointed at Jackson and then made the same jerking motion.

Jackson thought for a moment, then understood. "No, I'm not going to pull it out."

Bear rolled his eyes.

"You need anything? Other than getting the vent out?"

Bear looked back at Jackson and started to shake his head, then paused. A look of puzzlement crossed his face.

"Hold on, hold on," Jackson said.

He got up and left the room. Bear could hear him talking with someone just outside. When Jackson returned, he had a small dry-erase board and a marker.

Jackson placed the board by Bear's hand and gave him the marker. "Here, try this."

Bear's one-handed handwriting rivaled that of a Kindergartener, but Jackson could make out what he wrote.

STABBED?

"Yeah, you were stabbed," Jackson said. "We were going after Alvanitakis. You remember?"

Bear tried to wipe at the board. Jackson took it from him, erased what Bear had written, and handed it back. Bear scribbled again, writing one thing before crossing it out and writing another.

~~ALVA~~ ... ASSHOLE?

"Yeah, Alvanitakis stabbed you. Do you mean where he is? I don't know. He got away. I stayed with you."

Bear looked away again. The TV was on, mounted on the ceiling in the far corner of the room. Jackson thought he might be done and ready to relax. As he started to pull the dry-erase board away Bear stopped him, grabbing his hand. He looked at Jackson and made a wiping motion. Jackson nodded and erased the board. Bear wrote again, then nudged the board in Jackson's direction. He tapped the board, underscoring his message.

GET HIM.

Jackson looked up from the board and nodded.

"I'm going to. For you, for Nathalie, for everything. I'm going to."

FIFTY-SEVEN

JACKSON SAT in one of the hospital's many waiting rooms with a thousand-yard stare when a hand holding a Styrofoam cup full of coffee in front of his face broke his hypnosis. He looked up to see Special Agent Bailey standing over him, offering him the percolated beverage.

"You look like you could use this," she said with as tender a smile as she could muster.

Jackson took the cup from her. "What are you doing here? How did you know I was here?"

"I'm a special agent with the Virginia State Police. Believe it or not, I tend to hear about stuff like stabbings in suburbia."

"It was him, Bailey. George Alvanitakis. I couldn't see him clearly, so I can't prove it, but it was him. I was—*we* were—chasing him. He stabbed Bear."

"Yes, I know. A BOLO has already been put out to all agencies in the area, identifying him as a person of interest. Metro PD is working on getting a search warrant to hit his apartment."

"He's already long gone."

"Maybe, maybe not. We won't know until we look. Any word yet on Bear?"

Jackson took a sip of the coffee. It was better than he expected. "They're optimistic. He was lucky, they said."

"That's good." Bailey tried to sound reassuring. It wasn't helping.

"It's my fault," Jackson said. "I got him into this."

"Uh uh, don't go down that rabbit hole. The world is a fucked-up place. Unless you put that knife in his side, you're not at fault for anything."

Jackson said nothing, but he didn't buy that. All of this was because of him. Evan disappeared because of him. Nathalie was murdered because of him. Now Bear had been stabbed. Because of him.

Bailey could tell Jackson was falling down the very rabbit hole she'd just warned him about. She racked her brain for something to say.

Nurses and orderlies walked hurriedly back and forth. The harsh smell of chemical cleaners and disinfectants hung in the air. Machines beeped, and patients cried and moaned for loved ones over the quiet conversations of doctors and staff.

"I fucking hate hospitals," Bailey said finally.

"Me, too."

"Nothing good ever comes from them,"

Jackson snorted, looking down at the floor. "I got engaged in a hospital."

Bailey's eyebrows perked up. "No shit?"

Jackson nodded.

"To Nathalie?"

Jackson nodded again. "In Charlottesville."

"Was Nathalie a nurse there or something?"

"No, she didn't work there. It would've helped if she did, actually. I'd been in an accident. Traffic accident."

Bailey's face buckled into something between a simper and a

grimace. "Wow, must've really hit your head if you thought that was the right time for that."

Jackson chuckled. Looking up, he nodded, admitting the peculiar situation. He had hit his head, but not so hard that he didn't know what he was doing. He'd always been a man whose actions came out of necessity. Reactions to the situation at hand. It wasn't the most lovey-dovey of gestures, but then again, he'd never been mistaken for a romantic.

JACKSON WATCHED *as nurses and doctors rushed through the ER in a tumultuous weave. It had been this chaotic—busier than any Emergency Room he'd ever been in—from the moment the paramedics wheeled him in. He reached out, trying desperately to get anyone's attention. In truth, he'd have a better chance at plucking a fish out of a stream, but he tried anyway, sputtering like a skipping CD.*

"Excuse—Ma'am—If I could—"

Just when he was about to give up and lay back on his gurney, he heard a familiar voice.

"Jackson? Jackson?"

Nat called out from somewhere beyond the mayhem in front of him. He could just barely hear her over the busy hospital, but it was definitely Nat.

"Nat! Over here!"

"Jackson!"

A moment later, he saw her amber locks whip around as she scanned her surroundings, panic-stricken. A nurse pushed an EKG machine out of the way and finally, she saw him.

"Over here," Jackson said again.

Nat spotted him and jogged over. Dropping her coat and bag on a chair, she gently hugged him. Jackson grimaced in pain.

"Oh my God," Nat said. "Are you alright? I was freaking out. Some deputy called me with your phone and said you'd been in some accident and—"

"I know. I told him to."

"He'd barely tell me anything! And then I rushed over here, and the bitch at the front desk wouldn't let me back, so I had to sneak my way in, and then no one would tell me anything, and it's just been a mess."

Jackson couldn't help but laugh. Something about Nat's trepidation was sweet and endearing to him.

"What's so funny?"

Jackson winced from laughing. "No, nothing."

"Oh my god. Look at you. Are you okay?"

"I'm good, I'm good. Now that you're here."

"Are you sure?"

There was a knock on the sliding glass doors behind them and a nurse stepped in, looking down at a chart in her hands.

"Okay, Mr. Clay, I'm here to—" The nurse looked up to see Nat standing by Jackson's side. "Oh, I'm sorry. I didn't know family had come."

"This is Nat," Jackson said.

"Hi, I'm his girlfriend," Nat said.

The nurse nodded. "I see. Well, unfortunately, only family can be back here with patients. You'll have to wait in the waiting room, miss."

The nurse moved to usher her out, but Nat stepped away from her.

"Please, it's okay," Jackson said.

"I'm sorry, but it's policy. She'll have to leave."

Another nurse overheard what was happening and stepped in to assist the first. He, unlike the first, was six and a half feet tall, with arms as thick as Jackson's neck.

"Please come with us, ma'am," he said.

"Seriously, it's okay. She can stay," Jackson said.

Nat turned and looked back at him as she was led away. Jackson felt helpless watching her be whisked from the room. He tripped over his own words, trying to find the right thing to say.

"Stop! She's my fiancée!" he shouted.

The two nurses stopped and looked at him, then at each other.

"Please, she's my fiancée," Jackson said again.

"Even so, sir," the female nurse said. "Unless she's legally your wife."

"She's supposed to be by now. But this happened."

The two nurses looked at each other again. The male one shrugged and left to attend to other things.

"Alright," the female nurse acquiesced. "But I'm coming back in five to take you for X-Rays. And, no, she can't come with you."

Jackson smiled in thanks and nodded. Nat scampered back to his side, and the nurse slid the glass door to the room closed until it was just opened a crack.

Nat pulled up a chair next to Jackson. He took her hand in his and leaned over to kiss it.

"Jackson," Nat said. "You just lied to that lady."

"She'll get over it."

The two of them shared a laugh.

"So, what are we going to do when the real ballbusters come?" Nat asked. "I mean, I'm not actually your fiancée."

Jackson looked into her eyes. He'd thought about it ever more frequently until now it crossed his mind on the daily. Truthfully, he didn't know why he hadn't done anything about it yet. But something about getting run off the highway by a wayward semi convinced him there was no time like the present.

"Then let's get married," he said.

"What?" Nat asked.

"Marry me."

Nat laughed, but then saw the look in his eyes. He wasn't kidding. "You're serious?"

"I love you, and I don't want to have anything take you away from me like Nurse Ratched over there almost did. Marry me." Jackson squeezed her hand.

Tears formed in the corner of her eyes and she nodded fervently before the words came out. "Yes, of course."

Jackson pulled her in and kissed her, then rested his head against hers. It was their way of retreating into their own world. They held each other like that for a moment until Jackson suddenly pulled away.

"Oh no," he said. "You need a ring."

Nat laughed. "It's okay. Don't worry about it."

"No, no. I can't propose and not have a ring."

Looking around his ER room for a solution, his eyes fell on the piece of medical tape wrapped around his finger, holding an oximeter in place on his fingertip. "Here."

Jackson wriggled the piece of tape back and forth until it lost its stickiness. He slid it off and placed it on her left ring finger. There, it dangled, much too big.

The two of them laughed again. Nathalie leaned forward and kissed him.

"I love you," she said.

"I love you, too. Forever."

FIFTY-EIGHT

BAILEY HAD LEFT Jackson at the hospital and was just about to walk into work at Division Seven when her phone rang. She checked it, saw the area code was for western Virginia, and answered the call. "Special Agent Bailey."

"Special Agent," said a gruff voice, "this is Sheriff Bob Baldwin over in Bath County."

"Yes, hi, Sheriff. Thank you for getting back to me."

"Well I walked in this morning and one of my overnight deputies was all in a tiff about how the big, bad Staties had called last night. Said you had some case you were lookin' at that might concern us out here in Hot Springs."

"Yes, sir. That's correct."

"So, what can I do for ya?"

"I was wondering if anyone out there might be familiar with a George Alvanitakis. He may have also gone by his middle name, Adrien."

There was a silence over the line. Bailey looked down at her phone to check she was still connected.

When the Sheriff spoke again, his voice was quieter. And strained. "How bad is whatever he's done?"

The sheriff's serious tone gave Bailey pause. "Well, we're still looking into that, sir, but we have a strong suspicion he has, at the very least, stabbed someone. I was trying to get some background information. I see he has a slew of charges from when he was a juvenile."

"You're calling about the fire."

"I'm sorry, I don't follow. The fire?"

"The one that killed his sister and her child. It's all right there. The destruction of property charge."

"Maybe I'm not understanding. Are you saying George Alvanitakis started a fire that killed two family members?"

There was another pause. Again, Bailey checked her phone. "Hello? Sheriff?"

"I'll be straight with you, ma'am. George Alvanitakis was a menace to our society right up until the moment he left. And, yes, even though I can't prove it and the Commonwealth's Attorney never prosecuted it, I guarantee you he set fire to that house, killing his sister and niece."

"What drove him to do that?"

"Evil."

"Come again?"

"That's the only way I can explain it. Evil. Pure evil."

"Again, I don't follow."

"Special Agent Bailey, there are good apples and there are bad apples in this world, and then there's George Alvanitakis. George made our bad apples out here look like saints by comparison."

"You make it sound like he's a career criminal, but his adult record is spotless."

"Well, he left here as soon as he could, so I can't speak to it personally, but I'd have to believe it wasn't because he's been in church every Sunday. And he's smart as all get-out, too. It's half the reason we couldn't nail him for arson and murder when he was here."

Bailey thought for a moment. "Suppose I said Alvanitakis befriended a woman only to turn around and savagely run her off the road and kill her. Is that something the Alvanitakis you knew would be capable of?"

"Let me put it like this. Are you familiar with the dark core of personality?"

"You said the dark core? No, I'm not familiar."

"Well, believe it or not, I was a college boy, once. I went to JMU over there in Harrisonburg, studyin' psychology before I eventually moved on to public administration. Anyway, there's a theory in psychology of a dark core of personality. It's the idea that one single trait lies at the core of all of humanity's dark traits. Psychopathy, narcissism, sadism, so on and so forth. I never thought much of it. That is, until I met George."

"What exactly are you saying, Sheriff?"

"I'm saying, Special Agent Bailey, if there is a root of all evil, George Alvanitakis is cut from it."

The sheriff's words sent chills coursing through Bailey. Now it was she who fell quiet.

"Special Agent?" Sheriff Baldwin asked. "You hear me okay?"

"Yes, Sheriff. Thank you. I'll call you back if I need anything else."

Bailey ended the call, but those words hung with her.

If there is a root of all evil, George Alvanitakis is cut from it.

She thought of Jackson, back at the hospital, determined to get justice for his friend. She prayed he knew what he was up against.

FIFTY-NINE

WITH BEAR STABILIZED and out of surgery, Jackson decided to leave him to rest and take care of other matters. Chief among them was getting his truck back, which had been left in the parking lot near the soccer field.

Jackson opted to walk the two miles there, making his way through the suburbia that was Northern Virginia. Quiet, idyllic streets where the worst thing that happened at any given time was perhaps a nagging neighbor. It was a far cry from the nightmare Jackson was currently living.

He took the friendly suburban streets to a paved bike path that ran back to the soccer field. As Jackson crossed the field, he could see his pickup on the other side. The local county police had moved it into a parking space, locked it up, and given Jackson the keys at the hospital. He gave the truck a once-over, checking to make sure it had not been messed with by Alvanitakis or anyone else, and hopped in.

As he fired up the truck, Jackson noticed an older woman with her Yorkshire Terrier in the dog park next to the parking lot. It was the woman he'd sprinted past when he was chasing after Alvanitakis, the woman who seemed to live in the home with the detached garage Alvanitakis had been trying to access.

Jackson's first instinct was to ask the woman some questions, but he thought better of it. For all he knew, this woman was complicit in whatever Alvanitakis was doing. She could feed him lies and then turn around and tip off Alvanitakis. But while the woman was here, he could at least see what was in that garage.

He backed out and drove down the block to the house with the detached garage. He drove by slowly, looking it over. There was only one car out front—almost certainly the woman's—and he decided it was unlikely anyone else was home.

Remembering the nosy neighbor across the street that had spotted him last night, Jackson parked on the next street over and grabbed his lockpick kit from his things. He slipped on a dark gray hoodie, then found the pathway he'd chased Alvanitakis down behind the houses, and followed it back to the one with the detached garage.

Jackson climbed the wooden fence surrounding the house's property and lowered himself into the backyard. He stalked over and peered inside the windows. No one was home.

Since he wasn't sure there weren't any prying eyes about in the neighborhood, Jackson opted not to cut across the yard, choosing instead to follow the wood fence around the edge of it. When he got to the back of the garage, he crouched down and shimmied sideways to the door on the side. The door had a plain knob, but a metal latch above it was secured with a heavy padlock.

Jackson inserted his tension tool, then manipulated the pins inside with his pick until the cylinder turned. There was a metallic click, and then he was in.

He cracked the door open just enough that he could slide his body in, then shut it behind him. The garage was dark and smelled of mold and sawdust. He felt along the wall for a light switch, but found none. He walked deeper into the garage, raising an arm to feel above his head. When his hand found a metal chain, he yanked it, and a light bulb clicked on, painting the garage in a dim orange light.

The hairs on Jackson's spine pricked up in terror. To his right was a clothes rack filled with uniforms: Postal worker's blues; the rubber sleeves, gloves, and hardhat of a utility lineman; medical scrubs. As he flipped through them, a queasiness welled up inside Jackson, an inexorable tide of understanding: here were all his worst fears about George Alvanitakis, confirmed. He continued flipping through, past police officer uniforms, paramedic and firefighter outfits—even a pair of military dress blues.

Jackson pulled out another shirt and froze. He thought he might actually become sick. He forced himself to read the badge-shaped patch on the shoulder:

KINGS DOMINION PARK POLICE
HANOVER CO., VA

He looked at the other side of the garage. There was an old workbench with shelving against the wall. The shelves were lined with seemingly random objects, most covered with a thick coat of dust: A money clip; a pair of Ray Ban sunglasses; a hat; a necklace. He looked at each one, trying to figure out why Alvanitakis would have them out in the open like they were prized possessions.

Jackson reached up, feeling around on the top shelf, when something fell to the floor and bounced underneath the workbench. He crouched down and took out his phone,
shining it on the floor.
"Oh, god."
The light on his phone illuminated a tiny Adidas sneaker. Toddler size, and white, with the classic three stripes. The last time Jackson had seen a shoe like that was fifteen years ago.

Evan had been wearing them the day he disappeared.

Jackson fell onto his backside. His heart thumped in his chest like a beast desperate to break out of its cage. The world was spinning, and the garage was spinning inside that spinning world.

Then, as he tried to gather himself, his light shone on the back wall.

Polaroids stapled to the wood panels glared back at him. Not of happy family and friends, but very clearly strangers. Terrified strangers all with the same look in their eyes, a look that screamed they didn't know what was happening, or why it was happening to them.

Almost all of them were spaced a few inches apart from one another, but two in the bottom corner were practically on top of each other. The first was of a young boy. Evan. He was looking up at the camera. Not scared, but not smiling, either. Almost confused as to why his picture was being taken. Next to it was the sunken head of Nathalie. Unlike the others, she wasn't looking at the camera. Her hair was disheveled and matted with blood. Jackson couldn't see if her eyes were open, or if she was even alive, but it didn't much matter.

Jackson understood now. George Adrien Alvanitakis was the most unspeakable of monsters. More than a monster. He just might be the devil himself, Jackson thought. And this was his lair.

He had manipulated and deceived all these people.

He had killed all these people.

He had killed Evan and Nathalie.

PART SIX
CARNY GAMES

"One word frees us of all the weight and pain in life. That word is love." — SOPHOCLES

SIXTY

JACKSON DROVE STRAIGHT BACK to his cabin and started packing. No more overnight stuff—he was preparing to leave indefinitely. George Alvanitakis was almost certainly on the run, and Jackson was going after him. It didn't matter how long it took. A day, a week, a year, a lifetime. He'd spent this, the latter part of his life, chasing devils. Now, the one that took his son and ex-wife—the two things he loved most in life—had to be stopped.

Now he was going to end George Adrien Alvanitakis. Even if it meant ending Jackson Clay.

Jackson ransacked his drawers, throwing as many clothes as he could into a large backpack. When that was done, he emptied his pantry of nonperishable items and filled what water bottles he had. Then he grabbed any and all equipment he thought he might need. Some of it, like the FLIR monocle and handheld GPS, were already in the truck.

Opening his gun safe, Jackson took out his Smith & Wesson M&P 15 and his Sig Sauer Cross rifles. He grabbed three magazines for each, loaded them, then pulled out an extra ammo box of loose rounds for each.

Lastly, he went to the nightstand in his bedroom. Under a false bottom was another safe. He put his thumb on the biometric scanner and the safe unlocked. Jackson retrieved the gun inside. It was the Beretta pistol he'd had customized, silver with black accents and a black compensator. He ran his thumb over the initials engraved on the pistol grip.

E.R.C.

Evan Randolph Clay.

In another life, Jackson had planned to give it to his son when he was old enough. That life had died with his son. Now, Jackson would use this gun to take the life of the man who had taken Evan's.

By the time Jackson got everything loaded into his truck, it was almost midday. The sleet and freezing rain had finally let up, but the smoke-gray clouds remained, darkening the earth beneath them. Jackson headed back into his cabin one last time.

On his now-empty dresser was a framed 8 x 10 photograph of Nat holding Evan as a baby. It was the only picture Jackson had in his cabin. He took it, ripped off the back of the frame, and retrieved the photo from inside. Out at his dining table, he took a marker from his pocket, and wrote on the back of the photo:

THE LAST WILL AND TESTAMENT OF JACKSON CLAY

In the event of my death, I leave EVERYTHING to ARCHIBALD "BEAR" BEAUCHAMP. He'll know what to do with it.

Below that, Jackson signed his name and dated it. He flipped the photo over in his hands. Evan and Nat smiled up at him, eternally happy, the rest of what should've been very long lives ahead of them. Jackson studied their images, then closed his eyes, trying to take the images of happy Nat and Evan and replace them with the polaroids he'd seen in Alvanitakis' garage. He turned the photo back over, leaving it with the note facing up, and wrote one last thing.

I did it all for Evan & Nat

Jackson stepped to the open front door and took one last look around. The place didn't look lived in anymore, which was fitting: For all intents and purposes, he was moving. To where, he didn't know. But he was leaving this place. Forever, if necessary.

He turned off the lights and let darkness consume the cabin. Daylight flowed in from the windows, subtly hinting at the emptiness inside. It almost reminded him of the first time he'd stepped up to his and Nat's house in Richmond. But that had been a happy day. This was anything but.

As he climbed into his truck and left the life he'd rebuilt for himself behind, Jackson realized those happy memories were all he had left now.

JACKSON SAW *Nat waiting excitedly in front of their new house as he pulled up in a rented U-Haul truck. Nat waved frantically, and Jackson couldn't help but grin. He waved back, then positioned the truck so he could parallel park into a spot out front. Nat appeared in his side view mirror, brimming with excitement. Her reflection grew bigger and bigger as he backed up. She stood there in the street with her arms folded around herself as if to hold herself back. When he was finally in the parking spot, Jackson threw the truck into Park and hopped out of the cab.*

Nat fired forward like a racehorse out of a starting gate and threw herself into him. Jackson wrapped his arms around her and kissed her.

"Hey," she whispered.

"Hey yourself," he said.

"How was the drive?"

"It was good. I made good time."

Nat looked up into his eyes with the biggest smile he'd ever seen. They held each other like that for a moment before Nat pulled away, taking Jackson by the hand and leading him around the truck. Turning to him, she gestured with her hands, presenting their house as if she had hand-built it herself.

"Well, what do you think? Isn't it cute?!"

It was an unassuming two-story row house attached to the house next to it. It was painted a faded olive green, with white trim, and had a white picket fence around a small porch.

"It's great," Jackson said, smiling.

"Come on! Let me show you inside!"

Nat hopped more than she walked down the small concrete walkway and up the three steps to the door. She opened the front door, then stepped aside for Jackson to gaze into the house's interior. The front windows opened onto a good-sized living room that stretched back into a small dining area and larger kitchen. Directly in front of him, narrow hardwood stairs ran up to a second floor overhead.

"Hello," Jackson said into the void.

His voice bounced off the empty walls and Nat giggled. She came up behind him and slipped her arms around him.

"It's perfect," she said softly.

"It's ours." Jackson turned in her arms to face her. They shared another smile and Jackson leaned down to kiss Nat on the forehead. "Come help me unload."

Nat flashed a playful grin. "What? No movers?"

She knew Jackson hated hiring help. The man hadn't met a task he hadn't first thought he could do himself.

"Why waste the money when I have a big, strong, live-in girlfriend now?"

"Ha-ha. You better pay me with something, mister. I'm no free labor."

Jackson took a box under each arm off the back of the truck and turned to her. "How about a pizza from Chanello's and a six-pack when we're done?"

Nat leaned into him, asking for another kiss. "Make it a bottle of Pinot, and you've got yourself a deal."

Jackson kissed her. "Deal."

But the pizza and wine never happened. They only got about halfway through the truck when Jackson and Nat carried in the mattress. Jackson started up the stairs, but Nat turned and brought him and the mattress into the living room. There, surrounded by boxes and bags, they collapsed onto the mattress. Shedding their clothes, Jackson climbed on top of her. Nat wrapped her arms around his neck, biting her lip as she felt him inside her. Two lovers becoming one love.

Hours later, the sun had set over the James River and brought evening to their new home, but Jackson and Nat hadn't moved. They lay there on the bare mattress, holding each other under a fleece blanket.

"Do you think the neighbors heard?" Nat asked.

"I think my neighbors back at Fort Benning heard."

Nat laughed before burying her face in his chest.

"Are you cold?"

"Always."

"I can throw some clothes on, see if I can't get the heat running."

"No, stay here with me. A little bit longer."

Jackson obliged her request. From the early death of his parents to joining the Army straight out of high school, to five combat tours abroad, he hadn't known much peace or happiness in his life. But here, holding onto Nat, lying underneath their very first roof together, he felt both.

Nat turned over, putting her back to his chest, allowing Jackson's arms to envelop her. She ran her fingers over the tattoo on his forearm. It was a shield, the Army Ranger logo, with the words 75TH RANGER RGT written across a furled banner over top.

"My Ranger," she said.

Through the thin walls and single-paned windows, they could hear the city. Cars honking, sirens wailing, dogs barking, people laughing. In that world, they'd found each other and carved out this little corner for themselves.

The world could have everything else, Jackson thought. He just wanted Nat.

Her index finger followed the path of the lightning bolt across the shield before slipping down his forearm. Her hand found its home in his and they interlocked fingers, squeezing each other. With his free hand,

Jackson grabbed the blanket and pulled it over top of them. Nathalie bit her lip, smiled again, and backed herself deeper into his chest.

"I always feel safest here," Nat said. "With your arms around me. Like nothing can hurt me."

Jackson smiled, not just at the sentiment Nat shared with him, but at her softening voice. She was getting tired, fighting fatigue. She'd toss and turn or make small talk, doing anything to try and stave off sleep, even though it was a battle she never won. She'd rather be here with him than close her eyes and dream. Jackson loved that.

"Never let me go," she said quietly. "Okay?"

"Okay."

Jackson held her as they both drifted off.

SIXTY-ONE

WHEN MOORE OPENED the door to the BCI offices and saw Cotton immediately start toward him, he knew something had happened. If Cotton's hasty gait hadn't given it away, the man's expression would have. He'd never been much of a poker player, and Moore's wallet had benefited from that fact over the years.

Cotton intercepted Moore in the main aisle between desks and turned to walk with him. "Good morning. So, get this: Archibald Beauchamp, that friend of Jackson Clay? He was stabbed last night."

Moore looked at him with surprise. "Stabbed? Where?"

Cotton double-checked the police report in his hand. "Uh, left side of his torso."

"No, I mean, where did it happen?"

"Oh, Falls Church. Last night. And guess who called 9-1-1?"

"Jackson Clay."

"Bingo."

"Do we know what the stabbing was about?"

"No, apparently Mr. Beauchamp is indisposed and Mr. Clay was rather tight-lipped about the matter with local police."

"Sounds like him. Where are they? A hospital?"

"Virginia Hospital Center, Arlington. I called over there about half an hour ago. The nurse I spoke with said Clay had been there all night but she hadn't seen him recently."

Moore nodded. "Get your coat. We're going over there."

AN HOUR AND A HALF LATER, Moore and Cotton had made their way through the drudgery of morning rush hour traffic and arrived at the hospital in Arlington. Bear had been moved from the ER and was now in the Intensive Care Unit.

When Moore and Cotton walked into the ICU, they were immediately questioned by a skeptical nurse. "Excuse me, who are you two gentlemen?"

Moore showed her his badge. "I am Special Agent Booker Moore. This is Special Agent David Cotton. State Police, ma'am. We're looking for Archibald Beauchamp."

"Mr. Beauchamp is recovering from a serious stab wound. He needs to rest. If you need to speak with him, I can ask a doctor when that might be able to happen."

"With all due respect, ma'am, we need to speak with him *now*. This is in regards to an active homicide investigation, and possibly related to his stabbing."

"Even if I let you in, he can't speak with you—he's on a ventilator. Do you understand? He has a tube down his throat. He can't talk to *anyone*."

"Can he write on something?"

The nurse glared at Moore, annoyed. Two other nurses behind computers were now watching her, and Moore gathered the one he was talking to was in some position of authority or seniority.

"Quickly," she said. "I'll be watching his vitals from the monitor in the nurse's station. If I tell you it's over, it's over."

Moore raised his hands, surrendering and accepting the nurse's terms. She led them down the hall to a hospital room and opened the door quietly. Inside, Moore and Cotton saw Beauchamp laid up in a hospital bed. Sure enough, a pair of blue tubes extended from his mouth to a ventilator beside his bed.

"Mr. Beauchamp? These two men are with the Virginia State Police," the nurse said. "They say they need to ask you a couple of questions."

Bear looked at them groggily, then pointed at the tubes coming out of his mouth.

"I know, hon. I'll get you a whiteboard. Just a sec." She handed it to him, then turned and left the room. On her way out, she chided Moore. "Two minutes."

Moore ignored her and stepped toward Bear. "Mr. Beauchamp," he said. "I am Special Agent Booker Moore, this is Special Agent David Cotton. We're with the State Police."

With one hand, the burly man scribbled a single word for Moore and Cotton.

LAWYER

Moore smiled. "Mr. Beauchamp. You go by Bear, right? Can I call you Bear? Bear, you're not in any kind of trouble. We just want to understand what happened last night. Do you know who stabbed you?"

Bear used his meaty fist to wipe away what he'd written, then wrote something else.

SUCKMA

"Suckma?" Cotton asked. "Is Suckma a person? A place?"

With his free hand, Bear pointed to his crotch.

"I think he's inviting us to fellate him," Moore explained.

Bear pointed at Moore and gave him a thumbs up.

Moore ignored him. "Bear, don't you want who stabbed you to be brought to justice?"

Again, Bear wiped his board. This time, though, he scribbled out a longer message.

U ASSHOLES ARRESTED JAX—NO HELP

Moore shook his head. "I know Jackson didn't stab you, and I don't believe he murdered Nathalie McKenna. But I need to understand what's going on here, and I have a feeling it has something to do with last night. Am I right?"

Bear stared at the man but didn't write anything down.

"Please, help us help you. Hell, help us help *Clay*. Who stabbed you last night?"

Bear looked up at the ceiling. Cotton was ready to give up and leave, but Moore realized the man was weighing whether or not to help them. After a moment, Bear wiped his whiteboard again. He began to write something, crossed that out, then wrote some more and showed it to Moore and Cotton.

GEORGE ~~ALVANI~~—ADRIEN

At that, the nurse came bursting back into the room. "Okay, you had your two minutes. Time's up."

"Just a minute, ma'am," Moore said. "We're almost—"

"I said *now*, gentlemen."

She began to herd Moore and Cotton out the door. Bear made no attempt to tell her to stop. After some more pleading, she coaxed them out of the hospital room and shut the door behind her.

"That's enough for now," she said when they were out in the hallway. "If you need to speak more, you can do so later, when he's off the vent and a doctor says it's okay."

Before either Moore or Cotton could object, she left them to tend to other matters.

Cotton turned to Moore. "What do you think he meant? George? Adrien?"

"I'm not sure," Moore said. "Nathalie McKenna had a friend, Adrien Alva, but I don't know why he would stab Bear."

"You want to go talk to him?"

"Maybe, but not just yet. Where did you say the stabbing happened?"

"Falls Church, a couple miles from here. Police report said it happened near the East Falls Church metro station."

Moore nodded along. "Let's go check it out. There's something here we're missing."

SIXTY-TWO

JACKSON STILL WASN'T sure how he was going to find Alvanitakis, but he knew the first few places he'd look. He wanted to return to the garage in Falls Church and check it again. Even if Alvanitakis wasn't there, he could see if he'd come back in the interim and cleared anything out. That might give him a clue as to what the man was planning to do next.

If the garage was a bust, Jackson would go back to Alvanitakis' apartment, but there'd be no watching from afar this time—Jackson was going in, whether Alvanitakis was there or not. And if he didn't find Alavanitakis there, well, then hopefully something in the apartment might point to where he'd gone.

Jackson was running all this through his mind when he realized his gas light was on. Come to think of it, he couldn't remember the last time he'd eaten, either. It was time to refuel on all fronts.

Getting off the interstate at Haymarket, he pulled into a Sheetz gas station. As the pump filled his truck's tank, Jackson went in and grabbed a pastrami sandwich. Eating it beside his truck, the sandwich reminded him of Bear, and how he'd looked after Jackson through ... well, everything. He hoped Bear was doing okay.

Jackson pulled out his phone and called the hospital. After being transferred a couple of times, a nurse on Bear's floor answered.

"Hello?"

"Hi, this is Jackson Clay. My friend, Bear—er, Archibald—is admitted there. I'm his emergency contact."

"Oh, yes," the nurse said. "I remember you. What can I do for you?"

"I was going to head back that way. I just wanted to call and make sure he's doing okay."

"Yes, last I checked on him he was fine and resting. If you'd like, I can have the doctor give you a call the next time he comes through with more of an update."

"I'd appreciate that, thanks."

Jackson gave the nurse his number and ended the call. The gas pump clicked off behind him. He turned, put the pump away, and closed his tank. He had just walked around to his door when he felt his phone buzz in his pocket.

That was fast, Jackson thought. But as he pulled the phone out and looked at it, he saw the number calling had a 202 area code. Washington, DC. It wasn't the hospital.

And the last person he'd talked to on a DC number was—Jackson's heart rate quickened as he answered the call.

"Jackson, it's Harry Spencer."

Jackson was too caught off guard to say anything.

"The private investigator," Spencer continued.

"Yes, sorry," Jackson said. "What's up?"

"Well, you hired me to look more into Alva. I did some digging, and I have some preliminary info. Turns out that's not his name. Or legal name, anyway. It's—"

"George Adrien Alvanitakis. I know. I'm looking for him."

"That's handy because I found him."

Jackson felt a wave of adrenaline course through him. "You found him?"

"Yes I did. As a matter of fact, I'm looking right at him. Well, the car he's in, anyway. I'm tailing him. I called to see what you wanted me to do. After all, you're the client."

Jackson's mouth twitched into a snarl. Behind his wraparound sunglasses, his eyes hardened. "Tell me where you are."

SIXTY-THREE

MOORE AND COTTON drove over to the field where Archibald Beauchamp had been stabbed. Yellow police tape flapping in the early afternoon breeze caught their attention: Officers had wrapped it around three trees surrounding the exact spot of the stabbing, forming a triangular perimeter around it.

"I don't think we need this anymore," Cotton said. He ripped away one of the strands of tape and stepped through. He crouched down. "According to the report, he was facing this way, looking at Jackson across the field, when a man came up behind him and stabbed him."

Moore stood over him, looking at the blood-stained grass. "They confirmed it was a male suspect?"

"That was about all Jackson said. Male figure he couldn't identify in the darkness."

"Bullshit."

"I know." Cotton stood up and wiped off his hands. "The interesting thing is, four minutes before Clay's call to 9-1-1, they received another call just a couple blocks from here. Someone reporting a suspicious man outside her neighbor's house."

Moore scanned their surroundings. "Which way?"

Cotton pointed beyond the dog park next to the soccer field. "Down the road we turned in on. That way."

"Sort of the same direction where Clay supposedly was."

"You think it's a coincidence?".

Moore shook his head as his phone buzzed in his pocket. "No, I do not." He looked at the phone, then answered the call. "Cap, hey, what's up?"

"Book, when were you going to tell me you ID'd the second driver in the McKenna case?" Captain House asked.

Moore's brow scrunched together as he looked at Cotton. "I'm not sure I know what you mean. We didn't ID anyone."

"I'm looking right at it, Book. Someone ran over your things from Division Seven. The guy's file was right on top with his DC DMV photo. He's a dead ringer for the guy behind the second McKenna vehicle you pulled from the traffic cams."

Cotton caught the look on Moore's face and walked over. Moore put his phone on speaker.

"What's the name of this guy?" Moore asked.

"George Adrien Alvanitakis," Captain House said.

Moore looked at Cotton as he put the pieces together. "Adrien Alva."

"What?"

"Nothing. Sir, this is news to me. Can you send me this file on Alvanitakis, including the photo?"

"Yeah, give me a minute."

"Thank you, sir." Moore ended the call. The dumbstruck look on his face remained.

"Cap is saying a George Adrien Alvanitakis is our mystery driver in the other McKenna car?" Cotton asked.

Moore nodded. "That's what he says."

"George Adrien Alvanitakis. Adrien Alva. That's a hell of another coincidence."

"I don't think either is a coincidence."

Moore's phone buzzed with an incoming email from his captain. He opened it up and scrolled to the photo of Alvanitakis.

Cotton came around and looked over his shoulder. "That's our driver."

"Yes, it is."

"So George Adrien Alvanitakis is our killer. And the man who stabbed Beauchamp."

"Yes, he is."

"You want to take a closer look at that Suspicious Person call down the road?"

"Yes, I do."

SIXTY-FOUR

JACKSON DROVE as Spencer explained everything to him, his Dodge pickup weaving in and out of traffic like a slalom skier racing downhill to the finish.

"I'm in central Virginia," Spencer was saying. "A buddy of mine at the DC DMV got his name from the address on his license. I sat on the place last night. He returned sometime after midnight, then left early this morning. He walked up to a used auto dealership on New Hampshire Avenue and drove off in an older model Volkswagen. I had my associate chat up the dealer while I watched Alvanitakis. The dealer said Alvanitakis just paid four grand in cash for the car."

"Your associate?" Jackson asked.

"Don't worry, I pay him out of my pocket."

Money was the last thing Jackson was worried about right now.

"Anyway, I've been on him ever since," Spencer continued. "He took the Beltway into southern Maryland, then kept south on 301. Now, we've crossed back into Virginia, still headed south. When it became clear he wasn't driving around town, I figured I should call you."

"He's running."

"Do you think he killed Nathalie?"

"I know he killed her. And my son."

There was a pause on the other end of the line.

"Where are you now?" Jackson asked. "Specifically."

"Southbound on 301. We just crossed over the Rappahannock River into some small town."

"I'm coming to you. Don't lose him. I don't care if he makes you or not. He does *not* get away."

"You're the boss."

Jackson zigzagged his way across Northern Virginia, cutting through Manassas and crossing over Bull Run. Every ten or fifteen minutes, he'd call Spencer back for an update. Alvanitakis was still headed south on 301. Jackson figured he was avoiding the heavily patrolled interstate.

Just north of Dumfries, Jackson caught I-95 himself. On the open six-lane highway, he pressed down on the gas and the eight-cylinder engine roared to life, some three-hundred-plus horses charging after Nat and Evan's killer.

As he neared Fredericksburg, he called Spencer again.

"We're headed west now on some small county road," Spencer said. "I'm not sure where ... wait. Hold on. There's a sign. Ladysmith is ten miles ahead."

"I know Ladysmith. It's just off of the interstate."

By the time Jackson had gotten to Ladysmith, Spencer and Alvanitakis were further along central Virginia's backroads.

Finally, near Lake Anna, Jackson caught up to them.

"Still on him," Spencer said. "We're on—"

"Route 601," Jackson interrupted. "You're in a tan Tahoe?"

"Yeah. How'd you know?"

"I'm behind you. I see him. I've got it from here."

Spencer hesitated. "Are you sure? We've got him, and you obviously got something tying him to Nathalie's murder. Maybe we give the state police his location?"

"No police. This is between him and me now. Thanks for the help. Whatever's left in Nat's rainy-day money, consider a bonus."

Jackson saw the Volkswagen sedan crest the hill up ahead.

Nothing was going to stop him now.

SPENCER RELUCTANTLY HUNG up on Jackson and pulled off the road. A moment later, his SUV was rocked as Jackson's pickup flew by, rattling the naked branches that clawed at the road on either side.

He had an uneasy feeling in his stomach, like he'd just condemned a man to death. Maybe Alvanitakis was a bad man, maybe even a very bad man, but Spencer wasn't a judge or jury, and certainly no executioner. And he couldn't escape the feeling he had just sicced Jackson on Alvanitakis. Spencer wasn't okay with that.

Looking up a phone number on his phone, he punched it in.

"State police," a voice answered.

"Yeah, hi," Spencer said. "I have some information regarding the Nathalie McKenna murder."

SIXTY-FIVE

MOORE AND COTTON drove down the road to the address where the 911 call was placed. Outside the house, a woman who looked to be in her early fifties was knocking small icicles off her porch's overhang with a broom. When Moore and Cotton stepped out of their official-looking Explorer, the woman eyed them with suspicion.

"Hello, ma'am," Moore said. "We're with the state police. We understand you saw a suspicious person last night and reported it?"

"Yes, I did," the woman said. "Right across the street there. A goddamn peeping tom. The pervert was creeping up on Mrs. Garvis there. God knows what he would've done to that poor, old woman if I hadn't seen him."

"I see. And what happened after you called?"

"I went out and yelled at him. He took off down Mrs. Garvis' driveway. She even came out to see what all the commotion was. He ran right past her."

Moore looked across the street at the house that apparently belonged to Mrs. Garvis. It was a friendly-looking house, a Craftsman-style with a detached garage at the end of the driveway that ran down the side of the house. Both the house and its garage were painted a grayish blue with white trim and had an immaculately groomed yard. Moore couldn't figure out for the life of him why Jackson Clay would be interested in such a place.

Just then, Mrs. Garvis opened the front door to her house and stepped out, watching Moore and Cotton speak to her neighbor.

"There she is," the neighbor said. "Mrs. Garvis, these men are police. They're asking about last night, with the peeping tom."

Moore rolled his eyes behind his sunglasses. He waved at Mrs. Garvis as he and Cotton crossed the street. "Hello. Mrs. Garvis, is it? We're with the state police. I hear you had some excitement last night."

"Yes, we did," she said. "Though, I barely caught any of it. But one of them did run down the driveway right past me."

Moore glanced at Cotton, then returned his attention to Mrs. Garvis. "One of them? Do you mean there was more than one?"

"Oh, yes. There were two. At least, two I saw. One ran by me toward the back there, and that's when I saw the other one. They jumped over my back fence. One right after the other. It was the darndest thing."

"Do you know what they were doing?"

"No, I just saw one after the other. Right next to the garage right there."

"I see. If you don't mind me asking, what do you keep in the garage?"

"Oh, I don't keep anything. A fella rents it from me. For storage and stuff. He comes by every once in a while. He's never been a problem. Nice, quiet guy."

Cotton stepped away and walked down the driveway, looking around. Mrs. Garvis didn't seem to mind.

"What's the renter's name?" Moore asked.

"Oh, I have it in here somewhere. I'm not great with remembering anymore. Just a minute."

"Oh, ma'am, that's—"

But Mrs. Garvis disappeared inside her house. Moore took a step back and sighed in frustration. He was taking in the front of the house, waiting for Mrs. Garvis to return, when he heard Cotton call for him.

Moore looked around the side of the house and saw Cotton by the detached garage. He waved Moore over. On the side of the garage was a door, cracked open. An unlocked padlock lay in the icy mud just in front of it.

"Here you go, officer," Mrs. Garvis said from her driveway. "I have the name."

She was slowly waddling toward them and would be there in no less than a half hour. Moore put a hand up, asking her to stop.

"That's alright, Mrs. Garvis," he said. "You stay right there."

"Is something the matter?" Mrs. Garvis asked.

"It looks as though someone might've broken into your garage back here, ma'am. We're going to make sure everything's okay."

"Oh, goodness."

Cotton and Moore unholstered their pistols and flanked the open door on either side. Moore tried to peek in, but it was dark. Cotton read his mind and retrieved a small flashlight from his belt. When Moore looked at him and nodded, Cotton kicked the door open the rest of the way and moved swiftly inside. Moore was on his hip, covering his backside.

"State police!" Cotton barked. "Anyone in here?"

Silence.

Cotton looked around briefly with his flashlight, then started searching the wall near the door for a light switch. Moore's head bumped into a metal chain hanging in the middle of the garage. He yanked at it and a light clicked on.

Moore and Cotton's jaws collectively dropped. The garage was a house of horrors like nothing either of them had ever seen. They studied the wall of polaroid photographs, taking in all the helpless-looking faces.

"You want me to call the captain?" Cotton asked.

"I want you to call *everyone*," Moore said.

SIXTY-SIX

JACKSON WATCHED the Volkswagen sedan disappear over the hill on the road ahead. He pressed the gas pedal on his truck all the way down, and the old pickup accelerated even as it climbed the steep slope. As the hill topped out, all four wheels of the truck left the pavement before slamming back down onto it, groaning under the weight of the vehicle and fishtailing before Jackson regained control.

In less than a couple miles, he'd caught up to Alvanitakis and was now squarely on his fender—so close Jackson could see him look up in his rearview mirror.

That's right, you sonofabitch, Jackson thought. I'm right here.

Now, Alvanitakis sped up, but Jackson kept with him. He pushed forward until the grill of his truck was practically on top of the Volkswagen's rear. Jackson wondered if Alvanitakis had run down Nat just like this. He accelerated once more, ready to ram the sedan off the road, but it swerved.

Alvanitakis sped off the road at an intersection, cutting across a grassy corner and taking a left onto the adjoining road. Jackson slammed on his brakes and jerked the wheel. The tail of his pickup whipped around as he tried desperately not to overshoot the turn.

He came to a stop, tires spinning before catching the pavement once more, and then he was off, barreling after Alvanitakis again.

The road narrowed, and woods encroached on either side of the rural byway. Jackson could no longer see Alvanitakis, but he knew the man was somewhere just ahead of him, and Jackson raced to catch up with him again.

Around a slow-arcing bend, the road dipped and opened up onto Lake Anna. A snug, two-lane bridge crossed a narrow stretch of the lake and connected to a skinny isthmus on the other side. It was a quarter-mile stretch of road with nowhere else to go.

Alvanitakis had just made the mistake Jackson was waiting for.

Jackson pulled out into the opposite lane as he caught back up with Alvanitakis, and Alvanitakis swerved to block him. Jackson cut back right before Alvanitakis could block him a second time and came up alongside the Volkswagen. He stuck his Beretta out the window, pointed it at Alvanitakis' front tire, and fired off a round. The tire exploded, and the sedan careened right in front of Jackson. He turned into the sedan, clipping its backside, and slammed on the brakes.

Screeching to a stop, Jackson watched as the Volkswagen smashed into a guardrail on the other side of the bridge. The car twisted violently end over end, barrel-rolling twice and landing right-side up in the middle of the road.

Jackson pulled forward, closing on the wreck quickly. In an instant, he was out of the pickup, the MP 15 he'd kept in the truck's passenger seat raised and pointed in front of him. He moved carefully around the metal carnage, circling his prey. On the other side, Alvanitakis had just about managed to climb through his driver's window. He saw Jackson, gun raised, and tumbled out onto the road, struggling to his feet.

With his hands on his knees, Alvanitakis watched Jackson. His face was covered in blood and pockmarked with tiny shards of glass.

"What's wrong?" he asked between heaping breaths. "Hoped the crash would kill me?"

"No," Jackson said. "I was counting on this."

Jackson stepped toward Alvanitakis, whipping the rifle around and slamming the butt of it into the man's temple. Alvanitakis collapsed onto the ground, an unconscious pile of meat and bones.

Slinging the MP 15 around one shoulder, Jackson lifted the lifeless Alvanitakis and threw him over his other shoulder. He carried Alvanitakis to the bed of his truck and threw him in, securing a large camping blanket over the man's limp body.

Three minutes later, the first police cruiser arrived at the scene of the accident.

But Jackson—and Alvanitakis with him—was long gone.

SIXTY-SEVEN

IN FALLS CHURCH, Columbia Street was awash in police and law enforcement activity. Criminalists were combing the garage for forensic evidence, a small army of uniformed police officers were canvassing the neighborhood, and K-9 units had even deployed cadaver dogs, looking for possible bodies on Mrs. Garvis' property. In the middle of it all, Cotton and Moore were still trying to piece everything together.

"This is insane," Cotton said, looking around.

"A regular three-ring circus," Moore agreed. "Where are we with Mrs. Garvis?"

"She ID'd George Alvanitakis as the guy who rented the garage from her. He'd used the alias Adrien Alva. She said he paid her five hundred dollars in cash every month."

"That's less than legal."

"What do you want me to say? She's an old lady. She didn't see a problem with it."

Behind them, the loud *whoomp whoomp* of a powerful siren sounded as a black SUV rolled up to the scene.

"Jesus, is that who I think it is?" Cotton asked.

"The Director of BCI," Moore said. "Direct from Richmond."

Lieutenant Colonel John Guthrie was just under six feet tall, with receding gray hair and a round face that matched his frame. A small group of assistants and fellow officers surrounded him as he cut through the crowd of first responders, making his way to Cotton and Moore.

"Lieutenant Colonel," Moore said, extending a hand. "It's good to meet you, sir."

"Pleasure, Special Agent." The director's voice was gruff. "You two are Cotton and Moore, correct? You've been leading the McKenna case."

"That's correct, sir."

Guthrie gestured at the activity surrounding them. "This is quite the party you guys throw. I just got off the phone with the FBI, offering to assist. They want to send someone from the Behavioral Analysis Unit over here."

Moore shook his head. "Sir, with all due respect, we don't need to build a profile or anything like that. We have a good idea who's behind all this. Now we need to catch him."

"So, what *do* you need?"

"Honestly? Manpower, sir. A dragnet the size of the mid-Atlantic region."

"You'll have it. From what I understand, there's about two dozen photos in there of people known missing and presumed dead. Most of them here in Virginia."

"That's correct, sir. I worked a couple of the cases myself and recognize them."

"The Superintendent had a phone call with the governor about an hour ago. He doesn't like the idea of a serial killer running around the commonwealth. We'll have whatever we need. We just need to get the bastard."

"We will, sir."

The director nodded and stepped away as someone shoved a phone into his hand. He took it and started to talk to whoever was on the other end. A minute later he was back in the black SUV and being whisked away just as quickly as he arrived. As soon as the sirens faded into the distance, Moore heard his name being shouted behind him.

"Book, Book!"

Moore turned to see Special Agent Bailey trying to navigate the crowd.

"Bailey, what are you doing here?" Moore asked.

"I'm here for Clay," Bailey said.

Cotton's phone buzzed in his pocket and he stepped away to answer it.

"I know Clay didn't do it, Bailey," Moore said. "It was George Alvanitakis, a friend of Nathalie McKenna. Well, not much of a friend, apparently."

"Yeah, I know," Bailey said. "I put his file with your stuff at Division Two."

Moore stared at her. "*You.* You're why my captain called asking when we had ID'd Alvanitakis."

"I don't know about all that, but you've got a bigger problem."

"Bigger than a serial killer?"

"Yes. Clay."

"Why's he a problem?"

"Do you know where he is?"

Moore was about to dismiss her worries as paranoia when he realized the man had been curiously absent in all the recent drama: Clay hadn't been at the hospital, and he wasn't out here bothering any of them. Moore's lips curled into a worried frown.

"We've got the entire state looking for Alvanitakis," he said. "It's an army of cops versus one person."

"And that one person is Jackson Clay," Bailey said.

Moore fell quiet.

"Let me help you, Moore. Let me in on this. I know him. I can help."

Moore said nothing.

"Seriously, Book. Don't keep me on the bench here. Put me in the game."

"Fine, but no more stuff behind my back. From now on, I know everything you know."

Bailey nodded. Cotton ended his call and turned back to the two of them. He saw Moore and Bailey locking eyes and wondered what he'd missed.

"Everything okay here?" Cotton asked.

"Special Agent Bailey here thinks Jackson Clay has a head start on us hunting down Alvanitakis," Moore said. "She's going to help us find both of them."

"Funny you mention that," Cotton said. "That was the office. A private investigator named Harry Spencer called in a tip. He said Alvanitakis paid cash for a car in DC and headed down here into Virginia, last seen west of a small town called Ladysmith. The car is a 2003 Volkswagen Passat, fresco green with DC temp tags. And guess what? The Spotsylvania County Sheriff's Office just reported a suspicious crash at Lake Anna. Older model Passat, green, with DC temp tags. The car looked like it had flipped several times. There was no one with it when deputies rolled up."

Bailey broke eyes with Moore and looked at Cotton. "Jesus. It's Clay. Clay found Alvanitakis. Clay has him."

"We don't know that," Moore said.

"What else would it be? It's Clay, and you know it."

"We need to get to Spotsylvania. Fast."

Cotton pulled his phone back out and started punching in a number. "All these agencies ... I'll see if we have a bird nearby."

Seven minutes later, a state police helicopter landed in the field just feet from where Archibald Beauchamp had been stabbed. The three special agents jogged over to it and climbed in. As the helicopter took off and the scene on Columbia Street shrunk below them, Bailey looked out at the horizon. The rest of Virginia seemed to extend on forever.

Clay was somewhere out there, and she knew she had to save him. But not from Alvanitakis.

From himself.

SIXTY-EIGHT

JACKSON MADE HIS WAY SOUTHEAST, avoiding highways and following the main body of Lake Anna. Not only were highways more likely to be patrolled, but a groggy Alvanitakis coming-to in the middle of traffic was the last thing he needed.

He hadn't lied to Alvanitakis right before striking him with the butt of his rifle. He hadn't wanted the crash to kill the man. He wanted *this*. To bring Alvanitakis to *this* moment. Simply killing him would've been punishment without justice. Jackson wanted both.

The winding state road snaked its way through the lake region, cutting through thick woodlands before opening up and darting across one of the lake's many fingers, only to dive back into the trees on the other side.

As Jackson drove further, the shadows got longer. He'd been awake for more than thirty hours. Mentally, he was sharp, but fatigue was setting into his body. He wasn't in his twenties anymore, humping miles through the mountains of Kandahar. His body craved rest—and rest in one form or another would come—but not yet. He needed to finish this first.

Half an hour later, Jackson had left the lake region in his rear view but continued on down the state road. It took him through one small town after another. Places only people who lived nearby knew of. Bumpass. Beaverdam. And then, Doswell.

He was nearly there.

On the other side of Doswell, he took a small road over the interstate, the same road he and Bear had driven down just a few days earlier. The road pointed at the vast parking lot ahead before turning for the main gate. The gates were blocked by rubber cones. Jackson ignored them and ran them over, blowing through the gate. He made a sharp U-turn and headed for the entrance.

The skeletal skyline of Kings Dominion lay ahead.

BAILEY WATCHED THE SUN, low in the sky, as they flew into the heart of Virginia. The pilot had informed them they'd be at the Lake Anna crash scene in forty minutes. She prayed it was enough time.

Moore and Cotton spent most of the flight trying to coordinate with various agencies, getting resources and manpower into the area. As Cotton punched away on his phone, he stopped and showed something to Moore. Moore nodded to Bailey. Cotton reached over and got her attention.

"This just came in from Spotsylvania County," he said through his headset. "A black pickup was seen speeding away from the area of the wrecked Passat within minutes of the 911 call."

Bailey looked at Moore.

"Clay," Moore said.

"I told you," Bailey said.

"Well, what's he doing? Where's he going with Alvanitakis?"

"I don't know."

"You wanted in on this because you knew Clay. Well, this is Clay."

Bailey turned back to the window and closed her eyes, trying to think. She had two colleagues looking at her, expectant, with a helicopter engine roaring overhead. It was impossible.

"I need a map," she said. "Do we have a map or something in here?"

The co-pilot of the helicopter reached into a compartment and handed her a thick booklet.

"Road atlas for the state," he explained. "Don't lose it. We have it up here to reference when we need to."

Bailey took the atlas and flipped to the pages showing central Virginia. Lake Anna lay to the west, halfway between Fredericksburg and Richmond. There was nothing really except rural country until Charlottesville on the other side.

"Maybe he's just taking him into the woods somewhere," Moore suggested. "Work him over, then kill him."

"No, that's not Clay," Bailey said. "He's deliberate, methodical. Whatever he does, he does for a reason."

Moore reached over and put his finger on the yellow blotch labeled Richmond. "Didn't Clay live in Richmond with Nathalie McKenna? Maybe he's taking him back there."

"Maybe, but where? Their old place would almost certainly have people living in it. He'd have to figure that."

Maybe was good enough for Moore. He turned to Cotton. "Get in contact with Richmond PD. Tell them we have reason to believe Clay, with Alvanitakis, is coming their way. Notify headquarters down there and have them assist. I want the major arteries lined with troopers."

Bailey slid her hand over the map. Richmond made some sense, but not a lot. There had to be another answer. A better one. She ran her pointer finger in concentric circles around Lake Anna. Two laps around, her finger swooped across the word Doswell. She stopped.

"Oh my god," she said.

"What is it?" Moore asked.

She turned the map toward him, still pointing. "Nathalie's photo wasn't the only one in that garage Clay knew. There was his son, too. Evan. He was taken from Kings Dominion. *By* Alvanitakis."

Moore turned back to Cotton. "Who covers Kings Dominion?"

"Hanover County Sheriff," Cotton said.

"I want whatever they have over to the park right now."

Cotton nodded and got to work on his phone again.

Moore leaned forward and got the attention of the two pilots. "Forget the crash scene," he said. "We're going direct to Kings Dominion."

SIXTY-NINE

ALVANITAKIS CAME BACK TO CONSCIOUSNESS, lying flat on his back. Above him, an array of stuffed animals looked down, absent smiles on their cartoonish faces. He shifted his weight. He was on top of something hard and unforgiving. He turned and looked over to his left. There was some sort of booth or stall directly next to him. And beyond that, Jackson Clay.

Jackson sat on a bench, watching Alvanitakis. His face was emotionless, almost as if the man in front of him didn't register as human. In his hand, he held a large hammer. It looked to Alvanitakis like a sledgehammer, but different. Less menacing, in a way. Though, admittedly, it was plenty menacing in Jackson's hands.

"Do you know where we are?" Jackson asked.

His voice was low and steely cold. Alvanitakis took in his surroundings.

"Kings Dominion," Jackson said. He stood now and approached Alvanitakis from across a strip of paved walkway, dragging the hammer alongside him. "I'm surprised you don't recognize it. After all, you used to work here, didn't you? Or, at least, you dressed the part."

Alvanitakis tried to sit up, but couldn't. He could feel now his arms and legs were shackled down. He tried to look over the paunch of his belly at his feet.

"Fifteen years ago," Jackson continued, "I brought my family here. My whole, complete, *happy* family." He nodded over his left shoulder. "My wife, Nat, rode the Ferris wheel over there. My son and I were watching her when he disappeared."

Alvanitakis' gaze shifted from Jackson down to the hammer. Jackson brought the hammer around in front of him, letting its head hit the pavement with a *clunk*.

"When you *took him* from us," Jackson growled.

He waited for Alvanitakis to say something, but he didn't. He lay there, shifting his gaze between Jackson and the hammer, trying earnestly to wrestle his limbs free. Jackson imagined Alvanitakis' mind was churning, calculating how he'd escape all this.

Good, he thought. Let him put up a fight.

"Losing Evan broke us," Jackson said. "It destroyed our marriage. But that wasn't enough, was it? All this time later, you had to take *her*, too." He turned and sat down on the booth between him and Alvanitakis, angling himself so that he could take in the empty park grounds around them. "This was the beginning of the end, right here. I lost everything here."

Alvanitakis continued to squirm, still trying in vain to snake out of the restraints. Jackson knew his efforts were futile.

"You know what was the last thing we did before you took everything from me?" Jackson asked. "We played this game, here."

Jackson stood now and turned to face Alvanitakis. He flicked a switch behind the booth and everything came to life in a brilliant display of flashing lights and cheery music. "Evan loved these carny games." He lifted the hammer and dropped its heavy head on the booth's tabletop. "You like to play games, too, George. Befriending Nat, the mother of the boy you killed. Giving her a false sense of security before killing her as well. Lying to everyone about who you really are. Lying to *me*, acting like you cared about Nat. That you wanted to see her killer pay for what he did. But it was *you*. It was you all along."

Alvanitakis stopped moving. Jackson's words seemed to paralyze him. Jackson lifted his leg and put one of his boots on the booth and leaned forward. The lights overhead danced around him.

"What do you say we play one last game, George?"

THE HELICOPTER SET down on the large, empty parking lot in front of Kings Dominion. Moore, Cotton, and Bailey trotted out from underneath it, covering their heads. As soon as they were clear, the helicopter took off again. The three special agents shielded themselves from the rotor wash, their windbreakers whipping in the gale.

When the helicopter was gone, a uniformed sheriff's deputy jogged over to them. "You must be the state agents. We're getting everyone here as fast as we can. The first units on scene drove the perimeter. They spotted your black pickup near the employee parking lot."

Moore looked at Bailey.

"My god," she said. "He's really here."

"The call went out a half-hour ago," Moore said, turning back to the deputy and pointing at the small mass of officers and vehicles in front of them. "This is all you have so far?"

"We've got almost double what you see," the deputy said. "We're working to establish a perimeter. It's a large place."

Moore shook his head. "We don't need containment. This guy isn't interested in running. He's got what he wants. We need everyone we can get to sweep this place and find him."

"You want me to bring the guys on the perimeter in?"

"No, just get everyone else here to the front. Now."

The deputy nodded and stepped away, relaying orders over his radio. As he did, a dark blue SUV came up and joined the police vehicles out front. A man in jeans and a polo shirt stepped out and attached a holstered pistol to his belt. He walked over to Moore, Cotton, and Bailey and extended a hand.

"Shawn Flynn," he greeted them. "I'm the officer-in-charge for the county Crisis Negotiation Team."

"Sorry to call you in on your day off," Moore said, referring to the man's clothing.

"Well, I heard we've got a bona fide serial killer in town. That's more exciting than grocery shopping, that's for sure."

Moore nodded.

"Anyway," Flynn continued, "the rest of my team should be here soon, and we've got our High-Risk Entry Team being called up as well. What's the plan?"

Another man in off-day attire came around to them and placed a large map on the hood of Flynn's SUV. It was a layout of the theme park. Flynn called all the officers nearby over.

"Okay," Moore said, getting his bearings. "We've likely got two people somewhere on the grounds of the park. One is George Adrien Alvanitakis. We have an arrest warrant in his name for the murder of Nathalie McKenna. Based on new evidence, he has likely also killed several other people over a timespan stretching years. The second person is Jackson Clay. He is the ex-husband of Nathalie McKenna. It's also suspected now that Alvanitakis killed Clay's toddler son some years ago. We believe Clay has taken Alvanitakis, abducted from a car in Spotsylvania County, and brought him here. For what reason, we are not sure, but obviously, our worry is that Clay means to kill Alvanitakis."

"Good, let him off the asshole," an officer said.

Moore shot him a scornful look.

"Wasting time here," Bailey said.

"Yes," Moore continued. "We need to sweep the park, locate Alvanitakis and Clay, and deescalate whatever situation is taking place. Flynn, your team and the High-Risk Entry Team take point. We'll fan out, cover this, the north or front side of the park, and work our way south to the back side. Assume Clay is armed, so be careful out there. Everyone goes home at the end of this."

"Tactical Team from Richmond is here," Cotton said over Moore's shoulder.

Moore turned and saw men in full tactical gear disembarking from a large olive-green armored vehicle. "Okay, good. They can run point with HRET." He turned back to the group of officers around him. "Any questions?"

No one said anything.

"Alright," Moore said. "Let's go."

JACKSON POINTED at something above Alvanitakis. "Have you ever played this before?"

Red lines painted at even intervals and labeled with ascending numbers straddled a metal bar all the way to the top, where it connected to a bell. Suddenly, Alvanitakis understood what the large hammer Jackson held was for.

"It's called the high striker," Jackson said. He swung one foot after the other over the booth's counter and stepped up to Alvanitakis' lower half. "Most people think it's all about strength, but strength will only get you so far. Really, the key is all about momentum."

In one swift motion, Jackson brought the hammer behind him and swung it over his head, bringing it down and striking Alvanitakis' lower leg strapped to the lever. A loud crack, like a tree branch snapping, filled the quiet around them before Alvanitakis screamed out in pain. The puck on the metal bar barely lurched up a foot before dropping back down.

"It's all about how efficiently you can take your strength," Jackson hissed, "and bring it to strike the target in front of you." He reset his stance, bringing the hammer back before thrusting it down onto Alvanitakis' leg a second time. The man howled in agony again. "I saw the police report on Nat's crash. The way you sent her car flying off the road into that tree. You broke her leg just like this."

He brought the hammer back and swung a third time. Then a fourth time. Shards of broken bone began to break the skin, leaving a bloody pulp on the lever. Each time Jackson swung, the puck got a little higher with less and less of Alvanitakis to stop it.

"Because it was *you*! You all along," Jackson seethed. "Not just Nat. But my son, too."

Jackson swung again, nearly severing the leg altogether. Alvanitakis screamed again, but then it changed. His shoulders were bouncing in rhythm with his stomach, and Jackson realized the man was laughing.

"You," Alvanitakis said. "You ruined all the fun."

Jackson swung again and severed the leg. Alvanitakis only laughed harder. Jackson thought it might've been shock, but he wasn't sure.

"*Fun*?!" Jackson yelled.

"Yes," Alvanitakis said. "Fun. Do ... do you know how amazing it was? To listen to that dumb bitch cry about her dumbass son? Begging for whoever took him to bring him back? Not ... not knowing the whole time he was right across from her. Staring her in the eye."

He laughed again. Jackson stomped down on what remained of Alvanitakis' leg and the laugh devolved back into a caterwaul. Alvanitakis looked down and watched as Jackson undid the shackle on the severed leg, tossed the limb aside, and moved his other leg into position.

"Are you ready for round two?" Jackson hissed.

"She didn't have a clue," Alvanitakis said. "The dumb bitch didn't have a goddamn clue."

Jackson came over the top of his head and brought the hammer down on the other leg. It broke with the same sickly crack as the first. Alvanitakis' laugh became almost maniacal.

"Why'd you do it?!" Jackson shouted. "I want to know why!"

"It's all that idiot's fault," Alvanitakis said, trying to catch his breath. "Jeffers. That dumb fuck had to go and find god or whatever."

"You killed Nat because of Dale Jeffers?"

"No. I killed her because of you."

The words hit Jackson squarely in the chest as if Alvanitakis had a hammer of his own. He took a step back, righting himself. His brain couldn't form the words to ask for more, but Alvanitakis saw it on his face.

"I knew. I'd heard enough about you," Alvanitakis said. "She ... she had told me enough for me to know. If you got involved, it would only be a matter of time. I tried to tell her not to. But the dumb bitch wouldn't listen." He shrugged matter-of-factly. His grimace turned into a sly and unapologetic grin. "I had to do it."

Jackson lost control. He began wailing down furiously with the mallet. His strikes were errant, wild, but they did just as much damage anyway. A blow to Alvanitakis' knee. His hand. His hip. Several to the groin. Alvanitakis shook madly, laughing and screaming.

"Why?!" Jackson shouted. "And why Evan?! What did my little boy ever do to you?!"

Alvanitakis began to spit up blood. He turned his head, trying to let oxygen in. Jackson watched his eyes roll back, and he thought for a moment the man might finally pass out from the pain. He took the hammer and pressed its head down on Alvanitakis' severed leg to shock him back into consciousness.

"Why?" Alvanitakis said.

Jackson thought the man was now mocking him, and he started to load another swing when Alvanitakis said more in between spits of blood.

"Why ... why does anything kill?"

Jackson didn't answer him, not understanding.

"*Because*," Alvanitakis said. "Because it's hungry. Because there's a hunger. And it has to kill."

That was it. His explanation as to why he'd killed Evan, why he'd derailed Jackson's life and taken everything from him, was as simple as that. He did it *because he could*. Because he *wanted* to. That was it.

Jackson knew he didn't need to hear anything more.

He reached into the waist of his jeans and pulled out his Beretta. The Beretta with Evan's initials on it. The one he'd planned to give his son someday. The one he'd now promised himself would end the life of the man who'd taken Evan from him.

Jackson switched the safety off and pointed the pistol at Alvanitakis' head, prepared to deal the monster one final blow.

But the first officer in tactical gear stepped into view.

BAILEY AND MOORE moved down the main drag of the theme park together. Ahead of them were members of the state police tactical team. Cotton had gone with a separate unit and branched off to their left.

The empty park was eerie. International Street, designed to look like a worldly plaza or bazaar, was instead a ghost town. A large reflecting pool to their right, normally filled with fountains shooting water several feet in the air, lay dormant.

"Check these shops for any sign of a break-in," Moore said to the tactical team.

Two officers moved away and started checking doors.

"Alright, Bailey," he said quietly. "You're the Clay expert. Where is he?"

"I don't know," Bailey said.

"You know the man. If we're here because of his kid, where was his kid taken in the park?"

Bailey tried to think. If she had ever known those details, she couldn't recall them now. On the other side of International Street was the park's rendition of the Eiffel Tower. Around it, the park branched off in all directions.

"Could he be up there?" Moore asked, looking at the top of the tower.

"Negative. The bottom is secure, sir," a tactical officer said.

"Alright, we've got a lot of ground to cover and three ways to go. Let's divide and conquer. If you find Clay or Alvanitakis, radio it in."

The tactical team divided itself into three groups. Bailey saw a large sign labeled *Planet Snoopy* and thought it as good a guess as any.

She turned to Moore. "I'm taking left. Right is the far side of the park. Why don't you take middle?"

"Bullshit," Moore said. "You're staying on my hip."

"Well, I'm going left."

"Then so am I."

Bailey, Moore, and two officers flanked that way. As they moved into the kid-centric part of the park, they could see the tops of a roller coaster and the drop tower in the distance.

"Can we get on top of one of these rides?" Moore asked. "Get a vantage point over top?"

One of the tactical officers began to call in the request on his radio when the foursome heard a blood-curdling scream in the distance.

"Shit, was that one of them?" the officer asked.

"It came from over there," Bailey said. "North, northeast."

They picked up their pace, trotting past several kiddy rides and coming out onto what looked to be another main thoroughfare through the park. They heard a second scream.

Moore radioed it in. "Screams coming from near our end of the park," he said as they broke into a jog. "Somewhere east of the drop tower. Use it for reference."

A staticky voice came back a moment later. "I have a visual. Jackson Clay and George Alvanitakis. Clay has a weapon. Looks like a large hammer or mallet. He's assaulting Alvanitakis."

Bailey and Moore broke out into a dead sprint with the two tactical team members.

"Where?" Moore barked into his radio. "I need a location! Give me a location."

"Southwest of the Ferris wheel. Between it and the drop tower. Clay has Alvanitakis in one of those game stalls."

Bailey saw the top of the Ferris wheel. "Jesus, they must be dead ahead."

She ran as hard as she could, her pistol drawn and her feet thumping in rhythm with her heart. Every second felt like minutes. Hours. Get there, Jen, she said to herself, get there.

"Gun! Gun!" the officer said over the radio. "Clay has a gun. He's pointing it at Alvanitakis."

Two more tactical officers came from Moore and Bailey's right, also running. When they were about fifty feet ahead, the officers raised their guns. Bailey felt her heart lurch into her throat.

"Police! Drop the gun!" one of the tactical officers shouted.

Bailey covered the remaining distance in a matter of seconds. Coming around the side of the officers, she finally saw what they saw. A battered and bleeding Alvanitakis lay on top of some sort of carnival game a few feet off the ground. Clay was standing over him, pointing a pistol at his head.

"Everyone back!" Clay shouted. "I'll shoot him!"

SEVENTY

JACKSON WATCHED the officers spread out around him, making sure not to be in each other's line of fire in case they had to shoot. It didn't matter that George Alvanitakis was a monster, a sociopathic serial killer that had preyed on Jackson's loved ones and countless others like them. Here, in this moment, he was the man with the weapon. He was the danger. And he knew they'd use lethal force to stop him if necessary.

"I mean it," Jackson said. "Back up. *Now*. I'll shoot this man."

"We can't let you do that, Jackson."

Jackson turned to see a man in a polo shirt standing behind two heavily-armed officers. The man must've been the only officer there not pointing a gun at him.

"Let me guess," Jackson said. "You're the crisis negotiator."

"That's right," the man said. "My name is Shawn Flynn. I'm with the Hanover County Sheriff's Office. So, let's talk about what we can do to help you."

"Walk away. I've got this handled."

"Jackson, you know we can't do that."

Flynn's answer agitated Jackson. He squeezed the pistol grip harder. "Do you know what this man has done? To me? To others?"

"I have some idea, yes," Flynn said. "He killed your ex-wife. And probably your son, too."

"He *did* kill Evan!" Jackson could see he was making the tactical officers nervous. A couple were keying the mics on their radios, talking to one another. "He told me himself. He killed Evan. And Nat. And he's killed others. He doesn't get to do that and live."

Flynn tried to make his voice as calm as possible. "Jackson, you don't want to shoot him. We know he killed your loved ones. He'll be brought to justice for what he's done."

"What justice? A trial? Lawyers? Years of appeals? All the while he gets three meals a day and a roof over his head. No. He doesn't deserve that."

"That's justice, Clay."

"No. I'll hold him here, keep us all here, until he bleeds out."

"Jackson, let's not do anything we can't undo here."

Bailey felt their conversation stalling out. Flynn wasn't getting through to Jackson. Jackson needed a friendly face. Someone he could believe understood the kind of pain he was in. Holstering her pistol, she jogged around the semicircle of police officers to come up behind Flynn. There, she slid her way past him and the officers in front of him. They tried to keep her back, but she shrugged them off.

"Clay, it's me," she said.

"Bailey?" Jackson said. "What are you doing here?"

"Making sure you don't do something you'll regret."

"You think I'll regret killing someone like him?"

"Yes ... I do."

"Then you clearly don't know me as well as I thought you did."

Jackson took a step toward Alvanitakis and the officers, in turn, took a step closer toward him.

"Don't do it, sir!" one of the tactical officers shouted over Bailey's shoulder.

Jackson looked at him. Bailey stepped in front of the officer and forced Jackson to look at her instead.

"Clay!" she shouted.

Jackson stopped and looked at her. Hearing the desperation in her voice, it gave him pause.

"This isn't you," she said.

"You don't think I've killed before? Taken garbage like him off this earth before?"

"Not like this, you haven't. Maybe when others gave you no choice, but look at him, Clay. He's defenseless. And bleeding out. He's done. He's not going to hurt anyone. Not anymore. You won't be saving anyone. You'll just be killing him."

Jackson shook his head. "He doesn't get to do what he did and live, Bailey.".

"Remember Dale Jeffers."

"What about him?"

"You wanted to kill him, too. For what he did to Evan. Or, what you thought he did to Evan at the time. And you went to his house, ready to kill him. But you didn't, Clay. You didn't kill him. What happened?"

Jackson didn't say anything.

"You found that little boy. In the closet, right? You found him, and you couldn't bring yourself to kill Jeffers in front of that boy."

"What's your point, Bailey?"

"Not killing Jeffers in front of that boy gave you a second chance. You thought your world had ended when you lost Evan, but you found a reason to go on. You can do it again, Clay. Let Alvanitakis face justice for his crimes. *Real* justice. Not vengeance. Not this."

"Look around you, Bailey. Do you see anyone needing saving? Do you see any little boy watching?"

"Evan is watching right now, Clay. He's watching *you*. Nathalie, too. They're watching you *right now*. So, can you do it, Clay? Can you put Alvanitakis down with Evan and Nat watching?"

Jackson pictured Evan and Nat there, standing just off to the side of the officers. Evan looked at him confused, unsure of what his daddy was doing. Why he looked so angry. Nat stood behind Evan, her hands on his shoulders. A tear formed in the corner of her eye as her lips trembled. She didn't say anything but watched on with worry.

Seeing them there, imagining them witnessing all this, Jackson's gun became an unbearable weight in his hand. He had held onto his anger with a vice-like grip from the moment Bailey had called him, half informing him of Nathalie's death, half questioning him if he'd had anything to do with it. It had swelled with each passing day, from learning about Dale Jeffers' confession to meeting Brad McKenna, to ultimately finding the truth about the man who had gone by the name Adrien Alva. Now, that anger was an impossible weight sitting squarely on his shoulders.

Jackson was ready to let go.

Bailey saw this in his face. She took a couple of steps toward him. When she spoke again, her voice was soft. "It's over, Clay. Put the gun down."

Jackson knew she was right. George Alvanitakis would meet his maker someday, but it wouldn't be at Jackson's hands. Collapsing to his knees, emotion overcame him. Bailey walked over and knelt in front of him. She took the pistol out of his hand and placed it on the ground beside them. As the police officers rushed in, securing the scene, Bailey leaned forward and put her arms around Jackson.

"You did the right thing, Clay," she whispered in his ear.

Over her shoulder, Jackson could see police and paramedics tending to Alvanitakis, working to stabilize him. To save him. It was a grace he didn't deserve.

"It doesn't feel like it," Jackson said.

"I know," Bailey said. "It never does."

SEVENTY-ONE

JACKSON SAT ON THE CURB, handcuffed, in front of the park's main entrance. The sun had dipped beneath the skyline, covering the vast, paved plains in darkness as the twilight of dusk lingered overhead. This long day was finally ending. And, perhaps, the nightmare that had come with it.

He watched as, across the way, Alvanitakis was rushed to a medevac helicopter. As soon as the doors were closed, it took off, rising high into the cerulean sky above before turning and chasing the sunset. Bailey stood talking with two other men in state police windbreakers when she, too, watched the helicopter depart. As it disappeared behind Jackson, she walked over and sat down on the curb next to him.

"Is he going to make it?" Jackson asked.

"It's touch and go right now," Bailey said. "You really did a number to him."

"He deserved it and more."

"I won't argue with you there."

The two allowed a quiet to come over them as they watched the scene splayed out before them. The short-lived hunt for a serial killer followed by a hostage situation had drawn in a large police presence. Now, on the other side of it all, the first news trucks began to arrive.

"So, what happens to me now?" Jackson asked.

"They're deciding where to transport you. Jurisdictional bickering over who officially books you."

"No, I meant beyond that."

"Well, big picture? You've got some things to answer for."

Jackson nodded. "How bad, you think?"

"Probably depends on what doctors can do with Alvanitakis. I'm not the Commonwealth's Attorney, but I imagine kidnapping? Malicious wounding? If he doesn't make it …"

"Murder."

"Possibly. But more likely manslaughter."

Jackson, again, nodded.

"But I wouldn't worry too much. No one's going to be lining up to throw the book at a grieving father and ex-husband. Not when they learn what Alvanitakis did."

"I'm not worried about me."

Bailey sighed. "You rarely are."

She stood, wiping the dirt from her backside. Jackson looked up at her.

"Do me a favor?" he asked.

"Shoot."

"Make sure Bear is okay. That he gets home alright and gets everything he needs."

"I will."

Jackson looked down at the ground. "Thanks."

Bailey folded her arms and put one foot up on the curb. "I know it doesn't seem like it now, but you're going to be alright."

"I know."

"You'll find your way back from this."

Jackson didn't say anything.

"You're good at that. Finding things."

Jackson's shoulders lurched, and he snorted. He looked back up at Bailey. "Thank you, Bailey. For everything."

Smiling softly, she nodded. "I'll be in touch."

Twenty minutes later, Jackson was in the back of a Hanover Sheriff's patrol car, being driven to the regional jail to be booked. They had won the squabble over custody. An older deputy was behind the wheel. He had silver hair and a clean-shaven face. Jackson guessed the man was in his late fifties or early sixties.

As they headed down the road, they drove by the campground next to the park. Jackson saw the old woman who worked there with her pickup truck and recalled her telling him about the park police officer who'd escorted the boy away. He wondered now if that had been Evan, preyed upon by Alvanitakis in one of his many disguises. He'd never know for sure. Some truths had been lost to time.

As they came to a red light, the deputy glanced back at Jackson. Jackson met his eyes.

"You messed up that man pretty good by the sound of it," the deputy said.

"He killed my young son and my ex-wife," Jackson said. "What would you do?"

"Between you and me, I'd have finished the job."

Jackson didn't say anything back. A part of him still wished he had.

The deputy turned forward as the light turned green. "I'm sorry for your losses, though. For what it's worth."

"Thanks."

"Must've really loved your boy to do all this. Your ex-missus, too."

"I did."

"Where'd y'all meet?"

A warm feeling came over Jackson, thinking about the question. It started in his chest and rose until the smallest of smiles formed on his face. "A baseball game."

The deputy went on, asking questions and telling Jackson about how he met his wife, but Jackson wasn't listening. Even with Alvanitakis found, there was no bringing Evan or Nat back. That was something he'd have to learn to live with. He'd done it before. He hoped he could do it again. The happy memories helped. Like the day Evan was born. And the day Jackson and Nat got married.

And one night, almost twenty years ago, at a minor league baseball game.

"STRIKE THREE!" *the home plate umpire bellowed.*

Jackson and a group of his Ranger buddies threw their arms up in frustration.

"The game started at seven, blue, wake up!" Ramirez shouted.

The rest of them laughed. It was a warm, muggy Norfolk night in mid-May. Ramirez had convinced the lot of them to come up for the game. A lifelong Mets fan, he wanted to see a promising, young kid named David Wright who'd been called up to the Norfolk Tides. The potential for a bar scrap with some Navy boys convinced those less interested in baseball to tag along.

Now, though, Ramirez was indignant as the young Wright got rung up on strikes. He polished off the rest of his beer and crushed the can in frustration.

"Horse shit," he said. "Whatever. I'm getting a couple more. You guys want any?"

"Yeah, get me one," Jackson said.

"We'll come with you," their friend, Johnson, said.

Jackson stood up and let the others scoot out of the row. When they were gone, he had a handful of seats on either side of him to himself. He stretched his arms out, taking advantage of the extra space. He wasn't much of a baseball fan if he were being perfectly honest, but there was something relaxing about sitting in a ballpark on a warm night and taking in the game.

The next batter up swung at a fastball and clipped it, propelling the ball upwards like a mortar shell before it lost momentum and came careening back toward the stadium. Almost immediately, Jackson could tell it was coming into his section. Instinctively, he stood, watching the ball, ready to try and catch it. He moved slowly to his left, stalking it the way an outfielder gets under a pop fly. And when the ball came plummeting down within arm's reach, Jackson reached out and plucked it with one hand.

A woman screamed and Jackson realized then he had reached in front of her. She had her back turned, shielding herself from the ball's impact. Not only had he caught the foul ball, but he'd also stopped it from beaning the young lady.

Turning around, she locked eyes with Jackson. A couple of fans around them cheered, applauding the impressive catch. The woman smiled shyly, tucking her long, auburn hair back behind her ear.

"Thank you," she said. "I guess you saved me."

Jackson couldn't help but smile back at her. "I guess so."

An awkward pause began to form between them before the woman, thinking of something to say, jutted her hand out.

"I'm Nathalie."

"I'm Clay. Well, Jackson, actually. Sorry. Jackson Clay."

Nathalie giggled at Jackson stumbling over his words. "Well, thank you, again, Jackson Clay."

Jackson's sheepish smile hung on his face. "Not a problem."

"Do you make a habit of this? Saving girls at baseball games?"

"Ah, no. This is a first for me."

"So, I'm something special then?"

Jackson laughed. "Yes, you are."

"So, if I gave you my number, Jackson Clay, would you answer if I needed saving again?"

Jackson's mouth couldn't find the words to answer. His head bobbled in a nod.

Nathalie fetched a pen out of her purse and wrote her phone number on Jackson's forearm. "I'm going to hold you to that, Jackson Clay."

He looked down at his arm and then back at her. He'd seen beautiful women before, but there was something about her. Nathalie. A feeling she gave him. He couldn't describe it, but in that moment, he knew he'd do whatever it took not to lose it. As they locked eyes again, his smile widened.

"It's a promise," Jackson said.

Continue the story in *Happyland* and order your copy now, or keep reading for a sneak peek!
amazon.com/B0DV9YDM8Y

Join the B.C. Lienesch reader family and stay up to date on all the latest news!
https://www.bclnovels.com/newsletter

HAPPYLAND: CHAPTER 1

SPECIAL AGENT JEN BAILEY clenched the cold alloy frame of her service weapon in her hand. Resting her palm on the grip was a habit dating all the way back to her days as a trooper clocking speeders on Interstate 81. Now, she rode shotgun in one of the Bureau of Criminal Investigations unmarked Explorers, a part of a very different operation.

She looked down at the maps app on her phone in her other hand. Seventeen minutes away. The man driving the Explorer, John Pitts. Tall and broad-shouldered with short, salt-and-pepper hair, he looked over at her and grinned at her restlessness.

"Everything still good from when you last checked thirty seconds ago?" he asked.

Bailey ignored his remark. Pitts was a capable agent, but his true expertise was finding ways to get under Bailey's skin. They'd worked together ever since she'd joined the department's Human Trafficking Unit a year ago. In that span, she'd found the number of times she'd wanted to punch him and the number of times she'd wanted to buy him a beer about even. This latest quip might have just put the "punch him" desire ahead by a nose, though.

She was studying their progress on the app when her phone buzzed with an incoming call. She felt her heart lurch into her throat as she read the Caller ID.

Josephine

Bailey tapped the icon to answer the call. "Kristal, what is it?"

Kristal Hardy had unknowingly solicited herself to an undercover special agent in an apartment in Front Royal, Virginia seven months ago. Now, she was known to the Human Trafficking Unit as Josephine — a handle Bailey gave her from Josephine Bakhita, the patron saint of human trafficking victims — in an effort to conceal the fact she was now cooperating with them.

"Bailey! You've got to help me!" Kristal said in between labored breaths. "Something is wrong. Something is very, very wrong. They know!"

Bailey shifted with alarm in her seat. "Okay, just hold on," she said. "We're on our way right now." She motioned for Pitts to drive faster.

"It's not going to be fast enough!"

"It is, Kristal. Just breathe. I promise you, we're coming."

"Listen, you need to know. It's not just Shug. He's—"

Kristal's voice was gone. Bailey ripped her phone from her ear and looked at the screen. The call went dead.

"Shit!" she stammered under her breath. She looked up, thinking for a moment. Her fingers tapped frantically on the armrest built into the door. Maybe Kristal was right. Maybe they weren't going to be fast enough. She looked at Pitts. "Step it up. We're running it Code 3."

"Jen, they'll hear us com—"

"She's blown, John. They already know we're coming. Step it up!"

Pitts shook his head but reached over and flipped two switches. The lights and siren on their car announced their presence to everyone else on the highway. A second later, the convoy of unmarked cruisers behind them followed suit.

Bailey grabbed the radio from the center console and keyed the mic. "Be advised, our source may be under duress. We're going Code 3 the rest of the way. Someone coordinate with the Frederick County Sheriff's Office and have them start us some units."

"Copy, on it." A voice radioed back.

The convoy of a half-dozen cars snaked its way through the light traffic on the interstate before exiting onto the crowded streets of Route 50 in the town of Winchester. Pushing west, they headed for the rural hills just outside of town. Jen looked at her phone once more and clamped her fingers around the grip of her service weapon, unholstering it. They were two miles out.

Their target was the Mt. Olive Motel, a seedy-looking motor lodge that they'd learned through Josephine was being used to exploit trafficked women into sex work. The plan had been to serve a warrant and raid the place, taking Josephine into custody with everyone else and preserving her cover. Now, though, Bailey had no idea what they were rolling up on. As the highway meandered past a sloping hillside, the sign for the motel came into view.

"Here we go," Bailey said into her radio. "Trail cars cover the points of entry. Everyone else, follow us in."

A plot of small cabins, tenuously connected by one roof made up the whole of the motel. Their retro green and orange facade were indicative of the time they'd been constructed, with seemingly little to no upkeep done in the decades since. They were arranged in a crescent around an arcing drive and parking lot that climbed up a shallow knoll.

The fender of their Explorer nosed into the pavement as it shot onto the drive. Pitts led the three cars that followed him to the motel's office, nestled in the center, then jerked the wheel hard. Their Explorer swerved and came to a stop pointing at the office's front doors. The agents driving the other cars followed suit and maneuvered in to form a perimeter around the building.

Bailey hopped out to prepare to lead the lot of them up to serve the warrant when the office door suddenly creaked open.

"Movement! Movement!" one of the other agents shouted.

Pitts and Bailey took cover behind the doors to their Explorer, the other agents doing the same. Bailey waited a minute, her gun trained on the door. It stood half open, with no one and nothing visible inside; just a dark void.

"Virginia State Police!" Bailey called out. "We have a warrant to search the property. I need anyone inside to come out now, slowly, with your hands raised!" The whir of the cars' idle engines was her only response. Reaching into the SUV, she grabbed her radio. "Do we have Sheriff's Office units coming to back us up or what?"

"They're en route now. Couple minutes," an agent radioed back.

Bailey shook her head, frustrated. As she was about to repeat her orders to whomever was inside, the motel office door opened wider. Bailey got even lower behind her door. "You, in the office! This is the Virginia State Police! I need you to—"

Before Bailey could finish, a figure formed in the darkness, slim and feminine. As she stepped out, the rest of her features became visible. Her fawn complexion. Her dyed-blond hair showing its true color at its roots. Her round face inundated with makeup. It was Kristal Hardy. It was their Josephine.

She wore brown cowboy boots and low-rise jeans, but her torso was covered in something bulky and far less stylish. It took Bailey a moment to recognize what it was, but when she did, a chill came over her.

"Jesus Christ!" Pitts said. "Is that a fucking suicide vest?!"

Bailey's eyes focused on the vest. It looked to be something like a hunter's vest, albeit two sizes too big for Kristal. The whole thing hung off her bony frame. Around her abdomen, a wire — or several wires — ran to and from a row of canteen-sized canisters. Bailey looked up at Kristal's face. Her lips were trembling as her mascara began to drag behind the tears running down her cheeks.

"Kristal," Bailey said, taking a deep breath to calm herself. "Is that right? Is that an ... explosive around you?"

Kristal gave an almost imperceptible nod. "I ... I think so. I don't know. They put me in it."

Bailey dropped her head to talk into her radio. "Someone get the local bomb squad rolling *right now*." She looked back up at Bailey. "Okay, Kristal. Do you know if you can take it off?"

"I don't know. They grabbed me and put it on me, and then told me to wait for you all to come or they'd kill me."

"Alright, Kristal. That's okay. We're going to figure this out. I just need you to stay right there."

A QUARTER MILE AWAY, a man stepped out of the woods and into the parking lot for the Northwest Assembly of God. His hair buzz cut, he had two upside down revolver tattoos on opposite sides of his neck, framing his jawline. He looked back instinctively but knew he wouldn't see anything. That was the point, after all. Over here, they were hidden away from what was playing out at the motel.

The man reached into his pocket, fetched his phone, and called a number. Half a ring later, a voice answered.

"Where are we at?" asked the voice.

"It's done," the man said. "We left the bitch at the motel as a present for the cops. Your info was right. She tried to make a call as soon as we got to her."

"And the rest of them?"

The man looked ahead at a large Sprinter van sitting idle in the empty parking lot. "Secure, we moved them out before the cops came in. Had a couple of johns we had to scare off, but it shouldn't be a problem.

"What about Liles?"

"Also with us. Secure."

"You bring him to me."

"Understood. And the gift we left back at the motel?"

"Unwrap it." The line went dead.

The man grinned, flashing his yellowed teeth. He opened his contacts, scrolled to a number, and placed another call.

BAILEY HEARD sirens in the distance. Backup was coming. She locked eyes with Kristal and put her hand out in a stopping gesture.

"I just need you to stay right there," Bailey repeated. "Can you do that for me?"

Kristal nodded again. "Jen?"

"Yeah, Kristal?"

"I'm sorr—"

The blast kicked Bailey backward like a mule, throwing her the length of the Explorer and onto the pavement behind it. She heard muffled groans and voices, but couldn't make sense of them. Her mind tried to process everything, but it was like running underwater. What had happened? An explosion. The vest. Had it gone off?

Bailey rolled over. Pebbles stuck to her face like tar acne. The pavement was smeared with something slick. Oil? Blood? A combination of both? On the other side of the SUV, she could see Pitts pushing himself to his feet. She grabbed the wheel well of the Explorer and pulled herself upright. Smoke wafted out from somewhere beyond the Explorer. The engine of the sedan next to her was on fire.

Bailey crawled back to her open door, got her feet underneath her, and peered back over the door at the motel office.

Its windows were blown out and more smoke drifted upwards in spectral curls from somewhere inside. Debris was strewn over the pavement in front.

And amidst it all, Kristal Hardy was gone.

HAPPYLAND: CHAPTER 2

TWO HOURS LATER, Bailey found herself standing over a sink in one of the women's restrooms in the Frederick County Sheriff's Offices in Winchester. Kristal Hardy was dead — blown into a million pieces across a motel parking lot — and now the only keepsake Bailey had of her was the blood on the cuff of her blouse. She stood there, staring at it. Should she try to wash it off? It felt cruel, somehow, given everything that had just happened.

A loud knocking rapped on the door.

"Jen, you in there?" It was Pitts.

Bailey sighed and let her head drop. "Yeah, I'm just washing up."

"The big brass is here. They want to talk to everyone."

Bailey shook her head. Pitts always talked like he only played an investigator on TV. "Got it. I'll be right out."

She slapped off the faucet and looked at herself in the mirror, taking stock. Even by her standards, she looked tired. Her suit was untucked, wrinkled, and dirty, sitting on her athletic frame like hung laundry. The dark rings made her hazel eyes pop better than any expensive eyeliner could hope to, but they also looked like she'd gone twelve rounds with a welterweight boxer, and now the side of her neck was scraped from where she'd hit the pavement. She brushed her auburn hair back and studied the abrasion more closely before shaking her head in frustration. She left to join her team.

Bailey walked down a long, featureless hall to a conference room where Lieutenant Colonel Tom Girard stood waiting at the head of a table. Bailey's team from the motel was seated around the table looking as banged up as Bailey. With gauze wrappings and bandages interspersed throughout the team, they looked more like a motley crew that had been sprung from the local Emergency Room rather than a special investigative unit of the Virginia State Police. Windowless, oil paintings in gilded frames depicting battles from the American Revolution and Civil War adorned the walls behind them. Bailey extended her hand, bloody cuff and all, towards Girard.

"Sir," she greeted. "Jen Bailey, with Human Trafficking."

"Yes, I remember," Girard said with a kind smile. He looked at the blood stain, then up at her scraped neck. "Are you alright?"

Girard was the Director of the Bureau of Criminal Investigation, the Virginia State Police's investigative arm. Bailey didn't interact with him in her normal day-to-day, but she supposed a bomb going off just outside a town of nearly thirty thousand was reason enough to come out and supervise things. At least, until the media attention died down.

"I'm fine, sir," Bailey replied. "A few cuts and scrapes, but I'll live."

"Did you get checked out?"

"A paramedic looked me over at the scene. I refused further medical attention."

"You should probably be looked at by a doctor."

"I'm good, sir. If it's all the same to you, I'd like to get on with it."

His brow furrowed at her brusque response, but he motioned for her to have a seat. "Sure. So, the motel? You all were there to serve a warrant?"

"Yes, sir," Bailey slid into the seat directly to his left. "As you might know, we've been focusing our investigations on the Interstate 81 corridor. Because of its proximity to the inland port outside Front Royal and the numerous distribution centers throughout the Shenandoah Valley, it is a major thoroughfare for truckers, which also makes it a likely hotbed for trafficking activity."

"So, how did the motel play into that?"

"We developed a confidential human source. Kristal Hardy, whom we gave the handle Josephine."

"The woman that had the explosive vest strapped to her."

The image of Kristal mouthing, "I'm sorry" before being murdered shot into Bailey's mind, rocking her for a moment. "Yes, that's ... yes. Hardy was in a stable — or a group of trafficked sex workers — under the control of Sean Liles, also known as Sugar Bee or Shug."

"Liles was their pimp, essentially."

"Yes. Josephine was what is called a Bottom. While a trafficked sex worker herself, she was also a lieutenant of sorts for Liles to help manage the other girls. She informed us that the stable was operating out of the motel. Once we set up surveillance, we gathered enough evidence for a warrant to go in."

"Which brings us to today. So, what went wrong?"

"We're not entirely sure. As we were en route, I received a phone call from Josephine. She was panicked and sounding like they had found out she was cooperating with us. I made the decision to roll Code 3 the rest of the way. When we got there, we moved in and around the motel's office. That's when Josephine came out.

"With the explosive vest on."

Bailey nodded.

"So, they identified her as your source. Any idea how? Or by who?"

"No, sir. Obviously, it just happened and we haven't had time to get into it yet. Speculating, at this point, would be reckless."

Girard pursed his lips. "Still, an explosive vest seems heavy-handed for a local pimp."

"Liles used narcotics as a tool to keep his stable in line. Usually, it was bottom-tier junk, like meth. But Hardy told us a few months ago he started bringing in something new, something she'd never seen before. He called them Pepsis, like the soda. She was able to get us a tablet and we had it analyzed. Chemically, it's a new designer drug related to Pyrrolidinophenones. A psychostimulant similar to cocaine, but more refined."

"Again, this all seems above the pay grade of some dirtbag."

"Exactly, which was an angle we were very much interested in. Josephine said Liles didn't get the stuff from his regular distributors. Designer drugs are big money, so, naturally, we wanted to know if Liles had connections to a larger, more complex trafficking organization."

"You were hoping to flip Liles, expecting a bigger fish out there."

Bailey nodded again. "A bigger fish that was willing to set off an explosive vest to remain unidentified."

Girard put his hands on his hips, taking a deep breath in, then out. "Alright. I want you guys to pursue this. At the very least, it sounds like we now have Liles for Murder 1. That's a hell of a thing to hang around his neck, pun intended. I'm guessing it gets him to start talking." He leaned over and shuffled together his files on the conference table. "Of course, we have to find him first."

HAPPYLAND: CHAPTER 3

SEAN LILES BANGED his head against the SUV's window as the rocky road it traversed kicked him side to side. Any other time he'd let out a choice, four-letter word — or perhaps a string of them — but not now. Now, he was too scared.

He wasn't sure how long they'd been on the road — the hood over his head didn't exactly make it easy to keep track of time — but Liles figured, by the way he was jonesing for another hit, it had to have been a couple of hours.

The SUV slowed for a moment, then, as it returned to speed, the ground was smooth beneath its tires. *Paved road*, Liles thought.

"There," Nick Graves said from the passenger seat, directly in front of Liles. "Pull up to the doors."

From the moment they'd first met, Graves scared the ever-loving shit out of Liles. Now that he'd taken Liles on this masked field trip, the fear had only metastasized. Still, Liles didn't dare ask where they were or who was with them. Or the real question on his mind: was he going to leave alive?

The SUV came to an easy stop and everyone's doors popped open except for Liles. A moment later, someone opened his for him and pulled him out. They pressed him face first against the body of the car, took his wrists behind him, and bound them.

"Please," Liles now dared to say. "I'm not fightin' y'all. You ain't gotta do this."

"Shut up," said a gruff voice.

A pair of hands grabbed him underneath each arm and start to carry him forward, his feet dragging behind him. As the three of them crossed over some unseen threshold, Liles could make out through the mask that they had come from some place dark — likely outside — and into somewhere brighter. Then, a blend of smells hit him. The most dominant one was the unmistakable smell of horse shit.

The men turned with Liles, bringing him through another doorway before dropping him onto his knees. Someone behind him removed the hood, and for the first time since they left the church parking lot, Liles was able to take stock of where he was. The smells now made sense. They were in a barn, specifically in what looked to be a horse stall.

Liles counted five men in total around him. Nick Graves, with his twin pistol tattoos peeking out over the collar of his workman's jacket, three other men similarly dressed and equally menacing, and then a fifth man standing in the far corner. As he stepped into the single light overhead, Liles could see now he was different than the others. He was older; clean-shaven with hair slicked-back and slightly to the side and was dressed in a full suit save for the tie. The man stepped towards Liles so that he was now standing over him. Liles tried to look up at him, but was blinded by the light overhead.

"Sean Liles," the man said. "Sugar *Bee*." He chuckled. "Interesting nickname. Why do they call you that?"

Liles wasn't sure if he was supposed to answer or not. "I—I don't know, sir. It's just what they call me."

"A man often has nicknames when his own doesn't carry much weight." The man started to circle Liles. "And do you know where you are, Sugar Bee?"

"A ... barn?"

The man chuckled again. "Not quite. No, a barn is for storing farm equipment or livestock. Here, at the *stable*, we house our prized horses." He kept circling. "That's what it's called, no? Your roster of girls. A stable?"

"I—I guess?"

"An apt metaphor, I think. You keep them all under one roof, keep them safe. The only problem is being in close quarters with one another allows the opportunity for disease to spread. All sorts of diseases. Herpesvirus, Strangles. For all its beauty, nature loves to harbor just the nastiest things. The standard practice is to isolate and treat the infected. But every once in a while, you have one horse that is just ... *problematic*. For whatever reason, it can't get right. And then, that horse becomes a liability. That's when you really have some tough decisions to make."

Liles never considered himself particularly smart, but even he could see where the man was going with this. "Sir, I'm very sorry if I caused you trouble. I didn't even know ... about you."

The man stopped in front of Liles and once again stood over him. "That's just it. You don't even know *who I am*. And yet, you're threatening to spread your problems onto me, not unlike an infection." He crouched so that his face was closer to Liles. "Law enforcement are like a virus, *Sugar Bee*. They leech onto the dumbest and most susceptible of us and don't stop until they've gotten to those of us that have gone to great lengths to insulate ourselves."

"I didn't know Kristal was talking to the cops, I swear to god."

"Precisely my point. *You* didn't know." The man poked him sharply in the chest. "*You* didn't keep an eye on *your* stable. If it weren't for my sources, *you'd* be in handcuffs right now, probably singing like a goddamn soprano. Putting all of *us* — the ones you didn't even know about — at risk. So, now it's my problem."

"I'm sorry, sir. I—"

The man stood up. "Do you know how we put down a horse when it comes down to it? These days, people feel the *ethical* or *humane* way is to euthanize them. Drugs." He shook his head and sneered. "Admittedly, that would be fitting for you."

"Please, don't—"

"But I prefer the way my daddy showed me. And his daddy before him." Graves stepped forward and handed the man what looked like some kind of hardware tool. "It's called a captive bolt gun. That's just a fancy way to say it fires a bolt into the horse's skull, stunning it if not killing it outright. Crude? Maybe. But sure is effective. And *cost* effective. Hell, it doesn't even waste a bullet."

Liles began to quiver as tears welled up in his eyes and he released his bladder.

"Unlike you, Mr. Sugar Bee, I intend to look after my stable. And protect it. At all costs."

Liles opened his mouth to scream, but the man pressed the bolt pistol to Liles' forehead and pulled the trigger. In an instant, Sean 'Sugar Bee' Liles' life was extinguished. His body slumped forward before keeling over to its side. Graves stepped up next to the man, looking at the body. The man handed Graves the bolt pistol.

"The next time you sell extra Pepsis to some dipshit for a quick payday, it'll be you with a hole in your head," the man said. "You understand me?"

"Understood, sir."

The man nodded at Liles' body, grabbing a rag off a nearby hook, wiping his hands, and discarding it. "Clean all of this up. And once you get him out of here, I want the whole stall bleached."

"What do you want us to do with the body?"

"I'll leave that to you. But whatever you do, make sure he's found. I don't want any more prying eyes. This ends with him."

Graves nodded as he and the others got to work.

Continue the story in *Happyland*, grab your copy now!
amazon.com/B0DV9YDM8Y

Join the B.C. Lienesch reader family and stay up to date on all the latest news!
https://www.bclnovels.com/newsletter

ACKNOWLEDGMENTS

Writing this novel truly tested my confidence and abilities as a writer, and I could not have done any of it without a dedicated band of family and friends who supported me throughout the process. First, I would like to thank my mother, Debbie Bleviss, and my late father, Bill Lienesch, who passed away just weeks before this novel's release. Their support was unwavering not just in this but in all of my endeavors. Also steadfast in her support was my wife, Meg, who remains my greatest cheerleader and confidant. Third, I would like to thank my editor, Austin Shirey, whose adept editing eye did more, outside my own hands, to craft this story than anything. And finally, an equally special thanks is owed to David Voyles, who, along with Austin, my wife, and my mother, read early versions of this novel and provided invaluable insight and feedback.

ALSO BY B.C. LIENESCH

The Jackson Clay & Bear Beauchamp Series

The Woodsman

Country Roads

Chasing Devils

Happyland

Safe Harbor (Coming Soon)

ABOUT THE AUTHOR

B.C. Lienesch is an award-winning mystery and thriller author hailing from the nation's capital.

A former freelance writer, featured columnist, and editor for guysnation.com, he is an author-member of the International Thriller Writers and the recent recipient of three 2024 LitStar Book Awards including Outstanding Book Series for his Jackson Clay & Bear Beauchamp Series.

Born in Washington, D.C. and raised in Northern Virginia, he now lives in the same area with his wife, Meg, their two dogs, Kaia and Aria, and their three cats, Hitchcock, Ariba, and Savaneta.

Happyland is his fourth novel. He's previously written *The Woodsman*, *Country Roads*, and *Chasing Devils*.

Join the B.C. Lienesch reader family and stay up to date on all the latest news!
https://www.bclnovels.com/newsletter

Made in United States
Cleveland, OH
15 August 2025